PAMELA CALLOW

DAMAGED

MIRA®

ISBN-13: 978-0-7783-2750-9

Recycling programs
for this product may
not exist in your area.

DAMAGED

www.MIRABooks.com

Printed in U.S.A.

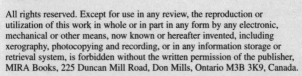

For my mother, the late Inge Luzie Callow,
who believed I could be anything;

For my husband and my daughters,
who were with me all the way.

1

Springtime in Halifax was not known for its warmth or sunshine. Nor was Lyons McGrath Barrett, one of Halifax's premiere boutique law firms.

Kate Lange allowed herself a one-minute break and gazed out her window on LMB's associate floor. Drizzle specked the glass, obscuring the line of cars snaking along Lower Water Street. Friday night rush hour was just beginning.

She turned back to her desk—an elegant mahogany-finished number with matching credenza—forcing her eyes to focus on the separation agreement spread out in front of her. The fourth this week. The twenty-seventh since she'd joined LMB. She grimaced. The irony was not lost on her. She'd left Marshall & Associates because of a preponderance of family law clients.

A rapid knock on the door broke through her thoughts.

Her pulse jumped in her throat.

It was Randall Barrett. Himself.

She'd never met LMB's managing partner before. He'd been in absentia during her job interview. She suspected it was because she was the former fiancée of Ethan Drake, the criminal investigations detective he believed sent an innocent man to jail. Two years before, Ethan investigated Randall Barrett's old soccer buddy, Dr. Don Clarkson, for the death of a critically ill patient. The media buzzed with the story: Had Dr. Clarkson misjudged the amount of morphine the patient could handle or had he perpetrated a mercy killing? The autopsy was inconclusive. The case hinged on the testimony of the patient's son, who claimed Dr. Clarkson had assured him his mother would not suffer any longer. Randall Barrett believed Ethan unduly influenced the teen.

Don Clarkson bankrupted himself with his defense but was convicted nonetheless. Randall Barrett stepped in to handle his appeal. But despite Randall's attempts to convince the Court of Appeal that Ethan had thrown the investigation, the appellate judges upheld the conviction two to one. Neither Randall Barrett nor Ethan Drake had gotten over it. The hostility ran deep.

Kate stood, smoothing her skirt. "Hello, Mr. Barrett." She gave him a brilliant smile, grateful she wore the new suit she'd bought with her last paycheck. It had been a toss-up between replacing her old articling clothes or the old kitchen piping, but the lure of the Jackie O–style suit had been too strong. When she heard the pipes groaning that night, she'd regretted her extravagance. But she couldn't bring herself to take the sleek cream suit back and ask for a refund. She'd learned a long time ago that there were no returns in life.

Now, eyeing Randall Barrett's exquisitely tailored gray suit, she was glad she'd kept it. He, of all people, needed to see that she belonged in this office, that her name would have a place on LMB letterhead. Because it didn't, not yet. Not for another two months.

And only if she cut it.

He smiled, showing off his strong, white teeth. It did nothing to ease her jitters. "Please, call me Randall." He raised a brow. "May I come in?"

She straightened. Flushed. "Of course."

He walked toward her, filling her office with plain, old-fashioned male virility. *Geez. Now I know why all the single women in the firm get flustered when his name is spoken.*

He stopped in front of her desk. A manila folder was tucked under his arm. In her heels Kate was almost as tall as he was, but his charisma gave him the benefit of a few extra inches. His brilliant blue eyes drilled into hers.

She forced herself to hold his gaze. It gave nothing away. Which was what she supposed she could expect. But it still rankled. Known for his keen analyses and eloquent arguments, she could learn a lot from him. If he gave her a chance.

His eyes sharpened, then drifted away, lazily scanning the piles of folders on her desk, resting for a moment on the stack of Reports of Family Law. "You busy?"

Now there was a loaded question. She had no doubt that he'd used that casual inquiry on every new associate who entered the firm's hallowed corridors. If she said no, she'd surely go to billable hours hell. And if she said yes, she'd sound churlish to LMB's top dog.

"Can never be too busy," she said.

A blond brow lifted. "Good." He tossed the file on her desk. "You've got a new client. She's waiting for you in the reception area."

He'd done this on purpose, wanted to test her. She flipped open the file, knowing Randall Barrett wouldn't be giving her what she wanted—that wasn't his style—yet unable to control the small hitch of hope that maybe, finally, she'd be able to show him that she was capable of so much more than the family law cases that had been thrown her way.

The file contained only one sheet of paper. Four words had been hastily scrawled in black pen: *Marian MacAdam. Custody matter.*

The sight of it filled her with disappointment, resignation. Resentment, even. But not guilt. That would come later.

She closed the folder carefully. The writing was on the wall. Randall had her firmly slotted in the family law group. All the platitudes her mentor, John Lyons, had given her about the probationary period being a time to assess her strengths and see where she best fit in the firm were bull. She hadn't received a single litigation, insurance or corporate case since she'd been here. Just family law. The pink ghetto.

She met Randall's gaze. His was cool. Amused, even. Damn him. He knew she was pissed off. And he liked it.

She circled her desk, crossing her arms. "I have only two months left of my probationary period."

A small smile curved his mouth. He turned and held open her office door, waiting for her to collect her latest family law client.

His lack of response was specifically designed to intimidate her, she knew. She strode through the doorway, knowing he was too much of a gentleman to walk in front of her, no matter his natural inclination to be one step ahead. Over her shoulder, she said, "When John Lyons *recruited* me—" the slight lifting of Randall's brows showed he hadn't missed her meaning "—he told me I'd be working in the civil litigation group." She began walking down the hallway.

"John didn't have the authority to tell you that," Randall said matter-of-factly, falling into step beside her.

She hoped her face didn't reveal how much that casual revelation threw her. Not long after she'd arrived at LMB she'd suspected John had less power in the firm than he'd like to think, but she never expected that the managing partner would come out and say it to a first-year associate. Partners usually stuck together.

"Why did you hire me, then?"

"We brought you in for a probationary period—" His careful choice of words was deliberate. Kate's stomach clenched despite her resolve to not let him intimidate her. "—Because we need to see where your strengths lie."

"I thought you'd seen them pretty clearly on the Robertson file." She'd single-handedly won the day for her David-like client, resulting in an offer of employment from John Lyons, who represented the Goliath insurance company.

"Yes, there's no question that John was impressed with your work on that file. But that was one case. We deal with a multitude of clients and issues at LMB. We need to be confident of your abilities to handle *both* the clients and the issues." Translation: she was now swimming in a much bigger pond and needed to prove she could be a shark like all the rest.

They approached the glass door that led to the reception area. She stopped, crossing her arms. "Unless you give me some civil lit files, you'll never know."

"You'll get your chance, Kate." Randall held open the door. "Do a good job on these files and we'll see if there's something we can give you from the litigation group." His eyes met hers. Piercing. Sharp. Looked right through her.

She wasn't fooled for a minute that he was interested in her. She knew he wasn't. He just expected her to respond to his magnetism like every other female he encountered.

Well, she did, if she was honest with herself. How could

she not? But he wasn't her type. Too cocky, too confident, too arrogant. And yet, there was a pull there. An awareness in her body that had everything to do with primal urges and nothing to do with self-respect. To respond physically to a man so sure of himself was humiliating.

She stepped around him and walked through the doorway into the reception area. The glass door closed behind her. Randall had not followed her.

She took a deep breath. Randall's patronizing "be a good girl" attitude had been hard to take. But he had thrown the bone she craved her way. She'd waited too long and desired it too deeply to walk away from it now. Because she knew if she forced the issue with Randall while she was still on probation he'd tell her to take a hike.

2

Her new client pushed herself to her feet when Kate approached.

"Mrs. MacAdam?" Kate asked, hoping she was wrong. She'd expected a middle-aged woman, but Marian MacAdam must have been well into her seventies. She wore a beautifully tailored camel overcoat that helped camouflage her stooped back. A pink-and-orange scarf was tied artfully around her neckline. Kate bet she drove either an Audi or a Mercedes. That was the car of choice for well-heeled Halifax matrons. The only thing that gave her away was her eyes. They looked anxious and tired.

"Yes," Marian MacAdam replied, her gaze sweeping over Kate. Uncertainty flashed across her face.

Kate put on a reassuring smile. "I'm Kate Lange." She held out her hand. Marian MacAdam grasped it, her fingers knobbed with arthritis but surprisingly soft and warm.

"My office is this way," Kate added briskly, holding the glass reception door open for her. They walked down the hallway, Kate forcing herself to shorten her stride, making small talk about the weather and the tulips. Marian MacAdam nodded, but said little. Her breathing came in shallow puffs by the time they reached Kate's office.

"Please, have a seat, Mrs. MacAdam." *Before you collapse.*

Marian MacAdam sank onto the blue upholstered chair. She glanced around, her gaze taking in Kate's stacks of legal books, the degrees mounted on the wall behind her, the picture of Kate's dog. Her eyes lingered on Alaska's goofy grin.

Kate sat down behind her desk. "I understand you have a custody issue you need some advice about?" She hoped maybe Randall had been wrong. Because if this lady did have a custody issue, it must be for a grandchild. And that was sure to be messy.

"Yes," Marian MacAdam said with an air of defiance. "I am seeking custody of my granddaughter."

Damn Randall Barrett. He really had it in for her. "I see. Does she live with one or both parents?"

Marian MacAdam hesitated. "She lives with my daughter-in-law. My son moved out two years ago, and they divorced a year later."

Kate began jotting notes. "How old is your granddaughter?"

"Fifteen."

"Fifteen?" Kate stopped writing and looked at her client. "What does she want to do?"

"She wants to stay with her mother."

Kate put her pen down. "Then why do you want custody?"

Marian MacAdam leaned forward. "Because her mother completely ignores her. She's always working. She has no idea where Lisa is most of the time." Disapproval tightened her mouth, puckering the loose flesh of her jaw. She was the picture of indignant outrage.

What Marian MacAdam didn't realize was that she wore the same expression as three out of four of Kate's clients. The anger, the blame—each side in a custody battle nursed their grievances. Kate listened to the diatribes, defused the pain, steered them back to the legal issues and dreaded the next client.

Maybe Lisa's mother needed to work to keep them going. Nova Scotia had a lot of deadbeat dads. Maybe Marian MacAdam's son was one of them—and she didn't want to admit it.

Kate knew how hard it was to swallow that truth. It had almost killed her twelve-year-old self to admit that her own dad had joined those ranks.

Kate knew her next words would not be welcome. "Mrs. MacAdam, the law does not like to take children from their parents. The parent has a prima facie right to custody unless you can prove the child is being neglected or emotionally harmed." She practically had those words memorized. Now came the clincher. She held Marian MacAdam's gaze. "Is Lisa being neglected or emotionally harmed?"

Marian MacAdam looked away. "She hasn't been physically neglected. But you might say she has suffered emotional harm."

"Mrs. MacAdam, there is a specific definition to that term. You would need to demonstrate that Lisa has severe anxiety, depression, withdrawal or self-destructive behavior—" And yet, as Kate knew only too well, emotional harm could be something far more insidious, far less obvious, something that spurred a teenage girl to ignore every warning her stressed-out mother ever gave her and allow the unthinkable to happen.

"I think she is using drugs," Marian MacAdam said softly.

Kate leaned back in her chair. "Are you sure?"

Marian MacAdam shook her head. "I don't have any proof…it's just a suspicion. She's unreliable, won't come to supper when she says she will, that kind of thing."

"Have you spoken to her parents about it?"

"Her mother keeps saying that Lisa doesn't have a problem, and, of course, Lisa won't admit to a thing." Marian MacAdam's voice hardened. "Which suits her mother just fine."

Kate felt a sneaking sympathy for Marian MacAdam's former daughter-in-law. It wouldn't be easy facing a mother-in-law's disapproval while trying to handle being a single parent.

"Have you tried speaking to your son about it? Maybe he can help."

Marian MacAdam's lip curled. "My son has no influence over his ex-wife. And besides, he travels all over the place. He's a partner in one of those big consulting firms."

"So Lisa lives with her mother?"

Marian MacAdam nodded. "Yes. Her mother works even more than my son." That sounded familiar. Kate's mother had worked two jobs to keep them going after her father's downfall.

"What does she do?"

Then Marian MacAdam dropped the bomb.

"She's a judge."

"A judge?" Kate tried to keep the shock from her voice. She'd created a picture in her mind of a down-at-heel single mother. Not a judge. "Which court?"

"She's a criminal court judge. You may know her. Her name is Hope Carson. She deals with all the scum." Her client's voice was edged with contempt. Kate smothered an inward flinch. Her father had been one of those scum. He'd brought them all down to that level. And Kate had spent the next eighteen years of her life trying to claw her way back up. Back to a place where people treated her with respect.

Respect wasn't something she'd gotten from Judge

Carson. Known by the criminal bar as the Faint Hope judge, Kate had only appeared once before her, just after she was admitted, when she handled anything that came through her previous firm's door. It hadn't been pleasant. Judge Carson was curt, impatient and had a sarcastic tongue. It didn't matter if you were a prosecutor or criminal defense, she doled it out to everyone.

And Judge Carson's mother-in-law wanted to engage in a battle to the death with her. The optics were a reporter's wet dream: they'd need to call in experts to provide evidence of Lisa's drug abuse and self-destructive behaviors. They would need to show that Lisa's parents—and, in particular, her mother—were failing to take any action. *What an unholy battle that would be.* It would be the talk of the bar, the media and her firm.

She'd be jumping with both feet into quicksand and dragging LMB with her. Goodbye career. They wouldn't want to engage in mudslinging against a respected criminal court judge.

She studied her client. There was an option.

One she'd never had to invoke before. But it was an option she was legally bound to discuss with this client.

"Mrs. MacAdam, if you are truly concerned that Lisa may be endangering herself, I have a statutory obligation to report Lisa's case to Child Protection Services."

Marian MacAdam jerked back. "No. This is family business. That's why I came to you. I want to deal with this privately."

"It's not a private matter when a child's welfare is at stake."

"You cannot go to Child Protection Services!" She spoke in the commanding tone of a woman used to getting her own way. But Kate could smell her desperation.

"Then you could."

Dismay flashed through Marian MacAdam's eyes. "No, I can't." Then she added, with a telltale bristle of defensiveness, "I'm not sure if I'm right about my suspicions."

Kate leaned forward. They both knew Marian MacAdam had just lied. "Why do you think you have a case for custody?"

Marian MacAdam shifted in her chair. "I'm not sure I have a case…"

Her client was a sharp lady. She realized she was on thin ice. If she admitted that Lisa's self-endangerment was grounds for custody, then she knew Kate would feel compelled to involve the authorities. Kate glanced at the little silver clock by her phone. It was 6:05 p.m. The meeting was now dead. She had no doubt that any question she asked her client would be hedged with *maybe* and *I'm not sure*, rather than a frank discussion of the facts as Marian MacAdam knew them. "…I just want Hope to take my concerns seriously."

Bull. It was time to take the gloves off. "Mrs. MacAdam, do you have any proof that Lisa is doing drugs?"

Marian MacAdam's gaze fell on the photo of Kate's dog. "No. I've never found any drugs or evidence of paraphernalia in her belongings. And she's never been…'high' when she's been to my house."

"Has she stolen money?"

"No."

"Disappeared at night?"

"I wouldn't know. She doesn't sleep over."

"What are her friends like? Are they the type to do drugs?"

"I'm not sure. Lisa doesn't have a gang of girlfriends."

"So why exactly do you suspect she's doing drugs?"

Marian MacAdam twisted her diamond-studded wedding band. It couldn't move very far. Her knuckles were too swollen. She dropped her hands to her lap. "She doesn't show up for supper when she's supposed to."

That was hardly an earth-shattering event for a teenager. "Does she have a good reason?"

"She claims she's at the library or some such thing. But I just have this feeling she's not telling the truth."

Kate put down her pen. "Mrs. MacAdam, you have a difficult case. First of all, the courts don't like to take children from their mothers. Secondly, the court would be wondering why your son isn't intervening."

Marian MacAdam glanced at the photo of Alaska again. Kate couldn't tell whether the picture of her dog was a comfort or a distraction to her elderly client. Finally, Marian MacAdam said, "Can I start a proceeding for custody?"

"You can start one, if you choose, Mrs. MacAdam. I just don't think your chances are very good."

Marian MacAdam's face tightened. "I thought you'd be able to help me. But it's obvious you are unwilling to do so." She picked up her purse and pushed herself to her feet. Her ankles swelled over the tight edges of her patent shoes.

"Mrs. MacAdam, please. I would like to help you. But you don't have a strong case unless you have proof of Lisa's drug use. Child Protection could help you."

"No. I'll find proof myself." She turned toward the door. Kate hurried around her desk and held the door open for her. It was after-hours, so she escorted Marian MacAdam to the elevators, her client's disappointment so palpable Kate felt a chill on her skin. Worse, though, was her own uneasiness about Lisa MacAdam. Kate knew how secretive teenagers could be.

They reached the lobby. Kate watched the elevator climb toward their floor. Fifteenth floor, sixteenth floor. She took a deep breath. She couldn't let Marian MacAdam go without trying one last time. "Mrs. MacAdam, Child Protection would be very discreet."

Marian MacAdam stiffened. "I don't want Lisa to be traumatized by some social worker nosing around in family business. She'd never want to live with me after that. And besides, she'd lie about it, anyway." Twenty-first floor. The elevator doors slid open. Marian MacAdam walked into its mirrored interior, then turned. "That's why I came to you, Ms. Lange. I thought we could keep it private this way."

The last thing Kate saw before the doors closed were tears blurring her client's watery blue eyes.

3

Kate watched the elevator carrying Marian MacAdam slowly descend. And with it, her spirits. What a crappy way to end the week. She strode quickly out of the reception area. Damn. Now she was left with a niggling doubt. It threatened to bring to the surface something she'd been trying to bury for the past two weeks. Something that had been surging in her memory like a slowly rolling ocean swell, gaining momentum as each day passed, threatening to swamp the even keel of her mind.

She breathed deeply. She wouldn't let it. She couldn't let it.

Damn. Maybe she should call Child Protection. But that was a big step to take. A very big step. One she didn't want to take when there was no tangible evidence of wrongdoing. Reporting that Lisa wasn't showing up on time to her grandmother's house for supper would become the office joke. They'd need a whole lot more proof that Lisa was being endangered before any judge would give an order removing Judge Carson's daughter from her care.

No. Kate would end up with egg on her face and Randall Barrett ready to scramble it for her.

She hurried down the long hallway to her office. The

corridors were hushed, the lighting muted. The workday was officially over. Except for all the worker bees who knew that the longer they stayed in the hive, the sweeter the honey would be.

Kate took one glance at the pile of paperwork left untended on her desk and headed to the snack station opposite her office. The coffee had been on the burner since at least 3:00 p.m., but what she needed was energy. Flavor, with several hours of work left to do, was a luxury.

She returned to her desk, settling into the chair, and kicked off her shoes. She tried to focus on the separation agreement she'd been working on before Randall Barrett had shown up at her door. But Marian MacAdam's tear-blurred eyes kept staring at her from the page.

The phone rang, shrill in the silence. She glanced at her watch: 6:56 p.m. Once upon a time, someone calling on a Friday night would have been a date.

She grabbed the receiver before it could ring again.

"Kate?" The cultured voice of John Lyons warmed her ear. She straightened. She hadn't heard from John for weeks. He'd checked on her a few times, but she hadn't worked on any files with him yet. And that rankled.

"Hi, John." She gripped the receiver.

"I realize it's late." John had such a pleasant voice. Warm, yet polite. Gentlemanly. Her hand relaxed on the phone. "Do you have any plans or can you come to my office?"

She hadn't had any plans since she'd ended things with Ethan on New Year's Eve. At 12:34 a.m. to be precise. Seven days and three hours after he slipped a ring on her finger with a kiss. One hundred and seventeen days ago. Every one of those days was carved into the wall of her heart.

Did John Lyons know about her failed engagement? "I can come up."

She placed the phone down. Reaching into her side drawer, she took a few swigs from her bottle of Maalox, wrinkling her nose. It should tide her over until supper. She pulled out a compact and brushed powder over her nose. Her face looked tired. More tired than a thirty-one-year-old should look. It was thanks to Alaska. That damned dog had taken over her heart in less than a week…and was waiting for her at home. Guilt ate at her. She snapped her compact closed and pushed down the guilt. She was still on probation. She couldn't turn down a partner, no matter it was Friday and Alaska hadn't been out for hours. When her probationary period finished and she was hired at LMB she would be able to ask if this could wait until Monday. But not yet.

She strode down the long hallway packed tightly with cubicles on the inner wall and spacious offices on the outer wall, relieved to see that Rebecca Manning had already gone home. *"People are saying that John Lyons only hired you so he could screw you,"* Rebecca had told her three weeks ago in the ladies' room. Kate had ignored her gossip, chalking it up to the disgruntlement the herd feels when the ranks are stirred up. But every time she got another family law file, Rebecca's words played in her head a little louder. Maybe she was getting those files because Randall believed John had hired her for purely personal reasons. And that would really get under Randall's skin, if there was any truth to the rumors about the way his own marriage had ended.

She straightened. She hadn't worked her tail off to be dragged down by two men who had no claim to her. To be found lacking because of her own inabilities was one thing; to be judged unworthy because of Randall Barrett's grudges against Ethan Drake and John Lyons was another. She'd show Randall that she was deserving of her position. Better yet, she'd make him glad she was at LMB.

She jogged up the stairs separating the associates' floor from the partners', her determination renewed and her anticipation rising. John Lyons' door was partly open. Kate knocked lightly. He cleared his throat, then called, "Come in."

His corner office was meant to impress, and it did. Ceiling-to-floor windows boasted an arresting view of the Halifax Harbour. The water was a dark, fathomless pool under the heavy sky. Two Queen Anne chairs sat on a Persian rug in front of a massive mahogany desk. It was a fitting accessory for LMB's senior civil litigation partner. He sat behind its broad expanse, his pale blue shirt immaculately crisp despite the lateness of the day. A plum-and-pewter-striped tie shimmered with subtle richness against his shirtfront. Kate was once again struck by John's gleaming head of silvery hair. Not too many men in their fifties could boast that. It had just the right amount of wave to brush smoothly off his high, academic forehead.

She darted a glance at the open folder on John's desk. One of the documents had a pale blue triangle stapled to the corner. A sure sign that a civil action had been started. Her skin tingled.

"Hi, Kate," John said, rising to his feet with his habitual courtliness. He waved a hand toward one of the chairs. "Please sit down."

"Thanks." She flashed him a smile.

He waited until she lowered herself in the chair, and resumed his seat. "So, how are things going for you? We haven't touched base for a while." John leaned back in his leather chair, his gray gaze solicitous.

She crossed her legs. "Randall's keeping me busy."

John nodded. "Has he given you some interesting files?"

She shrugged. "If you like family law." She wasn't going to pretend with him. She just hoped he couldn't see how the mention of Randall Barrett's name made her stomach tighten. The Maalox churned.

He gave her an assessing look. "I know it's not your cup of tea, but sometimes we have to do things we don't really care for to get ahead."

She searched his face. Did he realize how patronizing he sounded? He obviously had no clue about all the crummy minimum-wage jobs she'd done to get through university. "I couldn't agree more. But I thought we had a deal when you offered me a position here."

John nodded. "We still do. But the other first-year associates require delicate handling. The ones who articled with us." Kate's stomach sank but she kept her gaze steady. "Randall feels that after all the extra hours they put in during their articles, we owe it to them to make their career development needs our first priority."

The message was loud and clear: Randall believed that Kate hadn't earned her stripes at LMB yet. There was an even more subtle message, one she'd picked up from the cool smiles at the coffee station and the muted conversations in the elevators. LMB was an exclusive club. Entry to this club for junior associates was usually gained in law school, by possession of a high-octane combination of attitude, background and marks.

She hadn't made the cut in law school. Her marks fell in the critical second year when the large firms recruited their clerks, thanks to working extra hours to pay her way while dealing with her ill mother. Her mother finally succumbed to too many years of grief compounded by double shifts and heart disease.

But Kate managed to keep it together. She graduated with decent, but not stellar, marks. By then the only articling positions left were with poorly paid small practices.

Although they offered a wealth of hands-on experience, the salary was peanuts and career advancement was a new ergonomic chair. She wanted complex, challenging files. Something to sink her teeth into that would pave the way to a career with a six-figure paycheck and a seat on the bench.

Taking a position at Marshall & Associates was definitely going about it the long way. Crammed with overlarge antique furniture Madelyn Marshall had a passion for buying on weekend jaunts to Mahone Bay, the firm had a homey feel that reassured its walk-in everyday-joe clients. Kate's articling office had been converted from an old bathroom. It had borne the slight must of its previous functions. She'd kept the window open, even in the winter, promising herself that by next year she would not be at a firm where she had to hide long johns under her suit.

Getting her foot in the door in LMB was the first step. But it wasn't enough. She'd played the good girl for four months. She'd worked diligently on all those family files. It was time to let them know she wasn't going to take a backseat to the other first-year associates. "You haven't given me any other files except family law cases. How can I show you that I can handle the files if you won't give me any?"

John steepled his fingers together. Kate had the feeling he knew exactly how frustrated she was. "That's the point I made with Randall," he said finally. "I agree with you, Kate. You've worked here for four months and, so far, the reports have been good." He lowered his voice. "I had it out with Randall today. It's time to give you some litigation files."

Yes.

Triumph flushed her cheeks. But on its heels was unease. She didn't want the partners arguing over her. She wanted to be part of the team. She wanted to be cushioned

by the corporate safety net that a firm like LMB offered.
The last thing she wanted was to be the hot potato in a
power play.

There'd been whispers leaked from the partners' floor
that both John and Randall had been up for managing
partner last year. Randall had won the vote. Handily.
Judging from Randall's relaxed arrogance in her office
earlier, it was probably true. She studied John again. Strain
marked his suave features, making him look all of his fifty-
odd years. It must be galling for the lion who'd founded the
firm to be in a winner-take-all fight with the bullish Randall.

John leaned forward, his gaze intent. "Kate, I want you
to help me out on a file. You are probably aware that Trans-
Tissue, Inc., is one of my clients."

Her heart accelerated. Here it was. A chance to prove
herself. She flipped open her notebook. "TransTissue
makes surgical products, right?" She wanted to let John
know she'd done her research on LMB's clients before
she joined. She may be the protégée of a lion whose su-
premacy was on the wane, but right now he was the only
partner who was willing to back her. She'd do her best for
him. And hope that neither of them got gored by the bull
in the process.

His lips curved in a small smile, acknowledging her
efforts. "Correct. They are based in Toronto, but eighteen
months ago they opened a plant—if you wish to call it
that—in Halifax."

Kate nodded. "It was on the front page of the paper."

"It provided two hundred high-tech jobs, with the
promise of more opportunities as their product lines
develop." John spoke like a proud father. He picked up the
legal-size document with the pale blue triangle. "This is a
statement of claim filed against TransTissue this morning.

The plaintiff is a young man named Brad Gallivant, twenty-three years old, who claims he contracted hepatitis C from one of their products."

He handed the document to her. Kate skimmed it eagerly. According to the plaintiff, the defendant had negligently processed a tissue product that resulted in grievous personal injuries to him. "What exactly happened to Mr. Gallivant?"

John drummed his fingers on his desk. "He had arthroscopic surgery on his knee. The orthopedic surgeon used a tissue filler product to plug a hole in the cartilage. Several months later he tested positive for hep C."

"So the plaintiff is accusing TransTissue of supplying an infected product?" Kate asked.

"Yes." John closed the folder. "Of course, our client vigorously maintains that their products are up to standard."

"It couldn't be the filler, could it? Isn't it inert matter?" She tapped her pen against her lip. The defense was already taking shape in her head. God, she'd missed the fun of crafting an argument that wasn't an endless variation on custody support. "Wouldn't it be more likely that the disease was contracted either through a blood transfusion or from the plaintiff's lifestyle?"

"That's what our client says. But it's a little more complicated than that, Kate." There was a hint of amusement in John's eyes. "The products are not manufactured from inert matter."

Her mind raced. She knew she should know the answer to this. "Right. They make the products from live cells." She weighed the implications for the defense: they'd have to fight accusations of substandard laboratory procedures, infection transmitted by lab technicians—

"They don't use live cells," John said. "The tissue filler

products are made from—" a small smile curved his lips "—cadavers."

"Cadavers?" She stared at him. "They use dead tissue in surgical procedures?"

It was clear John had enjoyed shocking her. He nodded. "Yes. It's processed at TransTissue and then used in dental surgery, neurosurgical procedures and many orthopedic procedures. You know, hip replacements, ACL repairs, the list goes on."

"Ugh." Kate grimaced. She'd be a lot more careful about her joints from now on. Time for new running shoes. "Where does it come from?" At John's wry look, she added quickly, "I mean, where does TransTissue get the cadaveric tissue?"

"There are suppliers who harvest the tissue from bodies. Kind of like organ donors. The harvested tissue is sent to TransTissue to make into surgical products." His voice became thoughtful. "One body can go a long way to help a lot of people." He walked around his desk and handed her the file. "Here. Have a look at these notes and tell me what you think about this claim."

Kate nodded, slipping the claim into the folder. John sat behind his desk and flipped open another file.

She headed to the door. "When do you need it by?"

He smiled. "They're a top client. Have it ready for Monday."

4

Damn, damn and double damn.

Kate jogged through the dim parkade to her car. It was 8:35 p.m. She bet that Alaska was starving and upset by now. She threw her briefcase onto the backseat of her four-year-old Toyota sedan and slid into the driver's seat. The engine roared to life. She gripped the wheel tightly, weaving her way slowly through the near-empty parkade to the street.

It was dark, but it was a Friday night and Haligonians had spring fever even if the weather didn't. She was scared she'd hit some drunken university student celebrating the end of exams at the pubs connecting every street corner. So she crawled through the downtown core, her nerves on edge. She turned up Spring Garden Road, its bright, alluring storefronts swarming with Halifax's hippest.

She gritted her teeth in frustration at the pedestrians crossing the street willy-nilly in the dark. Did they have a death wish? It was only after she drove through the intersection of South Park Street that she relaxed. She was almost home. Her neighborhood bordered Hollis University, a pretty, leafy area in the south end of the city with century-old houses.

Drizzle sent little streams of wet scurrying across the windshield. It would rain soon. She hoped it would hold off until Alaska had been out in the yard. It was bad enough having a white carpet of husky fur all over her house, but it was even worse when it was wet and smelled of dog.

Five minutes later, she turned down her street. She pulled into her driveway. The house was shrouded in darkness. She'd forgotten to replace the burned-out porch light. Again. A street lamp illuminated the skeletal branches of a tall maple that waved disconcertingly around her opaque upstairs windows.

A familiar disquiet churned her stomach. *Stop it. It will be different in the summer. When it's still light at 9:00 p.m. and the trees are green.*

The thought didn't help her symbol of success feel any homier. Why couldn't she revel in the satisfaction of new ownership? Irritated with herself, she threw open her car door. Her house loomed over her. A movement flashed in the picture window.

She grabbed her briefcase and raced up the walk. Furious scrabbling on the wooden floor announced her arrival as she unlocked the heavy oak door.

"Hey, boy!"

With an excited whine, the pure-white husky threw himself against Kate. He was the only reason her house could claim to be a home. She hadn't realized it until he'd moved in.

She knelt down and buried her face in his soft fur. The dog licked her hand, then danced in circles down the hallway. There didn't appear to be a paper trail this evening. It never ceased to amuse her that she, a lawyer, would be the owner of a dog who seemed obsessed with leaving one, usually comprised of toilet paper but sometimes home decorating magazines. She followed the husky through the kitchen. And winced when she saw the puddle on the linoleum floor.

She cleaned up the mess, wishing she could wash away her guilt as easily. Now that she was on the TransTissue file, there would be many more evenings like this. She'd have to figure out something for this dog who'd adopted her. He gazed up at her, happiness in his blue gaze. Guilt stabbed harder. She scratched behind his ears. "Let's go for a walk."

His eager tail wagging lifted her spirits. Her dog's simple pleasures had become hers in less than a week. "Give me one more minute, boy," she called, bounding up the worn walnut staircase. She pulled off her work clothes, throwing them on the bed, and changed into track pants and a fleece-lined rain jacket. Alaska whined below.

"I'm coming!" She ran down the stairs, snatching the last apple from the fruit bowl. The husky bounced around her heels while she attached his leash.

"We're just going around the block," she warned him as they stepped outside. "We both need supper." Alaska's tail thumped a Morse code of agreement.

Drizzle fell onto her head. She forced herself not to pull up her hood. *You made the choice to live here. And besides, you don't need to hide. It's different now.*

Every fiber of her body ignored her pep talk, wanting to disappear. To shrink under the cover of her hood so no one would recognize her. But she wouldn't do that anymore. She'd remade herself. Created the future she'd always wanted. And today she had been given the chance she'd been craving for a long, long time. A chance to climb the ladder that, until now, had hung beguilingly out of her grasp.

She wouldn't let herself be dragged back down.

Was that why she moved back here? Some crazy impulse had hit her in January. Whether it was the need to clean out the cobwebs of her life, or celebrate her new job, it had fueled the purchase of this house on her old neighborhood street. An impulse she didn't care to examine but was sure a therapist would have a field day with. At the time, it was an act of defiance, of independence. Of proving to Ethan that she wasn't ashamed of who she was.

It was only after she recklessly bid on the house that it occurred to her there might be people living on her street, twenty years later, who would recognize her.

Alaska paused to sniff the hydrant. Kate breathed in the damp spring air, studying the houses lining the street. The dark hid the occasional sagging porch, old windows and peeling paint—a hallmark of the homes that had been converted into student flats.

When she'd lived on this street as a child, it'd been a family neighborhood. With kids her age, bicycles and skipping ropes strewn on the sidewalk. Now it housed either entrenched elderly or nomadic university students. It was both a relief and a source of sorrow to realize there were no reminders of her childhood here.

Her stomach growled. The caffeine from her coffee had dissipated, leaving her hungry and tired. "Come on, boy, let's get going. I'm starving."

The envelope on the car seat appeared empty, but Ethan Drake couldn't stop himself from glancing at it every few seconds.

He turned left, then slowed down, surprised to see the neighborhood Kate now lived in.

He frowned. Why had she moved back here after what she'd done? The fact he didn't know the answer ate away at him. Another sign that he really didn't know her, had never known her.

Her house was easy to find, close to the corner. Her car was in the driveway. Good. She was home. He couldn't deny the spark of satisfaction that she wasn't out on a Friday night.

He parked his Jeep on the street, grabbed the envelope and stuffed it into his pocket. *Walk slowly, take your time.*

Easier said than done. Now that he was here, need surged in him. The need to see Kate. The need to hear Kate tell him she was wrong. To see his suffering reflected in her eyes. To know that she was just as confused as he was about why things ended the way they did.

He deserved an explanation.

What if she doesn't give you one?

He ignored that niggling doubt and jogged up the porch steps. It was dark. The light had burned out. The cop in him noted this fact with concern. Kate needed to get it fixed.

It was a perfect opening line: *I was driving by and noticed your light was out...*

He shook his head.

You're an asshole.

She wasn't likely to fall for that. His pulse began to race. What would she do when she saw him on her doorstep? Would she invite him in?

Or would she slam the door in his face?

He'd said some pretty harsh things to her. But damn it, he'd been hurt as hell. The bubble that had enveloped him on Christmas Eve had been rudely burst one week later. "Auld Lang Syne" had had a whole new meaning by the end of New Year's Eve. Old acquaintances had refused to be forgotten, crashing the party with secrets in their pockets.

He ran his hand over his hair. Taking a deep breath, he pushed the doorbell.

Silence.

He pushed the doorbell again.

Silence.

The bloody thing didn't work. Just like the porch light. Kate needed a little help on the upkeep. He thrust away the obvious thought: if they were still together, he'd have this place sparkling by now.

He peered into the oblong windows flanking the front door. A light was on in the back.

He knocked on the door.

No responding footsteps inside.

Shit. Where was she? He peered through the glass again. It was cloudy with age and streaked with drizzle, but he would've been able to see movement if someone was home.

He knocked again.

No answer.

Heat suddenly flamed in his neck. Of course. What a friggin' idiot he was. Hard to believe he was a bloody detective when he couldn't put two and two together.

Kate's car was here, but she wasn't, because it was Friday night and some guy had come and picked her up and was taking her out to a nice restaurant, and he was standing on her front porch in the fucking freezing drizzle with a fucking envelope stuffed in his pocket.

He'd had it all planned out. What he'd say—"I found this under the sofa"—how'd he act. But she always seemed to pull the rug out from under him.

Man, how fucking stupid could he be?

No more stupid than you were on New Year's Eve.

He spun on his heel, taking the front porch steps two at a time, and stalked toward his car.

A large dog lunged toward him.

He leaped back. Not far enough. The dog jumped on him.

"Alaska!" The owner pulled futilely on the dog's lead. Ethan stared in disbelief. "Kate?"

Since when did she have a dog? Pain sliced through him. Anger added a satisfying sting. She'd never called him. Never apologized. Just left him scrambling for his engagement ring on the floor of Bob MacDonald's house.

Within weeks, she'd gone to the enemy camp and joined LMB. Then bought a house. Now a dog. What more could she do to show that he had meant nothing to her?

The dog's front paws were still planted on his chest. Ethan stared into its ice-blue eyes. He fought to control his anger. It wasn't the dog's fault. "Down, boy," he said, pushing him away.

The dog grinned and jumped down. Kate stepped closer. "Ethan?" The quiver in her voice betrayed her shock. Mist beaded tendrils of hair around her face. Her eyes shone with a clear amber light that pierced right to his heart. Shit, how could she still do this to him? When he knew, *he knew,* that the light in her eyes was deceptive. "What are you doing he—"

The dog poked his muzzle in Ethan's crotch.

"Alaska!" Kate cried, yanking his leash. The dog pulled his muzzle out and strolled over to a light pole, lifting his leg. A graceful arc of pee shone under the streetlight.

"Nice," Ethan said. If he hadn't been so angry, he might have seen the humor in this. The dog had summed up his relationship with Kate with brutal efficiency: sniffing his crotch, then pissing on the sidewalk.

He may have learned the hard way that he didn't know Kate the way he thought he did, but he definitely got this dog's vibe. "Where'd you get him? The Shelter for Delinquent Dogs?"

5

Kate stared at Ethan. Shock reverberated through her. Then guilt. Longing. Grief, pain, anger. Flooding her. Making her reel. She couldn't believe he was here. On her sidewalk. Waiting for her. Why, after all this time?

Whatever the reason, the sight of him set her heart jumping and skittering as if it was trying to run for cover and there was nowhere to hide.

There *was* nowhere to hide. That was the problem with Ethan. His presence was so large, so full of life, that it crowded out the safe place deep in her heart she burrowed into when things got too painful. The place she had found when she was ten, the place she had retreated to on a permanent basis six years later. The place he'd chased her out of for six heady months.

She finally was able to move her lips. "Sorry. He's not usually like this." Not only was that a lame excuse, it was a lie. She had no idea what Alaska was normally like. She'd only had him for a week, and she'd spent most of it at work. Why did she always feel she needed to cover things up when Ethan was with her?

He gave her an impenetrable look. "Maybe he's just misunderstood."

Was that an apology? Or was that his excuse for the names he'd called her? She stared at him, hoping she could figure out what the hell he wanted. He looked too good, damn him. His dark hair curled slightly in the drizzle, the collar of his jacket yanked up and framing his jaw. She'd loved tracing the scar on his chin, feeling the smooth line, straight and clean under the bristly stubble.

She found herself searching for the scar, her eyes hungrily absorbing the face she'd seen only in her memory for four months. He looked the same, yet different. There was a set look about his mouth. And his eyes... She couldn't figure it out, but they weren't the way she remembered them.

Neither was the rigid set to his shoulders. Ethan had never been one to let his tension show. But it did now. He had to have heard about her new position at LMB.

Her stomach clenched. He wouldn't take it gracefully. And why should she expect him to? She could just imagine his reaction when he learned that his ex-fiancée jumped to Randall Barrett's firm within weeks of throwing her ring in his face. Knowing her luck, he'd probably heard about it from Vicky.

Despite her resolve not to think about the fraud detective, Kate couldn't rid herself of the memory of Vicky's face after Ethan had confronted Kate on New Year's Eve. Those china-blue eyes, stark with mortification. Known for her unflappability, Vicky had never shown any outward malice toward Kate despite the fact her own relationship with Ethan had only ended several months before. But on New Year's Eve, it was a different story. With no happily ever after. Vicky had shocked everyone. Including, it would seem, herself.

Vicky had cornered her ex in a hallway outside the

bathroom. Kate hadn't seen it coming. She'd been getting a drink.

But upstairs, Vicky congratulated Ethan brightly on his engagement to the daughter of notorious embezzler Dick Lange.

Stunned, he'd confronted Kate. Kate had stared at him, drink in hand, her mind still trying to catch up to the fact that Vicky—cool, matter-of-fact Vicky—had played the woman scorned card. And had made Ethan look the fool.

But it was Kate who was left holding the bag. Had she planned on letting their kids visit Grandpa in the slammer? Ethan had demanded. It was irrelevant, she knew, that her father was no longer in jail. In Ethan's mind, he would always be a con.

He hadn't said much about her sister, Imogen, but his eyes told the story.

Vicky had even tried following Kate outside that icy night. Had it been to apologize? Kate didn't know. Vicky Moffatt would have to live with what she had wrought. Just like Kate did.

"So, how've you been?" Ethan asked, breaking the silence that Kate suddenly realized was growing longer by the second.

"Good." She nodded. "I bought a house."

His gaze swept over it silently.

Closed. That's what his eyes looked like. Closed. She followed his gaze, hoping he wouldn't notice that the porch railing had mold on it and the screen on one of the bedroom windows was torn. Hoping even more that he wouldn't know the significance of the address.

"Congratulations," he said. She hated how shuttered his eyes looked. They drilled into her without revealing a thing. She'd bet anything this was the same look he gave his suspects. "You've always wanted a place like this. And it's in your old neighborhood, isn't it?"

Damn. Vicky must have filled him in on that, as well. *Couldn't let it go, could you, Vicky, my girl?*

"Yes." She pushed a damp strand of hair from her face. She was sure by now her hair resembled waterlogged seaweed. *What a stupid, irrelevant thought. To worry about your hair when Ethan's come here to make you pay.* Because judging by his edginess, he wasn't here to kiss and make up.

"And you got a dog? I thought you weren't into attachments." There was no mistaking his bitterness now.

She lifted her chin. "I never said that."

"You said you didn't want to depend on anyone." He didn't add the rest she'd said that night: *that it was obvious she couldn't depend on him.*

"That's different."

"No." Ethan crossed his arms. "It's not."

He wanted to fight.

All the hurt she'd buried rose to the surface like fat in a boiling pot. Long-rehearsed responses to the accusations he'd hurled on New Year's Eve welled in her throat.

But she didn't speak. She'd had four months of pain searing its scabs onto her heart. Opening up old wounds just made the scars deeper. They'd damaged each other enough.

She tried to give a casual shrug. "I didn't 'get' Alaska. He found me."

"He found you?" Ethan's eyes narrowed. "Where, in the park?" As soon as the words came out, he looked as if he'd wished he could take them back.

She wished he could.

In the park. Where they'd met. Sunshine dappling through pine trees onto the graveled path. She was tying her shoelace, sweat dripping down her brow, her breath coming fast from the long run up Serpentine Hill. He was behind her; she'd noticed him down by the water, noticed him noticing her. When their eyes met, that was it. She had the sensation she had transcended her ordinary life and had entered a plane she'd never known existed. A plane where hope was suddenly, giddily, within her grasp.

"No." She struggled to speak through the tightness in her throat. "He used to live here. With the previous owner. When she died, he went to live with the owner's niece, but he kept coming back and sitting on the porch. I only adopted him last week." Rain trickled down Kate's neck. A damp chill settled around her. Along with a weariness. Couldn't Ethan see there was no point in this? They'd said too many things to each other that couldn't be taken back. The fragile trust they had forged together over six months of passion had been irreversibly severed. "I've gotta go." She turned up the walkway. Then added over her shoulder, "Please don't come here again."

The finality of her words seemed to shock Ethan out of his anger. "Wait." He lunged toward her. "I'm sorry. I didn't come here to argue with you."

"Really?" She didn't bother to hide her bitterness.

He reached into his back pocket and pulled out an envelope. "I found this the other night and thought you might be missing it."

Gold flashed as it fell from the open envelope onto the pavement.

Her breath stuck in her throat. A round gold circle gleamed against the wet sidewalk.

The ring.

He swore and dove to pick it up, holding it out to her on his palm. Her pulse jumped back into her veins. It was a gold hoop earring. She'd lost it a few weeks before the party.

She forced herself to breathe slowly. Had he seen her face when the earring fell? She hoped God was giving her this one small break and Ethan hadn't.

She picked the earring off his palm. His eyes remained fixed on her hand. He knew she was doing her best not to make contact with his skin.

"Thanks." She slipped it into her pocket. She'd throw it away as soon as she got inside. "I appreciate you returning it." She turned to go.

"Kate, *wait*."

She paused, pressing her hand against her side, twisting her fingers in Alaska's leash.

"We need to talk." He glanced at her house. Obviously hoping she'd invite him inside.

She shoved a soggy strand of hair behind her ear. "I don't want to talk. I think we've said enough." Before she cracked and the mess of her past came spilling out onto the sidewalk.

He crossed his arms. "That's the whole problem."

"What?"

"You think you've said enough when you've said nothing at all."

"There isn't anything more to say."

"I want answers, Kate. I want to know why you never told me about your father."

His eyes bore into hers. She could see he felt he was justified in demanding the truth. That it was owed to him. Her own anger began to simmer.

"I didn't need to say anything. Vicky filled you in pretty thoroughly, if I recall."

His jaw tightened. "Only because you didn't. How could you not tell me about your dad going to jail?" His voice hardened. "And about your sister?"

The weight in her chest got heavier. She hated what he

was doing to her. Bringing to the surface all the emotions she'd successfully smothered since they'd broken up. "I wasn't trying to…" She stopped abruptly. She sounded like a kid weaseling her way out of trouble. "It was never the right time."

"We saw each other several times a week for six months, Kate!"

"I know…" She'd wanted to tell him. She'd wanted to come clean about her past. But every time the moment seemed right, he'd hush her words with a kiss. And the kiss inevitably led to more…

He had been just as reluctant as she to burst the romantic bubble that had floated them beyond their pasts, their presents. He just didn't want to admit it. He wanted to blame it all on her.

The leash was twisted so tightly around her fingers she could feel them growing numb. It was good. Numb was good. Because if she wasn't numb, her anger would boil over.

She could feel his eyes boring into her. "So when were you planning to tell me? After I put my ring on your finger?"

His innuendo pushed her over the edge. "Are you suggesting I tried to trick you into marrying me?"

Christmas Eve, on his knee, his grandmother's ring. The memory punctured her.

She'd managed to say yes through her tears. Then spent the rest of the Christmas holidays in agony. Terrified he would reject her if she told him about her past.

It was his turn to look away. "I didn't mean you were tricking me…"

"Really? It sounded like that to me."

"It's just when you put two and two together…" He jammed his hands into his pockets. "When *were* you going to tell me?"

"I don't know!" Alaska sensed her agitation and whined deep in his throat. "I was waiting for the right time." How could she explain when she didn't know herself? It was outside her realm of experience. Everything. The sudden consuming passion, his adoration of her, his love of life that made everything seem vibrant, rich, good.

"There never would have been a right time for something like that." His brusque tone forced her back to the present. "You should have just told me."

"I knew it would ruin things between us." It had. She'd been right.

"It only ruined things because you lied to me."

"I didn't lie!" Her fingers curled into themselves.

"Lying by omission."

She stared at him. In the space of four months, he'd gone from being her lover to her accuser.

Her pulse began to pound in her temples. "You just can't deal with the fact that the future wife of a homicide detective has a father who is a convicted embezzler."

He crossed his arms. "It's not just your father, Kate."

She stiffened. She knew where he was going with this. Her rage flooded her. She welcomed it. "What do you mean?"

"I need to know what happened with your sister."

She raised her chin. "Vicky couldn't find the report?"

"Why are you making this so bloody difficult?" A corresponding anger tightened his face. "I just want to know what happened."

"You think I'm guilty, don't you? You think if I refuse to tell you, I did something wrong."

"It sure as hell makes me wonder!"

"You know what, Ethan? I'm tired of you treating me like a fucking suspect."

"And I'm tired of you treating me like a fucking idiot.

Didn't you even *think* about the fact all your 'secrets' were on the public record? That I would eventually find out?"

"Don't patronize me. You have no idea what I went through." She tugged on Alaska's leash and stumbled to the front porch stairs.

He called after her, "You're right. I have no idea. Because you won't tell me." His voice rose. "This is about trust, goddamn it. If you can't even tell me the truth…"

She stopped abruptly. She hadn't been able to tell him the truth four months ago. But, by God, she'd tell him now. Let him know just how lucky he was to have gotten away from her. She turned around. "You want the truth?"

He said softly, "Yeah. I do."

"Fine." *You're opening Pandora's box, baby, but it's your choice.* She took a deep breath. Made her voice flat. "Here's the story."

Her eyes forced him to hold her gaze.

"When I was sixteen I killed my sister."

He flinched. "The report says you were driving. The car crashed."

"I was speeding. I killed her."

It was as simple as that. A blink of an eye. A life gone.

"Are you satisfied now?" She didn't wait for an answer. Ethan had gotten the truth. Whether he could live with it was another question. She pulled out her house keys, fumbling. The leash tangled in her fingers.

"Kate. I'm sorry." His words sounded hollow.

"I don't think you are. You got what you came for. Now go."

"Kate…"

"Go!" She refused to look at him. She put the key in the lock. She heard him retreat haltingly down the walkway, his car door close, the engine squeal to life.

She pushed open the front door. The swollen wood stuck and then released suddenly. She pitched forward into the hallway. "Fuck!"

Alaska ran through to the kitchen, leaving muddy footprints and trailing his leash behind him. She caught a glance of herself in the antique hallway mirror. Her eyes, ringed with smudged mascara, stared back at her. She headed into the kitchen.

Alaska paced by his food bowl. He gave an expectant whine. She snatched his water dish from the floor. Water sloshed onto her fingers. "Fuck!" She banged the water dish onto the counter. Water splattered her T-shirt. "Fuck, fuck, fuck!"

Her fingers were shaking. She leaned against the counter, head down, breathing deeply until the anger leached from her body. So much for celebrating her new case.

When she opened her eyes, she saw Alaska watching her by his food bowl. "Sorry, boy," she said wearily. "You've been way too patient with me. I won't do this again."

She grabbed the bag of Kibbles 'n Bits from the cupboard, shame at her outburst overriding her anger at Ethan. She poured extra food into Alaska's bowl. He lunged forward and gobbled it hungrily.

She had no appetite, but she knew she should eat something. She needed protein for her run tomorrow morning. Not only that, the bottle of wine on the counter beckoned her, and if she drank on an empty stomach she'd end up on the kitchen floor.

She popped a frozen lasagna in the microwave. It was the last one. She needed to get to the grocery store. The thought of it exhausted her. She needed to get to bed. As soon as she ate, she'd have a hot bath and go to sleep.

Alaska gave his food bowl one last lick and began to

circle in front of the kitchen door. She let him out, watching the husky trot across the back porch down to the yard. He loved nosing around the overgrown shrubs, chasing the cats that slinked along the tattered garden bed. She turned from the door and poured a glass of wine.

The microwave beeped. She pulled her dinner from the oven. The pasta was limp under the unnaturally red sauce. The cheese looked stringy, not brown and bubbly.

A high-pitched howl split the air.

She started, tipping the tray. The lasagna slid over the plastic edge and fell to the floor.

"Fuck!"

There was another howl.

"Alaska?" The only sound she'd ever heard him make was whining.

A shiver snaked up her spine. She stepped around the splattered pasta and opened the back door.

Alaska crouched under the porch light, tiny drops of rain electrifying his fur. A low growl rumbled through bared teeth. His ears were erect, quivering.

She followed his intent gaze. And froze.

A hooded figure slipped out of her yard.

She ran across the back porch. A rotting board groaned under her weight. Alaska followed at her heels. When her stocking feet hit the steps, slick with rain and moss, she slipped and stumbled to her knees. By the time she scrambled to her feet, sanity returned. What was she doing? She shouldn't be chasing this guy. That was a job for the police. It was too late, anyway—the intruder had disappeared.

"Damn it." She stood panting in her yard. The street was empty. Quiet. Dark. Rain fell, washing away any footsteps that might have revealed themselves. She wrapped her arms around her middle.

Alaska nosed her thigh and she patted him. "Good dog." She walked slowly around the side of her house, glad for Alaska's presence, though she had to admit he wasn't attack-dog material.

She wished she had an alarm system but she wouldn't be able to afford one for at least another year, if then. The leaky roof and even leakier kitchen pipes had taken precedence. She stepped back inside. Alaska rushed by her straight to the lasagna. Within seconds it was gone. She couldn't eat, anyway. Fear constricted her stomach into a tiny ball.

Ethan. He was probably at home. She could call him and he would be at her house in five minutes. The cop in him would make sure she was safe.

Safe, but not forgiven.

She swallowed and reached for the phone.

The 911 operator answered on the first ring.

"I'd like to report an intruder," Kate said.

6

Monday, April 30, 6:21 a.m.

Kate watched Alaska trot across the dew-soaked grass of Point Pleasant Park. The ocean lapped its edges, funneling on one side into the Halifax Harbour, narrowing into the Northwest Arm on the other. By summer, the long blue arm of water would be dotted with dinghies, yachts and tour boats, people admiring the beautifully terraced properties of Halifax's finest homes.

She picked up her pace. God, it was hard today. Her body just didn't want to do it. But she needed to. She needed to get Ethan out of her head. She had woken on Saturday with a throbbing headache. Memories of chasing the intruder and giving the police a statement were like a bad hangover fueled by her confrontation with Ethan. For the first time in months she had skipped her Saturday morning run. Her run on Sunday morning didn't help dislodge the sluggishness in her limbs. She could barely concentrate on the TransTissue file. She had to force herself to sort through the facts and draft a memo to make John Lyons take note. The effort came with a price. Here it was, Monday morning, 6:21 a.m., and she felt completely drained.

Knowing that she had to go to LMB in less than two hours and prove her legal mind was as good—or better—than all the other first-year associates made her resent Ethan's unannounced visit even more. He had distracted her from the biggest file of her career. He had dragged her back to a place she had no desire to be.

He wouldn't let it go. He claimed he had come for answers, but she had seen his eyes. He wanted more than that. He wanted to make her pay for what had happened on New Year's Eve.

Her feet pounded in a punishing rhythm on the path. They had run together, their strides in sync. He loved running as much as she did. She had been used to doing it alone, letting her thoughts fly around her, but she had found herself enjoying his company. She'd think about the night before. How he'd seduced her with his reverential touch on her body. And then she'd feel the power in her body as she ran with him side by side.

How could she take one of those fairy-tale moments with him and ruin it with the sordid details of her past? Her past was something she kept locked in a very dark, deep box. Putting voice to it made it real again.

It had scared her. Terrified her. Admitting what she'd done to this man she loved so desperately. Ethan saw life in black-and-white. The only thing she saw in black-and-white was death. Everything else was shades in between.

In the gray of the early morning, the massive anchor of the sailors' memorial loomed a shade darker than the colorless water. Alaska skirted around it, then bounded across the wide stretch of grass toward the old stone fort. The fort had been one of the first lines of defense for Halifax during the two World Wars. It was crumbling now, overgrown with hillocks. Yet it retained a sober dignity, a memorial to long-ago trauma.

The fort was disintegrating. Just like the barriers she'd spent her adult life molding around her heart. They were suddenly becoming thin, porous, easily breached. It wasn't just Ethan. Although he'd given it a good hammering on Friday. The breach had started before that. When she realized she could never outrun her past. When she looked at the calendar and saw that the date was finally arriving.

The fifteenth anniversary of her sister's death. It gave her life a special symmetry. She had had fifteen years of being loved by her sister, and then had spent fifteen years living with the knowledge that she had killed the one who had loved her most.

A wind brushed her cheeks, damp and chill, pulling her out of her reverie. She glanced toward the horizon. Sure enough, a fog bank crept under the rising sun. Its edges smudged the dark band of fir trees on MacNab's Island. Within an hour it would billow over the water, blanketing the navigational buoys, concealing the treacherous Hen and Chickens Shoal off the end of the park that still caught yachts in its teeth. Then the low groan of the foghorns would fill the air. She usually liked the sound of them: deep, unearthly. So different from the shrill noises of modern technology.

But she was glad they weren't sounding today. She didn't need the mournful warning that the fog of her childhood was about to descend on her. That the ghost of her sister was running right on her heels.

She couldn't shake her. Nor could she shake the feeling that she was letting down another fifteen-year-old girl. One whom she hadn't met, but who appeared to be going down a road that Kate had glimpsed before. On the night of Imogen's death. When she found her fifteen-year-old sister in the back porch of a house party, with a mirror, a razor blade and a mound of white powder. She'd tried taking Imogen away.

And killed her instead.

She reached the fork at the end of the trail. Both paths were grueling uphill runs. She chose the one on the left. Serpentine Hill stretched out in front of her. It was steep. It was punishing. It was just what she needed. Alaska slowed down, angling into the woods to check out the squirrels. She pounded up the winding hill mercilessly. Just when she thought she could breathe no longer, the path leveled off, letting her heart catch up to the relentless pace her legs had set.

That was how she lived her life. Fast paced. Striving for success.

Because if you were successful, you'd be respected. No one could hurt you. No one could take that success away from you.

That had been her mantra for the past fifteen years. If she didn't have that, she didn't have anything.

LMB was her ticket to the kind of career she wanted. Thanks to the TransTissue case, she could sense success just around the corner. The easiest—and most prudent—thing would be to concentrate on that case. She'd done the ground-work over the weekend. She had a strong analysis to present to John Lyons this morning. She should forget about Marian MacAdam. After all, her client's last words to Kate were that she would find proof of Lisa's drug use herself.

But how could a seventy-year-old grandmother who lived a life of privilege know how to find proof of a teen-ager's illicit drug use?

She still didn't have the answer to that question when she ran through the park gates, Alaska trotting by her side.

Sweat left a damp patch on her back. To hell with it. As soon as she got to the office, she'd hand in her memo on the TransTissue defense to John Lyons. Then she'd call Marian MacAdam. She'd tell her that if she was really concerned about Lisa's well-being, they needed to contact the authorities right away.

To hell with Randall Barrett. He was the one who'd sent her the client. He'd have to live with it, too.

Her office phone rang. It was 8:55 a.m. Kate snatched up the receiver. She'd just called Marian MacAdam, but there'd been no answer. Maybe her client had been in the bathroom.

"Hello?"

"Kate, it's Mark." *Mark Boynton*. From the labor law practice. She straightened.

He cleared his throat. "I realize it's short notice, but I need someone to assist on a hearing today. Are you free?"

Her heart leaped. "Yes, of course."

"Great. Meet me in my office ASAP. I want to go over a couple of things before the hearing starts."

She put the receiver down, grabbed her briefcase and trench coat and hurried from her office.

As she walked down the hallway, doing her best to not swing her briefcase in excitement, she suddenly remembered her call to Marian MacAdam.

The hearing had gone well. Really well. Mark, a year away from partnership, had been pleased.

"You think fast on your feet," he'd said over a sub during the lunch break.

"These feet will run with anything you give me," she'd said, hoping he'd be impressed enough to throw her a lifeline out of the ghetto.

When she returned to her office just before 6:00 p.m., she checked her voice mail, then scanned the e-mails from her assistant. No message from Marian MacAdam.

In a way, she was relieved. She was tired; she wanted to get home at a decent hour for once—before Alaska peed on the floor.

And besides, what difference would a day make? The wheels of justice ground slowly.

It could wait until tomorrow.

7

Tuesday, May 1, 2:00 a.m.

He circled the silver sedan around the long building before rolling to a gentle stop beside the rear entrance.

No one was about. Nor should they be; it was the middle of the night. But you never knew.

He glanced upward through the windshield again. Yes. The grain elevators were a vacant shell. Cranes stood in the distance, frozen under the floodlights like Jurassic dinosaurs. A white fuzziness softened the hard metal edges. He frowned. The light was very bright. Too bright. It made things blurry in contrast.

He slid out of the car, easing the door shut, and padded around to the trunk. His pulse quickened.

Then froze. He heard a scuffling noise. His eyes scanned the long dingy building above. There was no light in the windows. Was someone up there? Watching him in the dark? He stared into the black recesses where the floodlights didn't reach. White fringed his vision. He squinted. There it was again. A movement. A scurrying.

His shoulders relaxed. A smile twisted his lips. He

should have recognized that sound. After all, hadn't he waited many nights for his prey in this very spot?

The rat strolled unhurriedly across the doorway and out of sight. Rats had brought him so much joy. How well he knew this species. Inside and out.

A rattle startled him. He glanced around quickly. Just the rat running into the garbage bin next to the building. He let his breathing slow.

Time to focus. He opened the car trunk. A faint light showed his prize.

He was good. Much better than he got credit for.

He reached into the trunk. His gloved hands glowed fuzzily against the darkness of his cuffs. He blinked. The blurriness remained. He ignored it. This was the moment. The culmination of his painstaking efforts. Nothing would ruin it.

He unzipped the plastic bag, so silently he felt—rather than heard—the vibration of the teeth yawning open. His hands slid under her. One hand behind the neck. The other at her groin.

She was easy to lift out of the bag, her body fitting compactly in his arms. He glanced around once more. There were houses and apartment buildings surrounding the granary. Ironic that such a noisy, rat-infested spot should be in such an expensive neighborhood, but that was geography. The granary was by the water. So were the houses.

The buildings were silent. It was if they knew he was coming and made sure their occupants were not straying. He hunched over his prize and walked quickly to the rear door of the granary. Blood spattered behind his shoes, gleaming in four little trails behind him.

Perfect. No one could miss her.

He laid her carefully on the ground and studied her one last time.

Her eyes stared at the black sky. They were empty. The drugs had taken care of the fear; his hands had done the rest.

Those hands had once been impotent. Futile. Unable to defend himself.

No. Don't think of it now. Don't ruin it. He clenched his fingers to stop the memory from taunting him.

Not now! His fingers dug into his palms. The effort, he knew, was in vain. His brain always overruled his body.

He was wrestling. Furiously. His eight-year-old self shrank under the blows of the fifteen-year-old.

"You are such a wimp," his brother panted, shoving him. He fell at his brother's feet.

"Don't you ever take my stuff again," Tim snarled, dangling the prize in front of his eyes. He closed them. It was too much. It wasn't fair. He always gave Tim his space. Never entered his lair. But when his brother had shown him the pocket knife he'd won at a school science fair, he couldn't help himself. It was everything he'd ever wanted. And would never be given. Pain warred with envy. He wanted it badly. So badly. The neat, tiny instruments that folded with utter certainty into impossibly narrow slots. He wanted that knife. He wanted to be the knife. To be able to fold into himself. And then pop out to dazzle everyone with his daring and precision.

He rolled away from his brother's legs and curled into a ball. He would prove himself one day. He would.

And he had. He had proven his mother wrong. And had shown it was not just his older brother who had talent.

A deep rumbling filled the air. A train sped by on the overpass. He ignored it and smoothed the skunk stripe in her dyed black hair. Then he stood and admired his handiwork.

It was flawless. How easily her limbs had separated from her body. There were no jagged edges. No hanging

threads of muscle, no torn tendons. They had all been precisely detached. All that was left was smooth bone under
even edges of flesh.

He nodded, pleased. She was perfectly straight. The
nipples on her small breasts made a symmetrical triangle
with the dark V of her groin. That was why he enjoyed the
younger ones so much more. Their bodies were not mis-
shapen from aging. Fewer surprises under the skin, too.
The muscles were firm, the bones strong.

Her shoulder and hip sockets gleamed wetly in the dark.
Pools of coagulating blood beneath the sockets made dark
memories of her limbs.

He pushed his excitement down. How long would it take
for the medical examiner to notice the little message he'd
inscribed in her glenoid cavity?

8

Ethan wove his Jeep around the line of cars inching away from the granary. This must be the early-morning shift of granary workers. A patrol officer urged them past, but they crawled along, craning their necks to peer beyond the bright yellow crime scene tape surrounding the site. Some sipped Tim Hortons coffee, others had a nervous puff. A few talked excitedly on their cell phones.

Ethan sighed. It wouldn't take long for the news to spread.

The good news was that they couldn't see anything. For that, Ethan was grateful. For the rest, he was not. He'd gotten the call from Detective Sergeant Deb Ferguson twenty-eight minutes ago. "Suspected homicide, the granary," she had told him. "The night watchman just called it in."

Ethan had thrown his legs over the side of his bed and forced his eyes to focus on the clock. It was 5:55 a.m. It felt like 3:00 a.m. He needed to get to bed earlier. Staying up flipping through his two hundred satellite channels was killing him. And he didn't even like TV.

"Here's the triangle," Deb continued. She was referring

to the Investigative Triangle, the command model they used for investigating cases. He straightened. "You're up for primary investigator." There was a pause. Was she hoping he'd thank her? He'd been waiting for months to be assigned primary investigator again. Ever since the Clarkson file. Ever since Randall Barrett had triggered an internal investigation into his handling of the witness. "Right." He made his voice noncommittal. But he couldn't hold down the satisfaction that washed through him. He was back in the fold. No, better than that, he was back on top again.

He stood. "Is the scene secured?"

"They're working on it. The patrol sergeant is taping off the area. I told him to secure everything inside the fence. We don't want another Surette case on our hands."

Ethan grimaced. They'd had a hard time living that one down. An inexperienced patrol officer had taped off a three-foot area around the body of gang victim David Surette. The bullet casings were found by a kid fifty feet outside the tape and taken to school for show-and-tell before the teacher called the police.

"I'll be there in half an hour," he said, heading to the bathroom.

There was a pause. "It's a nasty one, Ethan."

"Yeah?" The tone of the detective sergeant's voice snapped Ethan out of his precoffee fog.

"Young girl, mutilated."

"Shit." That'd be a magnet for the media. He wondered how many minutes it'd take for them to get wind of it. "The patrol sergeant better make sure the scene is nailed tight."

When he got to the chain-link fence surrounding the granary, Ethan spotted the white bunny suits of two Forensic Identification Services investigators—known as the "Ident guys"—just inside the yellow taped area. They were combing the outer perimeter of the granary lot, cameras and markers in hand. He pulled his Jeep in beside a van emblazoned with Forensic Identification Unit and hopped out. The command bus was sitting next to the gate, silent on the outside, but a hive of activity on the inside. Walker'd be setting up the computers right now.

Daylight burned through the fiery sunrise. How fitting to have a bloody horizon mark this young girl's death. *Red sky in the morning, sailor's warning*. At first, the childhood rhyme didn't register.

Then it did. More rain was coming. He rubbed his jaw, sloshing coffee over his knuckles. Shit. The Ident guys better work quickly before any trace evidence was washed away.

The patrol officer manning the gate was young. And from the looks of it, fresh out of the academy. The constable's eyes were stoic, but his face was pale. He would have been the first responder to the call. Ethan wondered if he'd seen a homicide victim before. He doubted it. All the more reason to assign him to guard the body when it was locked in the morgue. "Detective Drake, MCU," Ethan said, flashing his ID.

The constable glanced at it and opened the gate. "Detective Riley asked me to radio her when you arrived."

He nodded. Riley was the lead Ident detective. She ran a tight ship, and he respected her for that. No compromising of evidence on her watch. No one was allowed to enter a crime scene without her permission, except for the M.E. There'd been too many crime scenes that were compromised by police officers accidentally stepping on prints that were invisible to the naked eye or by leaving their own trace evidence. But with Riley, things changed. It made his job—and the prosecutors'—so much easier.

Riley saw him and waved. Ethan knew not to be fooled

by her small stature. She was tough, a triathlete in her spare time. She had more stamina—mental and physical— than the entire graduating class of the academy. She headed toward him, carefully following a path that he knew would be the same every time. Same way in, same way out. It kept contamination of evidence to a minimum.

She stopped in front of him. Alarm bells rang in Ethan's head. In the five years he'd known her, he'd never seen Audrey Riley show any emotional reaction to a case until it was over. But today he saw distress blurring her usual focused gaze.

"Here's the rundown, and it isn't good," Riley said, her hazel eyes locking his. "The victim looks to be approximately fifteen to eighteen years of age, been dead for several hours. She was discovered by a security guard." She crossed her arms. "Doubt he'll have a job after today. He admitted to falling asleep. Seems like he took a catnap every night."

"How long did he sleep for?"

"He claims he was asleep for twenty minutes around 0200, but he's an old guy. I bet it was longer."

"And what time was the victim discovered?"

"0540. The security guard called the police right away. He was scared shitless." A muscle flexed in her jaw. "He has shit for brains, too. He ran through the tire track the killer left. We can't get an imprint."

"That the only one?" From the flash of frustration in Riley's eyes, Ethan knew what her answer would be.

"Yeah. So far, it's the only trace evidence we've uncovered."

He stared at her. "That's it?"

"Yeah. The victim was naked, Ethan. No clothes, no ID, no fibers that we can find."

That meant the autopsy would be more crucial than ever. "Which M.E. is coming?"

"Guthro."

He relaxed. "Good. He'll find something. There'll probably be some trace under the nails—"

"Didn't anyone tell you?" Riley asked brusquely. "She was dismembered."

His heart dropped. "Deb was told she was mutilated."

"No. All her limbs were cut off."

"Shit," he said softly. "Have you recovered them yet?"

"Not yet." The way she said it, Ethan had no doubt the Ident guys would be digging holes in every inch of dirt until they did.

"So this wasn't the kill site?"

Riley shook her head. "Uh-uh. This site is pristine. You could have the Queen for fucking tea here. He killed the victim somewhere else and dumped her here."

"Damn." He stared past her shoulder at the crime scene tape. An anonymous dismembered girl, a clean dump site and rain about to fall on whatever trace evidence there was.

Halifax had never seen anything like it.

9

Marian MacAdam unlocked the door to her condo and rolled her overnight bag inside. Despite her attempts to make it feel like home, the condo had a still quality that she hated. No matter that she'd lived in it for almost three years, she couldn't get used to the confines of a high-rise. A house—or at least her house—had always seemed to breathe when she was gone.

Marian hurried through the living room and threw open the patio doors. The air was so damp it left a layer of moisture on her skin.

Part of her wished she hadn't come back just yet. Her plan had been to spend the week in St. Margaret's Bay, getting her cottage opened for the summer. Before her disastrous meeting with Kate Lange, she'd had visions of organizing the spare bedroom so Lisa could invite some friends to "hang out" there for the school holidays. She'd even looked into sailing lessons at the local yacht club.

But her meeting with Kate Lange had punctured those hopes. She'd spent the past three days halfheartedly making lists of jobs for the cleaning service, restocking the pantry and washing all the sheets.

Yesterday, she sat on the deck, the wind cool despite the sudden hit of spring heat. The fog had retreated to the outer islands. It would stay there for a few hours. She gazed at the water. Thinking about happier times. Thinking about her life with Roy. Missing him more than ever. Wishing she could talk to him about her meeting with Kate Lange. She'd wanted the lawyer to deal with her troubles, not heap more on her plate. She couldn't make her understand that calling Child Protection Services was the worst thing Marian could do to Lisa.

Wasn't it?

She had been so sure of that on Friday. Then over the weekend the doubts crept in. Just like the fog.

When her friend Margaret called last night to invite her for lunch at the art gallery today, she accepted with alacrity. Her doubts would not let her rest. Better to have some company. She wasn't sure if she would confide her troubles to Margaret; she'd see how lunch went.

The cottage seemed to breathe a sigh of relief when she had locked it up earlier this morning and ventured tentatively onto St. Margaret's Bay Road. The drive had been slow, the road windy and nerve-racking in its opacity, although the dense fog that hugged the curves didn't seem to slow down some drivers. Normally she liked to tune into the CBC radio morning show. But today she had needed to concentrate extra hard. She would never admit it to anyone, but driving was a bit difficult nowadays. She missed things that would suddenly rush at her and cause her heart to jump.

The call from the headmistress had been the third in the past two weeks. Hope put the phone down and stared at her hands. Her fingers clenched slowly into fists, then stretched out onto her desk. She breathed deeply. She had to be in court in five minutes. She needed to calm down. But it was difficult. The headmistress's insinuations had been offensive.

"Have you heard the morning news?" Ms. MacInnes had asked her.

Hope had. A homicide in the south end of the city. Police were refusing to provide any details until the victim's family had been notified, but witnesses claimed the victim had been a prostitute.

At first, Hope did not grasp why Ms. MacInnes had brought this up. But then it hit her. And she was outraged. She couldn't believe the nerve of the headmistress—*Head-mistress*—who was she kidding? A glorified public school principal, more like it.

Hope's voice became glacial. "What, exactly, is the relevance of that question in terms of my daughter's absenteeism?"

Ms. MacInnes paused. Hope felt a spark of satisfaction. It quickly died at the headmistress's next words. "It is very relevant if Lisa is using drugs again."

"She's not," Hope snapped. "There has been no proof whatsoever that she is using them."

"Besides the fact of her truancy," Ms. MacInnes said softly. Then she asked, "What does she do when she skips school?"

Hope inhaled sharply. "Her grandmother keeps an eye on her."

"I see." The headmistress did not bother to disguise her disbelief. "Lisa cannot continue to miss school, Your Honor. We have academic standards that must be met."

"I assure you that I am handling matters," Hope said stiffly. "Lisa will be at school tomorrow."

"Good. Perhaps we could arrange a time to meet about this…?"

"I will have my assistant call you." Hope disconnected the line.

She did not want to make the next call but she had to.

The phone rang. It jarred the stillness. Marian jumped. She had been lost in thought. Kate Lange had left a message on her answering machine just minutes before she had arrived home from the cottage. She'd left one the day before, as well. She wanted Marian to call her, but Marian hadn't—not yet. She decided she would talk to Margaret before she dove into those muddy waters.

The phone rang again. Insistent.

Was it Kate Lange? Marian's fingers hovered over the handle. She really didn't feel ready to talk to her.

The phone rang a third time. She hesitated. Maybe it was Margaret. She really should answer it. She snatched up the receiver.

"Marian."

Her heart sank at the sound of the crisp voice on the other end. "Yes." Why was Hope calling? Had her ex-daughter-in-law heard that Marian had consulted a lawyer about Lisa?

"I don't have much time—" *you never do when it comes to family* "—court is about to begin, but I wanted to check that Lisa was with you."

Dread crawled down Marian's spine. "I haven't seen her since last week."

"Lisa told me yesterday that she was having dinner with you. I assumed she stayed over."

How convenient. "No. I was at the cottage."

"Did Lisa know that?"

"Yes." *Why did you lie again, Lisa?* Marian silently wept for the child who had once had nothing to hide. "So she didn't come home last night?"

"No."

Marian's heart began skipping beats. She forced herself to calm down. "Where do you think she is?"

"I don't know. The school called five minutes ago to report her absence." Hope's voice was remarkable in its steeliness. Or maybe it wasn't remarkable. "But as we both know, she's gone off on her own before. She's probably at her friend's."

There was a murmur on Hope's end, someone had come into her office. Hope's voice became staccato. "Look, I have to go. I want you to call her friends. I'll recess court at 10:45 and call you."

"Yes, all right—" The dial tone buzzed in Marian's ear. Hope had hung up on her.

She put down the receiver and hurried over to her desk. Her address book was there. She hoped she had the phone numbers for all of Lisa's friends. Her stomach clenched with anxiety. Where had Lisa gone last night? And why hadn't Hope done anything about it until now?

This was exactly the behavior that had driven her to see Kate Lange in the first place.

She flipped open the book and began dialing.

Kate closed her office door and slid behind her desk. It was 10:25 a.m., although you couldn't tell by looking out the window. The rain had started. Everything was gray.

She picked up the phone. Her heart pounded as she dialed Marian MacAdam's number again. She had a feeling her client had deliberately not returned her phone call. But Kate couldn't wait anymore. Urgency thrummed through her. After hearing about the homicide on the radio this morning she knew she needed to act—before Lisa followed the same path as that dead prostitute.

"Hello?" Marian MacAdam said breathlessly.

"It's Kate Lange from Lyons McGrath Barrett." Kate stared at the Child Protection phone number she'd jotted on her notepad. Would she have to give an ultimatum or would Marian MacAdam call Child Protection herself?

"Yes? Are you calling about Lisa?"

Her tone wasn't what Kate expected. She thought Marian MacAdam would be haughty, reluctant. But there was no mistaking the desperation Kate heard. She swallowed her unease. "Yes. I'm calling about the meeting we had on Friday—"

"I haven't been able to find Lisa," Marian MacAdam said abruptly. "She's gone."

"Since when?"

"Her mother hasn't seen her since she went to school yesterday morning. She told Hope she was having supper with me, but that was a lie. She knew I was at my cottage."

"Well, I'm sure she's fine." Kate forced herself to sound reassuring. "She's probably at a friend's." Hadn't Kate done the same thing when she was sixteen? Snuck out to a party, taking her younger sister and her mother's car. But it had all gone horribly wrong after that. She pushed that from her mind. Lisa was probably cozied up with a friend cruising Facebook.

"I've called all her friends. No one's seen her."

The news report said it was a young prostitute who had been murdered. *What if it wasn't?* "Did anyone see her last night?"

Marian's voice was bleak. "None of her school friends have spoken to her for a few days, apparently."

Kate wiped her palms on her skirt. "Have you called the police?"

"No."

"You need to call them."

"I want to wait until Hope calls me back. She said she'd recess court at 10:45."

"Marian." Kate didn't know how to ask this, so she blurted: "Have you heard the news today?"

"No." Her client's voice became scared. "Why?"

"There's been a homicide. The reports suggest it was a prostitute, but—"

"It can't be Lisa!"

"But you don't know where she is."

"She's not a prostitute!"

"I know that." Kate tried to be gentle, yet she needed her client to see the urgency in this. "But the news report could be wrong. You need to contact the police."

"I'm going to wait until Hope calls. Lisa may have tried calling her this morning."

Clutching at straws. It was clear her client could not consider the alternative. That the unthinkable might have happened. Kate glanced at the clock. It was 10:33. Judge Carson should be calling soon. "All right, then. When Judge Carson calls, tell her if she hasn't heard from Lisa, then she needs to call the police. Or your lawyer will."

Kate hung up the phone. She knew, without a doubt, she had made the right call.

What she didn't know was if she had made it too late.

Kate found out twenty minutes later. Marian called her back. Her client could barely speak. Lisa hadn't called. But

Hope was dismissive of Marian's suggestion that the homicide victim could be Lisa. She wanted Marian to track down some of Lisa's old friends.

"It's a waste of time," Marian said, despair weighing her voice. "Lisa hasn't spoken to them for years."

"Why won't she call the police?" Kate asked. It seemed incomprehensible that a criminal court judge could not put two and two together when her daughter was missing and a dead girl had been found.

"Because then she'd have to admit to the police that she had no idea where her daughter was," Marian said bitterly. "She doesn't want to involve them until she has to. She said she wanted to look for her first ourselves."

"It's too late to be worried about what the police will think. If Lisa is not—" Kate paused at the sound of Marian's sudden sob. "I'm sorry. But Lisa's safety is paramount. Someone just killed a girl. If Lisa is still unaccounted for, we need to make sure she's safe." Kate picked up her pen. "I need a description of her I can give to the police."

Marion gave her the details in a numb voice, swallowing hard at the end. "You'll call me as soon as you know something?"

"Of course."

"I can't believe this is happening," she whispered.

Kate knew exactly how her client felt. She'd said the same thing fifteen years ago.

She hung up the phone and dialed Ethan's number before her courage failed her.

"Detective Drake." His voice was terse.

"Ethan. It's Kate."

"Jesus." He didn't hide his shock. Nor his anger. "This is a bad time to call, Kate. I'm on a homicide investigation."

"I'm not calling about what happened on Friday night," Kate said quickly. "I'm calling about the prostitute who was found murdered this morning. Is that the case you're on?"

"I'm investigating the homicide, but who said it was a prostitute?"

"That's what the media is saying."

"It's unclear."

Kate's heart lurched. If it wasn't a prostitute, then could it be Lisa? She took a deep breath. "Look, my client's granddaughter went missing yesterday."

Ethan's voice sharpened. "What's her name?"

"Lisa MacAdam."

"What does she look like?"

Kate read off the description: "Fifteen years old, five-foot-four, one hundred and ten pounds, dark brown hair with a blond stripe down the middle—"

"How do we reach next of kin?" Ethan asked abruptly.

"Oh, my God." Kate swallowed. She clutched the phone against her cheek. "Is it her?" *Please say no. If there is a God, please let Ethan say no.*

"Sounds about right." There was an unnerving mix of adrenaline and somberness in his voice. "Who are her parents?"

"Robert MacAdam and—Ethan, this is going to be a minefield—her mother is Judge Hope Carson."

There was a stunned silence. "Holy shit." He added softly, "We thought she was a street kid."

"No. Just a forgotten kid."

"Look, I gotta go. We need to get her parents down here."

"Right."

There was an awkward silence. "Thanks for the tip. I'm sorry it was your client's granddaughter."

"Me, too." She hung up the phone. She pressed her

palms into her eyes. How could she call Marian MacAdam? What would she say?

In the end, Marian MacAdam said very little. Just, in a tremulous voice, "Is it Lisa?"

Kate said softly, "The police need Judge Carson to ID the body."

Marian choked a sob. "I see." She swallowed. "I need to call Rob. He's in Singapore. I think... Oh, damn!" Her voice choked as another sob overwhelmed her.

The phone buzzed in Kate's ear.

Kate grabbed her purse and stumbled down the hallway to the elevators, ignoring the startled looks of the support staff. She got off on the wrong level of the parkade and had to climb up a set of stairs to find her car. Once in it, she rested her head on the steering wheel.

Why hadn't she called Child Protection sooner? Hadn't she learned from her own past? Why had she waited?

She'd been persuaded by Marian MacAdam's insistence that she had no real proof of Lisa hurting herself. But that was just scratching the surface. There were other reasons. Ones she hadn't wanted to examine but couldn't help drag out from under the cracked rock of her conscience.

They flailed her with their whiplike truths. *You were scared you'd hurt your client's case for no good reason if you called Child Protection; that you'd destroy the limited faith your client had in you; and*—this one made her heart curl in shame—*destroy whatever shred of confidence Randall Barrett had in your judgment.* She'd wanted to impress Randall Barrett with her smarts, not embarrass LMB with an unfounded call to Child Protection, bringing down the wrath of a client assigned by no less than the managing partner.

10

Tuesday, May 1, 11:00 a.m.

The granary hummed with tightly controlled energy. City workers had been let in to erect a tent over the nucleus of the crime scene. Between the rain and the reporter who had been caught hanging off a nearby apartment balcony with a telephoto lens, it was clear that the scene needed tighter protection.

And it would need even more if what Kate told Ethan was true. Cold sweat mingled with the rain on his skin. He knocked briefly on the door of the command bus and pulled it open.

Ferguson straightened. She'd been hovering over Walker's shoulder, both of them examining a digital photo of the victim's neck.

"Got anything?" Ferguson asked. A middle-aged woman of medium height, she looked like a big-boned Scottish milkmaid except for her eyes. She missed nothing and would put up with nothing.

Ethan exhaled slowly. "We've got a lead on the girl."

Walker swiveled his chair away from the computer and looked at him.

Ferguson's eyes narrowed. "And?"

"Pretty sure she's Judge Carson's daughter."

"Jesus," Walker said softly.

"Tell me about it."

"Who gave you the lead?"

Ethan's eyes met Ferguson's. "Kate Lange."

Walker's eyes widened. Without another word, he swiveled his chair back to the computer.

"How is she involved in this?" Ferguson asked sharply.

"She says her client's granddaughter went missing yesterday. Gave me a description. It sounds like the girl." He jerked his head in the direction of the crime scene.

"So her client is Judge Carson's mother?" Ferguson asked.

Ethan shifted. He'd been so stunned to hear Kate's voice on his cell—he hadn't spoken to her on the phone for months—and then even more stunned by what she told him, that he hadn't even thought of asking the exact relationship of her client to the victim.

A flush burned under his collar. Ferguson, he was sure, wouldn't miss it. "I don't know. She could be her mother-in-law, I guess."

"Why was she consulting Kate Lange?"

Ethan sighed. Man, he was an idiot. "I don't know. But I'll find out."

Ferguson threw him a pitying glance. "Contact Judge Carson. Find out if she's missing her daughter."

It was just after noon. Ferguson had called a quick debriefing for the team. Ethan walked into the war room at the station.

The tension was palpable. As he looked around the table at the detectives' faces, he knew they were all asking the same question: Was their naked, dismembered victim Judge Carson's daughter?

"Heard anything yet?" Ferguson stood at the front by the diagram of the crime scene.

Ethan shook his head. "I left an urgent message. But she was in court."

"You'd think if she was worried about it she'd just adjourn and call," Lamond muttered.

Ethan shrugged. "She never lets anyone off the hook." He took stock of his team. It was a good team. They had each other's backs. "Anyone else find anything?"

One by one, the detectives gave their status reports. No sign yet of the missing limbs. "Probably in the killer's closet," Lamond muttered.

"What about missing persons? Did you get a match on the victim's description?" Ferguson asked.

"We came up empty," Walker said. "No matches." He paused. "Maybe we should call Vicky. She never forgets a face."

Ethan threw him a sharp glance. Was that a dig?

Walker returned it with a "Sorry, but it needed to be said" look. Ethan forced himself to relax. The guy was just trying to do his job. It was well known at the station that Vicky had an uncanny knack of recalling people's names. They'd be negligent to not involve her.

"Okay, call her if the victim isn't Judge Carson's daughter," Ethan said.

"And," Redding interjected, "I did find a witness named—" he checked his notes "—Shonda Bryant, who said that she'd seen the victim down on Gottingen Street. At approximately 2200 last night."

"What was she doing?"

"The girl was buying E, but she ran out of money and was going home."

"So the killer could have lured the girl into the car and offered her more ecstasy…" Lamond murmured.

"She took it, and then got so high it would be easy to strangle her."

"So she was strangled?" Redding asked.

Ethan nodded. "She's got petechiae all over her face." They all knew the significance of that. Petechiae were little blood hemorrhages caused by lack of oxygen—a classic sign of strangulation.

"Sounds like a good theory," Ferguson said briskly. "Let's go with that until we know what the autopsy findings are." She turned to Redding. "Did this Shonda Bryant know the girl?"

"Said she didn't know her name. She was lying, but I couldn't get her to tell me any more."

"Who was selling the drugs?"

Redding shrugged with the loose-limbed ease of a former basketball star. "She says it was some guy named Darrell, but my sources tell me she's the dealer."

"Let's pick her up. Maybe that'll convince her to ID the girl. Also, check out the other kids on Agricola Street. Give them the heads-up. Tell them to keep an eye—"

The phone rang. Normally, the meeting would continue while someone took the call. But not today. Everyone fell silent.

Ethan sprinted to the desk at the back of the room. He dug under the crime scene photos scattered on top to find a notepad. Grabbing a pen, he jotted down the date and time. The phone rang for a third time. He snatched it off the cradle. "Detective Drake, Major Crime Unit."

"This is Judge Carson. You left a message."

Ethan inhaled sharply. "Yes, Your Honor. We are investigating a homicide of a young girl—"

"Is it Lisa?" she asked abruptly.

"We don't know. The victim has no ID."

"Then why do you think your victim may be my daughter?"

"We received a tip that your daughter had been missing."

Silence reverberated like an aftershock on the phone line. In a choked voice, she asked, "Who called you?"

"I'm sorry. I can't tell you that." He cleared his throat. "Can you describe her?" He prayed Kate was wrong, that Judge Carson's daughter was fat and blond, not thin and dark.

"Fifteen years of age, five foot four, black hair." There was a pause. "With a ridicul—with a blond stripe down the middle. And she had a scar on her left forearm."

They couldn't verify the scar, but the rest of the description was an exact match. His eyes met Lamond's. Ethan gave a slight nod. Lamond closed his eyes and crossed himself.

"Your Honor." He was dismayed to hear the hoarseness in his voice, but, Jesus Christ, it'd been one of the more disturbing sights in his career. "I regret to inform you that the initial description matches that of our victim. I need you to come to the morgue to identify the body—"

"How was she killed?"

"It appears to be a deliberate homicide."

"I don't want generalities, Detective. I want the facts. I want you to tell me how she was killed. Right now." Her voice was harsh and staccato in its delivery. It was a technique that she used to great effect on the bench.

He fought to regain control of the conversation. "Until we confirm her identity, I am unable to provide you with any specifics."

There was a sharp inhale on the phone. But Ethan knew she, of all people, would understand the need for holdback evidence. The specifics around the M.O. was the one card the police held. They could use that information to bait a suspect.

"Fine," she ground out. "I'll be at the morgue in twenty-five minutes."

Ethan knew the body—what was left of it—had already been removed from the scene. "We'll meet you there."

The phone went dead in his ear. He'd never been so glad for someone to hang up on him. He exhaled a deep breath.

"Man, that was tough," Lamond said. "How'd she seem?"

Ethan shook his head. "I don't know." No one ever knew with Judge Carson. She never let you. But one thing he knew for sure: she'd hang them by the balls if they screwed up.

Everyone in the war room knew it, too. The tension in the room rose a notch.

"Brown, start working on the warrant for searching the premises," Ferguson said. "Make sure every *t* is crossed. We don't want to get caught on a technicality with Judge Carson."

"Already working on it," Brown said. She flipped her portfolio closed with a sharp thud and strode with measured briskness out of the war room to her desk in the bull pen. Ethan knew without looking that Walker's eyes would be following her long, lean figure.

"Let me know when it's ready, Brown," Redding called after her.

"Give me twenty minutes," she said over her shoulder.

"Come on, Lamond," Ethan said. "We can't keep Judge Carson waiting." They filled out the paperwork for the key to the morgue's secure stall, impatience shivering through Ethan's muscles as he waited for the Ident detective to sign it out. The key in his pocket, Ethan hurried across the road with Lamond to the parking lot holding the police vehicles, jumped into an unmarked car and drove to the morgue. They made it in eleven minutes. Good. Ethan wanted to be first to arrive. He and Lamond had just reached the main doors when Judge Carson pulled into the parking lot.

"I came straight from my office," she said, striding across the wet asphalt toward him. She wore a stylish off-white trench coat, loosely belted at her trim waist. The rain began to make a darker pattern of wet across her shoulders. Her hair swung in a dark, sleek bob, threaded with silver and glistening with water. From a distance, she looked younger than her years. But her purposeful stride couldn't disguise the toll the past few minutes had taken on her. Her skin was pale and crepey. Hard grooves carved a path from her nose to her mouth.

Ethan ushered her into the foyer, out of the rain. Lamond stood next to him. Ferguson had assigned him the role of family liaison on this case, but Ethan knew he couldn't let Lamond deal with Judge Carson on his own. They couldn't afford any mistakes. No matter how much he liked the guy, he just didn't have the experience in homicide yet. New to plainclothes, he'd moved to homicide from sexual assault.

"Your Honor," Ethan said, "this is Detective Constable Lamond. He is the family liaison for this case."

Lamond stepped forward, sympathy in his eyes. "I am very sorry—"

She held up a warning hand, barely looking at him. "Let's get this over with."

Lamond stepped back. In silence, they signed themselves in with the commissionaire, then headed down to the path lab. Judge Carson's heels cracked sharply on the floor. She said nothing, her mouth clamped into a tight line, her gaze straight ahead. Tension vibrated from her body.

Ethan was sweating by the time they got to the double steel doors. He needed to prepare her for what she was about to see. He wasn't looking forward to it. The morgue attendant signed them in, then took them over to the viewing room.

He turned to Judge Carson. She was staring through the glass at the empty room on the other side. "Your Honor, there is something you need to know…"

She stiffened but continued to stare through the glass. He wished she would look at him. He could feel Lamond's gaze on his face.

He cleared his throat. "I am afraid that the victim's limbs were removed."

Her face paled, became clammy. He readied himself to catch her.

"Before or after the death occurred?" she finally said, her voice tight.

"We won't know until the autopsy has been conducted," Ethan said gently. "It's scheduled to begin in several hours."

She blinked. "How do you think she was killed?"

He'd refused to answer the question when he was talking to her on the phone at the station. But now, about to view the victim, he realized there was no point refusing to answer this question on the grounds of holdback evidence. Judge Carson would recognize the significance of petechiae. "We believe it was strangulation, Your Honor." He turned before she could ask him any more questions. "If you could please wait here, I have to unlock the stall."

"I'll come with you," she said. Both Lamond and Judge

Carson turned to follow him, Lamond bumping into Judge Carson's back. It was almost funny. But not quite.

"I'm sorry, Your Honor. But you must do the identification through the glass. Detective Lamond will wait with you." He glanced in Lamond's direction. Lamond stood by the door. A subtle reminder she was not to leave. Ethan pointed to the window. "We will roll the gurney up."

Judge Carson's lips pressed together in a thin line.

"It is part of homicide procedure to conduct the identification this way, Your Honor. It helps prevent any trace evidence contaminating the victim…"

"I know." She turned away. "Do your job."

He closed the door and went to the secure stall that held the homicide victims. He quickly located the girl's body, unlocking the tray. The morgue attendant placed the body on the gurney and rolled it up to the window.

How many times had he gone through this routine? Thirty, forty? He'd had to usher in the families of men with their faces shot off, women raped and stabbed, children beaten to death. It was all horrible. Some of it unthinkable.

Happened almost every day, if not in Halifax, then somewhere else.

And he had at least twenty more years of this to look forward to.

Judge Carson hadn't moved. She stared at the body bag through the glass, her eyes tracing the lines of the plastic shroud. Lingering over how it rose and then dipped abruptly just past the middle.

Her fingers curled into her palms.

He said loudly, "Are you ready, Your Honor?"

Judge Carson squared her shoulders and stepped closer to the window. She threw a warning glance over her shoulder at Lamond. He remained by the door. She gave a brusque nod. "Do it."

Ethan nodded to the morgue attendant. She unzipped the bag over the girl's face.

There was a split second of silence. Judge Carson's eyes swept the girl's discolored features. "It's her."

"You are sure?"

"Yes." She turned away.

That was that. No sobs of grief, no cries of distress over the bruising on Lisa's neck. No demands to see below her collarbone.

Ethan let the attendant zip up the bag and roll the gurney into the freezer. He locked the stall and hurried back to the viewing room. Judge Carson waited by the door, Lamond doing his best not to hover behind her.

The room was too small for the three of them. There was a smell in there, of high emotion desperately suppressed. But what that high emotion was, Ethan couldn't tell. Grief? Anger?

Guilt?

As soon as Judge Carson saw him, she walked out of the room toward the elevator. He fell into step beside the judge, Lamond half a step behind. "We need to trace Lisa's final movements. We have some questions for you."

Judge Carson kept walking, staring straight ahead. "I need to make some phone calls. I have to postpone the trial I was adjudicating. I'll meet you at the station in half an hour."

Ethan studied the strong profile, the smooth angles of her hair. She reminded him of a panther: fierce, her limbs moving with tensile strength. "We need to come to your home. Have a look in Lisa's room with my team."

She seemed on the verge of refusing, but then sighed.

"Get a warrant. I have very little to tell you, Detective. I have no idea where Lisa was yesterday. I was at work."

She headed out into the rain. Ethan watched the wet swallow her white form. Lamond gave a low whistle. "She's a toughie." Ethan said nothing. Who knew what was going on in her head? They'd have a better idea when they got to her condo.

As soon as he got inside his car, he called Ferguson on his cell. He didn't want this to go over the police radio. There were sure to be lots of interested folks tuning in now that news of the homicide had been leaked. "We've got a positive ID. The victim is Judge Carson's daughter, Lisa MacAdam."

"Jesus," Ferguson murmured.

"Has Brown got the warrant ready?" Ethan asked.

"Yes. Now that we've confirmed the ID, I'll get her to fax it right away. I gave the heads-up to the J.P. He's waiting for it."

"Send Redding over. He and Lamond can go through Lisa's room."

"Agreed. And Ethan…" She paused. He knew what was coming. A muscle under his eye jumped. Ever since the Clarkson case, the message had been drummed into him. "Be on your best behavior. We need Judge Carson's cooperation."

11

Ethan and Lamond met Redding outside Judge Carson's condo complex. "Here's the warrant," Redding said. "Brown went through it with a fine-tooth comb." He handed it to Ethan.

He read it carefully. The last thing they needed would be for the warrant to trip them up. But Brown had done a good job. It covered everything they needed. They were only going to do Lisa's bedroom this afternoon. See if they could figure out her last movements. If they found anything that would point to Judge Carson being involved in Lisa's murder—like blood samples or IMs with her friends implicating her mother—they'd get a new warrant and the Ident guys would come and do a thorough sweep.

Lamond looked around him and gave a low whistle. "Nice digs."

"Yeah." Really nice. One of the most luxurious condo complexes in the city. Where did Judge Carson get the money for that? Criminal court judges were government employees. Lawyers often took a cut in pay to sit on the bench.

Ethan glanced through the glass security doors to the main foyer. It was exactly what he expected.

A massive round pedestal table with an arrangement of orange lilies and some kind of ultramodern spiky greenery was the focal point. Gold-flecked marble on the floor complemented the massive gold-framed mirror that hung on the cream painted wall at the back.

Ethan picked up the security phone and rang Judge Carson's number. A sudden buzz announced the door lock being released. Redding grabbed the door before it locked again.

"Nice," Lamond muttered. He squared his shoulders. Ethan could guess what the younger detective was feeling. He'd been put in the role of family liaison but the victim's mother wanted nothing to do with him. And, in fact, could lacerate him with a glance. Not a comfortable position to be in. *Welcome to homicide, buddy.*

The elevator doors slid open and they stepped inside the mirrored lift. The judge had a penthouse condo. Ethan turned to his team. "Lamond, Redding, go through drawers, closets, under the bed, inside Lisa's stuffed animals, the usual. If she had a diary, read every entry. Go through her homework notebooks. Get on to her Facebook hangouts, her MSN chat lists, everything. And make sure you bag and tag *everything* you take. If Judge Carson turns out to be more than a grieving mother, we don't want her ramming improper evidence collection down our throats." The elevator neared Judge Carson's floor. "I'm going to take the judge through Lisa's final movements. If you need any backup, let me know."

They nodded. As soon as Lisa's identity was released, the papers would explode with this story. They needed to have all their ducks in a row.

They got out on the twelfth floor and walked down the hallway to the mahogany door at the end. Ethan rapped the gleaming brass knocker. It was shaped like a lion's head. The beast's eyes glared at him. It was the kind of welcome he expected from Her Honor.

Judge Carson opened the door. Ethan hoped his surprise at her appearance didn't show on his face. He realized he'd expected her to appear in full battle garb—severely tailored suit, sharp heels, immaculate hair.

Her hair was anything but. She'd obviously just come out of the shower. The sleek bob required a blow dryer to make maximum impact. And instead of her work clothes, she wore a pair of tailored denim jeans with a black turtleneck sweater in a fine silk knit that clung discreetly to her breasts.

If her outward appearance was not what he'd expected, the look in her eyes was. Challenge gleamed from their tawny depths.

"Your Honor, here is the warrant," Ethan said, handing it to her.

Judge Carson scanned the text slowly, holding it at arm's length, a slight frown between her brows. She read the faxed document word for word as if it were the first warrant she'd ever seen. She returned it to him and stepped back from the door.

He marshaled all his interviewing skills and walked inside. Redding and Lamond followed, hoisting their evidence kits and cameras through the doorway.

Judge Carson scrutinized the gear.

"Her bedroom is over there." She waved a hand upstairs. "My room is on the left. Hers is on the right."

Not once had Judge Carson referred to her daughter by name. Same as in the morgue. *"It's her,"* she'd said. Not, "it's my daughter," or "it's Lisa."

Just *her.*

"Have a seat, Detective Drake." Judge Carson walked down the steps into the sunken living room. A modern white L-shaped sofa and white fur rug were framed by two walls of floor-to-ceiling windows. They overlooked the Public Gardens, Halifax's jewel in the crown.

"Nice place," he said, settling himself on a chair, his back to the windows. Judge Carson sat on the sofa. Her dark clothing provided a stark foil to the white leather surrounding her.

Ethan looked around. Opposite the living room was a small but high-tech galley kitchen, separated by a smooth granite counter. It was remarkably uncluttered. No appliances sat on the counter, no dishes, no flowers, nothing. He wondered how anyone could function in a kitchen like that. He thought of his own kitchen: the fresh herbs growing on the windowsill, the sleek espresso machine and stainless-steel pasta maker gracing his counter. From the looks of this kitchen, Judge Carson never used it except to transfer her take-out food to real china.

But what about Lisa?

Where were the clothes strewn on the floor, the worn-out flip-flops kicked off in an untidy jumble, the magazines, homework, makeup, MP3 player and various other paraphernalia that marked the abode of a teenage girl?

He placed his notepad on the sleek cement-and-glass coffee table. It, too, was devoid of decoration. Just like the granite-and-copper mantel over the fireplace. Not a single photo.

Did Judge Carson actually live in this place or just drop in for occasional visits to check on her offspring?

"What kind of evidence have you collected?" she asked calmly.

Ethan leaned back on the sofa. Judge Carson was doing exactly what he expected: taking control of the interview, and asking questions that she, of all people, would know the police would not answer to the relative of a homicide victim. Not until they had their suspect in custody.

"We are still processing the crime scene."

"But surely you've found some evidence."

Ethan met her gaze. "Yes. We have." It was a lie.

"Was she killed at the granary?"

"I'm not at liberty to discuss our findings at this stage, Your Honor."

She recoiled as the implications of his words hit her. "For Chrissake."

She was about to say more, but Ethan said, "Can you tell me about Lisa's activities yesterday? We are trying to put together a time line."

Judge Carson closed her eyes. As if she couldn't stand the sight of him. Didn't matter. He had more important things to worry about. There was a brutal killer on the loose. They needed to catch this guy.

She opened her eyes. Her gaze was unflinching. "I have no idea what she was doing."

"Did Lisa go to school?"

"I expect so."

"What did she usually do after school?"

"Sometimes she went to her grandmother's. You should call her. Her name is Marian MacAdam." Her voice was flat.

"Her number?"

In the same emotionless tone, Judge Carson recited her mother-in-law's phone number. "Lisa told me she was having supper with Marian, but her grandmother was at her cottage yesterday."

"Did Lisa know that?"

"According to her grandmother, yes."

"So she lied to you?" Ethan watched Judge Carson's face closely. Would his question hurt her? Or anger her?

Neither. She shrugged. "It would appear so."

"Do you know where Lisa had supper?"

"No. I don't usually come home for supper, Detective. My work does not permit it. Lisa would either eat at her grandmother's, or make herself supper at home. Sometimes she would eat out with her friends." Ethan pictured the girl, coming home to an empty house, sticking a frozen supper in the microwave.

"What time would Lisa usually come home?"

"Around nine or ten o'clock. Sometimes later."

So this fifteen-year-old girl basically had no one to account to. Except maybe her grandmother.

He wouldn't make any judgments—yet—about this woman sitting in front of him, but his heart squeezed with pity for Lisa. He kept his voice as neutral as possible. "Did Lisa have a problem with drugs?"

Judge Carson dropped her gaze to her hands. They were square, capable hands. Strong. A small cut, still pink edged, marred one knuckle.

Finally she looked up. "This is not to be put in the file. Do you understand?"

Ethan understood all right. No one wanted a record of their omissions. Because when they were written down in stark black-and-white they began to look a lot like commissions. "Your Honor, your daughter is the victim of a homicide. We need to find out who did this to her. All information is pertinent. If I don't record it, we may miss a critical link." He felt slightly ridiculous telling this to Hope Carson, a criminal court judge, who would know all this already. But she wasn't giving him a choice. He and she both knew if it was something she didn't want put on paper, it was likely to be a critical link.

Her eyes scorched his face. She had been testing him, thinking she could intimidate him. He'd called her bluff. And she hadn't liked being spoken to like that. She was now weighing her options. Ethan waited.

"My daughter had some problems," Judge Carson said evenly. "She fell in with a bad crowd. She began using street drugs. But I know she stopped."

"How do you know that?" Ethan asked. How the hell could Judge Carson speak with such certainty after admitting she had no idea what her daughter had been doing every day while she was at work?

"Because I made sure of it. She had no funds to buy drugs. She also knew if she got caught with them she'd be sent away."

"Away? Where?"

Judge Carson's gaze became steely. As if remembering her daughter's reaction to this pronouncement. "To a boarding school."

"She didn't want to go there?" Ethan thought she might have found the prospect appealing: more company and regular meals.

A small grimace twisted Judge Carson's lips. "No. She wanted to stay near her grandmother."

"I see." And he did see how lonely Lisa's life must have been. "So you believe Lisa was not using anymore."

"Correct."

"We've had officers checking all the beats of the street kids, and we found a witness who reported seeing Lisa around 10:00 p.m. last night. Apparently she sold some drugs to her."

"But that's impossible… She had no money. None! I

made sure of it!" Judge Carson pushed a hand through her hair. "Unless…"

"Unless…?"

Her jaw tightened. "I suspect her grandmother may have indulged her and given her some pocket money."

Ethan began to write.

"I told you not to make a record of this!" Judge Carson reached over to grab the notepad.

Ethan placed his hand firmly on the page. "Your Honor, please do not make me have to charge you with obstructing an investigation."

Judge Carson recoiled with a sharp intake of breath. Somewhere in the tawny blaze of her eyes, Ethan thought he saw pain. He wasn't sure.

He rose. "Thank you for your cooperation."

Judge Carson stood. Her eyes burned into him. "If this information is leaked to the press, there will be hell to pay. I will personally see to it that you will wear this, Detective." Her face hardened. "And I don't think that's something you can afford, can you, Detective?"

He wouldn't rise to the bait. Judge Carson was trying to deflect her guilt onto him. He'd gotten the message loud and clear. Judge Carson was more concerned about her career than her dead daughter.

He wasn't.

12

Every time Ethan walked through the long, winding corridors in the basement of the Greater Halifax General Hospital, the word *bowel* sprang to mind. He knew his subconscious was bracing him for what was to come.

He glanced at Lamond. "You ready?"

He'd surprised Ethan by asking if he could come to the autopsy. Ethan had agreed. This would season him like nothing else.

The detective constable nodded. His expression of steely determination would have amused Ethan if he hadn't been so bothered by the case.

"Is this your first one?" he asked.

Lamond nodded again. "But I used to gut fish."

Ethan remembered thinking the same thing before his first autopsy. He hadn't wanted to listen to any advice from the senior officer then, and he doubted Lamond would want to hear it, either. But still, he'd be remiss not to give him the basics: "Get close enough to see but not too close. The smell can sometimes set people off. And make sure you stand near a garbage can."

They reached the end of the corridor. A sign on a large set of swinging doors said Morgue. Farther down was a single door with a smaller sign: Autopsy Suite. He headed toward it, dropping his coffee cup in a garbage can. He entered the room and reached for a scrub gown folded neatly on a metal shelf by the door. Lamond hung back at the doorway.

Ethan threw him an impatient glance and slipped his arms through the sleeves. "Remember, DNA contamination. We don't want to leave our trace on her. And besides, sometimes the blood can spatter. I hope you're not wearing your best shoes." He picked up his briefcase. "Although in this case, I'm not sure how much blood she has left."

Lamond hurriedly thrust his arms into a gown and followed him, the green edges flapping around his back.

A small cluster of people stood around the autopsy table. The medical examiner's assistant had just lifted the body bag from the gurney onto the metal surface. A member of the FIS team stood by, readying his camera.

The M.E. glanced over his steel-rimmed glasses at Ethan and smiled. "Right on time." His voice still retained the lilt of the Caribbean. It bounced off the stainless steel surrounding them, warming the room. His face grew somber. "It's a nasty case, Detective Drake."

Ethan nodded. "Tell me about it."

"Have you identified her?" Dr. Guthro asked.

"Yes." He was glad they had, but whenever they had a name to go with the body, it made it so much more personal. "Her name is Lisa MacAdam. A fifteen-year-old private school student. Her mother is Judge Hope Carson."

"My Lord." Even Dr. Guthro, a forensic pathologist who had seen a lot in his day, looked shocked. "How did this happen to her?"

"Good question. It's been a challenging crime scene."

"From what the FIS detectives have been telling me, you couldn't find any clothes or personal effects?"

Ethan shook his head. "Nothing. No clothes, no purse…" He glanced at the body bag. It sagged in all the wrong places. "… and so far we haven't been able to find her limbs."

"Obviously she was killed somewhere else." Dr. Guthro picked up his clipboard.

"Yes. We're hoping that there may be some trace evidence on her body." *Hope* was too mild a word. They needed something to go on. Now that the tire track was unusable, they had nothing. The fog had rolled in, making the search difficult. But even before that, the Ident guys had come up with very little. It was hard to believe that the dump site had yielded so few clues. It spoke volumes about the type of killer. He was smart. He was careful.

Dr. Guthro gazed over his bifocals. "The E.T.D. rules out fingerprints."

"Fingerprints?" Lamond threw an astonished look at the M.E. "She has no fingers."

Ethan frowned. "Dr. Guthro is referring to the killer's latents."

Lamond colored. "I didn't know you could get latents off a corpse."

Dr. Guthro nodded. "Latents are tricky to get off the skin. Since they usually only last for an hour or two after death has occurred, I'm afraid that is no longer an option for this victim."

Ethan swallowed his disappointment. He knew their girl had been dead for too long for the killer's prints—if he left any—to be lifted, but he had hoped Dr. Guthro might surprise them. They had so little to go with right now. "What time did she die?"

Dr. Guthro consulted his clipboard. "Based on the evening temperatures—which held pretty steady most of the night—we are estimating the time of death at approximately 2300 hours." He put down the clipboard and removed his reading glasses. "Let's have a look at what we've got, shall we?"

The assistant pulled the sides of the body bag open. The smell of dead, bloody flesh hit Ethan's nostrils. He glanced at Lamond. His eyes were wide.

I bet your fish never smelled like that.

Dr. Guthro stood poised over the body, inhaling deeply several times. "No cyanidic odor emitting from the decedent," he said into his Dictaphone.

He picked up a digital camera from a metal table and circled the body, taking photos of the naked corpse. "You've got a tough case," he said. "No clothes which might have trace evidence." His glance fell on the severed joints. "Not having her limbs is really unfortunate. I usually find excellent trace evidence under the nails."

Ethan looked at the girl. At *Lisa*. She looked inhuman without her limbs, like a mannequin. Yet she was all too human: the still-childish features, the defiant stripe of bleached blond in her hair.

"No sign of external injury on the torso," Dr. Guthro said, bending forward. "But the neck is a different matter. She was strangled. See the bruising?" It radiated from a thin red line around her neck.

"Looks like he used a ligature," Ethan said.

"I agree. The bruising shows even pressure was applied."

"Is that the cause of death?"

Dr. Guthro nodded. "Most likely. See the petechiae?" He gestured toward small red blotches that marred her neck. "They are quite extensive, around her mouth and—"

he pulled down her lower eyelid "—in the lining of her eyes." He gently rubbed a large cotton swab around the ligature marking, then placed it in an evidence envelope, noting the case, site and date. "Hopefully there is some residue left on her skin to indicate what the killer used to strangle her."

"Let's hope," Ethan said, his eyes tracing the smooth line circling her neck.

The M.E. and the Ident guy circled her body, looking, searching. The assistant turned the girl on her side. Then the other side. The killer had to have left *something,* some sign, on her body.

There was nothing. No semen, no hair. Nothing. Ethan shook his head. He couldn't believe it. Who was this guy who killed her? Clean dump site, clean corpse. He tried to ignore the sinking in his stomach.

"All right, let's see if anything was left in her hair," Dr. Guthro said encouragingly in the silence. He picked up a small black comb—it looked like the ones sold at the dollar store—and began to systematically comb through Lisa's hair. "Ah." Dr. Guthro used a pair of tweezers to carefully remove something. Ethan's pulse surged. Between the pincers was a thread, about a millimeter in length. "This looks promising."

"Right on," Lamond breathed.

Dr. Guthro dropped it into an evidence envelope and again jotted the case, site and date.

Ethan tried to not get his hopes up. "We'll have to rule out her clothes or her house." He allowed a small smile. "But it could be from the kill site."

The M.E. nodded. "We'll send it to the forensic lab for processing." Lisa's hair now lay neatly combed about her head. He plucked a hair with the tweezers and placed it in another evidence envelope.

Ethan stared at Judge Carson's daughter. "Did she fight the killer?"

Dr. Guthro shook his head slowly. "I don't think so. I don't see any sign of self-defense injuries. No abrasions, no cuts, no blood smears…"

Ethan frowned. Had she known her attacker? Or had she been drugged? "You will check her out for sedatives or date-rape drugs?"

"We'll do a full screen on her," Dr. Guthro said. "But you know as well as I do, if the killer used ecstasy on her, it won't be in her system now." Ecstasy was the drug of choice for rapists who wanted compliant victims, because it only lasted in the victim's system for about twelve hours, and they often had little memory of what happened. "For now, we'll get some swabs, see if any trace shows up." Ethan watched him swab around her mouth and around the gaping joints where her limbs used to be, using a fresh swab each time. He hoped one of those swabs would reveal under microscope the trace evidence they couldn't see: skin cells, semen, saliva. Something.

Dr. Guthro nodded to the assistant, who turned the body onto its side. "Lividity in the lower lumbar region and buttocks."

"What's lividity?" Lamond whispered.

"It's where her blood pools," Ethan replied impatiently. Lamond needed to get his shit together and read the manuals instead of *Men's Health*. He was in homicide now.

Dr. Guthro looked at Ethan. "She was supine when she was discovered?"

"Yes." Ethan looked at Lisa. Fifteen-year-old private school student. Daughter of wealthy, professional parents. Resident of an upscale condominium. The ridges of her spine showed through her skin. She looked so vulnerable. He wanted to throw a blanket over her.

He crossed his arms. He needed to be objective. Not let this victim get under his skin. For some reason, the longer he worked on this unit, the harder it was getting to keep his distance. He thought he'd get desensitized. But he'd only gotten more thirsty for retribution.

The assistant put her hand on Lisa's waist and pulled her onto her back. She took out a measuring tape and ran it along the side of Lisa's body. "Thirty-nine inches," she called out briskly. Then she looked at the scale reading on the autopsy table. "Seventy-nine pounds."

There was silence except for the sound of chalk scribbling. No one wanted to say what they were all thinking: in her case, these numbers didn't mean much.

Dr. Guthro slipped a swab in her mouth. Her jaw had dropped open before rigor mortis had settled in. Ethan was relieved they wouldn't have to break the rigor. He'd had to do it once at a funeral home to get a victim's fingerprints, and he'd never forget the crack each bone made as he unlocked the hand. Now whenever someone cracked their knuckles, his stomach lurched.

Dr. Guthro began combing Lisa's pubic hair with methodical thoroughness, plucking a hair and dropping it into an evidence envelope. He then picked up a long swab. Ethan forced himself to look as her genitals were examined and swabbed. He hated that invasion of her privacy. He could just imagine how a fifteen-year-old girl would feel to have all these strange men examining her. He clenched his jaw. He had to stop thinking about her feelings. She was dead. She had no feelings. He needed to focus on finding clues. Clues that would help them catch this bastard and make him pay.

He glanced at Lamond. The younger man shifted slightly on his feet. His eyes were glued to Dr. Guthro's efficient hands. His color was getting higher by the minute. Ethan was surprised. The guy'd come from sexual assault. But he'd never had to watch a girl getting the rape kit. He'd only had to read the reports.

Just wait. It's going to get a lot worse.

"No evidence of forced penetration in either the vaginal or anal regions," the M.E. said. "In fact, no indication of any sexual intercourse prior to her death. The hymen is intact."

"Intact?" Ethan started.

"Holy sh—cow," Lamond said at the same time. Then looked sheepishly at Dr. Guthro.

"Not your typical teenage rebel," Dr. Guthro said, a thoughtful look in his eyes.

"No." The discovery of Lisa's virginity unnerved Ethan. It brought to the surface all his protective instincts. He shoved his hands in his pockets. He'd taken a hard line at any punk who'd tried to mess around with his sister. Until she'd told him to stop scaring off her boyfriends. She could handle herself, she told him.

He bet this girl thought she could, too.

He was thankful for Lisa's sake that she had not been raped before her death, although the lack of sexual assault meant a potential source of DNA was eliminated. But it also shed some light on the killer's profile. He—or she— was likely not a sexual predator.

Dr. Guthro peered at the raw open wounds below Lisa's hips. He ran his finger lightly along the edges of flesh, pulling back the skin and tissue to reveal the bone. It gleamed under the large lamp.

He then looked at where her arms had been cut off. For several minutes he went back and forth between the wounds on her hips and her shoulders. "Her limbs appear to have been severed by a bone saw," he said, his voice puzzled.

"A bone saw?"

Dr. Guthro nodded. "Yes, like this." He held up a small handsaw. It resembled a saw Ethan had in his shed.

"How easy is it for someone to get a hold of one of those?" Ethan asked.

Dr. Guthro pursed his mouth. "Not too difficult, I would think. They are found in any hospital. It wouldn't take much to steal one." Dr. Guthro pulled the skin back on one of the hip sockets. "But it wouldn't have been used by just anybody. See this—" he pointed to the smooth bone beneath the pink tissue "— this is a very clean cut. It was done by someone who knew how to dissect a joint."

Ethan stared at the M.E. "You mean like a doctor?"

Dr. Guthro nodded. "Yes. Or someone who is familiar with anatomy."

He turned to Lisa's right shoulder. "There is one finding that is unusual. See this cut here?" He pointed to the joint.

At first glance it looked as smooth as the other cuts. But as Ethan stared at it, he could see a small marking on the bone. "Is that from the teeth of the saw?"

Dr. Guthro picked up a magnifying glass and held it over the bone.

Ethan leaned forward to peer through it. "It looks like two lines with a circle in between." He studied it for a moment longer, then stared at it incredulously. "Those aren't geometric shapes. Those are letters."

Dr. Guthro's fingers traced the small lines and curves engraved on the bone. "I think you are right. This one looks like an *L*."

"And the next one is an *O*," Ethan said.

"And another *L*," said Dr. Guthro.

"LOL."

"His initials?" Lamond asked.

"Could be. Or it could be an abbreviation for something."

There was silence. Then Ethan's eyes met Lamond's. *"LOL.* Laugh Out Loud."

"Jesus," Lamond murmured.

"So the killer left us a message," Ethan said. "A definite fuck-you if I ever saw one." The back of his neck tingled. This was no ordinary killer. Lisa MacAdam had not been killed in a fit of rage, or as a result of enflamed passion. She had been killed and dismembered in a clinical, dispassionate manner.

There was a psychological profile for a killer like that. Psychopath.

"How did the killer make the marking?" he asked Dr. Guthro.

"Looks like he used a scalpel." Dr. Guthro contemplated the bone. He pulled down his face shield. "Let's see what the internal examination tells us."

The assistant lifted Lisa's body slightly off the table and slid a rubber brick under her back. Dr. Guthro cut a large Y incision on her torso. A rotting, sweet smell added a new foulness to the air. Ethan's stomach churned. He had seen this procedure many times, but it still wasn't pleasant.

Lamond stepped back a little. Ethan noted he had moved closer to the garbage can.

Lisa's ribs were snapped with brutal efficiency by Dr. Guthro, and then the examination of her chest wall and abdomen began. Ethan watched silently as Dr. Guthro inserted a hypodermic needle into one of the veins below her clavicle. "Won't even bother with the groin," he muttered to himself. "Not much blood left." He extracted a small amount for the toxicology tests and the DNA standard they would use to confirm Lisa's identity—as well as rule out the victim's trace evidence against other trace evidence that might show up on or in her body—then sliced through the rest of the veins and arteries, removing her heart and putting it on a scale. Then he removed her lungs—"Doesn't look like she was a smoker"—and began to work on her abdominal organs.

When her stomach was sliced open, Ethan braced himself. The smell was awful. He glanced at Lamond. His face was pale and screwed into an expression that in normal circumstances would have made Ethan grin.

"It would appear from the gastric contents that her last meal was ingested at approximately 6:00 p.m.," Dr. Guthro said. He eyed the soupy mess. "Looks like hamburger and fries."

That did it for Lamond. Ethan bit back a smile. Lamond was addicted to fast food. Ethan didn't know how he managed to stay in shape. Watching Lamond hurry out the door, his shoulders hunched, Ethan wondered if this would cure him of his habit.

"Nothing unusual in here," Dr. Guthro said, ignoring the detective's hasty departure. His hands worked methodically in the girl's abdominal cavity. "No sign of internal injuries. No sign of drug overdose." He removed the rest of her organs. A cavity remained, reminding Ethan of the carapace of a lobster.

Dr. Guthro sliced a long vertical line through her neck and peeled back the skin. "The hyoid bone is crushed. Supports strangulation as cause of death." He glanced at Ethan. "But just in case, we'll check the brain for signs of trauma."

The assistant moved the block and slid it under Lisa's skull. Dr. Guthro stood behind the girl's head and deftly sliced her scalp from one ear to the other. He lifted the top flap of skin and pulled it down over her face, exposing her skull. Ethan forced himself to detach. *Do not think of this as a living, breathing teenage girl who was a daughter, a granddaughter. She is a victim.* Despite his efforts, his jaw clenched when Lisa's hair flopped onto her features like a Halloween mask.

The whirr of the Stryker saw drew Ethan's eyes away from her face. Dr. Guthro cut a "cap" in the bone and pulled it out of her skull. Her brain was exposed. "No sign of subdural hemorrhage."

He severed her brain from the spinal cord and pulled it out, making a sucking sound that Ethan could never describe but would never forget. Dr. Guthro placed the organ on the scale and left the assistant to record the data.

He stepped around the table to stand by Ethan and lifted his face shield. "We're done for now. We'll send the toxicology request stat. We should have the results by tomorrow morning at the latest."

Ethan picked up his briefcase. He longed to get some fresh air. "Thank you, doctor."

"You are welcome. I hope we come up with something."

Ethan nodded. "So do I." He walked toward the door. While he was removing his scrub gown, he glanced one final time at the autopsy table, now bloody. The assistant was placing the organs back into Lisa's abdominal cavity. Dr. Guthro was threading a needle.

Ethan watched him for a moment. It was the assistant's job to put the body back together. But Dr. Guthro never let them. He always did it himself, stitching the flaps closed as carefully as he cut them open.

Lamond leaned against the wall outside the autopsy suite. He managed a sheepish grin. "Sorry 'bout that. Won't happen again."

"I'm sure it won't," Ethan said. He slapped Lamond on the back. "Come on, let's get some supper. There's a hamburger joint on the way."

13

Ethan glanced at his watch as he pulled into the station. It was 9:08 p.m. Acid burned in his gut. He shouldn't have baited Lamond about the fast food. Now he was paying the price.

As soon as they got to the war room, Redding hurried over. "Drake, Lamond, the victim's grandmother, Mrs. MacAdam, is waiting to talk to you. She's been here about an hour." He paused. "She's been crying ever since."

"Where is she?" Lamond asked, squaring his shoulders for the second time that day. First Judge Carson, now Lisa's grandmother. It had been a long day.

"In the soft interview room." The soft interview room was reserved for families and children. It had upholstered furniture and a coffee table as opposed to the hard interview room, which was furnished with upright chairs and no table. The interviewer didn't want a barrier when interrogating a suspect.

"Look, Lamond, I know you are the liaison, but I think I should take this one. There are some things Judge Carson told me that I need to corroborate with Lisa's grandmother."

Lamond hesitated. His desire to prove himself was written all over his face. But Ethan needed to interview

Mrs. MacAdam. There was no point in both of them sitting there. There were too many leads to follow up. "In the meantime, get in touch with Mr. MacAdam and any other relatives who might have information."

Lamond nodded. "Right."

Ethan rapped quietly on the door to the interview room, and walked in. Mrs. MacAdam sat slumped on the sofa. A box of tissues and an untouched cup of tea sat on the low table in front of her.

Ethan walked toward her and held out his hand. "Mrs. MacAdam, I am Detective Drake."

She shook his hand. Her fingers were icy and limp.

Ethan lowered himself to the armchair opposite her. "Mrs. MacAdam, your granddaughter has been the victim of a terrible crime." She nodded, her eyes welling with fresh tears. He added quickly, "I realize this is a very painful time for you, but I ask that you do your best to answer my questions so we can catch the person who did this to her."

Marian MacAdam cleared her throat. "Of course." Her voice was firmer than he expected.

He began his round of background questions. All of her answers corroborated with Judge Carson's. It seemed that Lisa was free to do whatever she wanted most of the time. Mrs. MacAdam tried to keep tabs on her by inviting her over after school and staying for dinner.

"But I couldn't do that every day. I had other commitments…" She flushed. "You know, other friends, bridge club, this and that. Besides, I couldn't insist she come every day. Her mother has custody. That's why…" She stopped abruptly.

"Why…?" he prompted. The back of his neck tingled. She pursed her mouth. "You are going to find out, anyway. I was getting worried about Lisa. She had become erratic, wouldn't show up on the times I was supposed to see her, and—" she glanced down at her clasped hands "—and I think she had stolen some money from me."

"To buy drugs?"

The bluntness of his question seemed to both surprise and reassure her. "Yes." Her shoulders relaxed. "Lisa had been using drugs for a couple of years, on and off, since the time her parents separated. But I thought she had stopped. Then a few months ago, she seemed to be picking up all her bad habits again."

"Do you know why?"

Mrs. MacAdam shook her head. "No. She could be a moody girl. She got into that alternative stuff, you know, dyeing her hair and getting a tattoo…"

Ethan leaned forward. "A tattoo? Where?"

"On her ankle." Mrs. MacAdam shook her head. "She lied about her age at the tattoo parlor, and they never asked for ID. I had warned Lisa she could get some terrible diseases, but she didn't listen. You know what teenagers are like. They think they are immortal." Her eyes suddenly glistened with tears.

"What did the tattoo look like?"

"It was a cartoon. Of a dog." Her lip quivered. "She had a nickname for it. Rufus." She blinked rapidly a few times.

Ethan didn't want her dissolving on him. He changed the subject. "Did you ever give her pocket money?"

"No. Her mother did, though."

Ethan stopped writing and looked at Mrs. MacAdam. Judge Carson had told him that Mrs. MacAdam was giving Lisa money. Who was telling the truth? And why would one of them lie about it?

Mrs. MacAdam threaded a handkerchief between her

fingers. "I kept telling Hope not to, that Lisa would buy drugs, but she wouldn't listen. She told me that she had to give Lisa money to buy her meals." She leaned forward on her elbows. "Look, Detective, I'll be frank with you. I wasn't very involved in Lisa's life when she was young, but when Robert left the marriage, I felt I needed to step in. She never had a home-cooked meal unless she came to my house. It became apparent to me that unless she lived with me, no one would look after her."

The grandmother may look frail, but she had her head screwed on right. "Did you ask her mother if Lisa could live with you?"

Mrs. MacAdam's mouth twisted. "Ask Hope? She'd never allow it. People would judge Hope if she sent her daughter to live with me, and rightly, too."

"So what did you do?"

Mrs. MacAdam gazed at the wall behind his head, her expression wistful. "At first I thought if I just invited Lisa over, she would come." She glanced at him, her eyes seeking understanding. "But then I realized she was using drugs again. And Hope wouldn't do anything about it. Too concerned about how it would look to have a daughter in rehab when she's up for the Supreme Court."

His neck tingled again. Judge Carson was being considered for the Supreme Court?

"What did you do?"

Mrs. MacAdam straightened. "I went to see a lawyer."

He leaned forward. He could imagine how Judge Carson would react to that. "It was Kate Lange, correct?"

She nodded. "Yes."

He could see how this was unfolding. And it was a fucking mess. When Judge Carson found out about this, she was going to blow a gasket. "And…?"

Mrs. MacAdam wound the handkerchief tightly around her index finger. "She told me I didn't have a good case. That the courts were reluctant to remove a child from her mother, especially a teenager who didn't want to go."

He jotted down this information. Kate would have to be interviewed. *Shit*.

Marian MacAdam twisted her handkerchief. "I'd heard Lyons McGrath Barrett was a good firm, but I didn't feel Ms. Lange gave me good advice."

He leaned forward. "Why not?"

"She told me I didn't have a case unless I had proof that Lisa was endangering herself."

"Did she give you any advice about how to get it?" He watched her closely. Had Kate observed her statutory responsibility?

Mrs. MacAdam's eyes fell to her handkerchief. "She told me I could call Child Protection but I told her I didn't have any proof…"

"And did you?"

She stared at her handkerchief. "I didn't think I did…it was just a feeling." She met Ethan's eyes. Beseeching him not to judge her. It was a look he'd received so many times, he usually felt little sympathy. But in this case, he felt a twinge of pity. This woman would likely never get a full night's sleep again. "I didn't think a feeling counted."

She was right—in a way. It was hard to act without some concrete evidence. And yet, cops acted on instinct all the time. Feelings, as Marian MacAdam put it, could make or break a case.

"What about your lawyer?" He avoided saying Kate's name. "Was she going to call them?"

She shook her head. "I asked her not to. I wanted to keep the matter private."

"Why?"

"Because I knew that if Lisa found out I'd involved the authorities she wouldn't come live with me."

"You'd lose your case."

She hung her head. "Yes." Tears ran down her cheeks. The consequence remained unspoken but it was obvious what they both were thinking: *and now you've lost Lisa.* Marian MacAdam swallowed a sob.

"We need to find the person who did this to her," Ethan said firmly. He couldn't have her disintegrate on him. There'd be plenty of time—the rest of her life—to be subsumed in recriminations and loss. Right now he needed to get whatever information he could extract from her before time and grief blurred her memory. "We need to establish a time line."

She nodded, her head still bent. She closed her eyes for a moment. Then she took her handkerchief and wiped it over her cheeks. She stuffed it into her sleeve and straightened. "I don't have a lot of information," she said. "I was at my cottage." What she did know she recounted in a defeated tone. Ethan closed his folder. It was 10:07 p.m. They were both exhausted. He stood. "Thank you for coming in, Mrs. MacAdam."

"Can I see her?" she asked.

He picked up his file. "That's up to Judge Carson."

Tears welled in Marian MacAdam's eyes. "I was afraid you'd say that." She walked to the door, her body shrunken in her camel overcoat. Neither of them spoke as Ethan led her through the security door to the main foyer.

"Do you have an alarm system, Mrs. MacAdam?" he asked. She looked as if she would fall to pieces if anyone so much as tapped her arm.

"I live in a condo, Detective. There is good security in our building."

He nodded. "Make sure you use it." Given that Lisa's mother was a criminal court judge, and, in particular, Judge Hope Carson, there could be a number of killers with bones to pick.

Or cut off.

14

The rising sun sent a shaft of light under the blind, lightening the room to a cool blue. Sleep had proven a faithful accomplice to Kate's conscience, abandoning her to a night of insomnia while her mind twisted with recriminations.

She pushed the bedcovers back and sat up. Alaska had only been living with her for a short time, but he knew this was his cue. He padded over, his dog tags making a light jingle in the otherwise silent room, and nuzzled her hand. She rubbed his head. "You are the only good thing in my life right now, boy," she whispered.

She discovered how true that statement was when she opened her front door.

The morning paper lay on her front porch.

She picked it up and braced herself for what the headline would say. But it didn't prevent her heart from stopping in her throat.

Judge's Daughter Dismembered, the headline screamed.

Judge Carson's stark features, made even grimmer in grainy black-and-white, stared accusingly at her from the front page.

* * *

The few hours of sleep that Ethan caught didn't feel like any at all. He was on his third coffee, picked up from the gas station on his way to work. He pulled into the lot opposite the police station and parked the car. It was a perfect spring morning. The air was fresh, moist and full of promise. Ethan rolled down the window and breathed deeply. In the distance, Halifax Harbour spread out before him. Blue, sparkling, beautiful.

Some things never seemed to change, despite the death and depravity that he investigated every day. It comforted him to know that he could still find beauty. Because he was scared that one day he would look at the harbor and see just blue water. Cold, polluted water.

He picked up the paper and glanced at the clock on the dash: 7:38 a.m. He had just enough time to skim the paper before the case meeting.

He knew what the headlines would say—the phone had been ringing since yesterday morning. The *Halifax Post*'s usually cynical crime reporter eagerly asked him about the girl's death, probing for as many salacious details as he could get.

Still, he flinched when he read the large bold print on the front page: Judge's Daughter Dismembered. He thought of Judge Carson when she saw that headline. It would anger her. But would it also wound her? Or would it give her a secret satisfaction?

He was bothered by her interview yesterday. She was so angry. She showed very little grief. That wasn't necessarily a sign of guilt; many people were paralyzed by grief and unable to show it. It would swell inside until it erupted when the grief stricken were least prepared. Judge Carson might adjudicate a case five months from now and find herself swallowing sobs as she gazed at the shaved head of a Hells Angels member. Maybe he'd have a tattoo of a dog on his skull. Maybe that would remind her unexpectedly of her own child.

Nonetheless, he'd interviewed a lot of victims' families and something about Judge Carson was off.

He hadn't really considered her a strong suspect until Marian MacAdam told him Judge Carson was in line for an appointment to the Supreme Court. That was a big step up from the criminal court. Supreme Court justices were chosen based on their legal acuity and their character. He suspected Judge Carson would easily ace the first criterion, but given Mrs. MacAdam's description of Judge Carson's family situation, he wasn't sure about the other. Would having a drugged-out daughter and a nasty custody battle with her own mother-in-law be grounds for excluding her from the race? He guessed that no one wanted to appoint a justice to the Supreme Court with that kind of baggage.

So it came to this: How far would Judge Carson be willing to go to secure that appointment?

From Mrs. MacAdam's point of view, she was already willing to sacrifice her daughter's well-being and not send her to rehab for fear of public scandal.

But would she actually kill her daughter?

And dismember her?

Mutilating the body would be a perfect way to cover up the crime.

Yet, it was hard to believe that a mother—and a criminal court judge—could commit so heinous an act on her own flesh and blood.

Which, of course, was the perfect reason for doing it.

He ran his mind back over the information she provided. It was very little. She was vague about a lot of the time line.

A picture of her hands floated in his head. They were strong hands. One knuckle bore a cut.

And Lamond reported that Lisa's father had been overseas for the past fifteen days and was not due back for another ten. Thus, nicely out of the picture.

He washed his muffin down with his coffee and hopped out of his car.

Judge Hope Carson was officially on the list of suspects.

He headed through the heavy wood doors of the police station, swiping his pass through the security door, and strode down the hallway. He tipped his coffee cup into his mouth and discovered he'd drunk it all. Cursing under his breath, he tossed the cup into the garbage can.

Ferguson stood at the white board, jotting notes. He slid into a seat at the boardroom table next to Lamond. Ferguson stared one last time at the map, then turned to the group.

"All right, then," she said. "The media is already whipping the public into a frenzy, so we have no time to lose. Walker and Lamond, you take the street kids and prostitutes. Lisa MacAdam's grandmother thinks she started using a few months back. Find out when, who sold to her, who she hung out with, and whether anyone had a reason to hurt her."

Her gaze turned to Ethan. He knew what was expected of him. They'd already discussed their tasks earlier this morning via cell. "I'll check out all the offenders on release that Judge Carson put away," he said for the benefit of the team. He'd wanted to be out in the field, checking leads, not sitting on a computer tracking ex-cons. But he was good at this. And right now, he had to prove he was not only a team player, but a team leader. He pushed back his chair. "Everyone know their tasks?"

The team nodded. He walked toward the door. "See you at 5:00 p.m."

Ferguson intercepted him outside the war room. "Before you go…" She lowered her voice. "I had one of the guys run a check on Kate…"

"You did what?"

She returned his outraged stare with a coolness that Ethan knew he needed to regain. He breathed in deeply. "What did the check show?"

"The previous Friday night she reported an intruder in her yard."

His pulse pounded. Kate had reported an intruder? Why hadn't she called him? "What time?" he asked. His voice was hoarse. He swallowed. "What time did she report the intruder?"

"About 2150."

He felt the tension leave his shoulders. It was after the time he'd seen her, but still…the realization that she'd called patrol instead of him was like a punch to his gut.

She's moved on, buddy.

But he hadn't.

He'd swallowed his pride, gone to her new house. Tried to make her see that they couldn't just leave things the way they were. He'd hoped she'd apologize, that she'd throw herself in his arms and tell him that Vicky had gotten it all wrong. That she was the woman he'd fallen in love with.

But she didn't.

He should never have fallen for a lawyer. Lawyers were trained to champion a side. They represented a client, not the public. They deliberately turned a blind eye to justice. It infuriated him when an accused got off on a technicality, practically given permission to go out and hurt someone else.

Kate had tried turning the tables on him and telling him that *he* had the problem. He wasn't the one with the stained past. Her father had been feeding a spiraling gambling addiction; she'd been speeding. They'd both thrown the dice—and lost.

She also had been everything he'd ever wanted in a woman.

He was fucked.

"We're going to have to talk to her, Ethan."

He nodded. "Right."

Ferguson's face became more intent. "I don't want you calling her."

He crossed his arms. "Is she a suspect?"

Ferguson shook her head. "No. But we can't afford to have the media spinning this. I'm going to do the interview myself."

"Right." He picked up his clipboard, pretending an indifference he didn't feel. "I'm going to start the court record check."

"Good." She paused. Her eyes sought his. "If I learn anything, I'll let you know."

Ethan nodded. He turned on his heel and left the room. He needed some privacy to sort out his thoughts. Without the team watching his face.

How had Ferguson guessed that his first instinct would be to call Kate and give her the heads-up? Despite everything that had gone down between them, he wasn't prepared to have her ambushed.

And yet, as Ferguson had told him—had that been an oblique warning in her gaze?—Kate hadn't called him about the intruder on Friday night.

She'd chosen to not involve him.

The message was loud and clear. Kate wasn't calling him for help. She had opted to go the official route.

He would do the same.

* * *

"The police are here to see you," Liz announced. Kate glanced up from her work. Her nerves were so taut that she was shaky. Her icy-blond assistant looked surprised for once, but Kate wasn't. She knew why they were calling. Relief seeped through her, mingling with trepidation. She wanted to know what happened to Lisa and yet was scared to find out.

Because she would finally know how terrible her guilt would be.

"Send them in," she said. She closed her file and pulled out the MacAdam folder, her hands suddenly sweaty. Two police detectives came in.

This pair was older than the ones who came to her house on Friday, more seasoned veterans of the police force, dressed in civilian garb.

"Ms. Lange, I am Detective Sergeant Ferguson," said a woman about ten years older than Kate. She held out her hand, her open, freckly features belying a steely grip and even steelier gaze. "And this is Detective Constable Redding." He nodded, his bloodshot eyes inscrutable in his weathered face.

"Please have a seat, detectives." Kate tried to look calm, but her palms were sweating like crazy. She sat down and rubbed her hands furtively on her skirt.

The officers pulled up the two seats by her desk until they were directly in front of her. Detective Redding took out a portfolio from his briefcase and balanced it on his knee. He clicked his pen. That seemed to be a signal for his partner.

"Ms. Lange, you are aware that the granddaughter of your client Marian MacAdam was found dead on Tuesday morning?" Detective Ferguson asked.

Judge's Daughter Dismembered. Kate could never forget that headline for as long as she lived. "Yes."

"We believe she was the victim of foul play," Detective Ferguson said.

"The paper said she'd been—" Kate's tongue resisted saying the word; she forced it out "—dismembered."

Detective Ferguson nodded. "Yes."

Kate swallowed. "Do you know if she was conscious when it…happened?" Her mind refused to let go of the images of Lisa's final moments. A killer cutting off an arm. A girl whimpering in disbelief. Then agony. Crying for her mother, her grandmother, *someone,* to help her. Eyes begging for mercy. How long would it have taken her to lose consciousness?

She suddenly became aware of Detective Redding watching her. There was a flash of sympathy in Detective Ferguson's eyes before she shook her head. "We cannot give details, Ms. Lange."

Kate's hands clenched. She knew the police couldn't give out information while they were searching for a suspect. But she *needed* to know.

"Lisa had been hanging out with some street kids the day she disappeared," Detective Ferguson said.

"I see."

Detective Ferguson watched her closely. "Lisa's grandmother told us she was concerned enough about Lisa's activities that she came to you for advice about getting custody from her daughter-in-law."

Kate breathed out slowly. "Yes, Detective, that is correct." Breathing made no difference. The guilt churned regardless.

"And what advice did you give her?"

Kate's gaze sharpened. Nice try, Detective. "Solicitor-client privilege prevents me from sharing that with you."

Detective Ferguson raised a brow. Kate could see that she had known full well Kate wouldn't divulge the details of the meeting.

"Well, you must have had a good reason for not involving Child Protection…"

Detective Ferguson was fishing. Kate knew the detective was hoping she would try to defend her advice, and thereby reveal information about the file. But she held her tongue. She would repent silently. Not share her remorse with two homicide detectives.

"Although you did call the police yesterday morning, correct?"

"Yes." *Too little, too late.* The thought was reflected in Detective Ferguson's gaze.

"Why?"

"Because I'd spoken to Mrs. MacAdam and she told me Lisa was missing. And I'd heard the news report about the homicide."

"Why didn't you call Child Protection sooner?"

"Without revealing the details of my discussions with Mrs. MacAdam, I was assured that she had no proof Lisa was endangering herself." She knew what she said, on the surface, sounded reasonable. But inside her conscience was firmly on the homicide detectives' side. *Why didn't I call them sooner?*

Detective Redding fished through his briefcase and pulled out a document. Kate recognized it as the statement she gave to police on Friday night. "You told Constable Drummond that you had an intruder at your house on Friday night?" This was the first time he had spoken and his voice was surprisingly deep and penetrating.

"Yes."

"Did you see the intruder?"

Kate shook her head. "No. He wore a hooded coat. It was long. His back was to me. He ran away before I could see his face." But he hadn't really run, Kate remembered. He had just…left. Gone out through the gate. Same way he had come in.

Detective Ferguson leaned back in her chair. "Quite a day you had, Ms. Lange. You chase away an intruder—not recommended, by the way, you should call the police—and earlier that evening you meet with the grandmother of a girl who is murdered only a few days later."

"I know."

"That's quite a coincidence."

"Yes." But there was no explanation for it. She just happened to be in the wrong place at the wrong time.

Detective Redding closed his portfolio and clicked his pen. The interview was over. "If you remember anything else that may help us in our investigation, here's my number." Detective Ferguson sized her up one final time before giving Kate her card. "And keep your doors locked, Ms. Lange. Until we determine whether your intruder and Lisa's murderer are linked, you could be at risk." With those parting words, the detectives left.

Kate closed the door and sank in her chair. Her mind was going in circles. The meeting had been fruitless for both sides. Neither had gleaned anything more.

She just needed to know one thing.

Had Lisa suffered?

She'd hoped the detectives would give her a hint. But they were too experienced to give anything away that would jeopardize their investigation.

Her mind scrabbled for the only other option. Would Ethan take pity on her and tell her if she called him?

He hadn't called to warn her about the police detectives

coming. He hadn't tried to warn her that there could be a link between the intruder and the murderer.

She closed her eyes and pressed her fingers to her temples.

15

Thursday, May 3, 4:00 p.m.

"This is not the way we do things at LMB," Randall said. He flipped open the file Kate passed him. His handwriting jumped out at him. *Marian MacAdam.* He'd had no idea when he took her call what chaos that unassuming name would wreak. Damn, why hadn't he remembered she was Hope Carson's mother-in-law?

He skimmed Kate's notes, noting her even, scrawling hand, feeling her stiff presence across from him. She'd given him the file with a flash of defiance and anger. It diverted him for a moment from other, more telling, signs. She looked a little worse for wear. Her usually luminous skin was marred by dark shadows under her eyes. But it was the expression in her amber gaze that warned him. As if she was ready for his attack and wouldn't let him see how much it hurt.

He tried a different approach. "I realize I referred Mrs. MacAdam to you, but she did not inform me of her relationship to Judge Carson."

"I wondered that," Kate said. Her tone was as stiff as her back. "But it didn't matter. It would have been difficult for her to proceed with a custody application. She didn't have much going for her."

"I see." He paused for a moment, finding himself strangely unsure of how to proceed with her. He brushed a hand over his hair. "Look, Kate, I believe you gave Mrs. MacAdam the appropriate advice—" She glanced away. *She doesn't think she did.* He filed that knowledge away. "—but you failed in your duty to the firm. You should have come to me and told me about the delicate nature of this case."

She straightened her back. Met his gaze head-on. A direct, clear gaze that seemed to look into him. Which was distinctly unnerving.

"As far as I was concerned, there was no case."

Unrepentant.

He fought to hide his response to that. She needed to understand that she was part of a team now. A team that was only as strong as its weakest link. He couldn't indulge her defiance. "It doesn't matter what you believed." His subtle emphasis of the word *you* was noted by the tensing of her shoulders. He relaxed a little. He could get under her skin just like her gaze seemed to get under his. "You are operating in one of Halifax's best firms. You are no longer in a two-person practice. You need to be cognizant of the firm's reputation."

"Trust me, I was very concerned about it." He thought he glimpsed self-loathing in her eyes. She dropped her gaze. When she raised her eyes again they gleamed with a fierce determination. Kate was not going to let him see how upset the MacAdam case made her. She probably believed he'd think she was weak.

He'd have to work at it to make her crack.

He softened his tone. "Why didn't you come to me, Kate? I referred Marian MacAdam to you."

She lifted her chin. "It didn't seem there was anything

to report." What she didn't say, but he'd seen it in a flash of her eyes, was that he'd be the last man on earth she'd come to for advice.

Hurt—unexpected and unwelcome—stabbed him. It startled him, threw him off his stride. Making his next words harsher than he intended. "You mean the fact that you had a client who was concerned her granddaughter was endangering herself and you didn't think that was worth reporting? If not to me, then to Child Protection?"

She paled. "She told me that she had no proof."

"Did you tell her Child Protection could get it for her?"

"Yes." Her voice sank to a whisper. "Yes. I did."

"Then why didn't you call them?"

"I wasn't sure I should." She looked out his window. But her gaze was inward. Searching her soul.

He waited. He needed to know why she'd made this decision. He had an obligation to the firm to test her on her professional abilities.

Finally she said, "She wanted to keep the matter private. She was concerned that Lisa wouldn't want to live with her if she notified the authorities…"

"But, Kate, if the girl was endangering herself, you had a legal obligation to report it!"

"I know!" Her eyes blazed at him. "Don't you think I know that?" Her tone changed abruptly. "The only behavior that Mrs. MacAdam could point to was that Lisa wasn't showing up for supper on time. Hardly out of the ordinary for a teenager."

"Do you think she was telling the truth?"

She glanced away. "I couldn't tell. When I informed her about my duty to report to Child Protection, she became upset. And I wondered if that influenced the rest of the meeting. I wondered if she was holding back."

"So much so that you changed your mind and reported your concerns to the police yesterday?"

"How did you know that?" She stared at him, shock making hollows under her cheekbones.

"Child Protection told me." He'd been just as shocked. It had taken all of his skill to keep it out of his voice and assure them that he had every confidence in his new associate Ms. Lange.

She drew back in her chair. "They called you?"

"Yes. They are investigating whether you met your statutory obligations. Apparently Mrs. MacAdam hadn't given you the same version as she gave the police." His eyes drilled into hers.

"Oh, my God." She became so pale that he almost got out of his chair to steady her. He forced his pity down. She was in an unenviable position. Heartrending. But years of experience had taught him that the moment when his emotions were most likely to erupt was precisely the time they needed to be held firmly in check. He could not let her see how profoundly sorry he felt for her. The firm's reputation depended on his ability to judge her objectively. But it was obvious that this latest piece of information was news to her. It would appear that she'd been screwed by her client.

She straightened that steel spine of hers and said, chin up, "So what did you tell them?"

That's my girl. Fight back. The thought flashed through his mind, unnerving him. Again. "That I was going to speak with you and phone them afterward."

"I see." Her eyes searched his face. After a long pause, she asked quietly, "What are you going to tell them?"

What his gut had been telling him all along. "That you acted appropriately." He finally let her see the sympathy he'd been holding in check.

There was a slight loosening of her shoulders.

"Kate, they may want to have an independent opinion."

"I understand."

"But I think, in terms of your client, you did the right thing."

Tears suddenly welled in her eyes. He had an uncontrollable urge to give her comfort. Put a hand on her shoulder. Draw her to him. Feel her damp eyelashes on his skin.

Jesus. What was wrong with him? He drew back in his chair.

She looked away. "Thank you." She rose from her seat.

He couldn't help himself. He lifted a hand. "I'm not done yet."

She sank back to her seat, averting her gaze until her eyes were dry. Relief brought a tinge of color back to her cheeks. It was clear to him that she'd been suffering all week.

He knew why the suffering would be so acute.

She didn't know this—and he would never tell her—but he knew all about her sister. And her father. He'd been the inadvertent witness to her life story. His mother had been the manager of the bank her father had defrauded.

That knowledge had given him all the more reason to resist John Lyons' desire to hire Kate. That, and the fact he sensed John Lyons had more than just a mentor's interest in his new hire. He studied Kate. Was there anything going on? She'd worked hard to rise above her past. He admired her for that. More than he would ever let her know. But his admiration would corrode in a heartbeat if she allowed herself to be seduced by John Lyons. She ought to know—after all, didn't everyone know? His lips twisted bitterly—how he would feel about an affair in his firm.

She watched him with an expectant look on her face. There was a small light in her eyes that hadn't been there earlier. He hated to crush it, but he had an obligation to the firm. "Judge Carson is now calling us and demanding to know why her mother-in-law was seeking legal advice behind her back just days before her daughter was murdered." He paused. "She's furious that you called the police about Lisa's disappearance."

"How did she know that?" Did Ethan tell her? Blood rushed to her cheeks.

"Apparently your client admitted it."

Kate stared at him. Marian had betrayed her. But then she thought of the elderly matriarch squaring off with her daughter-in-law and she knew she couldn't blame Marian. "I'm sure Judge Carson wrung it out of her."

"And she's trying to wring it out of us, too."

Kate inhaled sharply. "She would know that we couldn't divulge anything."

"Her daughter's dead, Kate," he said gently. "She finds out from the police that her mother-in-law is sneaking around, trying to get custody of her daughter, and three nights later her daughter is murdered and dismembered. I think most people would want answers."

"Especially if they feel they are to blame." The minute she uttered the words, he could tell she knew it was the wrong thing to say. She added quickly, "I only meant that there was some suggestion by Lisa's grandmother that Judge Carson was not involved enough in her daughter's life. That Judge Carson might feel guilty about this."

Did Hope feel guilty? She'd never seemed dogged by life's reproaches. But this wasn't a reproach. This was a full-out assault. And she seemed to be reeling under it. "She's making up for it now," he said. "She may not have been involved when her daughter was alive, but she sure as hell is involved now that her daughter is dead." He paused. "Kate, I have to warn you, Judge Carson is out for your blood. By calling the police before she did, you showed her up."

"I was worried about Lisa."

"I know. But your action underlined her inaction."

Her eyes searched his. They were so translucent. If he stared into them long enough, what would he find? "What do I do about this?" she asked quietly.

She was asking for advice. He had managed to break through at least one line of defense. Unexpectedly, he wanted her to trust him. "There's not much you can do unless Mrs. MacAdam comes back, seeking advice. Keep me in the loop this time."

"I will." She shifted on her chair. She wanted to leave. He could sense that. But he couldn't let her leave until she understood that he was, as of this moment, on her side.

He walked around his desk and leaned against it. "Kate, you were put in a very difficult situation, partly through my own oversight. I'm sorry."

"That's okay." She stood hurriedly, bending over to pick up her notepad. Her skirt tightened smoothly against her buttocks.

His nerves leaped in response. He pulled his gaze up to her averted face. She turned to go. "You know, I didn't come from the silver-spoon background most people think I did."

That stopped her in her tracks. Whether it was the intimacy of his tone or the information he revealed, he could tell he'd thrown her for a loop. A softer, kinder Randall? she was probably thinking in amazement. He took advantage of her confusion and added deliberately, "I never knew my father." She froze. "My mother worked her way up through a bank. She made me read Shakespeare," he added, to see if she would smile. She did. Slightly. It urged him on. "I won a scholarship to Hollis U, then to Harvard Law School. I think you know the rest."

"Yes. You have had an impressive career." She put a hand on the doorknob and looked back over her shoulder. "I want one, too."

He took in her steady, clear gaze. "I believe you will, Kate. You've made it this far. Try not to make enemies." On impulse, he shared his own code. "If you do, take no prisoners."

She gave him one final, impenetrable look. Then she left.

He stared at the spot where she had stood. Kate Lange could well become a fine lawyer.

As long as she stayed out of trouble.

And between Lisa MacAdam's murder, Child Protection Services' investigation and Judge Carson's wrath, that seemed unlikely.

What the hell happened in there?

Kate walked back to her office, completely confused. When she first sat down in front of Randall Barrett's desk, she'd felt as if she was back at elementary school, perched on the edge of a hard wooden chair in the principal's office, being told by a censorious Mr. Ginley that young ladies *did not* put snowballs down the boys' pants.

Except Randall Barrett was nothing like Mr. Ginley. Her former principal had been fiftyish, balding, portly and reeked of aftershave.

Randall Barrett was none of these things. As every warm-blooded female in Halifax was only too aware. He'd been a coup for LMB when he joined the partnership. He had been brilliant at law school, graduating top of his class from Harvard. The Chief Justice of the Supreme Court of Canada handpicked him to be his articled clerk. After being admitted to the bar, he litigated the big securities cases on Bay Street. Until his star was suddenly eclipsed by his divorce. He returned to Halifax.

He'd probably thought he was leaving it behind him in Toronto, but the scandal rags of Halifax couldn't resist sinking their teeth into a prime catch like Randall Barrett. His impressive net worth was gleefully dissected along with a profile of his adulterous wife. She had blamed her affair with another lawyer in her Toronto firm on her husband's overriding work ethic. Kate figured his ex-wife must have had serious grounds for her complaint. Because, for the life of her, she couldn't see why any woman married to Randall Barrett would seek sexual satisfaction elsewhere. He reeked of virility.

Even in her state of shock, or perhaps because of it, his proximity pounded at her reserves. And she hated that.

When she was summoned to Randall's office, she was convinced she was about to be fired. No firm, especially one with the kind of rep that LMB had, liked to have a lawyer whose cases resulted in probes by the police and Child Protection Services. She'd gone into Randall's office on the defensive, not willing to let him see how desperately she needed someone—him, her boss, the firm's managing partner, one of Halifax's best legal minds—to acquit her conscience.

The glimpse of sympathy in his gaze at the end of their meeting had almost been her undoing. It had been a split second, a look that passed between the two of them and left her reeling. Stunned. Disgusted with what she'd wanted to do.

She'd wanted to bury her face in his shirt, inhale its crisp cotton, feel her tears dampen and warm the tension between them. She knew that he would give her that comfort.

And more.

She had seen it in his eyes. The brilliant blue had taken on an intensity, charged with heat, edged with fire.

What the hell is the matter with you? She strode down the hallway to her office, her thoughts furious, jumbled. *He's the managing partner for God's sake. You don't screw your boss. You'd be committing career suicide—not to mention emotional hara-kiri—in one single leap.*

She stalked through her doorway and shut the door. *He doesn't even like you.*

That stung. *And what about Ethan?*

She stared out the window. She had no answer to that.

Disgust mushroomed in her chest. She was yearning for the comfort of Randall Barrett to absolve her of her mistakes, knowing that if she had only acted differently a girl might not have died.

And in such a horrible, grotesque manner.

How could she live with that? She sank into her office chair and lowered her face in her hands.

She knew in that place deep inside her where hard truths could not be eroded by a sympathy-laden glance that she'd made a terrible mistake.

And she didn't know how to make it better.

16

Saturday, May 5, just before 1:00 p.m.

A long line of cars marked the street where St. Mark's Cathedral was located. News trucks hogged the prime parking spots, their satellite dishes gleaming in the watery spring sunshine.

Kate glanced at her watch and picked up her pace. Lisa MacAdam's funeral service would begin in twelve minutes. She was glad she'd walked. The parking would be a killer. And she had no doubt she'd get caught in the glut of mourners at the end. She wanted to be able to leave quickly.

Each strike of her heel on the pavement matched the pounding of her heart. The knowledge that she'd have to sit through Lisa's funeral had left her edgy. Nauseated. Terrified.

But it was her act of penance.

Most of Halifax's legal community and what appeared to be all of Lisa's high school had shown up. Dark-suited legal eagles swept past swarms of teenage girls huddled together in the parking lot. The girls held hands or hugged one another. Kate was a little surprised to see so many of Lisa's classmates. Hadn't Lisa been a bit of a loner? She wondered if the girls were more distressed at the loss of Lisa or by the shattering of their innocence.

She remembered Gennie's funeral. The other girls, watching her. The circumstances beyond their limited experience. She'd hurried past them, hoping for a touch on her sleeve, but none of the girls had moved. They'd just stared at her. Some with pity in their eyes. Some with blame. These girls, these friends of Lisa's, knew nothing of Kate. Yet she found herself hurrying past them, unable to meet their gaze. Just as she had fifteen years ago.

A news camera panned over the mourners. Several reporters stood off to the sidelines, mics tucked discreetly in the folds of their jackets, ostensibly respecting the grief of the attendees, while scanning faces, hoping to see if someone was willing to put their grief into words.

Kate wasn't. Never would.

Marian MacAdam sat down on the pew next to her son. She felt him shift slightly away from her. His reticence toward her had always made her heart constrict. She had learned over the years that the more she lavished her only child with love, the less it was returned.

Despite her own antipathy toward her daughter-in-law, Marian had thought Hope had suited Robert. But strangely, Hope hadn't been enough for him. Two years ago he surprised everyone by walking out the door.

And Robert hadn't been enough for Lisa. Marian liked to believe that he had loved his daughter but his career, his all-consuming jet-setting power-hungry career, had prevented him from acting on that love. Otherwise, how could she explain how indifferent he was to his own daughter's suffering?

And she didn't mean Lisa's final moments. She meant

all the moments leading to this. All the times Lisa'd asked her daddy to fly home to see her in the school play, all the times Lisa'd asked her father to take her with him, all the times Lisa had stopped asking because she knew the answer would never change.

When Robert walked out that door two years ago, he checked out for good. He never admitted it—he played lip service to the custody agreement—but the reality was that he was never home. And Marian suspected he liked it that way.

How, Marian wondered, had she managed to raise a son who could abandon his own flesh and blood?

But now he sat by her side. Viewing his daughter's coffin with the same drawn expression as he'd viewed her remains yesterday.

Hope sat on the pew opposite them. She had not acknowledged them. In fact, she'd barely acknowledged anyone. She sat by herself. She stared straight ahead.

At the same coffin.

Encasing the remains of a child that no one had loved enough to save.

Marian closed her eyes.

Kate walked through the heavy oak doors of the cathedral. She blinked, her eyes adjusting to the dimness after the brightness outside.

Several people stood in the vestibule, taking in their bearings like Kate. There was a couple, the man balding and the woman tastefully outfitted, and then another fair-haired man who stood off to the side. They were all dressed in suits, which suggested friends of Judge Carson, but Kate recognized none of them. The couple looked as if they'd graduated at least fifteen years before her, although the blond man was younger. Almost as one, they moved toward a small red-haired teenager handing out programs of the service, her pale blue eyes lined with black but rimmed with pink. It was strange how an event could connect people in a way they never would have imagined a week ago. Now here they were, an older couple who led the way, and a younger man who courteously allowed Kate to walk ahead of him through the doorway.

Then all their paths parted as they stepped onto the bloodred carpet that bisected the pews. A strange hush swallowed their footsteps. It was the hush of the living who wanted to be silent like the dead girl on the altar, but betray the fact that their hearts are still beating by the nervous flipping of the program pages, the uneasy shifting of bodies on pews, the whispered words of greetings as they found a familiar face in the throng.

Kate didn't look around to see if she knew anyone. She hoped no one would see her. She wanted to be by herself.

She slipped into a pew near the back. There were very few spaces left. The teenage girls she'd seen in the parking lot had better hurry up and get in the cathedral, or they wouldn't get a seat.

She glanced down at the program.

Lisa's gaze met hers. Kate's breath stopped in her throat. Lisa looked like a typical teenager. And yet she didn't. There was something in her eyes, a pain that went deeper than the usual teenage angst, a loneliness that Kate understood only too well.

She wished she'd met her.

She wished she'd helped her.

She wished she could change places with her. Give this young girl her life back.

But she had wished that before.

It hadn't changed a thing.

* * *

Ethan stood at the back of the cathedral. The funeral was set to begin in approximately one minute. The mourners had been ushered in from the parking lot and were now settled into the pews.

His eyes rested for a moment on the back of Kate's sleeked head. She hadn't seen him. But he'd seen her. Oh, he'd seen her. His nerves had jolted through his body as she stood hesitantly on the threshold of the church. She wore a little black dress, with a cropped jacket that reminded him of Audrey Hepburn. It hung around her hips—she'd lost weight since they broke up; he hadn't noticed that last Friday because she'd been wearing a raincoat. The starkness of her clothing also accentuated her pallor. As usual, she wore very little makeup, but her lips had a pale pink sheen that reminded him of the inside of a seashell.

She didn't look left or right. Just walked over to the closest pew and slipped into it. Within minutes she was joined by a muted group of teenage girls who'd exchanged looks of dismay at having to sit so far in the back.

There must be at least five hundred people here. He pressed his lips together.

Four hundred and ninety-nine mourners.

And, the team fervently hoped, one killer.

Contentment swelled within him. And satisfaction. It'd been a good week so far.

He'd gotten another case. Again.

That's what careful planning did for you. The weather forecast had held true—their accuracy for predicting rain was usually about ninety percent in his experience—and the girl had been found on schedule.

Fortune had thrown a little luck his way. The girl was a

judge's daughter! He liked to think it was fate telling him not-so-subtly that he would exact justice for the wrongs done to him. Dr. K had almost fainted when he found out.

It just goes to show that fortune favors the bold.

And to cap off his week, he'd come to her funeral to savor the moment. He usually didn't get this pleasure. Most of his patients were lost to their families before he began his procedure. Hardly any had funerals, and when there was one, there were so few family members he would have stood out.

He sat still, feeling the energy of the mourners. Pain, shock, disbelief.

Fear.

He absorbed it.

It filled his cells, transmitting an energy to his muscles that only his body could accept. Getting his fingers ready for the painstaking, precise work they excelled at.

His gift.

The world was just seeing it now.

He basked in the energy around him.

He glanced across the aisle. Three little schoolgirls sat with tears smudging their makeup. Lovely, firm bodies on two. The third was out of shape. He bit back a sigh. The muscles might be flaccid, but there was always something to learn from it. He had to remember that.

And then the woman next to them. He couldn't believe his luck when *she'd* arrived at the church. She was a class act, a lawyer by the looks of it. Again, it was a sign. He walked into the church next to her, breathing in her faint scent of lavender. He bet her muscles were nice and smooth, her flesh firm under that dress she wore.

If he killed her, the legal community would begin to wonder if they were being targeted. A deviation from his plan. But a tempting one.

He pictured laying her body out. He smothered the giggle that threatened to break through his lips and glanced at the woman. A whitish aura outlined her face.

He blinked.

When he looked again, the aura had gone. But her face was pale. Her eyes glowed like pools of warm whiskey. Hot toddy. He felt the blood pulse through him, his dick grow hard.

Stop. *Stop.*

He needed to be pure, sterile. Clean.

He would never be accused again of having an inappropriate relationship with his patient. He would never be called a dirty little bastard again. Right, Mom?

He scanned the crowd. There were other girls here. Ones whose eyes were already deadened. Like that black girl over there in the corner.

His gaze was drawn irresistibly back to Whiskey Eyes.

He'd have to wear sunglasses if he found her on the street. Her eyes were so clear. They looked right through him.

And he didn't like that.

The service was interminable. Marked by poignant eulogies, reflective yet hopeful hymns and the solemn words of the officiating clergy who had baptized Lisa fifteen years ago and had never seen her since.

Kate had sat through a service similar to this. The year her sister died was the same year Lisa was born. You'd like to think that the eternal circle of life was kicking in, providing some order to the universe but, as life would have it, Lisa died a tragic death, too. Kate had no doubt there was another baby being born who would face a similar tragic death in fifteen years, whose passing would rend the fabric of her family and leave them unraveled.

God, why did it have to happen?

God didn't answer.

She bowed her head. The program sat unopened on her knee. Lisa's eyes met hers. But this time they were brown, deep. Fringed with darker lashes. Filled with laughter. They were always laughing eyes. Playful, flirtatious Imogen. Gennie. Wanted to be grown up, like her sister. Wanted to be part of the in crowd.

Those eyes had been glazed with drugs on a Friday night, tinged with defiance. Until their car rounded the corner too fast. Then those beautiful brown eyes rolled in wild panic, first at Kate, then at the guardrail. Within a few seconds, they were unseeing. How could Kate walk away from that accident, literally wrench open the door and stumble out of the car, but her sister be lifeless, her body smashed and bloody?

It was all about angles and impact and speed. That's how the accident reconstruction experts looked at it. Kate looked at it differently. It was about one moment of careless judgment, one minute of pressing the gas pedal too hard while trying to make her sister understand that she needed to find new friends, ones that didn't sneak off onto the back porch and snort up. Had it been frustration that had made her foot press too hard on the pedal or one drink too many? She'd never know. How ironic that she'd been trying to save her sister from making bad choices, when she herself had made not just a bad choice, but a fatal one.

Had Gennie suffered? Had there been agonizing pain before the final oblivion?

The organ began to play a mournful dirge. The refrain was familiar. Tears swelled in Kate's throat. Bile was right behind it.

She needed to get out of here.

She looked wildly around. She was boxed into the pew

by three girls, all of whom sat in tears. Mourners were rising slowly to their feet, folding the programs into their purses, murmuring phrases like, "It was a beautiful service," to one another.

Kate stood. The air pressed in on her. Floral perfumes, citrus aftershave. Some really cheap cologne worn by the girl next to her. Her breakfast pushed up through her esophagus.

Ethan sat in one of the pews on the side. The rest of the team had distributed themselves at various preassigned spots. Walker and Lamond had filmed everyone entering the cathedral and were now watching the exits. Redding and Brown were videotaping the cars and license plates in the parking lot, as well as the side streets. After Ethan saw Kate go in, he chose an aisle seat slightly behind and to the side. He told himself it was an optimum vantage point to observe the mourners. It also happened to be an optimum vantage point to observe Kate. He'd caught her staring at the picture of Lisa MacAdam. She had a look of such stark anguish in her eyes that he felt a pang of sympathy.

And with that came doubt.

Maybe she hadn't put her firm first over Lisa MacAdam's interests. Maybe she had tried to do the right thing.

If she hadn't, she sure as hell was paying the price for it now.

The organ filled the church with a deep, nasal chord that vibrated through his body. The service was ending.

Kate rose from the pew, her face a shocking white against the jet of her dress. The program slipped from her fingers. She didn't notice.

Her jaw was rigid. She gripped the pew in front of her.

Jesus, was she going to faint?

He leaped from his seat.

* * *

Whiskey Eyes looked as if she needed a shot of whiskey herself.

Her face was white, even whiter than the aura surrounding it. He blinked again.

She stood shakily, her fingers curled around the edge of the pew. The tendons stood in rigid lines over her knuckles. Fine, strong tendons. He could almost make out the white of the bones underneath. His fingers itched to trace them with a scalpel.

Would she faint?

If he was quick enough, he could catch her.

He could take her outside.

To his car, he'd tell anyone who asked. Away from the crowds.

He patted his pocket. Good.

He'd remembered his sunglasses.

He longed to put them on right now, to block the white lights that danced around his vision, but he could wait.

He watched the woman, his body poised to jump from the pew as soon as the moment presented itself.

Fortune favored the bold.

17

Kate stumbled past the first girl, stepping on her foot. The next girl swiftly tucked her feet under her, but the last…

The bile was right there in the back of Kate's throat. Pushing its way in a wave that was building, building.

The last girl had placed her bag down by her feet. Kate's heel caught the strap. She lurched, falling forward into the aisle. Out of the corner of her eye, Kate saw a man—blond hair, gray suit—reach for her, but another man darted forward, blocking him.

"Kate?" Ethan grabbed her elbow, steadying her.

"Ethan?" Her heart simultaneously lifted and sank. It didn't help the nausea. She took a deep breath. She wanted to appear strong. Not grief stricken and on the verge of vomiting.

The first group of departing mourners was closing in. Kate glanced over her shoulder to see if she could see the blond man, to thank him, but he had gone.

Ethan led her quickly toward the vestibule. "Are you okay?"

"Yes." No. She wouldn't admit it to him. She felt disoriented, people swarming around her as they made their way to the sweet fresh air outside. Sweat beaded her brow. She tried to shake Ethan's arm away but his fingers tightened.

"I need to talk to you." He pulled her across the vestibule toward a side door that led to the church basement. Kate saw with a start of surprise that Lamond stood by the door. His eyes widened.

"Wait," she said. Lamond had opened the door for them. "Let's talk outside."

"Please." Ethan's voice had an edge of desperation. "We don't have a lot of time."

Lamond's big brown eyes signaled his agreement.

"Fine," she muttered. All she wanted was to sit down and let the nausea pass.

The mourners had left the church. Marian MacAdam knew she should be in the vestibule, thanking the hundreds of people who had come to pay their respects to Lisa.

But she was frozen. Immobile. She could feel nothing within. Nothing without, either. When she finally pushed herself to her feet, she could not feel her legs.

She swayed.

A hand steadied her. She looked down at the fingers clasping her black wool sleeve. It was her son's hand.

She waited for it to fall away.

Instead, his fingers curled protectively around her elbow.

She glanced at him in surprise.

His eyes met hers. And finally her tears came.

Flowing as freely as the ones that ran down his gray cheeks.

Ethan led Kate through the basement door of the cathedral, helping her down the stairs. Lamond closed the door behind them.

The air was damp, musty. The chill snapped her out of

her nausea. She steadied herself on the railing, moving her arm so Ethan's hand would fall away.

He pretended not to notice and led her to a small cloak-room. Low hooks marked the wall. Lambs and ducklings frolicked on the wall above them. A forgotten Dora the Explorer backpack lay in one corner.

She turned and faced him. He looked all business, his dark suit and midnight-blue tie bringing out his European good looks. Longing stabbed through her in jagged thrusts. She still wanted him. And that was the worst.

"We need to talk," he said. Alarm bells went off in Kate's head. He'd shown up at her house on Friday night, saying the same thing. And then had thrown one accusation after another at her.

She wasn't going to let him do that again. Offense was the best defense when it came to the way he made her feel. "The only thing I want to talk about is why you threw me to the wolves," she said curtly.

"The wolves?" Surprise, then guilt, swept through his eyes.

"Yes. The wolves. How do you think I felt, being ambushed by your team and knowing full well you could have called me but you didn't? Especially after I'd called you about Lisa MacAdam!" That had really hurt.

His face tightened.

Good. She'd pissed him off.

"Why didn't you call me about the intruder you reported last Friday night?" he shot back.

She stared at him. "Because you'd just finished accusing me of lying to you. Remember?"

A flush rose in his neck.

Her temples throbbed. She wanted to go home and bury her face in Alaska's fur. "I need to go."

"Wait. I need some information."

Her heart sank. "I can't help you."

"I think you can. I need to know if Marian MacAdam told you anything that would give Judge Carson a motive for murder."

Gooseflesh shivered down her arms. "You think Judge Carson killed Lisa?" She rubbed her arms reflexively, stunned by his question.

"She is on my list of suspects."

"But why?" How could Judge Carson commit such a horrible crime to her own child? She was so shocked by Ethan's accusation that she didn't see the trap he was setting for her.

"That's what I'm hoping you can tell me."

The headache tightened into a band around her skull. "Solicitor-client privilege prevents me from saying anything, Ethan," she said softly. She searched his face for understanding. All she saw was a man who'd had too little sleep and enough disappointment this week to etch lines around his generous mouth. "You'd have to ask Marian MacAdam."

"I already asked her. She couldn't tell me much except that you felt she didn't have a good case for custody. I want to know why."

"I can't disclose the details." The lambs frolicking on the wall behind Ethan's head had an alarming perkiness. Too white, too fluffy, too innocent of the wolf at the end of the path.

He didn't bother to hide his frustration. "Were you influenced by the fact that Lisa's mother was Judge Carson?"

"No."

"Then why didn't you call Child Protection?" The question came swiftly and with the unerring aim of a snakebite. "You have a statutory duty."

"I know that." She glared at him. "I didn't think at the time there was evidence that Lisa was endangering herself."

"Child Protection doesn't think so."

"What, exactly, is your point, Ethan?" His ruthless attack and her own guilt fanned her anger. "You know damned well I can't disclose anything. I did the best I could."

His lips tightened. "A girl died." He added softly, "I'm not convinced she had to."

She felt the blood drain from her cheeks. "You think I'm to blame?"

"Do you?"

The lambs froze on the wall.

"You bastard." She spat the words. "You are so fucking sanctimonious. You believe the worst of everybody."

"That's not true."

"Yes. It is." She felt the anger and hurt spilling free. She relished it. "I made some terrible mistakes in my life and I pay for them every single day, Ethan. Every. Single. Day. I don't need you to be my judge and jury."

"I'm not trying to be."

"You treat me like I'm a suspect."

"No. I don't."

"You interrogate me as if I've committed a crime."

"I was giving you a chance to make amends, Kate."

"Make amends?" She was not going to stand there and let him heap more guilt on her. "You fucking bastard!"

She pushed past him. He grabbed her arm. His fingers were hard. "I'm not done with you."

She looked at his face. It was hard. Angry. Bitter. As if he wanted her to pay. And she knew this wasn't about Lisa. This was about them.

"Let go of me!" She wrenched her arm.

He grabbed her other arm and pulled her to him. "I'm not done yet." His mouth ground against her jaw, seeking her lips.

She twisted her face away. "Ethan, stop it!" She pushed her hands against his chest. "Let go of me or…I'll scream!" *Jesus.* Couldn't she do better than that?

"Please, Kate." His voice sank into a whisper. "Please."

She heard his pain. Her own pain, clawing her now, overwhelmed her. She closed her eyes. Allowed herself to feel his chest against hers. His hands loosened their hold on her arms. His lips softened. All she was aware of was their warmth sliding along her jaw. Seeking her mouth.

Her breath caught between her lips, moist and suddenly desperate to feel his mouth on hers. Desperate for the sure oblivion they would provide.

His hands slid around her waist, pulling her closer.

She could not do this anymore.

She could not ignore everything that was wrong about them for momentary oblivion.

She stiffened.

"No, Kate," he whispered. "Don't."

"Ethan, please," she said, pushing him away. He resisted for a moment. But when she pulled back, his hands fell. "Don't do this."

He half turned from her. Breathed deeply. Ran his hands through his hair, then turned back to her.

"I don't know what happened there." No apology, Kate noted. She knew what happened. He wanted to make her pay. In the currency he knew would cost her the most.

He shoved his hand through his hair again. "We need to catch Lisa's killer. Make her pay for what she did to her."

Lisa's face, twisted in agony, flashed through Kate's mind. She closed her eyes. Her heart raced. Pain and guilt swamped her. She forced herself to breathe slowly.

"If you could tell me what you know about Judge Carson's behavior toward Lisa…"

She hugged her arms. "I don't know anything. That's the truth."

"Can I see your notes? There might be something in them." *Something you missed.* He didn't need to say the words. But they both knew it.

She tried to remember her meeting with Marian MacAdam. It hadn't seemed to yield anything important. But she didn't know what evidence the police had uncovered. Maybe there *was* something in her notes that would be the missing part of the equation. She stared at the lambs. They didn't deserve to be butchered.

"Okay," she said finally. "You know I'll be disbarred if this is ever revealed."

Ethan's face softened. "I won't tell a soul." He reached out to touch her arm. Then stopped when he saw her pull back. His hand fell to his side. "Thank you."

She wasn't ready to accept his gratitude. He'd hammered her too hard with her own conscience. He'd manipulated her as deftly as any of his suspects. And he'd tried to exact the steepest price he could from her: her dignity. "In return…"

He stiffened. "In return?"

She crossed her arms. "I need some information."

He hadn't been expecting that. She'd boxed him just as neatly as he'd boxed her. And she could tell by the hardening of his gaze that he didn't like that.

"What is it?" he asked warily.

She said softly, "Did Lisa suffer?"

He let out a deep sigh. Whether it was relief that she wasn't asking something that would jeopardize the investigation, or whether it was from the knowledge her question brought, she didn't know. "According to the

M.E.'s report, she was drugged. Then strangled. The dismemberment came afterward."

"So did she suffer?" Every part of her being was focused on him.

"Probably very little."

She closed her eyes for a moment. Her nausea swelled with relief.

A cell phone rang.

They both checked their pockets, an awkward silence descending between them. "It's mine," Ethan said, opening his phone. "Drake here." He listened for a moment. "Right. I'm coming." He flipped it closed and stuffed it in his jacket. "I've been called in. Ferguson wants to go over the guest book and review the footage."

"The footage?"

"Yeah, we've got security cameras on all the exit points. To see if we can get a visual on the killer."

"You think he was here?" A small shiver snaked across her scalp.

Ethan nodded. "Yeah. I do."

She walked up the dim stairwell, aware of Ethan's large frame behind her. Lamond opened the door for her. "Deb's on her way, Ethan."

"Yeah, she called me." Ethan turned to Kate and spoke softly. "I need that package ASAP."

"I'll get it for you tomorrow morning. Come to my house around ten."

"Thanks, Kate." He infused a little warmth in his voice, but it didn't penetrate her hurt. She'd seen the way he'd looked at her. She knew what he'd been thinking: first her sister, now Lisa. "You should go now." He glanced over his shoulder. When he saw Deb approaching, he added under his breath, "We need to keep this between us." He gave her a gentle push on the small of her back. "Pretend we just crossed paths. Take the main doors. Don't look back."

She hurried into the vestibule. She didn't stop until she'd gone through the double doors and felt the sun on her face. Ethan's words echoed in her head. *Don't look back.*

The irony of it didn't escape her. She'd spent her whole life trying to get ahead. But in the end, she was always looking back. She was always trying to outrun her mistakes.

18

He got out of bed and padded into the living room. He'd had a good nap after the funeral. It had refreshed him.

He grabbed a beer from the fridge. The funeral program sat on his coffee table. He picked it up and studied Lisa MacAdam's face. It wasn't a great picture of her; she'd looked better in the flesh.

He closed his eyes, his finger lightly stroking her photo.

The urge was back. Sooner than before. Much sooner. Normally after one of his nights out he'd be exhausted, moody, withdrawn. Happy to get back to his job and his routine.

But not today. He took a long swig from the bottle.

It was the funeral that did it. Seeing all those young girls. Young, firm bodies. Unlined skin, gleaming hair. Just like the dolls.

He'd already gone through his six-year-old neighbor's collection of dolls. At first, her mother would buy her a new one. And he'd steal that one, too. But her mother starting accusing her of being careless, and she stopped replacing them.

He had to find more dolls to steal. He discovered it was quite easy at the local department store. No one suspected a seven-year-old boy would want a doll.

After he'd finished with them, he'd burn their limbless bodies in the woods. He loved watching the synthetic hair curl and then fall off.

The arms and legs he kept under his bed. In a shoebox. Every night before he went to bed he'd pull them out and stroke them under the cover of his sheets. The smooth plastic, pliable under his fingers, soothed him, helping to ease the loathing he felt for his mother. Until the next day.

When he was older the limbs had a special purpose.

A special pleasure.

Then Tim found them.

"You freakin' weirdo," Tim said, grabbing a handful.

"No! D-D-Don't!"

His brother snickered. "If you can say it without stuttering, you can keep them."

That just made the stutter worse. And his brother knew it.

He eyed his painstakingly assembled collection mashed in his brother's fist. If he could just grab them...

"Say it!" Tim commanded.

He shook his head.

His brother smacked him across the face with the plastic legs.

It hurt. His cheek flamed pink.

But it wasn't the smarting of the blow that made him angry. It was the knowledge that his brother had used his only pleasure to inflict pain on him.

Anger shot through him. "I-I-I'm g-g-g-g-gonna—"

Tim laughed. "You gonna make me pay?" He began bending the limbs. "How? With your doll collection?"

He threw the limbs on the floor and began jumping up and

down on them. "Ooh, I'm so scared. Little brother's dollies might get angry." When the limbs were crushed to his satisfaction, Tim walked to the door. "Don't make me laugh."

Then he left.

He'd never stolen another doll again. Instead, he began hunting live specimens—rats, stray cats, raccoons. He worked on specimens for years, trying to develop his skills until he was ready for his ultimate dissection.

His brother.

Tim's funeral was one of the happiest days of his life. His mother had wept, mourning the loss of her beloved first son, the genius of his pathetic family.

There had to be sacrifice for genius. How many times had he heard that, as the family scrimped to pay for the extras that came with having a firstborn who was a prodigy.

It would have been perfect. Except he wasn't the firstborn.

He had been an "accident." His lips twisted. There were no accidents. There were just mistakes. And his mother didn't like it when anyone else made them. She showed her displeasure in ways that he didn't want to remember. His brother never had to worry about that. Everything Tim did came naturally. With ease, grace, precision.

Everything he'd done had been the opposite. Except when he picked up a blade. It focused his energies, turned his clumsiness into smooth, deliberate motion until it was like an extension of his brain, his heart. His soul.

His brother had finally seen the power in him.

Had finally recognized his talent.

Had finally seen that he was deserving of sacrifice, too.

His brother just hadn't realized that he was the sacrifice.

Until it was too late.

His pulse thudded with remembered pleasure. He never had to hear his brother's laugh again.

He finished his beer and wiped his mouth with the back of his hand. Within minutes, he was dressed, briefcase in hand.

He locked his apartment carefully. No one was allowed in it.

He slipped into his car, putting his briefcase into the empty slot between the front seats.

He was ready.

Ethan ran toward Serpentine Hill, pacing himself, relishing the fact it was Sunday morning and he could do a longer run. Point Pleasant Park was wet today. A torrential rainfall last night had eradicated the weak sun that shone at Lisa's funeral.

The air was incredibly fresh. A damp breeze cooled him down. He needed it. He'd been running for the past hour, ruthlessly pushing his body through the last ten Ks. Frustration still thrummed through him. He'd been sure they'd get a lead on the killer at Lisa's funeral. But everyone who attended had checked out: Lisa's friends, Judge Carson's colleagues and neighbors, lawyers, the funeral employees, the media.

And then there was Kate. Seeing her had totally thrown him off. He'd been trying to focus on the job. And then she'd arrived. He'd never felt so confused in his life. Everything was usually clear-cut. Black or white, blue or yellow, but not a fucking kaleidoscope. That's what Kate did to him. She mixed everything up until he wasn't sure what color he was seeing, what emotion he was feeling.

He turned up Serpentine Hill. It was a steep, windy path that cleared his head like nothing else. The first time he saw Kate, he'd turned up this hill, not suspecting that his life would change that instant. One look into those amber eyes and he was a goner. She just pulled him in deeper and deeper until he felt as if their souls were touching.

That's what he'd tried to recapture yesterday. It had shocked him, his impulsive grab of her.

But she'd tried walking away.

And it was one time too many.

Not when her client's granddaughter had been brutally murdered. Kate hadn't seen Lisa's body on the gurney in the morgue. He had. And he didn't think he'd ever forget it.

And when he held Kate against him, felt her breasts push against his chest, her rapid breath moistening his cheek, his pain erupted. He wanted to grind his mouth into hers, push her against the wall and lose himself in the sweet nirvana he knew she could give him. He needed something to remind him of all that was good and hopeful when every day he faced evil and hopelessness.

He was just one guy trying to draw a line to protect the innocent. And when he failed to protect them, all he could do was solve the crime and make the perpetrator pay. An eye for an eye.

And that didn't mean he believed the worst about everybody. Kate was wrong about that. He didn't. Not yet. He'd believed the best about her. What really hurt—and if he was honest with himself, what really scared him—was that his gut had been so wrong about her. That knowledge had eaten away at him for the past five months.

Now he felt a lightening. She'd pushed him away but she'd also made a promise to him. She was willing to put herself on the line to redeem herself. To redeem her profession. To redeem his belief about her.

He glanced at his watch: 8:57 a.m. Kate had told him to meet her at her house at 10:00 a.m. She'd have the notes for him to read.

The kaleidoscope was shifting into focus. The hill had done its job. It began to level off. He didn't slow down; he didn't try to catch his breath.

"Randall Barrett." He uttered his name automatically, wondering who on earth could be calling him this early on a Sunday morning—at his office, no less.

"Randall, it's Judge Carson." Her voice was tight. The only indication of her feelings. But Randall knew the signs. She was angry. Everyone knew that when Judge Hope Carson was angry the explosion would be of nuclear proportions. He had learned that the hard way eighteen years ago. He planted his elbows on his desk, his mind racing. It would take all his diplomatic skills to defuse her. Especially since she had used her formal title on the phone.

"Your Honor. How can I help you?" He quelled his uneasiness with the reminder that she needed his sympathy right now. The funeral yesterday had been devastating. Immersing himself in his usual Sunday morning catch-up at the office, he'd had a hard time keeping his mind off it. Any parent sitting in those pews could not help but think of their own daughters. For once he was glad his kid was living in Toronto with her mother.

"You mean like you've helped already?" Judge Carson's bitterness lashed at him.

He stiffened. "I told you I'd look into the matter and I did."

"What did you find? That my mother-in-law acted within her rights?"

He closed his eyes. Unbidden and entirely unwanted, an image of Hope Carson swam behind his lids. Not her now, in her judge's chambers, dressed in her black suit with her severe salt-and-pepper bob and grooves between her strong brows. No, he suddenly saw her as he first saw her eighteen years ago, walking into the law school, her red wool coat blowing open, laughing carelessly with a friend. From behind her tortoiseshell glasses, her eyes burned through him. Tawny and hungry. Gleaming with intelligence. She was a tiger.

Tyger, Tyger, burning bright…

They dated for three months. She had seared him with her caustic comments about the professors, her friends, his friends and even him. He had learned she could take what she dished out. He had fallen in love with her strength, her callousness, her fierceness.

But she wasn't interested in a relationship. And especially with him. She couldn't dominate him. He couldn't dominate her. In the end they were too much alike. There was no give and no take. Just attack, attack, maim and eventually kill.

He had relegated their relationship to a very distant memory. Now it returned. He didn't like the knowledge it brought with it: they were both newly single.

Why had she called him?

"Did you look at your associate's file?" Her voice brought him rudely back to the present. The way she said *your associate* made it sound like an unsavory part of his bodily functions.

He frowned. "Yes. She handled everything correctly."

"Are you sure?"

"Yes." He remembered the look on Kate's face when she handed him the file. Anger, defiance and resentment had flashed through those strikingly translucent eyes, along with something else he couldn't put his finger on. He suspected John Lyons had been right about her. Kate was made of stronger stuff than he had first thought.

Hope may not realize that her nemesis was a lot like her, but he did.

"Look, Your Honor, Kate did her job."

"But did you?"

"Of course."

"Then why the hell did you pass my mother-in-law over to a first-year associate instead of seeing her yourself?" Randall knew exactly what Hope was accusing him of: by sending Marian to someone other than him, there were now written notes—a paper trail—detailing Hope's inadequacies and Marian's concern about Lisa. If Randall had met with Marian, he would have grasped immediately the connection between Marian and Hope, and the notes would have been briefer and less detailed.

His frown deepened. He'd screwed up. Referring Marian MacAdam to a new associate had been a brash and stupid move. If he was honest with himself, he had been focused on swamping John Lyons' most recent acquisition with as many family law files as he could get his hands on. Anything to give John Lyons the message that he wasn't top dog any more.

"It seemed a reasonable decision at the time, Your Honor," he said, his voice low and smooth. As soon as he said the words, he knew he'd taken the wrong approach.

Her voice became a snarl. "Don't bullshit me, Randall. You screwed up. If that file gets leaked everyone is going to think that I drove Lisa to her death." Her voice wavered but she steadied it. "I won't allow Marian to win this one."

"Marian didn't win the last one, Your Honor. Kate Lange advised her to not proceed with the matter. She saved your as—your reputation." And the firm's, he realized. She hadn't deserved the dressing down he had given her.

"That's bullshit. She destroyed my reputation," Hope said tightly. "With the police. She should never have called them. I will never forgive her for that."

What you mean is you'll never forgive yourself. But would she ever realize that? Or just hate Kate for showing everyone that her mother-in-law's lawyer cared more than she did? Knowing Hope, it was a bitter pill that probably would never be swallowed.

"Just make sure that file doesn't contain anything the media could use against me."

Her words reverberated between them. He stared at his law degree mounted on the wall opposite him. He knew what Hope was demanding. To do what she wanted, he'd have to violate not only his legal ethics, but his own personal ethics. Not to mention betray Kate Lange's trust.

He lowered his voice. "Hope, don't ask me to do this…"

"Please." There was a catch to her voice.

He closed his eyes. This woman's only child had been horribly murdered. And from Kate's notes, there would be no question Hope had let the girl down before she died. Maybe Lisa had been in the wrong place at the wrong time because despair over her mother had sent her there.

"Randall, I'm asking this as a personal favor." Her voice was bleak. He couldn't imagine—refused to imagine—being in her shoes right now. She had enough to live with. She didn't need the whole city to be aware of her failings. Especially since he'd heard a rumor that she was being considered for the empty spot on the Supreme Court. That might be the only thing to get her through this ordeal.

"All right," he said softly.

She inhaled sharply. It sounded suspiciously like a sob. "Thank you." The phone went dead.

Randall placed the receiver down and stared at it for a long moment.

He pushed back his chair and rose heavily to his feet.

Kate's office was on the floor below him. He headed down the hallway.

Twice he paused, ready to turn back to his office. What he was about to do went against everything he had worked for, everything he stood for. But then his mind invariably returned to Hope's daughter, lying in a coffin with her toy dog. Hope's daughter, who had died a horrible, unimaginable death. How could any parent live with the knowledge that they had failed their child when they needed them most? From the sound of Hope's voice—bleak and hopeless and angry—the knowledge was eating away at her. He couldn't make her suffering worse. He had been spared. His own child was safe and happy in her blue-and-green bedroom in Toronto, surrounded by her stuffed animals and people who loved her. He didn't really believe in God, and yet he couldn't help but hope that this act of charity toward Hope might keep his daughter safe from the wolves that prowled the streets.

He turned down the corridor toward Kate's office. It was quiet, the air-conditioning turned off for the weekend. He half hoped she'd be in her office. Then he'd be saved from the decision he had made.

But she wasn't. Her chair was empty. Although when he stepped into her office he had the sense she was there, leaning against her desk, those long legs crossed at her slim ankles, arms folded. Watching him, disappointment and betrayal written in those startling eyes of hers. Eyes that could ignite his pulse.

He frowned. She had gotten too far under his skin. He didn't know how it had happened, but it had. It had to stop. He could not get involved with her, with any lawyer in his firm—not after what his wife had put him through—but especially her. John Lyons' protégée.

He didn't want Kate Lange in his head anymore.

He strode toward the filing cabinet and found what he was looking for. He knew without a doubt that Kate would put two and two together.

She'd get the message loud and clear.

No one took a stand against the bull without getting gored.

19

Damn. Kate couldn't believe it. It was 9:21 a.m. on a Sunday morning and Randall Barrett's car was already in the parking lot. Didn't the guy have a life?

She drove up another level of the parkade and left her car in the dimmest corner. Her errand would only take a few minutes, but she was taking no chances.

She took the elevator to LMB's associates' floor and ran her security pass through the reader. Her palms broke out in a cold sweat.

The halls were hushed as she hurried down the corridor. She breathed a small sigh of relief. No one else was working this morning. Except, of course, Randall Barrett.

She turned the corner and strode into her office, heading straight for the file cabinet. She pulled out the MacAdam folder and flipped it open.

Her fingers began to shake.

The folder contained only one sheet of paper. The one Randall had given her, with the simple notation *Marian MacAdam. Custody matter.*

What had happened to the rest of the file? Panic made her fingers clumsy. She pawed through the folders and Post-it notes in her drawer. No notes.

She racked her memory. The last time she'd seen the notes was the day the police detectives had come to her office. She remembered putting the file in her filing cabinet.

She opened the filing cabinet again. This time she combed through every file from *A* to *Z*, searching in the folders and between them to see if the notes somehow had fallen in.

They hadn't.

Where were they?

She dropped to her hands and knees behind her desk, looking under the credenza, her desk, chair, and behind her bookcase. No sign of them.

She stood. Her glance fell on the clock. It was 10:03 a.m.

Her heart sank as her panic rose. She couldn't even write out another copy. The harder she thought back to her meeting with Marian MacAdam, the more blank her memory became.

The clock ticked another minute: 10:04 a.m. Ethan would be at her house right now, wondering where she was. She grabbed the folder, Marian MacAdam's name blurring in front of her eyes and ran to her car. As she drove down the ramp, she noticed Randall's car was gone.

Her mind whirled.

She had been about to breach her own legal ethics by giving the notes to Ethan to read. Now someone had beaten her to it.

It could only be one person.

Randall Barrett. He wouldn't be worried about the repercussions of being caught.

He had a personal relationship with Judge Carson.

His ballsiness took her breath away.

He knew that she could only challenge him if she was willing to lose her job.

She wasn't. She had mortgaged her life to LMB.

Pain tightened her chest. Why had he done this to her? After that look she'd caught on his face in his office, she'd thought there had been a rapprochement of sorts. She'd thought he'd be willing to comfort her. Hell, she'd thought he *desired* her. There had been a moment of awareness between them that had shaken her to the core.

And now he stole from her.

Her heart twisted.

Damn him. Damn him for making her feel like this. She clenched her teeth and forced the pain of his betrayal down.

She wouldn't confront Randall Barrett about his theft.

But she could never trust him again.

She pulled into her driveway. Ethan was standing on the porch, leaning against a post. He had a coffee in each hand. He gave her a small smile when he saw her.

Her stomach churned.

"Hi." He was freshly showered, his hair still damp at the ends. His T-shirt showed his fit physique. She could almost feel the soft cotton warmed by his skin, the broad rounded muscles of his shoulders underneath.

She stepped carefully around him, putting her key in the door. "You'd better come in."

He straightened at her tone and followed her inside. Alaska padded toward her, ready for his welcome. She scratched his ears hurriedly.

"Look," Ethan said awkwardly, "I'm sorry about what happened yesterday. I don't know what came over me."

"It's okay," she said, although they could both tell from her voice that she didn't mean it. She rubbed her arm.

Ethan handed her a coffee. "I bought this for you."

"Thanks," she said.

Silence was a black hole of recriminations between them. Who would fall into the abyss first? she wondered.

"Did you bring the notes?" Ethan asked.

His question gave her the answer. She'd be the first to make the plunge. "I brought the file."

"Good." He relaxed, sipped his coffee. Waited expectantly.

Here goes. She took a deep breath and blurted, "The notes are gone."

He stared at her. "Gone? What do you mean, gone?"

"They aren't in the file. Look." She thrust the file folder at him, wondering in the next instant why she did so. It only contained a single piece of paper with one line scrawled on it. Ethan flipped open the cover. His lips pressed together. He looked up at her. His eyes searched her face. "So what happened to them?"

She shook her head. "I don't know. I searched all over my office, under the desk, in the drawers—" She stopped abruptly. She was babbling. "I don't know."

"Did you change your mind?"

"No. I was going to give the notes to you."

"So you didn't destroy them?"

"No."

"Hide them?"

"No!"

"Give them to someone else."

"Ethan, I told you I don't know what happened to them!"

"So someone stole them." He gave her a skeptical look.

"I guess so."

"Who would do that, Kate?"

"I don't know." She didn't want to voice her suspicions about Randall. With the bad blood between Ethan and her boss, it would be adding oxygen to a wildfire. This was between her and her managing partner. And there would come a time when she would make Randall account for this. He wouldn't get away with it.

"You don't know?" Ethan's eyes gleamed. "I think you do."

She took a sip of her coffee. It scalded her tongue. "No. I don't."

He studied the page in the folder. "This isn't your handwriting, is it, Kate?"

She looked away. "No."

"Who assigned you the file?"

She hesitated for a second. It was fatal.

Suspicion tightened his face.

She answered with quiet resignation. "Randall Barrett."

He slammed the folder shut. "That bastard. He took the notes."

"You don't know that, Ethan."

"Yes. I do."

"Why would he do that? He assigned me the file because he had no interest in the client, Ethan!" She was panicking now. Would Ethan confront Randall? She didn't want to think about the fallout of that. She'd be exposed, fired, thrown out on her butt, lose her income, her house, her reputation, all because she'd tried to assuage her conscience and help Ethan with his investigation.

What a tangled web we weave when first we practice to deceive...

"Really? Maybe he assigned you the client for another reason."

"Like what?"

"'Cause he wants to screw you." His deliberate crudeness was meant to offend.

A heat rose in her chest. She glared at him. "That's so off base you have no idea." She hoped he couldn't see the truth of what he said in her eyes.

"So why are you protecting him?"

"I'm not!"

"Yes. You are." He took a swig of his coffee. "Has Barrett made a pass at you yet?"

You jerk. That hit too close to home. "No. He has more finesse than you."

Ethan's face tightened. "I told you—"

"Randall didn't even hire me." She cut him off, her voice razor sharp. She wasn't going to stand there and let him point fingers. Time to set the record straight. "John Lyons did. And the fact you could suggest that I was hired for a reason other than my skills shows how little you knew me. Just because Randall Barrett made you doubt your abilities on the Clarkson case doesn't mean he doubts mine!" She stopped abruptly, her chest heaving. The lies never seemed to stop coming when she was around Ethan.

"You think I'd worry about some arrogant bastard when the Court of Appeal said he was full of shit?" His voice reverberated with a bravado that didn't quite reach his eyes. He was lying, too, she realized with a start. "And now you've gone to work for him and his fucking firm."

"I don't have to explain my career decisions to you." *Now.* Her eyes challenged him to refute this new truth.

"It was a big mistake, Kate," he said curtly. "You can't go work for a bastard like that and not get smeared by the shit he mucks around in." He shook the file folder. "Case in point."

She crossed her arms. "I was prepared to muck around in it for you."

His lips tightened. "We need to find Lisa's killer."

"So that makes it okay? When it's for the greater good?"

"Yes. It does." He dropped the folder on the hall table and opened the front door. "Goodbye." His tone was heavy. Final. He wouldn't be showing up on her doorstep again.

He was almost at his car when his cell phone rang. He

waited until he got into the front seat, then answered the relentless chime. "Detective Drake."

"Ethan, it's Deb."

"Yeah?" He started the engine. He wanted to get away from Kate's house. ASAP.

"I'm calling in the team." Her tone was clipped. "We've got another victim."

20

Kate sat back on her heels.

She'd rushed to her office this morning, dropping her purse and falling to her knees in front of the filing cabinet. *Please*, she prayed. *Please let them be there*. At 3:04 a.m. last night, she'd awoken with the chilling certainty that she had forgotten to look through the *N* folders. The notes were there. Misfiled. Or maybe she'd been wrong about Randall. That he'd only taken the notes to photocopy so he'd have his own record when Child Protection grilled him.

But the notes weren't there. Of course not. Never trust those dead-of-night certainties. They were just ghost whispers of what might have been.

Here she was, on her knees in her office, coming to grips with more than one unpalatable truth. The managing partner of one of Halifax's finest firms had stolen her notes, breached a fiduciary duty, snatched her confidence, her trust and, most importantly, her hopes. In one quick grab.

She pressed her face against the cool metal of the upper cabinet. And Ethan believed she was either lying to protect herself, or to protect Randall—because he thought she was having an affair with him.

That one hurt. First Rebecca Manning, then Ethan. Both insinuating she had done the rounds with the senior partners' beds to get hired on. As if she wouldn't be hired on ability alone. She'd worked her butt off, taken every crummy family law file thrown at her, to prove she was worthy of being at LMB.

And what had happened? She'd dropped the ball and let down her client, her firm, herself. And a young girl had been murdered.

Her direct line rang. She glanced over her shoulder at the clock on her desk. It was 9:01 a.m. It felt more like noon. Not a good way for the week to begin. That was the problem. It didn't feel as if last week had ended.

She staggered to her feet and picked up the phone.

"Kate Lange." She cleared her throat.

"Ms. Lange, this is Marian MacAdam."

Shock made her legs weak. She sank into her chair. Had Marian MacAdam learned somehow that Kate's notes were missing? Guilt rushed in where shock ebbed.

"Mrs. MacAdam. What can I do for you?"

Marian MacAdam's voice was strained. "As you are probably aware, my granddaughter's funeral was on Saturday."

"Yes." Kate cleared her throat again. "I went. It was beautiful."

"Yes, it was." Marian MacAdam's voice was tight. "But that is not the reason why I am calling."

So, she *was* calling about the missing notes. Kate's body went into red alert: pulse racing, body temperature rising. "Yes?"

"You know that the night Lisa was killed she had

returned to her old haunt—" Marian MacAdam cut off the word abruptly. "Lisa returned to the street corner where she bought drugs."

"Yes." Kate became aware of how cool the phone receiver felt against her cheek. "I read about it in the paper."

"She met with some friends." Marian MacAdam paused. "One of them came to the funeral. A black girl named Shonda."

"I see." The funeral was a blur for Kate. She didn't remember any of the faces except for Ethan's.

"Although I partly blame these so-called friends for encouraging Lisa's habit, I cannot blame them for what happened to Lisa."

Whom do *you blame?* The insistent voice of her conscience jumped into the conversation. *Yourself, for claiming you had no proof of self-endangerment? Hope Carson, for driving Lisa to it? Or me, for not doing anything about it?*

"This girl Shonda was very upset about Lisa's death," Marian MacAdam continued.

"We all are," Kate said softly.

"She told me some concerning things after the funeral." Marian MacAdam's voice dropped.

Kate breathed in deeply. There was a subtext in Marian MacAdam's voice, a hidden message that Kate hadn't yet deciphered. But she sensed the code was about to be given to her.

"She told me that Lisa wasn't the only street kid to disappear."

Kate's heart dropped. But she forced herself to sound unconcerned. "Really?"

"She said there were others."

"It's not unusual for street kids to come and go. They're a pretty transient population."

"That may be, but she seemed to think there was something more to it."

"Did she tell the police?"

"Yes, but they told her there wasn't much they could do."

"Why is that?" Kate couldn't imagine Ethan ignoring a lead like this.

"Because there was no proof that the girls were killed. And they'd been missing for months."

"So maybe there's no connection to what happened to Lisa."

"Perhaps. But I told her that I thought there'd be someone willing to look into this for her."

Kate's heart nosedived. "You did?"

"Yes. I thought you might be willing to help."

"Mrs. MacAdam, I'd like to be of service to you, but…" *But what? But I don't want to get my hands messy?* She closed her eyes. The guilt could no longer be held down. Marian MacAdam had her by the balls, and her client knew it. She swallowed. "What exactly do you want me to do?"

"Shonda's nervous of dealing with the police, given her background." Marian MacAdam paused delicately. "You know, living on the street." Kate understood how this girl could feel. How once you were branded no good, it was so much more difficult to ask for help. "Maybe you could find out who these missing girls are and work as a kind of liaison with the police."

A humorless smile crept across Kate's face. Marian MacAdam had no idea how the police operated. And how much the police wouldn't want her, in particular, involved.

"I'm not sure if that will work—" She rubbed her forehead. She was always making excuses with Marian MacAdam. She owed this woman. The debt was there.

Acknowledged. Being called in at this very moment. Maybe she could meet this girl Shonda and find out if her concerns were legit. "Okay. How can I find her?"

"She is living in a place on Gottingen Street. Here is her number."

Kate jotted it down. "I'll get back to you."

"Thank you." It sounded like the devil himself had answered her. But she had a feeling it was more the reply of an avenging angel.

She had been given a chance at redemption.

But not before she made a sacrifice. If Randall Barrett found out she was sticking her nose further into Lisa MacAdam's case, she knew what that sacrifice would be. She'd be ousted from the firm. She'd lose her shot at a decent career and the salary that was paying for her house. She doubted she'd get another job in a big firm.

She was taking her future and throwing it out the window. Her rational, logical brain had been hot-wired with guilt, short-circuited by a desire to make amends.

And maybe, just maybe, she'd be able to live with herself again.

The break had come quickly, courtesy of Vicky. She was good, no denying it. Her uncanny recall for people had once again connected a face to a criminal record.

"The girl's name is Krissie Burns," Ferguson had announced in the war room. It was 9:11 a.m. The room was buzzing, everyone getting that surge of adrenaline that comes with a break.

Redding clapped Vicky on the shoulder. She stood next to Ferguson, her dark hair pulled into her habitual ponytail. Ethan stood at the back, watching her. He hadn't spoken to her since New Year's Eve. She'd avoided him at the station, pretending not to see him when they crossed paths in the hallway.

He wondered why. Was she ashamed of the way she'd behaved? Hell hath no fury like a woman scorned. And yet he hadn't really believed her capable of that. She'd always seemed to be a sensible kind of woman, pragmatic, straight shooting, never one to mince words. Not malicious.

He grimaced. He hadn't believed himself to be capable of being so cruel to someone he thought he loved, too. And yet, he'd been a bastard to Kate. Had she deserved to be treated that way? He still couldn't tell. The kaleidoscope was spinning madly, shifting into focus for seconds, then blurring again. Giving him glimpses of what he thought was Kate's guilt, then shifting to reveal another facet of the case that made him doubt all his previous assumptions. No sleep and too much coffee wasn't helping.

"The victim has a record as long as my arm," Vicky said. Her china-blue gaze flicked around the table, skimming past Ethan before they could make eye contact. He wondered if that would always be the case. It saddened him. He had once loved Vicky. Not with the same kind of devouring passion that he'd experienced with Kate. But there had been pleasure, and he remembered with a pang the soft whimpers she made as he ran his tongue over those muscular thighs that were encased in soft, creamy skin.

But it hadn't been enough. When she pushed him to move in with her, he realized that Vicky wasn't the one for him. It had been difficult to break things off, knowing they would still be in the same division. But she'd taken it like the cop she was.

No question she'd screwed up big-time on New Year's Eve. Confronting him in front of his division and spilling the beans about Kate's family had given her a bad rep with some of the other officers. But she'd also forced to the surface the secrets that Kate had kept from him. She'd had the guts to tell him when Kate hadn't. And he respected Vicky for it.

"Krissie Burns has been in and out of prison for the past several years, prostituting and shoplifting to support her habit." Vicky produced a computer printout. "This is what we have on her—no fixed address since her last incarceration, but known to frequent Windmill Road and Agricola. Her pimp is a guy by the name of Darrell LeBlanc. She went by the street name of Kristabel." She sat down, closing her file folder.

Ferguson marked the large map mounted next to the white board. "So we've got two similarities with these victims. Krissie strolled the same area where Lisa bought drugs. And her body was found in the south end. This time at the Camp Hill Cemetery."

"Next thing we know he'll be burying her for us," Lamond said, his brown eyes glum.

"I doubt he'll use another cemetery," Ethan said. "But he's got a reason for using the south end. We just have to figure out why."

"So he's changing dump sites," Ferguson said, "but not his M.O. In fact, his M.O. is practically identical to his first killing—the victim was strangled, dismembered and left naked."

She flipped open the M.E.'s report. "The M.E. believes that a ligature with a smooth surface was used to strangle Krissie. Just like Lisa. The time of death is estimated at 1:51 a.m. The victim had one identifying mark, a tattoo on her left shoulder blade. It was a large red heart with the words *In Smack We Trust*." There were a few snickers. Ferguson paused until the team was silent. "Her limbs were dismembered with a bone saw, and the killer notched *LOL* on her—" she glanced down at her notes "—glenoid cavity."

"Just like Lisa," Redding said.

"Just like Lisa," she confirmed. She looked around the table. "This guy has an agenda."

"What about trace evidence?" Ethan asked.

Ferguson shook her head. Frustration tightened her features. "It rained that night. Heavily. It washed away whatever tracks the killer might have left."

"That guy must have a subscription to the weather channel," Lamond muttered.

Ethan stared at him. "Holy shit. The killer is following the weather. He's making sure that the dump site gets rained on."

The team exchanged glances.

"I think you're onto something, Ethan," Ferguson said. "Brown, keep track of the weather forecasts. I want you checking every three hours." The weather could change at the drop of a hat in Halifax. Especially in the spring.

Ferguson glanced at her watch. "Our next debriefing will be at 1200. And in the meantime," she said, her face turning grim, "keep praying for sunshine."

21

Kate rounded the corner quickly, avoiding eye contact with any of the associates behind open office doors. She wasn't in the mood to make small talk. What was the point trying to make friends, anyway? She was likely going to be kicked out on her butt. Between the Child Protection investigation, the missing notes and the appointment she was about to keep, things didn't look promising.

She pushed the button to the elevator. The door opened. The elevator was empty. Except for one person.

Randall Barrett.

He smiled at her.

Her pulse jumped in her throat.

"Kate!" Was it her, or did his voice sound a little strained? She hesitated. She did not want to share an elevator for the next twenty floors with him.

"You going down?" he asked. His tone challenged her. Her eyes swept his face. Not a shred of guilt to be seen. Either he was a damned good actor or he didn't steal the notes.

Or...

Things were going exactly as he wanted.

She straightened. "Yes." She stepped into the elevator, careful to keep as much distance as possible between them. She pressed the P1 button. He'd already pressed the button for the pedway.

"How are you doing, Kate?"

She turned to face him. He was looking at her with concern.

She felt a slow flush building in her chest. With it rose her anger. She hated the fact that she responded to his solicitude. *Bastard.*

"Fine." Her voice was curt.

"Has John Lyons called you in about the TransTissue file yet?"

"Yes."

"Good." He rocked back on his heels. "It's an excellent case, Kate. One every associate in the firm lusted after."

"I know." She knew what he was doing—confirming her loyalty despite his perfidy. Reminding her that he was the one who could make or break her.

She studied his eyes. They were so penetrating it was hard to look at them without feeling as if every inch of her soul was being carefully, thoroughly scrutinized. She wasn't sure, but she thought she saw a shadow of regret.

"The TransTissue case is groundbreaking. It will set legal precedent."

"Yes. I'm very excited." She hadn't thought about it all weekend. And she should have. It might be the only thing that could save her now.

"It's the chance you asked me for, Kate." She couldn't miss the warning in his voice. "Do a good job on it."

The elevator button dinged. It was Randall's stop. As the door slid open, Randall said softly, "Don't worry about

Child Protection. I've dealt with it. They are satisfied you acted appropriately."

He gave her a quick, strangely tender smile, and left.

The door closed behind him.

Kate leaned against the elevator wall. Her legs were shaking. She took a deep breath.

Had he taken her notes?

The glimpse of regret in his eyes suggested he had. But that he hadn't wanted to. Then why would he do it?

Hope Carson. He had said she had called him. Had she asked him to take the notes? And why would he risk his professional reputation to appease her?

The elevator rushed down to the parkade.

She had the sudden impression she was falling into the rabbit hole.

The knock on the door startled Shonda. It better not be the cops. She hurried to the window, hugging the wall as she craned her neck to peer through the glass.

Relief flooded through her. She ran down the stairs and opened the door.

A woman's eyes searched hers. "Shonda?"

Shonda stepped back. "Who are you?"

"My name is Kate Lange." The woman had a smooth, low voice. "I was told by Marian MacAdam that I could find someone by the name of Shonda here." Marian MacAdam? What the fuck? She took a deep breath.

"Why'd she send you?" she asked brusquely.

Kate Lange smiled. It was warm and friendly. Not too many people looked at her like that. Not anymore.

"I'm a lawyer." She handed Shonda a business card. It looked real fancy. Shonda stared at it. The words in the big blue letters were jumbled, but she guessed Kate Lange's name was underneath because the words started with *K* and *L*. Kate Lange added, "Marian MacAdam thought I might be able to help."

She looked at Kate Lange. This woman was offering to *help* her. No one, not since her first grade teacher, had ever offered to help her.

What should she do? Darrell would go ballistic if she let a lawyer in. But he blew her off when she told him about all her friends. He thought the pills were fucking with her head. The police weren't listening, neither. The only person who had listened to her was that old bitch in the black suit. Lisa's grandma. She was the only person Lisa'd ever said anything nice about. Everyone else was just "them."

Shonda felt a pang of grief. Something she hadn't felt since the night she pushed Vangie into that car.

"You can come in," she said to Kate.

The lawyer flashed her a reassuring smile, stepping into the dim hallway. Shonda chained the door behind her and led her upstairs. Since she'd started dealing, she'd had enough money to get her own little studio above Darrell's place. She liked not being in with all the girls. They bitched and fought and took her shit without asking.

She glanced around, suddenly aware of the unmade mattress on the floor in the corner, the dish of pills sitting on the table next to a box of baggies. She'd been in the middle of counting when the lawyer arrived.

She sat on one of the vinyl chairs she'd snatched on garbage day. It had a big gash down the middle of the seat, but it beat having nothing to sit on. The lawyer sat on the other chair. It wobbled when she crossed her legs. The woman planted her narrow feet on the floor and fixed her gaze on Shonda.

"You knew Lisa MacAdam?" she asked. No bullshit from this woman, Shonda thought.

"Yeah."

"Did you see her the night she was killed?"

Shonda forced herself to meet the lawyer's gaze. "Yeah."

The lawyer leaned forward. "When?"

Shonda crossed her arms. "Look, I already gave my story to the cops."

"I'm not a cop, Shonda," Kate Lange said, with a weird twist to her lips. "I'm just trying to get the facts."

"I sold Lisa some pills and then she got killed." She shrugged. "Just like the others."

"We'll get to the others in a minute. What time did you sell Lisa the pills?"

"Around ten o'clock." Shonda shrugged again. "Shit, I don't know for sure."

"Let's assume it was ten o'clock. What happened then?"

"Lisa took the pills. She went off with some friends. They were goin' to someone's place."

"And?" Kate Lange prompted gently.

She hadn't freaked out about her selling Lisa the pills, Shonda realized. She slumped back against the chair and began to play with the hole in her T-shirt. "She got high. I saw her later. She was by herself."

"What was she doing?"

"She was walking home." She had watched Lisa skip down the street. Lisa'd stopped and given her twenty bucks for one last hit, then headed south.

"Was that the last time you saw her?"

Jesus, how many fucking questions did this woman have? She wasn't used to talking this long. "Yeah."

"Tell me about the others."

The lawyer's eyes rested on her face. Kate Lange's eyes

were like clear, bright pools. Like a kid's. The other girls always looked at her with eyes that were hard and dull like old marbles. "There were two other girls who went missing."

"Since when?"

She thought about it. Since when? She never thought about time in months anymore. It was all about the day she was in. When she'd have to get out of bed, when she'd eat, when she'd deal, when she'd get high. That was it.

"Was it just recently?" Kate Lange asked. "Like in the past few months?"

She shook her head slowly. "No. Vangie disappeared when I was fifteen."

"How old are you now?"

"Seventeen." Was that surprise on the woman's face? She hunched her shoulders.

"So this girl named Vangie went missing several years ago?"

"Yeah. She got in a car with some guy and no one saw her again."

She still remembered that night. Vangie'd been holed up in her room. If she'd known how strung out Vangie had been, she'd never have gone to the apartment. But it'd been a freezing September night, the mist soaking her through and it hadn't even started to rain. She didn't want to spend another night huddled under the overpass. The damp, the cold, the darkness. It never changed. Never got better.

She'd thought Vangie would help her. But Vangie'd had too many rocks and Darrell was pissed that she was huddled over her dirty sheets, her wig all hangin' over her face.

The look in his eyes when he saw her made her stomach turn over. She'd stood in the dim living room, not sure whether she should just leave but the warmth had glued her to the spot. Then Darrell uttered the words she'd sensed had been growing like maggots in his small brain for a while. "*If Vangie don't work, you're gonna.*"

Shonda didn't waste any time. She strode into Vangie's bedroom. Vangie was kneeling on the floor, her head on the mattress. A glass tube with a tiny piece of rock in it was lying between her fingers.

"*C'mon, Vange. Get your ass off the bed,*" *Shonda said. She'd slid her hands under Vangie's pits and pulled her up. A smell wafted off Vangie: stale, bitter, used.*

Shonda'd seen Vangie wasted before, but not like this. Vangie swayed on her feet against Shonda. Then her whole body spasmed. But she said nothing. Nothing. Just stared past Shonda's shoulder. Usually when Vangie was high she'd be all excited and loud, shouting and singing and partying. It was the only time she'd smile, because she'd forget to hide her broken teeth.

Darrell's cell phone had rung and he strode out of the room. Over his shoulder he yelled, "*Get the bitch outside.*" *He threw a ten-dollar bill at Shonda.*

"*Sure thing,*" *Shonda'd said. Vangie leaned against her. Pity and revulsion flooded through her. Vangie smelled like something else. But she was so thin. And small. Shonda hadn't realized how tiny Vangie was. Like a little broken bird on her shoulder.*

Shit. She couldn't be feeling all sorry for her. She was a crackhead. She smoked rocks instead of eating.

Shonda'd pulled Vangie more roughly than she intended across the room. Vangie muttered, "*I'm a bird.*"

"*You crazy bitch,*" *Shonda'd said, and picked up the ten-dollar bill Darrell had left for her. She stuffed it into her pocket, guiding Vangie past the old sofa with the stains bigger than the faded flowers. They reached the door. Vangie looked around her, as if trying to figure out something.*

They went outside. It was so quiet, Shonda'd heard her stomach gurgle. She could almost taste that burger. And she hadn't tasted much in the past two days. Drizzle fell. Damp coated the north end street in a greasy sheen. The smell of the container pier, of oil and rancid seaweed, filled Shonda's nose. Her stomach roiled.

She'd led Vangie to her corner. No one else was there. All the other girls had already gone with johns. Shit. It better not be a quiet night. Vangie needed to make some money for Darrell. Shonda didn't want him asking for no money back.

A car cruised slowly down the hill, toward them. Relief made Shonda's head buzz. Looked like Vangie had a customer. And that meant she'd make some dough for dickhead.

That meant Shonda had done her job and could buy her burger, her fries, her milk shake.

She'd propped Vangie against the telephone pole. Mist shivered on the coarse strands of Vangie's wig, silvery and damp. It shrouded her head in a spider's web.

Goose bumps had prickled Shonda's skin. Vangie's lips looked sunken and shriveled in the unforgiving streetlight. Like a death's-head. Shonda'd groped in her pocket for her lip gloss. The car had stopped at the lights thirty feet away. She had just enough time to smooth the gloss over Vangie's cracked lips. She tilted Vangie's chin in her hand. Her heart unexpectedly contracted with concern. Vangie's skin was friggin' cold.

"You okay, Vange?" she'd asked.

Vangie swallowed.

The lights changed. The drizzle turned to rain as the car drew nearer, like the headlights were performing a magic trick. Damp crawled over Shonda's bare arms, up under her skirt. The car slowed down in front of them.

It stopped.

She'd waited for Vangie to make her move. To sashay over in her heels and show her scrawny leg, maybe flash her red thong.

She did nothing. The man in the car waited.

"C'mon, Vange," she'd said.

Vangie'd muttered to herself.

The passenger's window slid down. "You workin'?" the man had asked from the dark recesses of his seat.

Shonda couldn't see his face but she sensed his impatience. "Yeah," she said quickly. She'd grabbed Vangie's hand before the man could say anything more. He opened the door, and Shonda propelled Vangie forward on her heels, pushing her into the car. She shut the door before Vangie could say anything. The car drove off.

The queasy feeling had churned Shonda's stomach again. The whole deal seemed off, different from the other times, wrong somehow. Maybe it was because Vangie'd been doing too much crack. It was changing her. Maybe she shouldn't have put Vangie in the car.

"Did you report this to the police?" Kate Lange asked.

Shonda focused back on the lawyer's face. She bet Kate Lange had probably never had a run-in with a cop in her life. To a lawyer, cops were friends, looking after the rich folks. But to Shonda, they were a threat. Runaways don't go to no cops. "No."

Kate Lange showed no surprise at this answer. She shifted slightly on her chair. "What did she look like?"

Shonda tried to picture Vangie in her mind. "She was real small. Old."

"Anything that made her special?"

"Nah—" she started to say, but then a picture shot through her head. Vangie putting those fucking red shoes on. The fluttering tattoo covering her skinny ankle. "She had a tattoo. It was a bird…"

Kate Lange leaned forward. "What kind of bird?"

"Shit, I don't know." She stretched the hole in her shirt bigger. She used to know the name of it. "It's a small bird. With little wings that fly really fast."

"A sparrow?"

Shonda flashed her a look of disgust. "Nah. It sticks its nose into flowers."

"A hummingbird!"

"Yeah." Their eyes met in a look of mutual satisfaction. Shonda looked back down at the hole in her shirt. "It was orange and red. Real pretty."

Kate Lange wrote this down on a notepad. "Anything else?"

Jesus, would she stop with the questions. "No."

"And there was another girl?"

Shonda felt the pressure growing inside her. She needed another hit. But a vague memory crept across her brain. Karen…Karen what's-her-name. She was supposed to meet her a few months ago after turning tricks to buy more dope but she never showed up. Shonda had been too high to worry about it.

"Karen," Shonda said. "Karen went missing. We figured she'd gone out west…" She shrugged. "Turns out the cops said she'd died of ex… of being out in the cold too long."

"Marian MacAdam said you told the police this and they did nothing about it."

"I told the cops about Karen. And Vangie. They told me it was so long ago it'd be hard to track her down. They wanted me to make a missing persons report."

"Did you do that?"

"Yeah." Shonda remembered the small black words. A

woman cop had helped her fill in the blanks. She shrugged again. "But the cops did nothin'. And now Krissie's missing."

"Krissie?"

"Yeah. She's another girl I know. No one's seen her since Saturday night. But sometimes she goes home to Cape Breton to see her mother."

"Do the police know that?"

"I'm gonna call them if I don't see her…" She bit her lip. Krissie also went on smack binges. She wasn't going to tell the lawyer about those. But she didn't want to call the police and get Krissie dragged into the hospital. Krissie would be so pissed with her.

Kate Lange stood. "Thanks for talking to me, Shonda. I'll check on those missing girls for you. What are their last names?"

"Vangie's last name was…" She searched her memory. It felt like she was stirring sludge with a stick. "White. I mean, Wright." She pursed her lips. "Don't remember Karen's."

Kate Lange took out another card and jotted a number on it. "This is my direct line. Call me on it if you remember Karen's last name." She handed it to her. "Thanks very much, Shonda."

"What're you goin' to do about all this?"

"Once I track down the reports, I'll see if there's something the police might have missed. Then I'll call you." The lawyer glanced around the room. "Do you have a phone?"

She stood and patted her pocket. "I got a cell. Here's my number." She recited it while the lawyer wrote it down. Then the lawyer headed for the door. Shonda unchained it, scanning the street before letting her by.

"See ya."

Kate Lange stopped on the sidewalk. "Call me if you have any more concerns, Shonda. I would like to help."

You can't help me. The thought flashed through her head. She steadied herself against the door. Fuck, she needed a hit. "Yeah."

"Goodbye."

She closed the door and leaned against it. Darrell would be back soon. She got to fill those baggies.

22

Kate drove back to her office, idly listening to her car radio. Her mind was on her conversation with Shonda. The girl was a drug addict, but her concern about her missing friends was genuine. She sorted through the facts: the first girl to go missing was Vangie Wright, about a year and a half ago. Then another prostitute by the name of Karen disappeared. But she apparently died of exposure in February…so that girl was accounted for. And the last girl—Krissie Burns—just went missing thirty-six hours ago. All these girls were transients and drug addicts, girls who easily moved around and fell through the cracks when they used. It didn't mean they were victims of foul play.

"Breaking news," a chirpy female announcer on the radio said excitedly. "A serial killer is on the loose on the streets of Halifax!" She paused for dramatic effect.

Kate shook her head. The radio stations were getting really desperate for listeners if they had to resort to pronouncements like that.

"Yesterday we reported that police found the body of a young woman. They are viewing the death as suspicious," the announcer added in an I'm-a-serious-news-anchor voice.

Kate's scalp prickled. She turned up the volume. "We

have just learned this hour that sources close to the scene have indicated the young woman was killed in a similar fashion to fifteen-year-old homicide victim Lisa MacAdam."

Suddenly the announcement of a serial killer preying on Haligonians didn't seem so preposterous. Could the victim be the prostitute whom Shonda said had disappeared on Saturday night?

Kate waited for more details, her pulse racing. "And now a look at sports," the news announcer intoned.

"Damn," Kate muttered. Until she knew who the murder victim was, she wouldn't be able to get the missing Krissie Burns out of her head. She hurried back to her office. Ignoring all her messages, she checked the local news sites on the Internet. But there was no further information.

Now what should she do?

Call Ethan.

But after their last meeting it was the last thing she wanted to do.

She could call the police.

She bit her lip. She could just imagine *that* phone conversation. Yes, I'm the lawyer who gave bad advice to the first murder victim's grandmother and then reported her missing. I'm also the ex-fiancée of one of your detectives. You know, the one who humiliated him in front of your division on New Year's Eve? Now I have information that may show you guys aren't on the ball…or at least Vicky isn't.

They'd love that. Just as much as Randall would. His pointed warning flashed through her mind. *Do a good job on the TransTissue file*. She was still waiting to hear back from John Lyons about her memo. But what with the events of the past week, she'd barely thought about TransTissue's defense, hadn't even dug into the piles of research mounded on her desk. And if she really wanted to impress John Lyons, she should be determining the evidence needed to support their position. Panic welled inside her. She wanted this case. She wanted to do a good job. Not just to assure herself a spot on the LMB letterhead, but to prove to herself—especially after the Marian MacAdam debacle—that she actually was a good lawyer.

But she couldn't ignore what Shonda had told her.

If the second murder victim was Krissie Burns, then maybe Shonda's other missing girls were related to this case, too. The police needed to be given the heads-up.

She reached for the phone. Her stomach clenched.

Ethan's cell rang as he was pulling out of the halfway house parking lot. Frustration seethed in him. Tracking down the ex-cons Judge Carson had put away was looking more and more like a dead end with the discovery of a second victim. Krissie Burns's connection to Judge Carson was nil. Unless the murderer had been bitten by bloodlust and had begun to pick off other prostitutes for the fun of it, Ethan was wasting his time.

"Drake," he said into the phone.

"It's me. Kate." Her voice was low, strained.

His body reacted before his brain did: his heart accelerated, a vein pounded in his temple. Despite himself, despite his rationalizing that Kate was the wrong woman for all the right reasons, his heart squeezed painfully. He bit down on his bottom teeth. He couldn't afford to feel this way about her. Especially after the way she pushed him away. She was in Randall Barrett's camp now. And she couldn't risk going against the bastard. He had to remember that. His grip on the steering wheel tightened.

"Hi." He forced his voice to sound businesslike. "Did you find the notes?" Although Judge Carson had moved down the list of suspects, he still wanted the notes. Just to tie off loose ends.

Just to make sure that Kate kept her promise to him.

"No."

His disappointment angered him. He should have known better.

She hesitated. "But I've got some information. It might be pertinent to the MacAdam case."

"Just a sec," he said curtly. "I'm gonna pull over." A convenience store was just ahead. He slid into a parking spot. "So. What kind of information do you have that wasn't in the notes?" He allowed a derisory edge to sharpen his voice.

He could feel her tension over the phone. It fueled his own in a perversely satisfying way.

"I had a phone call from Lisa MacAdam's grandmother. She met a girl named Shonda at Lisa's funeral who told her some other girls went missing. Other prostitutes. One of them was named Krissie Burns."

"Krissie Burns?" His contrariness evaporated. That was victim number two. If this girl Shonda had actually seen the killer pick up her friend… "You sure?"

"Yes." She paused. "Was Krissie Burns the girl whose body was just found?"

He hesitated. It was confidential information, and Kate was officially—and unofficially—off-limits.

His conscience won out. She'd called him in good faith. "Yes. We're still tracking down her family."

"How did you ID her?"

"Vicky remembered her from her criminal record."

"Oh." That one word spoke volumes. Vicky had also remembered Kate's father from his criminal record.

"She gave us our break, Kate," Ethan said softly.

"Yes. I understand." Her voice was cool.

"Did this girl Shonda report her suspicions to the police?" he asked abruptly.

"She hadn't reported Krissie Burns's disappearance because she said sometimes she went to see her mother in Cape Breton. Apparently there were two other girls—"

"When?" He tensed.

"One was a long time ago, at least eighteen months. But Shonda only reported her missing a few months ago when her other friend disappeared."

"Neither of them have been heard from since?" His mind was racing. Eighteen months ago. Could the killer have been operating since then?

"The girl who went missing a few months ago—her name was Karen—was found dead. Of exposure."

Ethan exhaled slowly. So at least one of the missing girls wasn't a victim. And her death fell right between two missing girls, breaking up the chain of disappearances. "And the other one?"

"Her name was Vangie Wright. She's still missing. But the police told Shonda that she took so long to file the report she'd be hard to track down."

"That's true, especially if she lived on the streets. We'll have to determine if this Vangie Wright is even related to the case." He stared out his car window. He knew what he was going to say next would rankle, but damn it, he had a job to do. "I'll pass this on to Vicky. If anyone can track her down, it'll be her."

There was silence. "Can you let me know what she finds out?" The unspoken message was clear: Kate wasn't about to call Vicky herself. "I told Shonda I'd get back to her."

The implications of this slammed into his exhausted brain. "You've spoken to her already? I thought you'd gotten this information from Lisa MacAdam's grandmother." He fought to keep his voice calm. "Kate, this is a homicide investigation. We can't have you interviewing potential witnesses. You know the best information comes from the first interview. It needs to be done by an experienced investigator."

"I'm sorry." She didn't sound sorry to Ethan. He knew once she got something in her sights, she was relentless about tracking it down. That had been a quality he'd admired in her. Until now. "I promised Marian MacAdam I'd talk to Shonda because she said the police weren't doing anything about it."

"And you believed that?" He didn't bother to hide his anger. Too little sleep, two murders too many and too few leads weren't helping. "You think we'd just ignore the only lead we've got? You think we're a bunch of idiots, Kate?"

"Don't be ridiculous."

"Did Randall put you up to it?" It'd be just like the bastard to mess around in a police investigation. He'd done it before. If he knew Ethan was on this one, it'd be all the more reason for him to get in the middle of it.

"No. Of course not."

"Then why are you doing this?"

She inhaled sharply. "You really don't think much of me, do you?"

He couldn't answer that. He didn't know what he thought about her anymore. Finally, he said, "Stay out of this, Kate. There's a psychopathic killer on the loose. Leave it to the police to handle. Stay away from Shonda."

She could not jeopardize a homicide investigation because of personal demons. Two young women were dead. And he was scared—yes, he'd admit it, he was scared—that there'd be a third. Soon. His eyes scanned the sky. When would it turn leaden and menacing with rain?

"I can't, I made a promise—"

Kate needed to understand just how high the stakes were. "Damn it, Kate, there are young girls' lives at risk here—"

"I know—"

"And you are jeopardizing them!"

"No. I'm not."

He drew in a deep, frustrated breath. "Already you've potentially ruined our best source of information on the case by speaking to Shonda, and now you want to call her again and share confidential information. It could affect the whole outcome of our investigation. It could cause the killer to either not be caught or, worse, be released for lack of evidence." He knew that she would understand the implications of this.

There was a painful silence. "I was just doing what I thought was best."

He sighed heavily. "Leave it to the police. We're the good guys, remember?"

23

A gleaming black truck with an enclosed bed in the back pulled into Kate's driveway at exactly 7:00 p.m. That was a good sign. He was right on time.

She'd gotten home ten minutes before, her briefcase crammed with her neglected TransTissue research, the disastrous phone call to Ethan still running through her head. He'd been right about everything. But he couldn't see that she'd tried to do the right thing, too. He thought she had ulterior motives. He didn't understand that she was doing this to try to help victims, just like him.

The truck door swung open and a young guy in his twenties stepped out.

Whoa. She'd seen this guy before. Tall, blond, muscular. He strode toward the house, hips swaggering slightly. She smoothed back the corner of the living room curtain before he could spot her.

Alaska jumped excitedly at her heels. She didn't get many visitors, so anyone showing up on her front porch was worthy of delirious excitement. It was infectious. She felt a bit excited herself. It helped smother the loneliness that had suddenly hit her.

A brisk knock announced the new dog walker's arrival.

She swung open the door, hoping that the Doggie Do dog-walking service would assuage her guilt at leaving Alaska alone for so long.

"Hi," the guy said, smiling. He had a great smile, warm and friendly. "I'm Finn Scott."

"Hi. I'm Kate." She opened the door wider. "Please come in."

He walked in, his gaze taking in Kate in a slow, languorous sweep. Was that a look of appreciation in his eyes? Her cheeks grew warm, surprise mingling with a foolishly girlish glow. Being checked out was a welcome balm to her ragged ego after dealing with Ethan today.

Finn turned to Alaska. The husky wagged his tail and nosed Finn's hand. Just his hand, fortunately. She still remembered the way he had greeted Ethan. It had been a prescient foreshadowing of every interaction she'd had with her ex-fiancé since.

"This is Alaska," she said to Finn. She allowed herself a proud smile.

Finn knelt down and looked into the dog's eyes, scratching him behind the ears. Then he stood, ignoring the white fur coating his faded Levi's. Alaska leaned against his legs. "I'll take you out in just a minute, buddy," he said.

He turned to Kate. "I always like to take them out on their own the first time, so we get used to each other before I introduce him to all the other dogs. Where's his leash?"

"Right here." She passed it to him, already feeling reassured by this man. He seemed to know instinctively how to handle dogs. She'd quizzed him on the phone about his dog-handling experience and his program, feeling slightly ridiculous about how much reassurance she needed that Alaska would be in good hands.

Finn took the husky out the door. The dog obediently

trotted by his side. They walked down the block, around the corner. He had a relaxed but purposeful stride. Alaska obviously had warmed to him. She had, too. Ten minutes later, he was back. She watched them come inside. How in the world had he gotten Alaska so completely under his thumb in ten minutes? "You're going to have to show me how to do that," she said with a rueful smile. "He pulls me like a sleigh."

"You have to let him know who's the lead dog," Finn said. "It's all in the body language. Look at my shoulders. See how relaxed I am?"

Did he realize she'd been looking at his shoulders since he'd gotten out of his car? A flush heated her chest. His shoulders were broad, solid, well developed under his white T-shirt.

Like Randall Barrett's.

Shit. She was really losing it. There was no question. First Ethan, then Randall, and now one look at Finn and she was suffused with a desire to feel the hard body of a man.

She looked away. "Yes. I can see that."

He removed Alaska's leash. "Go get some water, boy." The dog went into the kitchen.

"You've got a very special dog there," Finn said.

She smiled, bemused at the effect the dog walker had on Alaska. And on her.

She was being pathetic. *You're just feeling weak and vulnerable, that's all.* The events of the past week had made her doubt everything she'd ever done that was good in her life and forced her to remember everything she regretted.

She'd never felt lonelier.

"I'm so glad you could come tonight." Then realized how that could sound. She rushed on, "It's really important to me that Alaska gets some company during the day. I'm at work until at least six…"

Finn responded with an easy smile. The smile prodded her memory again. She could feel it coming into focus. Wait…it was there…teasing her mind…

The funeral.

He looked like the man who'd walked in with her at the funeral. He'd tried to help her when she made her embarrassingly hurried exit, but Ethan had cut him off.

She studied him. He was wearing jeans and a V-necked pullover but in a suit…?

"You look really familiar to me," she said, then felt a small burn in her cheeks. She was sure he got it from all his single female clients. She didn't want him to think she was just like all the others.

His eyes crinkled at the corners. They were blue-green. Nice eyes. "Hmmm…you look familiar, too."

Did he mean it or was he just playing along? She made her tone businesslike. "Were you at Lisa MacAdam's funeral on Saturday?"

He started. "Yeah. Were you?"

"Yes."

"It was really awful what happened to her." He shoved his hands in his pockets. "Lisa was a nice kid," he added softly.

It was her turn to be surprised. "You knew her?"

"One of my clients lived on the same floor as she did. She used to come over and visit the dog. She loved dogs." A light flush tinged his tanned face.

Kate noted it, puzzled. Then she realized why he'd reacted the way he did. It wasn't just dogs that the fifteen-year-old girl had loved. She'd had a crush on the dog walker. It was only natural, given his rugged blond looks, his way with animals. Probably happened to Finn all the time.

"Did you spend a lot of time with her?"

He shifted uncomfortably. "We were friends. She was a nice kid underneath it all."

"Underneath what?" She suddenly needed to know what this dead girl had been like. What had driven her to that street corner.

He seemed to understand that. "Underneath the tough skin. You know, the dyed hair, the makeup." His eyes were haunted. "She tried so hard to be like the other girls, you know, flirting and stuff, but really she was still a kid. She had this tattoo…"

"A tattoo?" That didn't sound very kidlike.

"It was a dog. One she'd met when she was eight, she told me. She'd loved this dog, wanted one so badly. But her mother wouldn't let her get one." He looked away. "It was cruel. I would have taken it for walks for free…" His gaze swung back to Kate. "She was just a kid, you know?"

"I know," Kate said softly. A kid who never had a chance to be a kid.

Sadness settled between them, drawing them together with the unnatural intimacy of the grief stricken.

"You know what really gets me," he said suddenly, "was seeing her grandmother put her stuffed dog in the coffin. I'll never forget that."

That ragged, dingy dog with one ear. Kate had tried to block the memory. The toy dog had somehow settled itself into the hollow of the dead girl's neck. Her protector.

Kate blinked away tears. What was happening to her? She was about to fall apart in front of a man she had just met. She flashed him a quick glance. He didn't look in such great shape himself.

She cleared her throat. "I wanted to thank you, you know, for stepping out to help me at the end of the service…" She trailed off. There was no mistaking the bafflement in Finn's eyes. "It wasn't you?"

"No." He gave her an apologetic smile. "Sorry."

Kate's mind raced. He looked so familiar. Then again, if you lived in Halifax long enough, half the faces you saw were familiar.

Finn turned to the door. The strange mood was broken. He said with forced briskness, "I'll pick up Alaska at ten a.m. tomorrow and then again at three-thirty."

"Great. I wish I could be home by five, but with my job…"

He smiled, a slow, reassuring smile that eased Kate's guilt. "Don't feel bad. The dogs enjoy the companionship."

"Oh. I almost forgot." She picked up a spare key that she'd left on the hall table and gave it to him. "The lock is very old, so you need to jiggle it a bit…"

"No problem." He put the key on a ring with about ten others. Kate noticed he had a leather thong wrapped twice around his wrist. It was worn and rugged, sexy against his strong forearm. "Most of my clients live in the south end, and most have old locks. I'm used to them." He gave Alaska one final scratch. "See you tomorrow, boy."

"If you have any problems, here's my work number." She handed him her card. The embossed letters glimmered in the hall light. "And I'll leave a check for you under the plant." She gestured to a geranium that sat on the hall table. It was wilting and needed to be deadheaded. He must think she was incapable of caring for any living thing. And then she wondered why she cared what he thought of her.

He tucked her card in his pocket. "I doubt Alaska will give me any trouble." He held out his hand. "It was nice meeting you."

She shook his hand. His fingers were warm and strong around hers. Before her imagination could taunt her with any more images of a man's hard body comforting hers, she pulled her hand away and held open the door.

She watched him walk toward his truck. He had a cute butt. He had a cute everything. And he loved dogs.

She closed the door. *You are so screwed up. Wasn't it bad enough that you almost threw yourself at your boss? That you almost let Ethan kiss you? Wasn't that humiliating enough? Now you're eyeing the dog walker?*

But Finn was different. He wasn't dangerous in the way that Ethan or Randall were. He didn't threaten the fragile sutures of her lacerated heart.

She leaned against the door. It didn't matter that Finn was too young for her. Or that she hired him to look after her dog. He had made her feel like she was a woman who was desirable. Physically and emotionally.

She hadn't felt that way in months.

She fed Alaska and boiled an egg for herself. Half an hour later, she emptied her briefcase onto her kitchen table and got to work. It was time to do what she'd been hired to do.

At 12:08 a.m. she pushed her chair back and stood, stretching. Satisfaction spread through her as she tidied the papers littered on the table. The cases looked promising. Good enough to give TransTissue a solid defense.

Alaska watched her from his vantage point by the kitchen door. His tail thumped encouragingly. He wanted to go to bed and was waiting for her to say the word.

"Okay, boy, time for bed." He pushed himself to his feet and lumbered down the hall.

She followed him, switching off lights. She had lived in the house for more than three months and still wasn't used to the noises. Late at night was the worst. Long shadows cloaked the corners of the hall. As she walked toward her bedroom, floorboards creaked, their moans sounding strangely human to her ears.

Ever since the intruder had been in her garden ten days ago, the noises had bothered her. Even Alaska seemed on edge, getting up at night to prowl the house. No wonder she was always tired.

She switched on the overhead light in her room. The light didn't break through the shadow in the corners, despite the pale blue walls and white trim. Kate had thought the blue would look fresh and modern. Now she regretted her color choice. The room was so cavernous, the cool shade made it look even colder and barren. Her wicker bedroom furniture appeared meager and sticklike under the ten-foot ceilings. Only when she'd snuggled down under the covers did she feel warm.

It was going to be difficult to get out of her bed at 6:00 a.m. for her run. She had stayed up too late and tomorrow she would pay the price.

Alaska was performing his nightly circles on his bed when she crawled under the sheets. Within seconds, she fell asleep.

The howl cut through her dream.

24

Her mind hovered between consciousness and sleep.

The second howl brought her straight out of bed.

"Alaska!"

She grabbed her robe and ran down the stairs, shrugging it over her pj's.

Alaska howled again. He was in the kitchen.

Goose bumps shivered down Kate's arms. She had only heard Alaska howl once before. That time he had been outside the kitchen door.

She ran into the kitchen. Alaska had scrambled onto the counter and was frantically pawing the window. Kate followed his gaze.

Someone was in the backyard.

She could just make out the hooded form, bent over the ragged garden in the back. The intruder was digging.

Fear prickled along her neck.

Was this Lisa MacAdam's and Krissie Burns's killer?

She needed to call the police.

"Be quiet, Alaska," she hissed. She wanted the intruder

caught this time. So far, it seemed that he hadn't heard Alaska's unearthly howling.

She pulled the husky off the counter. A movement caught her eye.

Someone walked through the garden gate. It was a woman. Elderly, her back stooped, her white hair glowed in an unearthly halo around her head. She walked slowly, but purposefully, across Kate's yard.

What was this woman doing? Couldn't she see there was a killer fifty feet away from her?

The lady walked right by the kitchen porch.

Kate grabbed the mop and threw open the bolt on the kitchen door. She ran onto the porch, wincing as her toe struck an uneven board.

"Jesus!"

The elderly lady stopped in her tracks and shot her a shocked glance.

"Watch out!" Kate leaped down the stairs, holding the mop out in front of her. "There's someone in my garden!" She gestured over her shoulder. "Quick! Come into the house. I'm going to call the police."

As she spoke, she had the sensation she was still in the kitchen, watching a wild version of herself waving a mop and ranting. The elderly lady appeared completely unaffected by Kate's panic.

Kate glanced over her shoulder. The killer remained by the garden. Unmoving.

She slowly lowered the mop. Alaska stood by her knees, his ears pricked defensively, a low growl building in his throat.

"My dear, I am very sorry to disturb you," the elderly lady said. She glanced nervously at Alaska. "And I am sorry if my sister frightened you."

"Your sister?" Kate echoed, stunned. That hooded shape in her garden was not a psychopathic killer, but an elderly lady?

The lady nodded. "Yes, that's my sister." Kate stared at the intruder. All she could see was her back. From the distance, and in the dark, she could have sworn it was a man, and a large one at that, under the hooded coat.

The lady continued, "We haven't been introduced. My name is Enid Richardson. I live down the street with Muriel."

Kate stared at her. The Richardson sisters. Here, in her yard. She hadn't realized they were still living, let alone in the neighborhood.

Enid Richardson held out her hand. It was pale and translucent in the porch light, but there was a cordlike strength in the tendons. Kate shook it, praying that Enid Richardson wouldn't remember her. "It's nice to meet you, Mrs. Richardson. My name is Kate…Lange."

"Kate Lange?" Enid Richardson's gaze swept over her. Her eyes lingered on Kate's face. Kate shrank into the worn folds of her bathrobe. "I thought the eyes were familiar." Enid smiled. "I remember you now. What dear little girls you and your sist—" She stopped abruptly. Sympathy welled in her eyes.

"Yes. Well." Kate looked desperately around her. Her gaze fell on the hooded figure of Muriel Richardson. She said quickly, "Why does your sister keep coming to my yard, Mrs. Richardson?"

"It's Miss Richardson," she said. "But please call me Enid." She smiled, then looked at Muriel's kneeling form. "My sister has Alzheimer's. She used to play at this house as a child. Now she gravitates back to it." She sighed. "The older I get, the more I see how the mind returns to its childhood. In the case of my sister, her mind is so confused she seeks comfort in simple things." She gestured around her. "She likes to dig in the garden."

Sensing that danger had passed, Alaska began sniffing the yard.

"Is your dog friendly?" Enid asked, stepping between Alaska and her sister. Kate quickly followed her to where Muriel Richardson knelt.

Alaska ignored them both. A patch of soggy leaves was proving to be of immense interest.

"Yes. He's been good so far," Kate said. She rubbed one foot over the other. The ground was freezing.

"Oh. Is he new?" Enid looked at him with renewed interest.

"I adopted him a few weeks ago." Pride laced Kate's voice. He was a beautiful, gentle giant. "His name is Alaska."

"Did he live here with Margery Thompson?" Enid asked. "I think she had a dog that resembled him."

Kate nodded. "Yes, he kept coming back to the house after she died, so I kept him."

Enid pursed her lips. "I never understood why an old lady would get a young frisky dog like him. It didn't seem fair." She shrugged. "But I bet he was company."

Kate smiled. "He is good company. He keeps me on my toes." She thought of the shredded magazine she had found under the kitchen table this evening. "And he enjoys a good read."

"Well, I'm sorry we interrupted your sleep, Kate." Enid smiled apologetically. "We'll be getting back to our beds." She walked over to her sister and gently took her arm. "It's time to go home, Mil." Muriel let Enid pull her to her feet. She was tall, surprisingly tall for an elderly lady. Enid looked small and frail next to her.

"Muriel, this is Kate Lange," Enid said. Muriel didn't

look up. Her gaze was transfixed by a clump of wet earth she held in her hand. Very slowly, she mushed the icy soil between her fingers.

"Hello," Kate said.

"I want a cup of dirt," Muriel blurted loudly. She curled her fingers into her palm.

"Yes, dear." Enid patted her arm. "I'll make you some when I get home." She led Muriel slowly toward the gate. "It was nice to meet you *again*, Kate." She gave a little smile. "I am sorry we scared you."

"No problem." Kate smiled back. "I'm glad you found your sister."

Enid paused at the gate. "I hope she doesn't disturb your sleep again. I keep the doors locked, but sometimes Muriel remembers how to unlock them."

"It's okay." Kate's feet had turned numb. Six a.m. was getting closer and closer. "Nice to meet you."

"Drop in for a cup of tea sometime, dear," Enid said, leading Muriel out the gate.

"Thank you." Kate watched the two ladies leave. The larger sister was being led carefully down the driveway. Despite their height differences, and the fact that Muriel's mind was no longer whole, they walked in step, obviously used to being together and taking comfort from that fact.

Kate wondered if Imogen would have been taller than she. If they would have remained friends as they grew older. If they would have been companions in old age.

She turned and walked into her house. Her feet were like blocks of ice. She wished the numbness would extend to her heart. Because try as she might, she could never make the pain go away.

Tuesday, May 8, 1:00 p.m.

By lunch, Kate had eleven voice mails waiting to be heard. She'd been out of the office all morning, arguing a motion at family court. She briefed her client, grabbed a take-out salad and an Americano, and took it back to her office to eat. After a few sips of the espresso drink, her energy returned. She'd only gotten about four hours of sleep last night. When she opened the paper this morning, the headlines blared: Rain, Rain, Go Away, Say City's Women. And in smaller print: Police Advise Women to Stay in on Wet Nights. The police warned that the killer was using the weather to his advantage. Fortunately, the forecast was good for the week. A welcome reprieve for both the police and the city's soggy residents.

Putting the voice mails on the speaker phone, she ate her salad while scribbling down phone numbers. The first six voice mails were the usual: lawyers needing to exchange information or set up meetings and clients wanting updates. The seventh voice mail stopped her in her tracks.

It was a young girl's voice, hesitant, rough sounding, in complete contrast to the educated adult voices that had filled her message box. "It's Shonda. You told me to call if I remembered the name of that dead girl Karen."

Kate picked up her phone receiver.

"Anyway, it came to me all of a sudden. Her name is Karen Fawcett."

There was a click, and then Kate's voice mail went into its usual spiel. She replayed the message, wrote down Karen Fawcett's name, then deleted the record.

The dead prostitute's name blurred in front of her eyes. Shonda had come through for her. She hadn't come through yet for Shonda.

Should she try to track her down? Ethan had warned

her—no, he'd ordered her—not to. To leave this to the police. She could jeopardize the investigation; she could inadvertently let a killer remain free.

But Karen Fawcett wasn't a missing person. She was dead. And the cops believed she died from exposure. So she wasn't even on their radar. Kate wouldn't be jeopardizing their investigation if she kept her promise to Shonda. And right now, keeping her promise was the only thing she could hold on to.

All she needed to do was confirm that the prostitute died of exposure. The easiest way to confirm it would be her death certificate. But when she looked it up on online, she discovered that information was only accessible with permission from her next of kin.

She stared at her computer screen. There was another potential source of information. Karen Fawcett's obituary. It might say something about the circumstances of her death. And it was in the public domain. Kate rubbed a hand over her face. She hated reading obituaries. She'd hated reading them ever since she'd had to help her mother write her sister's. She hated seeing all those names associated with platitudes like they "fought a courageous battle." It was never a battle they won.

Her fingers hit the keyboard with a fierceness that was meant to bolster her courage. Within minutes, she had located the local paper's archives for the obituaries. Satisfaction overrode her reluctance. Karen Fawcett was in the database.

Kate scanned the sparse text. Karen had died last February. There was no mention of cause of death, although the obituary said Karen Marie had been taken to her Lord "suddenly." It was eerily familiar to Imogen's obituary in terms of its obliqueness. No one had wanted to spell out the fact Imogen had been killed in a car crash. Given who was driving.

The obituary was pitifully short. Either Karen's family didn't have the money to spend on the text, or they had little to say about their dead child. Kate drummed her fingers on her desk. Charitable donations often indicated what had caused the death. But no charity was mentioned. The only guidance given to mourners was that Keane's Funeral Home was handling the burial service.

A knock on the door made her swing her chair around.

"Your one o'clock canceled. She rescheduled for tomorrow," Liz announced. Her eyes flickered over Kate's computer monitor.

Kate nodded. "Right. Thank you, Liz."

Liz threw one last look at the screen before leaving.

Kate shut down the computer. *Another dead end.* If she hadn't been so disappointed, she might have enjoyed the gallows humor of her thought. But now she had nothing to tell Marian MacAdam and Shonda. She'd wanted to be able to reassure them that Karen Fawcett's death was as innocuous as the police believed.

She rubbed her temples. There was one last avenue: the funeral home that had handled Karen's remains. Maybe they would be able to give her some information. She jotted down the address.

Her fingers stilled. She stared at what she'd written. She'd been to that funeral home before. It had been called O'Brien's fifteen years ago.

All of her ghosts were coming home. She just hoped they wouldn't want to linger.

25

Kate slung her purse over her shoulder and tried not to look self-conscious as she walked through the hallway of her firm. It was 4:45 p.m., early to be leaving. Certainly the earliest she had ever left LMB before. She bet none of the other first-year associates had left yet.

The traffic was heavy in the downtown core. It was 5:20 p.m. before she drove up to the front of the funeral home. A large, deep building, it had been transformed from a brick monolith to a Grecian-style mansion with white siding and massive columns. She would never have recognized it as the one in which her sister had lain.

Kate rang the bell next to a massive double door. Her palms were sweaty despite the cool air. She wiped her hands hurriedly on her skirt.

The door swung open. For a moment—a split second that made Kate catch her breath—she'd expected to see the erect figure of Mr. O'Brien, the previous funeral director, standing in the shadow of the door frame.

Instead, a blond woman in her forties held open the door. "Hello. May I help you?" she asked. Her voice was rougher than her clothes. She wore a chic, chocolate-brown suit with pinstripes in pale pink that covered a sturdy frame. Brown suede pumps and chunky gold earrings were her sole accessories.

Kate guessed this was Anna Keane, the self-made businesswoman who had bought the aging funeral home from Mr. O'Brien and grew it into one of the largest and most successful funeral parlors on the Atlantic coast.

"Ms. Keane?"

The woman smiled. Her teeth glowed ultrawhite against her shiny lip gloss. "Yes."

"I'm Kate Lange, from Lyons McGrath Barrett. I was wondering if I could ask you a few questions." At the mention of her firm's name, Kate saw the woman's tanned face tighten. She probably thought she was being sued for a botched embalmment. Kate added with a placating smile, "I'm not here representing a client."

This reassurance didn't warm up Anna Keane. "Why don't we talk in my office," she said, her voice stiff. She ushered Kate into the foyer.

Kate looked around. Her heart, which had begun pounding as soon as she'd pulled into the parking lot, now began to beat crazily. The air closed in on her. Like when she was sixteen.

Breathe. You did it before. You can do it again.

Anna Keane walked quickly. Kate picked up her pace. Out of the corner of her eye she noticed the interior had been updated in typical understated yet tastefully elegant funeral-home decor that was the current style. And yet she could have sworn when she'd walked in that it'd been the same dated furnishings of fifteen years ago.

Anna Keane led Kate to her office. It was graciously appointed, with a gleaming mahogany desk and navy chairs. Rather like Kate's own. It was an uncomfortable realization. Business was business.

"Please have a seat." Anna Keane pointed to a round conference table in the corner. A vase of white forget-me-nots was placed precisely in the middle. Kate sat down.

Anna Keane lowered herself in the chair opposite. "Why are you here?" She smiled after the question but Kate wasn't fooled. Anna Keane wanted to take control of this discussion. And despite the funeral director's cool composure, Kate sensed that her presence rattled her. She wondered if Anna Keane had any idea that the feeling was mutual.

"I'm doing some background checking on several women whose families were your clients," Kate said. Her voice sounded high, tight.

Breathe slowly.

Anna Keane's gaze sharpened. "Oh? And for what purpose?"

"More for my own conscience than anything else." Her voice, thankfully, came out more assured this time.

"You realize that we cannot divulge private information about our clients, Ms. Lange."

There was no getting around it; she'd have to be frank with Anna Keane if she hoped for any information from her. "Okay, here's the story, Ms. Keane. I know the family of Lisa MacAdam." The only sign that Anna Keane recognized the name was a slight raising of her brows. "Her grandmother was told by a friend of Lisa's that several other girls had gone missing." Anna Keane's brows rose a fraction higher. "All of them have died, except for one. Two of them had their remains managed by your funeral home."

Anna Keane leaned back, her eyes fixed on Kate. "Who were these girls who went missing?"

"Krissie Burns, Lisa MacAdam and Karen Fawcett." Krissie's identity had been announced in a press release this morning, so Kate knew she wasn't giving away anything she shouldn't.

"I certainly recognize the name of the first two girls." She shook her head. "What a tragedy about the MacAdam girl."

"Do you remember anything about Karen Fawcett? She would have been another street kid or prostitute. She died last February. Your firm handled her service."

Anna Keane gave her a weary smile. "We handle the remains of a lot of people like Karen. More than you can imagine." She shrugged. "I thought it would be a small contract when the city asked for tenders to handle the remains of indigents. If I'd known I'd have so many, I would have charged more. We certainly don't make any money, Ms. Lange."

"Why is that?"

"Our contract just provides the basic cremation and interment. If the family suddenly appears—and you'd be surprised how many want to mourn someone they rejected while they were alive—they often want the extras to make up for the years their loved one lived on the street. So they ask for a service, flowers, an urn. They have to pay for those. Most of the time, they have no money." She paused. "When the grief seems genuine, I write the extras off as a charitable donation."

There was a ruminative look in Anna Keane's eyes that made Kate suddenly think, *She's a lot softer than she lets on.*

"Do you remember anything about Karen Fawcett and her family? The police told Lisa's friend she had died of exposure."

Anna Keane closed her eyes for a moment. Kate noticed the fine lines around them. There were grooves around her lips, too. It couldn't be easy facing death every day.

She opened her eyes and caught Kate studying her. "If

I recall correctly, Karen Fawcett was young? Maybe eighteen or twenty?"

"That sounds about right."

"They found her frozen on a golf course." Anna Keane leaned back in her chair. "Another young girl who had a drug habit that she fed by prostituting herself."

"How did you know she had a drug habit?"

"If she's the one I'm remembering, she had needle marks on her arms. In fact, the veins were shot. We found more marks between her toes. She was a real junkie."

This woman must know a lot of the dead's secrets. It was an unnerving thought. Kate hoped her body wouldn't have any secrets to betray when she died.

"What about her family?"

Anna Keane shook her head. "She was just a straight contract delivery—cremation and interment in the city's lot. Her family showed up later." She shrugged. "That's all I can tell you, I'm afraid." She rose to her feet.

Kate stood. "Thanks very much, Ms. Keane. I appreciate your help."

Anna Keane walked her to the door. "I hope I put your conscience to rest." She gave a crooked smile. "Even though morticians are supposed to handle the remains of the dead, I find I spend more time dealing with the remains of the living."

Kate stared into Anna Keane's light brown eyes. She wished she'd known Anna Keane when Imogen died. The funeral director seemed a genuine straight shooter, not dripping with fake concern or the barely concealed disapproval of Mr. O'Brien.

She held out her hand. "I think families would be very fortunate to have you help them at such a difficult time."

"Thank you, Ms. Lange." Anna Keane led her to the main doors.

Anna Keane opened the door. Kate suddenly remembered Shonda's other friend. "Have you ever heard of Vangie Wright? She's the friend of Lisa's that no one can account for."

Anna Keane shook her head. "Sorry, Ms. Lange. I've never heard of her." She smiled again. "Believe me, in my business, that's a good thing."

26

Kate stared through the windshield of her car at Keane's Funeral Home. Relief washed through her. She'd made it through the interview without embarrassing herself. It had been strangely cathartic. The changed interior, the more modern, compassionate female funeral director. It had helped erase the memory of the dim room in which Imogen's smashed body lay, of Mr. O'Brien's stiff disapproval whenever she arrived.

More than anything else, it had been Mr. O'Brien's manner toward her sixteen-year-old self that had shown her how much her life had changed. She'd gone from attractive, promising young woman to irresponsible, fatally flawed teen. It had been a swift but shattering fall from grace.

She leaned back in her seat. Her limbs were weak. She hadn't realized until now that she had half expected to see Mr. O'Brien appear at her elbow as she walked through the funeral home foyer. The fact that he hadn't, that he no longer owned the business, that she would no longer need to see the censure in his gaze, lifted a weight off her chest she hadn't been aware of until it was gone.

She'd done what she'd promised to do. She'd tracked

down Karen Fawcett. Everything checked out. That was an even bigger relief. If it hadn't, she would have had to call the police. And she could just imagine how Ethan'd react to her latest update on her involvement in the MacAdam case.

She dialed Shonda's number. Anticipation quickened her pulse. She'd go home after this and relax. Have a glass of wine and read the remaining home-decorating magazine that Alaska hadn't shredded. Unless he'd eaten it today—

"Yeah?" Shonda answered in a bored tone.

"Hi, Shonda. It's Kate Lange."

"Yeah?" Shonda's voice rose a notch.

"I followed up on the girls you told me about."

"Girls?" The plural came out slurred.

Dismay quelled Kate's excitement. Shonda sounded like she'd been using.

"You know, the missing girls you told me about a few days ago," she said carefully. She wanted Shonda to understand what she was telling her. "Krissie Burns, Karen Fawcett and Vangie Wright."

"Oh. Yeah. Right."

Kate hesitated. "There is some bad news about Krissie."

"Yeah. I heard." Shonda's voice was dull, emotionless. "The cops've been around asking questions."

"I'm sorry."

There was silence on the other end. She visualized Shonda's face. The round, childish cheeks. The shuttered, watchful eyes. Intelligence glimmered in their brown depths, suffocated under layers of neglect, fear and drug abuse.

Kate cleared her throat. "I passed on the information about Vangie Wright to the police. They have someone looking into her missing persons report."

"Yeah. I know. That blond guy."

"Blond guy?"

"Yeah. He had some dogs… Did y'know Lisa was crazy 'bout dogs?"

"Yes, I heard." A blond guy with dogs who knew Lisa. Her fingers clenched around the phone. "Was the guy's name Finn?"

"Uh-huh." Shonda's voice was trailing off.

Why was Finn asking Lisa's friends questions? Kate thought again of Lisa's funeral. She'd been sure he was the guy who'd tried to help her. Yet he denied it. And now he was playing private investigator. Why? Ethan would be furious if he knew some guy was snooping around on his turf.

Shonda breathed heavily, quickly, into the phone. Kate was losing her. She needed to focus. She needed Shonda to stay on the line until she finished her report. She needed this to be over with. "I tracked down the funeral home where Karen Fawcett was cremated and they confirmed her death was not suspicious."

"Yeah." This was barely more than a mumble.

"So that's good. But, Shonda, the other victims appear to be in your circle of friends. Be caref—"

The cell phone went dead.

Kate stared out the window. The stream of cars going by her window had gotten thinner. Should she have told Shonda about the link between Lisa's and Krissie's homicides?

No. The media had already reported it. It was up to the police to warn these girls. She'd never live with herself if she inadvertently screwed up their investigation.

Her next call was much shorter. Marian MacAdam listened to her report with little comment. "Thank you for looking into this," she said. "I'm disappointed you couldn't come up with more. Especially since that prostitute has been found murdered."

"I am not a detective, Mrs. MacAdam," Kate said. The clock on the dash showed it was past six-thirty. She was still in her car, sitting by the curb. "And from what I understand, the police are following all these leads. They don't need me to do their job for them."

"No." Marian MacAdam sounded suddenly weary. "I suppose not." There was a pause. "Is that all, Ms. Lange?"

It could never be enough for Marian MacAdam. Nothing would ever fill the trench her guilt had dug in her heart. Kate understood. Her own trench remained as empty and ragged as it had fifteen years ago.

"Yes," she said softly.

Dust had already settled on the room. Even in the dimness of twilight, Hope could see the motes floating lazily, undisturbed and indifferent to her presence.

Her heart thudded. *Calm down. You can do this.*

She had to do it. She had to prove to Marian that she could confront Lisa's belongings, that she had nothing to feel remorseful about.

A note had appeared in Hope's mailbox at work yesterday. *I would like to have returned the music box I gave Lisa for her eighth birthday.* The note was unsigned.

Hope had crumpled the note and thrown it in her wastebasket. When she came home from work today, she downed three glasses of Scotch. She'd had one more with supper before rising heavily to her feet. Her legs had resisted the stairs, her heart pounding so loudly when she reached the landing by Lisa's room that she had to stop. She leaned against the wall.

You have to do it. You can't let Marian win.

She took a step into Lisa's bedroom. It still bore the marks of fingerprint powder. She scoffed to herself. The cops lifted prints in Lisa's room but they had nothing to match them to. Not one bloody fingerprint had been found on Lisa.

Her eyes fell on Lisa's bed. Still unmade. The chartreuse chenille cover lay crumpled at the foot, the sheets bearing a faint rumple from her body. She stepped toward it. Then stopped. The rumpling was more likely caused by the police rifling through the bedding, looking for drugs.

Hating the weakness that threatened to topple her to the floor, she crossed the room. Woodenly. Like a puppet. She forced herself to study the detritus of Lisa's life, the posters on the wall—when did she get the Andy Warhol?— realizing she hadn't been in Lisa's room for weeks. If not months.

She would not weep. Because it would never stop. Marian knew that and that was why she sent the note. She wanted Hope to go into Lisa's room; she wanted Hope to pick up Lisa's things; she wanted Hope to repent, repent, repent.

I will not. I will not succumb.

Her lips twisted when she pulled the music box from the shelf. She had never told Marian that Lisa had ignored the gift. Lisa wasn't into ballerinas and tutus as a child. Marian hadn't known that because she hadn't bothered to get to know her grandchild. She was just as guilty as Hope.

Sure you can have the music box, Marian. It meant nothing to Lisa, just like you meant nothing to her.

She retraced her path across the room. Her fingers shook. The box slipped. It fell to the hardwood floor with a discordant tinkle. She broke out into a sweat.

She needed to lie down.

But if she lay down in here she would never get up.

She snatched the box off the floor. The clasp opened and something fluttered to the floor.

No. No. Lisa had never used this box. It had meant nothing to her.

Then who had put a photo in it?

She picked up the picture. What was left of her heart disintegrated. She knew who put the photo in the box.

It was Lisa. And the box must have meant something to her, because the photo was dog-eared and creased from much loving. There was even a few water stains marring the ink on the back. She didn't want to believe they were tear marks but she couldn't deny that they were.

Her own tears started then. Large hot angry tears.

They coursed down her face, landing on Lisa's eight-year-old features with such force that the weakened paper bent. She wiped the picture across her breast.

She stared at it one final time. She didn't remember this photo being taken. It looked as if it had been at someone's cottage. Lisa was sitting on a lawn, hugging a large unkempt dog. Happiness shone in her round features.

Hope realized she had been so used to Lisa's defeated gaze that she had forgotten her daughter hadn't always looked like that.

She read the childish handwriting on the back of the photo. *Me and Rufus.* A large heart enfolded the inscription.

Tearstains smeared Rufus's name but it didn't matter. She remembered now. She remembered Rufus. She remembered Lisa talking about him. So much so that she finally forbade Lisa to bring up his name anymore because she was so tired of hearing Lisa talking about that damned dog, of Lisa begging her for a dog of her own.

She snapped the music box shut. She stuffed the incriminating picture in her pocket. She wanted to destroy it, crumple it up, shred any evidence of the mother she had been.

She had put her own ambitions in front of her daughter's needs. Not to mention her husband's.

Now her daughter was gone. Her husband had left long ago.

All she had left was her career. Her own hopes. And those hopes were high, right now. The Supreme Court was within her grasp. As long as she wasn't pulled under the muck with Marian's sneaky backroom manipulations.

After all, hadn't she given up everything, including her chance at salvation, for her work?

Lisa was dead now. Hope's mistakes would remain buried with her. Only she would know how deeply entrenched they would remain on her soul.

She closed the door to Lisa's room softly behind her. On Monday, she would ask the cleaning service to begin packing up Lisa's room.

27

"We've got a problem," John Lyons announced. "But it's not insurmountable."

He was sitting at the head of the boardroom table, a file folder spread out before him. Kate lowered herself into the chair on his right. It was 10:07 a.m., and John Lyons had called her up to one of the smaller conference rooms.

Her heart thudded loudly in her ears. Had he called her to talk about the MacAdam case? She furtively scanned the papers in front of him. Then relaxed. She could clearly see the statement of claim of Brad Gallivant. Her eyes fell on another document with a pale blue triangle stapled over the corner. She straightened. "Looks like the other defense has been filed."

"Yes, we just received it." John handed her the document.

She flipped through it. "Doesn't hold any surprises, as far as I can see." Dr. Ericson, the orthopedic surgeon who operated on Brad Gallivant's knee, and the Greater Halifax General Hospital, known in the city as the GH2, claimed that the injuries caused to the plaintiff were solely attributable to the cadaveric tissue supplied by TransTissue, Inc. "So what's the difficulty?"

"I just spoke to their counsel, Morris MacNeil." She waited for John to give his usual smirk. Morris MacNeil always brought that out in him. But not today. Instead, John gave her an assessing look. "He's claiming there's a case in the U.S. that blows our defense out of the water. And…"

A case she hadn't found? Sweat pricked her armpits.

She forced herself to keep her cool. Morris MacNeil had a reputation for blowing a lot of hot air. She arched a brow. "And?"

"He thinks he has a new plaintiff. Someone else who claimed to have gotten hep C from a bone filler. Gal by the name of Denise Rogers."

"I see." This was getting worse by the minute. "When are they going to file?"

"Morris is just doing up the claim, he says."

"And what about this U.S. case?" She hated asking. She should know the answer. She should have unearthed that case, analyzed its facts, distinguished it in a memo and presented it to John Lyons. Before Morris MacNeil called him and caught him unprepared.

It must have been embarrassing for her mentor. She'd let down the one man who'd believed in her. Her cheeks burned.

"According to Morris, the U.S. appellate court recently came down in favor of a plaintiff who contracted syphilis through cadaveric transplant."

"Same procedure?"

"Yes."

"I see," she said softly. Even though the U.S. legal system was not one the Canadian courts relied on for legal precedent, in a case involving state-of-the-art medical procedures the U.S. decision might have some weight.

"How did the plaintiff prove the syphilis came from the tissue?" she asked. "In most cases it would be difficult to pin down a sexually transmitted disease on knee surgery."

"They found that the tissue processing procedures were below standard." John leaned forward. "How many U.S. cases did you research for our defense?"

She straightened. "I pulled up a few, but they were inconclusive. It was too difficult to determine the cause of the disease. Nothing was ever nailed on the tissue processor. I thought we had a pretty good defense."

"Until this case came out."

Was that a dig? She flushed. "I'll do an online search for the case." She hated how defensive she sounded. "But if the decision was based on substandard tissue processing procedures, we can clearly distinguish it."

John twirled his pen. "I think we'll be okay," he said slowly. "But Morris and the plaintiff's lawyer both want to visit TransTissue and see the procedures for themselves."

Cocky bastards. "Fine. Of course, we'll want to conduct a discovery on Brad Gallivant to explore whether he could have contracted hep C some other way." She gave a little smile.

John returned the smile. She relaxed. He wasn't going to hold this against her. "You read my mind. I'll call Trans-Tissue and set up something. How are we doing with the surgical expert?"

Kate exhaled slowly. "I've got a confirmation from her. She had a look at Brad Gallivant's medical records and says there isn't any record of a blood transfusion. So it seems unlikely he contracted hep C during surgery. But it is something he could have picked up from a high-risk lifestyle. Drug use is one of the risk factors."

"Let's get that discovery scheduled." John steepled

his fingers together. "Then we'll know if our Mr. Gallivant has been gallivanting around."

Kate bit her lip as she scrolled through the U.S. case that Morris MacNeil had bragged about. Morris, blowhard that he was, had one-upped her. It was mortifying. A firm like LMB prided itself on its superior legal skills. Why hadn't she been aware of this decision? John hadn't asked her, but the question had hovered like a Michelin blimp in the conference room.

She had a lot to prove on this file. To John, to her firm, to her colleagues, to herself. And to Randall. He'd already made a point of letting her know that. She couldn't allow herself to be distracted by Marian MacAdam's guilt trip or by her own childhood ghosts. The whole point of getting a job at a firm like LMB was to prove she could amount to something, that she deserved people's respect. Not their pity or condemnation. But that's all she'd get if she ended up getting the boot at the end of her probationary period. She couldn't hack it, colleagues would whisper. She wasn't good enough.

And not only had she been given the opportunity to work on a civil litigation file with an expert like John Lyons, but this file in particular was one lawyers dreamed about. It was an exciting, groundbreaking case. She had an opportunity to create legal precedent. How many lawyers could brag about that? It would cement her reputation and guarantee her a place on LMB's letterhead.

She could not blow it.

She read through the U.S. decision twice. It was comforting to know the case was decided in the plaintiff's favor solely on the grounds that the tissue processor had been negligent in its processing procedures. The company had failed to screen the tissue properly. Namely, it failed to run viral blood-screening tests. It was only a matter of time before some nasty bug or disease would find its way into their products.

She sat back in her chair. She needed to see TransTissue's procedures manuals and tour the plant. *Before* the other parties.

If TransTissue was processing the tissue properly—which she fervently hoped they were—then it led her to the next question: Were their suppliers? TransTissue got their tissue from tissue brokers. Who, exactly, were these people? She'd never heard of any companies that specialized in tissue harvesting.

What really concerned her was the fact that the regulatory framework governing tissue donations was brand-new—and hands-off. The regulations placed a great deal of faith in the abilities of tissue processors to monitor their own activities. The onus to discover and report an adverse event, such as the transmission of a virus through a tissue product, was placed on the tissue processors and others in the supply chain. Assuming an adverse event was discovered and subsequently reported, the government then expected the tissue processor to conduct their own investigation and report their findings.

This would be the soft spot for her client. Morris MacNeil had already found it. Now he would begin hammering away at it.

She picked up the phone and dialed the number John had given her.

"Melinda Crouse," a perky voice answered.

"Melinda, it's Kate Lange from LMB. John Lyons told me to call you about some information I need."

"Of course. I was expecting your call. What can I do for you?" she asked cheerily.

"I'm going to need your procedures manuals."

There was a pause. "All of them?" Her voice was a little less cheery.

"Yes."

"Okay. Will do. I'll have them copied and couriered to you tomorrow."

"Great." Kate infused her voice with gratitude. "And one more thing…"

"Yes?" The enthusiasm was definitely muted now.

"I need to see the records that came with the tissue used to make Brad Gallivant's and Denise Rogers's knee filler. Denise Rogers is a new plaintiff," Kate added. "In fact, I'd like the records for every batch that was made on the day their fillers were made." That would rule out any screwups before or after the filler was made that could have affected the quality.

"Um…I wasn't told anything about that. I'll have to check."

"Please do. I need it ASAP." The U.S. case had left a niggling fear.

"Okay, Ms. Lange. I'll get right on it." She didn't sound too hopeful. "It's just that those records are confidential. We have a duty to protect the donors, you know."

"Yes. I understand. But all this information is protected by solicitor-client privilege. I won't divulge it."

"Oh, right." Her voice had regained its perkiness. "I forgot about that. It shouldn't be a problem, then."

Kate hung up the phone. She stood, pacing to the window, then back to her desk. She wanted the records now. She wanted to get the case on track and leave the other parties in the dirt.

It was time to show Randall and John what she was made of.

28

Thursday, May 10, 2:45 a.m.

He backed the car down the boat ramp until the rear was about five feet from the water's edge. The Arm was flat, black. No moon lit its edges tonight.

He opened the door, then stopped. White lights flashed across his eyes. They settled around the periphery of his vision with comfortable familiarity. Everything he looked at was circled in pulsating dots. He blinked, his fingers massaging his temple.

Why was he here?

The white receded. He exhaled heavily and opened his eyes. His gaze fell to the dash. The clock spelled out the time in eerie fluorescent green: 2:45.

It had been 11:38 when she'd climbed into the passenger's seat. At 11:59 her beseeching eyes had beseeched no longer.

He knew now why he was here.

He glanced around. It was such a pretty neighborhood. He liked to walk through here sometimes, choosing which house should be his. Sometimes he even sat on the wharf next to the boat ramp and stared across the water at the

Armdale Yacht Club. The boats were so clean, so elegant, beautiful instruments of speed and precision.

He should have finished his residency this year. With a newly minted surgeon's salary he would have been able to afford one of these gracious homes that lined the Arm. Instead, he was toiling away for Dr. K.

Pain acidulated his blood. He had been a star medical student. *A star.* Had earned a spot at a top surgical residency program.

He had proven his mother wrong.

And then it had been ripped away from him. He'd planned to appeal the committee's decision, but his advisor warned him they were out for blood; there were suspicions he'd stolen fentanyl from the supplies room, he was told. There was the time he'd harassed one of the surgical nurses, he was reminded in a lowered voice. Then that little incident with the mentally challenged patient… and the drunk… The advisor shook his head. Don't waste your time, he said. What he meant was: get lost. And good riddance.

His mother had laughed. Laughed in his face when she heard. "I always said you were a dirty little bastard," she said. "Bet you couldn't even say those long words without your tongue tripping over them."

That's when he picked up his first girl.

It took care of the urges for a while. Until he began working for Dr. K and took on new responsibilities. Then the urges began to flood him. Building and building until he could resist no more. But instead of breaking him down, it made him stronger. Powerful. In control.

He hurried around the car and opened the trunk. She lay there. Young, pretty enough in life if you liked the type. Too much makeup for his taste. So much more beautiful when the whiteness of her bones and the pinkness of her flesh were revealed.

He reached toward her.

He snatched his hands back.

His hands were bare. He had forgotten to glove his hands. Sweat broke out on his forehead, his bowels loosening at his close call.

How could he have forgotten that?

He rushed around to the driver's side, snatching the pair of latex gloves that were tucked under his coffee holder. He had never, ever forgotten to glove before.

What was wrong with him?

He slid the gloves on, double-checking that they were a snug fit, and threw one last look around him. The street was still quiet. Not a soul stirred.

Especially hers.

He lifted her from the trunk and laid her carefully on the ramp. Blood trickled slowly down the slope. It slid into the black water.

She wasn't quite straight. The slope made it difficult to position her. But he didn't have time to fuss.

The white had slipped back. It was pulsating in slow circles around his vision.

He put the car into Drive and eased up the ramp.

Fortunately, it wasn't far to drive home.

"Hello?" Randall glanced blearily at the fluorescent blue numbers of his sleek clock radio: 3:46 glared at him.

"Randall?"

"Yes." He sat up in bed. He recognized the voice and bit back a groan. Was this a bad dream? "Hope...I mean, Your Honor—"

A raspy laugh mocked his confusion. "For Chrissake take the stick out of your arse, Randall. Call me Hope."

He blinked. She was drunk. Howling drunk. "Look, Hope, why are you calling me—?"

"Did you get the fucking notes?" she cut in.

He lowered his voice, "Yes." He put the thought of Kate's accusing eyes in the elevator out of his head. He did what he had to do. But it had been harder than he thought.

"What did you do with them?"

"I shredded them."

"At your office?" Her voice rose a notch.

He sighed. "No. At home."

"Phew." She suddenly laughed. "I knew I could count on you."

His face twisted. He got Hope's number loud and clear: single, newly bereaved and isolated by both her family and her profession. It wasn't easy being a judge. You had to keep yourself above your former colleagues.

"Is that all, Hope?" he asked briskly.

"No. No, it ishn…isn't." She took in a gulping breath. "You know, you were a great fuck. Did I ever tell you that?"

"Yes."

Her voice caught a little. "Was I?"

Randall squeezed his eyes shut. He hated the note of vulnerability in her voice. He needed to end this, now, before she lost her last remaining shred of dignity.

"You were amazing." He said it softly, but there was no question of his sincerity. He meant it. She had been amazing in bed.

He felt her relax over the phone.

"Now." He resumed his brisk tone. "It's time for some sleep. I'll bet you have a full docket tomorrow." He hoped this would remind Hope of her chosen station in life. Of her need to be careful of her conduct.

"Yes." She soundèd suddenly deflated. "It is time for bed…" Her voice trailed off, then it strengthened. "I made it and I have to lie in it."

The phone buzzed in Randall's ear for a full minute before he placed it back on its cradle.

The tiger had turned on itself.

29

The discovery of a third victim threw public relations at the police department into full damage-control mode. The media wanted to know what the police were doing to find this sicko and why hadn't they already caught him?

It was a nightmare for Deputy Chief Forrester. Which meant it was a nightmare for the criminal investigations unit. Reporters were violating the crime scene tape and trying to steal photos of the bloody trail leading into the Arm.

When Ethan saw photos of the latest anonymous young female victim he felt sick. Angry.

Wednesday had been a sunny day.

They thought they'd have more time. Brown had been assiduously following the weather forecasts while the team scrambled to follow the meager leads from the first two homicides.

It was now 7:00 a.m. More than twenty-four hours had passed since an early morning jogger had made the grisly discovery at the boat ramp on Jubilee Road.

He picked up the crime scene photos from the board-room table. The dismemberment of the latest victim's limbs was the same. But the rest was different. She had long, fine, pale brown—almost blond—hair. It was in a ponytail. Wisps hung around her face. She was heavier, much heavier than Lisa or Krissie, with large breasts, and a stomach that had several rolls of puppy fat. She had one of those dangly belly button rings that seemed to be the latest trend with teenage girls. Her face had been heavily made up. Now the mascara was smudged around her eyes, and several smears of black ran down her cheeks. Her pale silvery lip gloss was a bizarre contrast to her waxy skin and petechiae-marked flesh.

There was one more difference between the killer's most recent victim and the last: her face showed more terror.

The killer was amping up his game.

Ferguson walked into the war room and stood at the front of the boardroom table. The team quickly took their seats. "Okay, we've got to put a stop to this guy," she said brusquely. "Brown, what have you come up with to profile this guy?"

Constable Liv "Copper" Brown was the resident profiler on the team. Before she'd joined the force, she'd done a master's in behavioral sciences. At six-foot-one in her sock feet, with a lean physique and a coppery head of hair, Brown was used to commanding attention. She looked around the table. "All signs point to the usual basic profile for a serial killer—white male between the ages of twenty-five and thirty-four."

Ethan thought of Judge Carson. "How can you be sure he is a man?"

"All the victims are young females. The first two even shared certain physical characteristics—slight build, longish hair. His fantasy is built around that."

Unless the killer was one very sharp judge who knew

that she could mask the killing of her daughter by choosing other victims like her. And that, by doing so, everyone would assume it was a guy who did it.

"Have you been able to pinpoint any habits we could use to find him?" Redding asked.

Brown grimaced. "None yet. He's obviously highly intelligent. And highly organized."

"And yet he picked a different physical type of victim this time…" Ferguson said. "Is he becoming less organized?"

"I think so. He also didn't wait for the weather to turn, either. From the cases I've looked at, when the killer starts to deviate from his known M.O., it's a sign the need to kill is driving his impulses."

Everyone knew what that meant. They might finally get a break.

Ethan leaned forward. "What do you think is the killer's fantasy?"

Lamond sniggered. "Why don't you tell us yours and we'll see if they match."

Brown grinned, then said, "The victimology is crucial here. We need to know whether our guy is targeting certain physical types. So far we can see that he likes young women. But Lisa MacAdam and this unknown girl were very different physically." She skimmed her notes. "This brings me back to the M.O."

"They were the same," Ethan said.

"And this is where our guy deviates from the typology."

"In what way?" Ferguson asked.

"Normally, a power-control killer wants to inflict maximum fear and pain on his victims. He needs to magnify his self-worth by reducing the victim to worthlessness."

Ethan nodded. "I know what you're getting at. According to the medical examiner, the killer didn't dismember the girls while they were alive. Nor were there any signs of torture on their heads or torsos."

"So could the self-gratification come after death?" Ferguson asked.

"I suspect so." Brown flipped her notepad closed. "And he's using the *LOL* signature to send a message."

"The last laugh," Ethan muttered. "And it's on us so far."

Ferguson stood. "Right. So the killer doesn't live in the south end. Maybe he works there?"

Brown nodded. "Yes."

"At one of the hospitals?"

"Most likely."

"Lamond, any success in IDing victim number three?" Ferguson asked.

Lamond shook his head. "No. No one's called about her yet. Patrol's been canvassing the neighborhood but Sergeant Wilkins says he needs to pull them in for foot patrol."

Ethan glanced at Ferguson. They both knew the stress Wilkins was under. They needed patrol to do the canvassing, Wilkins needed more patrol to respond to the panic seizing the city. And not only to reassure citizens. Halifax's criminal underbelly had seen the opportunity and had upped their game—there were several drug-related murders and an increase in vice activity since the first murder had splashed across the papers. As every cop knew, most crimes were ones of opportunity. And the opportunities had been huge these past two weeks.

"It's been twenty-four hours." Ferguson pressed her lips together. "She is probably another street kid. Walker, what did Vice have to report?"

"Vicky says she didn't fit any of their kids, but these kids move around so much, she couldn't be positive. The victim could be from out of town."

Ferguson nodded. "We'll have to wait it out. We can't rule out that her family's away." She picked up her folder. "In the meantime, I want Walker and Redding to hit the streets. Warn all the regulars. There's a pattern. They need to understand that they are at risk." She turned to Ethan. "Any success with the ex-con lead?"

"Nothing yet. I've checked out eight suspects. None of them is capable of doing this. And all have alibis. Guess our halfway house system is working." He smiled wryly.

"What about ex-cons who've been out for longer?"

"I'm getting to them next. I've got about five on my list." Ethan pushed back his chair and stood.

"Let me know when you've tracked them all."

"Right." He left the station and got into his car. The list sat propped on his dashboard. Five more dead ends to go down. But, he knew—and Ferguson had reminded him— a good cop had to explore every avenue. Who knew what turd was going to be turned up in the process?

30

When news of the third victim was reported by the media on Friday, the city had reeled in shock. The police upped their foot patrols in the north and south ends; residents were being advised to use extreme caution. Early-morning joggers banded together into running groups. There was a feeling of joining forces in the face of adversity, like after Hurricane Juan devastated the city in '03. Parents carpooled their kids home instead of letting them walk.

Kate skimmed the day-old paper. The headline was yet another dramatic eye-catcher: Rain or Shine, Body Butcher Strikes Again. Who got paid for those headlines? One of the articles about "protecting the children" caught her eye. She sipped her coffee. These kids weren't the ones in danger in the first place. It was the other kids, the kids no one cared about, the kids who bummed money, used drugs, got kicked out of school and generally fell through the cracks. These were the ones being chosen by the killer.

Despite the theme of strength in adversity that ran through the newspaper's articles, it didn't conceal the fear and anger. No one could believe that someone was getting away with ruthlessly picking girls off the street and brutalizing them. No one knew where a body would be left next. No one wanted to look out the window in the morning for fear of making a grisly discovery.

People were getting spooked.

Everyone had theories, and a lot of people thought they'd seen the guy—"he was in a big truck cruising down Barrington Street," "he drove an old, broken-down Chevy... I saw him in the park," "I think he's a guy who used to work for the post office—he was really weird."

If the newspaper was able to round up these witnesses, Kate could just imagine the number of people clogging the police hotline.

She wondered how Ethan was doing. This case was getting to him. She had seen it in his eyes. It almost made her forgive him for the way he treated her about the notes.

Alaska whined, pacing restlessly by the door. She put on her running shoes. It was time to take the new man in her life for a run. The problem was memories of the old one kept dogging her.

She ran for an hour. She was just returning to her house when a woman's voice called, "Kate! Kate!" She threw a startled glance around her. From a sagging front porch, a woman waved her hand.

Kate smiled and tugged on Alaska's leash to stop. "Hello, Enid," she called from the sidewalk.

"Lovely morning, isn't it?"

"Yes." The sun had stroked silver on the water this morning.

Enid stepped toward her. "Why don't you come in for a cup of tea?"

Kate hesitated. "I have Alaska with me."

"Oh, tish, that's no problem. I'll keep the cats upstairs. He can come inside."

"Well…" Kate thought of her empty house. All she had waiting for her was a vacuum cleaner and a duster. She smiled. "That'd be nice."

"Oh! Lovely!" Enid said, sounding surprised.

"I'll just leave Alaska on the front porch." She tied his leash loosely to one of the posts. She could just imagine his reaction to being in a house full of cats. He'd think he was in heaven.

"Be good," she said to his alert face. His tail thumped. He turned away and began sniffing the porch.

Enid held the screen door open for her. Kate noticed it was about the same vintage as her own door. She stepped inside the large foyer. It was dim, but not oppressively so. The old walnut floors gleamed discreetly with polish. She wondered what her floors would look like with a bit of elbow grease. She wished now she'd had them stripped and varnished before she'd moved in, but she had been too impatient.

On the far wall, a massive antique mirror caught the light from the old ship's lantern that hung from the middle of the ceiling. She started. The mirror had also captured her reflection. She hadn't recognized herself for a minute. Her figure was trimmer than it had been for a while, which pleased her, but there were sharper angles to her face. She wasn't so sure about those.

"I'll go make the tea," Enid said, smiling. Her teeth were crooked but well kept. Her smile lit her fair skin with an inner glow. Why hadn't Enid married? She had such a vivacious air about her.

"That sounds wonderful."

"Why don't you have a seat in the living room," Enid said. "Muriel is in there." She ushered Kate through a large arched doorway into a room that seemed empty. Then Kate realized that Muriel was sitting on the piano bench. Her back was to the keys.

"Mil, do you remember Kate? She lives in the Hansens' old house."

Muriel gazed at Enid earnestly. "Mother says we need to be home by five o'clock and not a minute later."

"Yes, Mil. Don't worry, we won't be late." Enid turned to the sofa. "Shoo, shoo, Brûlée."

Kate threw a startled glance at the sofa. A caramel-colored cat lay curled on an overstuffed brocade pillow. The cat threw her a baleful look and jumped off the sofa. Enid gestured to Kate. "Make yourself comfortable. I won't be a minute."

Kate settled herself gingerly on the sofa. There were a lot of pillows, covered in various shades of cat hair. She gazed around the room. Brûlée lounged under a brocade footstool, which looked too fragile to support anyone's feet.

Sitting at right angles were a velvet-covered sofa and love seat in a beautiful shade of deep cherry red. Kate studied them. The color was so vibrant, so youthful, yet not at all out of place with the room. They looked fairly new. Only a few scratches marked the bolster.

Muriel blew her nose. Kate glanced over her shoulder and gave her a tentative smile. The old lady was dressed in a long plaid skirt with a heather-green cardigan. She looked like many of the elderly ladies Kate saw around Halifax, except she wore a pair of Scottie dog hair barrettes, the old metal type. They were upside down.

"Hi, Muriel," she said.

Muriel stared at her, her gaze searching Kate's face. "Mother says I have to be home by five o'clock today."

"Okay." Kate smiled tentatively.

"But I want to stay longer!" Muriel's face twisted in distress.

"Now, we'll just talk to Mother about it, Mil." Enid walked into the room, her birdlike body stooped over a large tray. Kate jumped to her feet to help her lower it to the coffee table. "Thank you, dear," Enid said. She prepared a cup of tea for Muriel. "Why don't you come over here, Mil? I have some nice tea and those shortbread cookies you like."

Muriel's face brightened. She left the piano bench, lowering her tall body onto the red love seat. Her hand slid back and forth over the velvety seat. Brûlée jumped up next to her. She fed him part of her cookie and he slid onto her lap.

Enid poured Kate and herself some tea, then sat down on the sofa next to Kate. She lowered her voice. "I wanted to talk to you. I need some advice."

Kate glanced at Muriel. She was humming softly to herself, stroking Brûlée.

Enid followed her gaze. "She won't notice. And if she does, I don't think she'll understand." Enid put her teacup on her saucer. "Yesterday I went to a funeral home to make arrangements. For myself and for Mil."

Kate guessed what was coming. She quickly ran through in her head the type of estate provisions Enid and Muriel should have: wills, powers of attorney, joint accounts.

"Is everything all right with Muriel?" she asked. She didn't know much about Alzheimer's.

Enid gave her a wry smile. "As can be expected. Mil is declining. But my doctor told me my heart is acting up. He tells me that every ten years or so. This time, though, he's sent me to a cardiac surgeon." She took a sip of her tea. "I haven't decided whether I'll go under the knife or not. But it seemed like a good time to get everything in order in case something happens to me." She glanced at Muriel. Worry pulled down the lines of her face. "I contacted a nursing home and put Mil on a waiting list. Then I went to a funeral home to put in place funeral arrangements for when something happens to one of us."

Kate noted she'd said "when something happens to one of us," not *if*. She studied Enid's face. Under those blue-veined eyelids were eyes that had seen a lot in their time. Right now they gazed at her with a look of calm resolution. Kate supposed if you live for eighty-odd years, uncertainties became less uncertain.

Enid leaned forward. "I spoke to the funeral director and she put all the paperwork in order. Then she asked if I'd like to donate my body to science. I must have mentioned I'd been a nurse, because she told me that she thought with my background I'd be interested in helping medical research."

"Is that something you'd support?" Kate asked. She wondered how she'd feel if she was asked to give up her body in the aid of science.

"Well, once she told me that this research would help people with neuromuscular disorders, I was interested to learn more. She gave me the donation forms. I signed one for myself, because after the things I've seen, I'd like to know that this old bag of bones—" she waved a self-deprecating hand over herself "—might serve some higher purpose."

"That's great, Enid," Kate said. She thought of her sister. She'd been too damaged to be an organ donor. It would have given some comfort to her mother to know that the precious life she'd nurtured hadn't gone completely to waste. But Kate had been driving too fast for that one small consolation.

Enid leaned forward. "But then the funeral director said that maybe my sister might be interested. I told her that we'd never know, because she is no longer capable of telling us her wishes. This is where it gets worrisome." She placed her teacup on the table. Her gaze rested fondly on Muriel's face. Muriel was staring at the cat, her eyes transfixed by the movement of her fingers over the cat's fur. "The funeral director told me that I could sign the consent form for her. I said I didn't think so. But she was very persistent, said that if I had power of attorney I could sign for her. She filled out the form and tried to get me to sign it right then and there."

Kate straightened. "Did you?"

Enid shook her head. "No. It didn't feel right. But afterward I wondered about it. Maybe she was right and I had the legal authority to do it. That's why I thought I'd ask you."

Kate brushed her fingers free of crumbs. "I'm glad you asked. You don't have the legal authority. If Muriel had put her wishes in her will, and you were the executor, you could do it. But the power of attorney only grants you decision-making authority over her care while she is alive."

"That's what I thought!" Enid pursed her lips. "You know, I had the distinct impression she was trying to trick me. I've a good mind to go down there and ask for my money back."

Kate bit into a cookie. "Which funeral home was this?"

"Keane's Funeral Home."

Kate choked down her bite. Keane's Funeral Home? "So it was Anna Keane you were dealing with?"

Enid nodded, and poured more tea. "Yes."

Kate stirred milk into her cup. She was surprised to hear that Anna Keane had tried to take advantage of Enid. "Maybe it was a misunderstanding."

Enid shook her head. "No. She was lying to me. I know it."

"I wonder why…maybe she is trying to help this researcher."

"At my expense?" Enid snorted. "I've made up my mind. I'm going to go there on Monday and demand my money back."

Kate took a sip of her tea. She wasn't sure if Anna Keane had tried to trick Enid. Maybe Anna Keane really believed that Enid had legal authority. Kate hoped so. She had liked Anna Keane; she provided a difficult service with compassion. Kate knew how valuable that was. The funeral director deserved the benefit of the doubt. She put down her teacup. "Would you like some company?"

Enid smiled eagerly. "That would be lovely."

"I'm in court all day Monday. Why don't you come over around four-thirty on Tuesday? Then we can drive together." Kate stood. Her muscles had stiffened. She moved slowly to the door. "Thank you for the tea."

Kate felt Enid's pleased gaze on her back as she followed her to the front porch. A small glow of corresponding pleasure spread through her. "I'll see you Tuesday."

31

Sunday, May 13, 3:00 p.m.

Judge Carson swung open the door to her condo. The afternoon sun blazed behind her. It took a second for Ethan's eyes to adjust to the brightness. When they did, he saw she gazed at him with a glacial expression that was designed to establish who was in charge.

"This better not take long," she said. "I'm extremely busy." She stepped back reluctantly, her hand still on the doorknob. Ethan walked past her. He breathed in deeply. Was that a hint of Scotch on her breath?

Judge Carson crossed her arms. It had the effect of tightening her blouse against her breasts. Her shirt was a white fitted number, buttoned right at the spot where her breasts swelled. She had tucked the shirt into a pair of dark jeans that cupped her curves.

Her tawny eyes flickered over him.

And over him again.

He shifted away from her.

"Have a seat, Detective Drake." Judge Carson turned toward the sunken living room. The view from the two walls of windows was stunning. The Public Gardens spread before him. Budding greenery and spring tulips swayed in a light breeze. Couples drifted through the meandering paths. He and Kate had done the same thing less than a year ago.

He settled himself on a chair, his back to the windows. He wanted to check out the rooms, not the view. Judge Carson sat diagonally opposite him on the sofa. She raised her brows inquiringly. "You said you had an old case you wanted to discuss with me?" Her voice was brusque.

"Yes—"

"The Arnold case, I presume?"

There she went again. Trying to wrestle control of the interview.

Ethan leaned back and crossed his legs. He was going to set the pace. Not her.

His eyes traveled slowly around the room. Everything was the same as last time: bare, white. Not much had changed except what was on the long granite counter separating the living area from the kitchen. A crystal whiskey decanter sat on a small tray. The matching crystal glass was visible behind a pile of files on her stylish computer desk. The glass looked empty. Recently? He couldn't tell from where he was sitting if it was clean or used.

Judge Carson watched him from the sofa. Her face was expressionless. She leaned back, mimicking—or mocking?— his body language, stretching her arm along the back. Shadow and light played on the curve of her breast. "I'd offer you a drink, Detective Drake, but I know you're not staying long."

He smiled and laid his notepad on the table. His leisurely appraisal of her home had unnerved her. It surprised him. He thought she was cooler than that. His mind swung back to the lion's head on her door. He could think of no better symbol for her desire to guard her home. But from what?

"No problem. As you guessed, I'm here about the Arnold case."

Mark "the Shark" Arnold was the only ex-con that Ethan hadn't been able to track down and eliminate from his list. He'd served his full sentence with no chance of parole for a grotesque murder fifteen years ago, when he was nineteen. His victim had been his girlfriend. He'd raped her, strangled her, then cut her up and thrown her body into the Atlantic Ocean. The only problem was, he hadn't gone far enough out to sea to dump her remains. Some of her body parts got caught in a fishing net. In a morbid postscript, a shark had also been caught in the net. His girlfriend's torso was found in its belly. Hence, Mark Arnold's nickname.

It was a gruesome case, and he had been punished to the full extent of the law. It had been the most sensational murder in Nova Scotia until now. Ethan looked it up and discovered a disturbing fact: Judge Carson had been Mark Arnold's defense lawyer. Had he been angered at the harshness of his sentence? Did he blame Judge Carson, fresh out of law school? Or did he harbor a hate toward teenage girls?

Now he was back on the streets. His prison records indicated that he had received training in the plumbing trade.

Judge Carson's gaze sharpened. "You think he did it?"

Ethan raised a brow. "I don't know. But I wanted to make sure you knew he was out."

She gave a bitter laugh. "Oh, yes, I knew, Detective. I checked it myself."

When? Before she killed Lisa? It would be a perfect deflection away from her. Maybe Brown had been on the wrong track.

"Has he been in contact with you?"

She shook her head. "No."

"Do you know if he was in contact with Lisa?"

She paled at the mention of Lisa's name. Her glacial demeanor was a lot thinner than he had thought. Was it the booze chipping away at it?

Or guilt?

Guilt could seep through the iciest hearts, weakening resolve in the most unexpected places, until the right question made the guilty crack and fall through the hole. They spent the rest of their lives drowning.

"Not that I am aware." Her voice was steady, clipped.

"Did he ever threaten you?"

"Yes."

Ethan picked up his notepad. "When?"

"The day he was sentenced. He thought I hadn't argued forcefully enough for him. He told me that when he got out, he'd make me pay."

Ethan searched her face. Her eyes met his. Strong, fierce, but not evasive. He'd be damned, but he believed her. "Did he give any specifics?"

She gave that harsh laugh again. "No. But he had lots of time to devise something."

"You knew him." Ethan leaned forward. "Do you think he was capable of carrying out this kind of crime?"

She looked away. Ethan followed her gaze and saw that it was on the whiskey decanter. She glanced back at him. She had seen his eyes following hers. She straightened. "I don't know," she said flatly. "He wasn't that bright. He killed his girlfriend in a fit of anger." She snapped her fingers. "It was a classic crime of passion. But for some killers, once they do the first kill, the next one is easier. He already had experience with dismemberment. And he had fifteen years to formulate a plan. I think it's possible."

She spoke in a dispassionate tone. She could have

been arguing the facts before a judge. Ethan watched her closely. Again, there was no artifice. Her body language was open.

Despite himself, he was beginning to doubt his suspicions about her.

"Do you have any idea where he might be? He was released over a year ago. He stopped reporting to his parole officer three months ago."

"Figures." Her mouth twisted. "No. I have no idea. I seem to recall he had some family on the south shore, but who knows? It was fifteen years ago." She shrugged. Her blouse gaped a little. Ethan kept his eyes on her face.

She rose to her feet in a fluid motion. "You'll forgive me, but I have work to do."

Ethan stood. "Would you mind if I had a look around before I left?"

She crossed her arms. Her eyes, which had lost their hostility over the course of Ethan's visit, hardened. "I've had enough police digging through my house. Check the reports, Detective. It's all there. Hair samples, fingerprints, photos."

His jaw tightened. He knew it was all there. It wasn't the same as looking at Lisa's room with a fresh set of eyes, two homicides later. "Right."

She headed to the door. He walked the long way around her sofa so that he'd cross by her computer desk. He scanned the stacks of files. He found the whiskey glass.

So she had been drinking before he came.

He turned toward the door, giving the desk a final sideways once-over. A letter caught his eye. *Department of Justice, Government of Canada* was scrolled across the top. He made out the words *We are pleased to confirm...* before Judge Carson's voice interrupted him.

"I asked you to leave, Detective."

He turned smoothly toward her. "Of course, Your Honor. Or should I say, Madam Justice?"

She flushed.

That's a once-in-a-lifetime occurrence.

"Don't be impertinent."

He slid his notebook into his pocket. "I'll call you if I track down Mr. Arnold. Please let me know if you see or hear from him."

"Don't worry, Detective. I'm not a fool."

"Don't worry, Your Honor," he ever so gently mimicked her tone. "You would never be accused of that."

He closed the door behind him and left the building. He hadn't been able to read it all, but he was sure that the letter had confirmed Judge Carson's appointment to the Supreme Court Division.

He bet she wasn't the first drunk judge to grace that bench.

32

Tuesday, May 15, 10:00 a.m.

Kate eyed the three-foot-high pile of binders on her desk. Melinda Crouse had kept her word. The screening and tissue processing procedures were now awaiting her.

But what she wanted was in a thin kraft envelope on top of the pile. She picked it up and pulled out a sheaf of reports. A Post-it note was stuck on top, with a note written in a rounded hand: *The donor reports and blood-screening reports you requested for B.G. and D.R., M.C.*

There were twelve sets of reports, two pages each. The first page of every report was the donor eligibility report, headed with the name BioMediSol. Kate had never heard of BioMediSol before, although it had a postal-box address in Halifax. From what the client had told John, BioMediSol was a tissue supplier or harvester, a company that literally removed the tissue from donors and sent it to TransTissue to process. They sent the tissue with a donor eligibility report and a blood sample.

Establishing donor eligibility was the first stage in screening whether the tissue could be harvested for biomedical purposes. The report determined the donor's medical status and cause of death. If the donor had a chronic disease, or had died of cancer or an infectious disease, then he or she would not be eligible to donate tissue.

Kate skimmed the first donor eligibility report. The donor's name was blacked out, but the rest of the information was intact: gender, age, preexisting medical conditions, risk factors, cause and date of death.

She studied each of the twelve donor eligibility reports carefully. So far, so good. The donors had passed Bio-MediSol's eligibility criteria with flying colors. None were too old, all had lived pretty healthy lives, none had died of diseases that would render their tissue useless.

It ruled out BioMediSol as the cause of Brad Gallivant's hep C. They'd done their end of the screening.

She flipped to the second page of the reports. These were the blood-screening reports filled in by TransTissue. Their private lab tested each blood sample that accompanied the tissue for hepatitis B, hepatitis C, HIV and syphilis. The screening measured the antibodies or antigens in the blood for each virus. The count was recorded in a numeric value, referred to as a titer in the medical profession. For HIV, a positive result would be any titer over 1.0. So if a donor's titer was 0.23, he would be HIV negative. The donor's titers would need to be within the acceptable range for each of the four viruses in order for the tissue to be eligible for processing.

Kate studied the blood-screening report for the first donor. None of the first donor's titers was above the acceptable range. In fact, all were well below normal. Reassured, she examined the next. And the next. All fine.

The fifth donor's HIV titer startled her. It was 0.53—a higher value than the titers of the previous four donors, whose titers were in the low double digits. But still acceptable. She flipped to donor number six. Back to a low double-digit HIV titer. Same with donor number seven.

When she reached the report for the eighth donor, she stopped. The donor's HIV titer was 0.53. Just like donor number five.

She checked the ninth donor. The HIV titer was also 0.53. Puzzled, she flipped through the remaining three reports. Those donors' HIV titers were also 0.53.

How could they all have the exact same titer, not off by even one one-hundredth?

Her pulse accelerating, she compared the hepatitis B titers for each of the five donors. They were identical. So were the hepatitis C titers. And the syphilis titers.

She stared in disbelief at the reports.

How could five donors' titers be exactly the same for four different viruses?

They couldn't.

It wasn't possible.

She flipped through them again. She hadn't misread them. Five donors had the exact same titers for all four viruses.

Why hadn't TransTissue noticed this?

She picked up the phone to call Melinda Crouse. Then she put it down. It was time to visit TransTissue in person. Because if she was wondering about what the hell was going on over there, she had no doubt Morris MacNeil would be, too. Good thing he didn't have the blood-screening reports yet.

She glanced at her watch. It was 10:30 a.m.

"I've got a couple of client meetings," she told Liz. "I'll be back at lunchtime."

TransTissue was located in a new building in an industrial park in Dartmouth, Halifax's twin city. Kate drove over the bridge connecting the cities. The deep blue water of the

Bedford Basin on the left side of the bridge gleamed today with the full promise of May sunshine. She headed onto the highway, taking the exit ramp to the industrial park.

There was probably a very good explanation for the reports, but she couldn't think of any as she sped through the endless intersections of the industrial park, looking for Blue Ridge Crescent. Something niggled at her.

She made a wrong turn. She'd never been this far into the industrial park before. Blue Ridge Crescent was on the farthest side of the park, bordering a pine forest. She turned down the road. It was long and curving. Empty. A paved road surrounded by evergreens. Just when she was starting to wonder if she had the wrong address, she glimpsed a large, four-story building fronted with reflective pink-tinted glass windows. She drove toward it. As she got closer, she noticed a separate square building squatting behind its counterpart, two tall metal chimneys spouting grayish smoke into the sky. The smoke plumed lazily against the blue, then dissipated slowly through the upper reaches of the pines.

She parked her car in the area marked Visitors' Parking. Grabbing her briefcase, she walked into the main building's foyer. It looked more like a hospital than an office, with pale blue and green furnishings set against spotlessly white walls. A set of framed posters were placed predominantly on the main wall, showing the range of TransTissue products. One caught her eye: NextGeneration Bone Filler. That was the product used in the plaintiffs' knees. Even though she'd done extensive research on the use of bone fillers, it still blew her mind that cadaveric material was being used in so many medical procedures.

Kate walked over to the security desk. The guard watched her approach. His eyes flickered over her. No bantering with this guy.

"I'm here to see Melinda Crouse. In public relations."

He nodded, looked up the number and dialed. Kate waited, glad she hadn't called ahead of time. She wanted an element of surprise.

The guard spoke for a minute into the receiver, then hung up the phone. "She'll be right out." He handed Kate a visitor's tag on a lanyard. "Please sign in."

She was disappointed to see she was signing a fresh page of the visitors' log. She'd hoped to scan the list of visitors to see if Morris MacNeil had already "dropped by."

"Hi." Melinda Crouse's perky voice materialized at Kate's shoulder. She turned around to see a young woman in her mid-twenties greeting her with a warm, if puzzled, smile.

"Hi, Melinda." Kate held out her hand. Melinda grasped it limply. "Sorry to drop in on you, but I received the information you sent me and had a couple of questions."

"Sure, no problem," Melinda said, with a smile as perky as her voice. "We can talk over here." She pointed at a small reception room just off the foyer.

"Great." Kate followed her, studying her from behind. She wore an off-the-rack tailored navy suit, with pointy-toed shoes that were worn at the heels. Her blond hair was carefully streaked and pulled off her face.

The reception room looked like one of those rooms the hospital set aside for family members to pray or grieve. It had several comfortable armchairs in pale green velveteen, with an oak side table. A water cooler was tucked in the corner.

Kate settled herself in one of the chairs and pulled out the reports from her briefcase.

Melinda sat opposite her. "Did you get everything you needed?" she asked.

Kate smiled. "Yes, thank you. I wanted to run through

a couple of things with you. First of all, were there only six batches of NextGeneration tissue filler made on the same day as the plaintiffs' batches?"

Melinda nodded. "Yes. We traced the batch numbers for the knee filler to the donor records I sent you."

Kate held up a donor record. "Is there any chance the donor records were filled out by TransTissue instead of BioMediSol?"

Melinda shook her head. "No. We require the tissue supplier to fill in the form."

"Who reviews these forms?"

Melinda straightened, a look of uncertainty on her face. "Um…it goes to the screening division. They check all that stuff and then the product is sent to processing." She smoothed her skirt. "It's all in the manuals I sent you."

"Great." A movement in the foyer caught her eye. A brown-haired man with broad shoulders straining his suit turned the corner and was gone.

"Is that where the processing division is?" Kate asked, pointing in the direction of the disappearing man.

Melinda nodded. "Yes."

"I've always been curious about it. Do you think you could give me a tour?"

Melinda smiled and jumped to her feet. Her relief at no longer having to answer questions was palpable. "Sure thing!"

Kate shoved the reports into her bag and followed the young PR woman. They walked past the security guard and around the corner. Melinda swiped her security pass through the sensor, pulling open a set of white-painted metal doors.

Kate walked through them. The doors fell closed behind her. There was a hum in the air, almost visibly shirring the fluorescent lights overhead.

"We can't go to the part where they make NextGen, because you need to be suited up and stuff," Melinda said. "But I can show you how they make some of the pure bone products."

"All right." She was disappointed. She wanted to watch how the filler was made, see if there was a weak link in the chain that Morris would undoubtedly hammer at. "Can I come back and see it?"

"Um…you need to get approval from the CEO. It's a restricted area." Melinda gave Kate an apologetic smile.

Kate frowned. "Why?"

"Oh, because of the sanitation protocol. You know, everything has to be kept germfree and all that." Melinda paused in front of a large window, which overlooked a room that looked like a laboratory. "Here's the FADAL."

"The what?" Kate stared at her. It sounded like she said, "The fuh doll."

Melinda smiled and pointed to an eight-foot-tall rectangular machine with a long steel table running through the middle. A large drill was mounted over the table. "The technician uses CAD software to program the FADAL, so the bone is precision cut."

As Melinda spoke, a woman in a white lab coat lined up a bone on the steel table. She ignored Kate and Melinda staring through the window. After punching some buttons on the machine, she lowered the drill. White dust floated around her masked face. When the dust cleared, Kate saw that the bone had been cut into even dowels.

"I presume the bone has already been screened for disease?" Kate asked.

Melinda nodded. "Yes. We take the blood sample that's sent with the tissue and test it. Once it's cleared, the tissue is cleaned off the bone, and then it's sent here for processing."

"What are the bone dowels used for?"

"These ones will be used for lumbar fusion."

At Kate's questioning look, Melinda added, "It's a common spinal surgery. We also make dowels that are used for ACL surgery to aid in graft-to-bone healing."

The technician placed the dowels in a container.

"What happens after the product is made from the bone?" Kate asked.

Melinda smiled proudly. "All of our products go into our debug system afterward."

"What's that?"

"It's like a big washing machine. It cleans the bone really well and it comes out free of germs. Some of the products are freeze-dried after that. Then they are ready for shipping." She glanced at Kate. "We label each product with the batch number so we can trace it to the donor or donors."

"Can the debug system get rid of HIV or hepatitis?"

Melinda nodded. "I think so. But it's not really an issue because we screen the blood for it before we process the tissue. And the broker screens the donors to make sure they don't have the disease before they harvest tissue from them." She smiled brightly. "So that's the tour. Any more questions?" She turned and began walking back to the foyer.

Kate heard footsteps behind her. She glanced over her shoulder. It was the broad-shouldered man.

"Just one," she said to Melinda. "But I think we should finish our discussion in the conference room—"

"If I may," the man behind Kate interjected.

He stepped next to Kate, studying her with shrewd brown eyes. Melinda threw him a flustered look. "Oh, Mr. Duggan, I didn't see you—"

Kate met the CEO's gaze. He was youngish, in his forties, with football-player features that had aged well.

"It's quite all right, Melinda." Mr. Duggan gave her a brief smile.

Kate held out her hand. "Mr. Duggan, I'm Kate Lange."

He took her hand in his. His handshake was firm and warm. "Ms. Lange, I've heard a lot about you." He smiled. His teeth were even and white. "You come highly recommended. I understand you are helping John mount a watertight defense for us."

Kate smiled. "I hope so. I wanted to see the bone filler processing facility."

He nodded. "We'll try to arrange that. Now, what was the question you had for Melinda? Perhaps I can answer it for you."

"I received the donor reports for the plaintiffs' knee fillers. Five of the donors have the exact same serology results. Same titers. I'm wondering how that is possible."

He could not hide his shock, although he tried. "The exact same?"

"Yes. Do you think it's possible that BioMediSol might have sent you the same blood sample for five of the donors?"

Melinda gasped. Bob Duggan threw her an irritated look, then turned to Kate. "I shall look into it. This is extremely unusual. I can assure you that our screening director reviews every serology report prior to the tissue being processed. Perhaps there has been a paperwork error…"

"I hope so." She held his gaze. "This kind of error can have very unpleasant consequences for TransTissue, not to mention the patients that receive the allograft."

She hadn't meant to sound so sanctimonious, but his obvious shock had sent her anxiety about the defense skyrocketing.

Bob Duggan frowned. "I am well aware of that, Ms. Lange." He walked her to the front door. "Please return those reports by courier today." He pulled the door open for her. "I'll have someone contact you about touring the NextGen processing area."

"Thank you." She left the building, mulling over Bob Duggan's reaction to her discovery. He'd been as horrified as she was.

Damn.

Hopefully, Bob Duggan would review the reports and find a reasonable explanation for the identical serology results.

Otherwise, they were screwed.

She glanced in her rearview mirror as she drove down Blue Ridge Crescent. The noonday sun turned TransTissue's pink-tinted windows into a fiery shield, blinding her view of Bob Duggan. The hair on the back of her neck prickled. She may not be able to see him, but she felt his eyes on her.

33

Kate placed the phone down. It was 2:48 p.m. She'd managed to reach a friend of hers from her waitressing days who now worked in a pathology lab. Her friend had confirmed, as Kate had guessed, that it was nearly impossible for five people to have the exact same viral screening results.

TransTissue's paper trail was fatally flawed.

The case had fallen apart in front of her eyes.

She dialed John Lyons' number. He answered on the first ring. "Can I talk to you for a minute about the Trans-Tissue file?" she asked, her heart pounding.

"Yes, in fact, I was going to call you about it." His voice was cool, preoccupied. Disquiet edged along Kate's nerves. "Come on up."

She gathered the TransTissue file and walked quickly to John's office. "Hi, John." She made sure her voice sounded confident despite the time bomb she had tucked under her arm.

He gave her a small smile. "Sit down, please, Kate."

She sank into a Queen Anne chair facing his desk, balancing the TransTissue file on her knee. "What's up?" Something was. Instead of the usual warmth she had grown to expect from her mentor, his gaze was perturbed.

"I had a call from Bob Duggan," he said. He watched her closely.

She kept her gaze steady. "I met him this morning."

"What were you doing at TransTissue?" His tone wasn't accusing, but it contained enough of an edge to put her on the defensive.

"Checking out a few facts. Before Morris does," she added pointedly.

"Bob told me that you had all kinds of reports sent to you, and then questioned the veracity of them."

"I had asked for the donor blood-screening reports for the batches of knee filler products made the same day as the plaintiffs'."

His gaze didn't soften.

Alarm bells went off in Kate's head.

"I did it so that I could be sure there hadn't been some slip in the manufacturing chain that would negate our defense."

He steepled his fingers together. "But you accused them of falsifying the reports."

Falsifying reports? Her mind raced back to her conversation with Melinda, then with Bob Duggan. She'd asked both of them if they knew why five of the reports were identical. There had been no accusations. She straightened. "John, I didn't accuse them of falsifying reports. But there *is* a problem—"

"I know." His tone was flat. "Bob told me that the PR gal had made a photocopying error and sent you five copies of the same serology report."

"Did he, now." Her fingers tightened their grip on the file. "That's not what he told me. He asked me to send the reports back to him so he could investigate the matter. I just sent them." Why was Bob Duggan trying to make her look bad? "Look." She handed the photocopy she'd made of the reports to John. "See how these titers are identical?"

John picked up the reports and flipped through the top five. He placed them carefully back on his desk.

"I agree. They are identical." His gaze sharpened. "Due to paperwork error. Simple as that." His tone implied she should have figured that out without needing TransTissue's CEO and her boss to tell her.

"I agree. It could be a simple photocopy error." It was the easiest explanation, but her research of the U.S. cases wouldn't let her leave it at that. "We need to see the originals. Without the names or ID numbers blacked out."

John folded his arms. "Do you seriously believe that TransTissue was falsifying documents?"

She met his gaze head-on. "I don't think TransTissue is falsifying records. However, I think that their supplier might've been sending in fake blood samples."

John's brows rose, a look of incredulity on his face. "Were you watching *CSI Miami* last night?"

A flush heated her cheeks. "I came across this in my research of the U.S. cases. Whenever the tissue processors got in trouble, it started with the suppliers. They were harvesting contaminated tissue and falsifying the donor reports."

John leaned back in his chair and studied her. She couldn't read his expression. After his *CSI* barb, she was tensed for anything. "So you think that TransTissue has a bad supplier and is ignoring the problem?"

Relief surged through her. He was finally getting it. What she didn't understand is why it took him so long. He was well-known for his abilities to ferret out the weak links in much more complicated chains of evidence than this. "That is one possibility. Have you heard of a company called BioMediSol?"

John frowned. "Vaguely. Why? Were they the supplier?" He picked up a pen and rolled it between his finger and thumb.

She nodded. "Yes. And the blood samples they sent to TransTissue for testing came up with the exact same results, five times out of twelve."

He sighed softly. "As Bob Duggan said, it was a paper-work error." He put the pen down and held her gaze. "Kate, you have got to understand something. You are on shaky ground. TransTissue has above-standard industry screen-ing procedures. They have a rigorous selection process. They have a health care professional who personally approves all tissue." He shrugged. "They happen to have a PR gal who made an error."

She squared her shoulders. "Like I said, it's not Trans-Tissue themselves that worry me. It's their supplier." She didn't understand why John, the veteran litigator that he was, wasn't more concerned. "Better us than Morris MacNeil. Because I'll bet he'll be asking."

"Perhaps." John picked up the pen and snapped it back in its holder. "But the problem is, you have managed to annoy a major client of LMB. They want you off the case."

"What?" She felt the blood drain from her face.

"Yes. I've tried to smooth things over. But I can only do so much." His eyes met hers. "I think you are an excep-tional woman. In every respect—"

She kept her features stony as he began the spiel of re-jection she knew was coming.

"—But you are walking on quicksand. First, the Lisa MacAdam debacle. Randall came very close to firing you."

She swallowed but held John's gaze.

His expression softened. "Did you know that Randall and Judge Carson were once an item?"

She stared at John. "No."

"It was a long time ago. But those are the ties that bind people."

Randall Barrett and Hope Carson, once lovers. Had that former relationship been enough to let Hope compel him into stealing her notes?

Would he really put his professional ethics aside for the sake of an ex-flame?

She exhaled slowly. Hadn't she let Ethan guilt her into doing the same thing?

John clicked his pen. Kate's gaze snapped back to him. She forced herself to concentrate. "The real issue is that you've antagonized a major client."

"I was trying to get the facts straight. The reports seemed fishy—" She stopped abruptly. She couldn't afford to lose her cool. She'd already staked too much on this job, this case. She smoothed a finger slowly over the file folder. "I guess I should have been more diplomatic in the way I phrased my question to Bob Duggan."

"Yes. You should have. But—" his expression hardened again "—I called you in for a different reason."

Was he going to fire her for antagonizing their client? LMB had let go of associates for lesser trespasses. She braced herself.

He leaned forward. "I advised Bob Duggan that we should settle."

"What?" She started, her fingers reflexively grabbing the file before it slipped off her lap.

John gave her a slight smile. "He accepted my advice."

She stared at him. "But we haven't even conducted the discovery!"

"I know. We'll save our client a considerable amount of money."

She breathed in through her nose. It was supposed to calm her. It didn't. "I don't understand why you want to settle at this juncture. It will cast them in suspicion."

John spread his hands on his desk. "Kate, it's simple." His tone rebuked her, as if she should have figured this out without him having to explain it to her. She smothered her irritation. This was her mentor, her champion, the man who had given her the golden egg. He had never spoken this way to her before. He had never made her feel as if she was out of her league. Until today.

Was this a taste of things to come?

John pointed to a blue-cornered document on his desk. "We've now got two plaintiffs: Denise Rogers filed today. TransTissue doesn't want the publicity. They've posted record profits—which is quite a feat in our current economic climate—and are in the process of buying several tissue banks in the U.S. This is a period of growth and excitement for them. They are considered industry leaders." He spoke like a proud father. "To enter into a lengthy lawsuit—no matter how innocent we know they are—is not in the best interests of the company. Bob was very concerned that they'd be pulled away from their expansion to deal with this."

"What are the terms of the settlement?" she asked, her tone flat. The bubble had been burst. Rudely. Without warning. Without a safety net. All that work, all her excitement at being on a ground-breaking case, was gone. What was left was the sticky reality of her job at LMB: family cases.

"Good financial remuneration for the plaintiffs, sealed with a nondisclosure clause." John stood. "I can handle it from here, Kate."

He smiled. Kate knew it was meant to take away the sting of dropping her from the case. She didn't smile in return.

"You've done good work, Kate. Never mind your screwup with Bob Duggan. I'm confident you won't do it again. You're a quick study." He paused. He was waiting for her to thank him for his faint praise, thank him for looking past her bumbling error, thank him for keeping her safe in this den of lions.

She rose to her feet and headed to the door. "So. Case closed." She forced a light tone.

He gave her a relieved smile. "Case closed."

She turned the door handle.

"And, Kate?"

She glanced back at him.

"I'll give you a call if something else comes up." But would anyone else in the firm be interested in her now that John had dropped her from the case? She doubted it. When Randall heard about this, she would be associate non grata. If she wasn't fired first.

"Thanks." She closed the door behind her. Her feet moved automatically down the hallway to the stairwell.

She walked by Rebecca Manning's office. The door was ajar. Out of the corner of her eye she glimpsed Rebecca behind her desk. Her smooth blond head was tilted, the phone cradled to her ear while she wrote on a LMB notepad.

Kate continued walking, hugging the TransTissue file to her chest. A bitter smile twisted her lips. Rebecca had predicted this outcome. What she hadn't predicted was the manner in which it would be done.

John Lyons had indeed screwed her.

Kate wondered if he'd enjoyed it.

34

"Damn," Kate muttered as she pulled into her driveway. She glanced again at the clock on her dash: 4:44 p.m. She was fourteen minutes late, but she bet it had seemed like forever to the two ladies standing on her front porch.

She climbed hurriedly out of her car and strode up the walk, her trench coat flapping in the breeze. It was one of those unusually warm May afternoons, when the sun finally commits to spring. Kate knew that a day like this was illusory, that the sun would disappear like a sleight of hand into the fog, and suddenly it would be cold again. But right now the sun beat on the back of her neck. "Enid, Muriel! Hi!"

She ran up the steps to where the elderly sisters stood. The casualness of her generation weighed upon her: in Enid's day people were punctual and didn't use excuses like "my voicemail was crazy."

Enid grasped Kate's hand. "Hello, dear."

Kate smiled, relieved that Enid didn't seem upset. "Sorry I'm late." She put the key in the lock, twisting it past the sticky part until the lock released. The heavy door groaned open. Kate braced herself for Alaska's welcome. But the hallway was empty. Eerily so.

"Alaska?" She hurried into the kitchen.

No sign of him.

"Alaska?" She rushed through the living room.

There was a lot of hair on the carpet, but no sign of him.

Then she remembered. This was the time that Finn took Alaska for his supper-time walk. She let out a breath. Man, she was a lot more stressed than she realized. The day had really gotten to her.

"Is everything all right, Kate?" Enid asked from the porch.

Kate turned, her nervous energy draining and leaving her limp. She wiped a sweaty hand on her skirt. "It's fine. I forgot that Alaska is out for a walk with his dog walker." She pushed the screen door open. "Please, come in. I just need to grab something and we can go." She had a book upstairs in her study that she thought Anna Keane might like. It was a guide to legal instruments published by the legal education society. It might give Anna Keane some guidance about consent issues.

Enid and Muriel stepped into the hallway. Kate hurried upstairs. She longed for it to be supper time. She longed for a glass of wine. She longed to tell her troubles to someone. Six months ago, she would have had Ethan to pour her troubles to. But now she had no one to tell about her ego-bruising, pride-wounding meeting with John Lyons.

How had she ended up with no friends? All work and no play. It was a cliché, but like most clichés, it started with an essential truth. She'd been too busy, first with articling, then with Ethan, and now with LMB, to keep up her friendships from law school. She'd assumed she'd make friends at work. But she'd been too big an outsider and too big a threat for her colleagues. Oddly, the only person who'd extended any warmth to her was Randall Barrett. And now she knew even that support was like the spring sunshine. Deceptive in its warmth and quick to retreat behind the chill fog of ambition.

She glanced at herself in her bedroom mirror. Her cheeks were flushed, her hair mussed. She quickly threw on a fresh blouse, smoothed her hair and hurried downstairs.

The sisters were no longer there. She glanced around the foyer, puzzled. Then she heard voices from the kitchen.

"Mil, please come out."

"No! I'm busy."

She hurried into the kitchen and stopped abruptly. Muriel was kneeling by the old broom closet in the pantry, pulling out a dustpan. She threw it behind her. Around her lay scattered a mop, a bucket, several pristine scrub brushes and three bottles of cleaners.

Kate prayed Muriel hadn't found a dead rodent. That was the last thing she needed. Although it wouldn't have been the first rat she'd encountered today.

A broom skittered by her feet. Muriel leaned farther into the closet. An empty paint can rolled across the floor.

Enid threw Kate an apologetic look. "I'm so sorry. I went to the bathroom, and when I came back, Muriel was in your closet."

"What's she doing?" Kate asked, looking at the mess in dismay. She stuck out a foot to stop the rolling paint can and picked it up.

"Mil, please get up," Enid said. She tugged on her sister's arm, but she was no match for Muriel's size.

"Get a sun bright," Muriel called, her voice muffled.

"A what?" Kate asked, stepping closer.

"A flashlight," Enid translated.

"I have one over here." Kate hurried to the kitchen drawer. "But what is she doing?"

"She is looking for a hidden staircase we used to play on as children." Sadness muted the sky blue of her eyes.

Kate glanced at the clock. The dog-bone-shaped hand had moved past the five. "We have to get going."

Enid lowered her voice. "I'm concerned she might lose it if we force her to leave."

"Lose it?"

"She can have these violent outbursts. Don't worry," Enid said hurriedly at Kate's look of concern, "she's never hurt me."

Kate frowned. She could either let Muriel tear apart her closet or deal with the tantrum of a demented lady. Tension pushed against the walls of her chest. What had she done to deserve a day like this? First Bob Duggan, then John Lyons, and now Muriel. "Is she almost done?"

Something snapped loudly inside the closet.

"I think so," Enid said with a wry look.

Kate turned on the flashlight and stood behind the old lady, sweeping the light around the closet. She stifled a gasp. Muriel had pulled away one corner of an old bookcase that had been propped on the floor and nailed to the back wall. It was only about three feet high, a rickety old thing, and the middle of the shelves sagged under the weight of ancient paint cans. Kate had meant to clean it out when she moved in. But like most of her good intentions about her house, she hadn't gotten around to it. LMB had taken over. Now the cans lay in haphazard piles on the floor around Muriel's feet.

Muriel gripped the edge of the shelf that had been loosened and pulled again. A sharp cracking sound startled them both. One of the sides of the bookcase broke off and fell to the floor with a crash.

"Help me," Muriel said. Kate reached around her and

gingerly pulled the pieces of the shelf out. She tried to not let her dismay show on her face. She'd have to buy another bookcase now.

"Ah," Muriel said. She leaned forward and ran her finger along the back wall.

"Did you find it, Mil?" Enid asked, peering over Muriel's other shoulder.

Kate aimed the flashlight at the now-empty space. The wall was painted a dark brown. In the dim light of the closet it was hard to make out anything.

Kate peered deeper into the shadows. "Is that a door?"

Muriel ran her fingers along the edge of a small cupboard door. It was about the same height as the bookshelf, and had been painted over to blend in with the walls.

Enid clapped her hands. "You did find it after all!" She turned to Kate. "This door leads to a secret passageway."

A shiver ran up Kate's spine. She didn't like the sound of that. At all. It hadn't seemed real until now. Now it had all kinds of unpleasant potential. "Where does it go?"

"It leads to a set of stairs. They end in the linen closet."

"Upstairs?"

"Yes." Enid smiled dreamily. "We had such fun playing in it with the Hansen children. We used to pretend the linen closet was a turret and we had to rescue the princess."

Muriel grunted, her shoulders straining as she tried to loosen the door from its seal of paint. She pulled again. The door popped open a few inches. Kate marveled at her strength. She was incredibly strong for her age.

Dusty, stale air escaped from the crack. Kate shone the flashlight inside. Muriel and Enid strained to see. A heavy cobweb hung above the door. Muriel pushed it away impatiently.

Enid gripped Muriel's shoulder. "It hasn't changed much, has it?"

Muriel shook her head. Tears swam in her eyes. "We had so many happy times, Enie," she whispered.

"I know." Enid pulled gently on Muriel's arm. "We have to go now. Ms. Keane is waiting for us. Perhaps Kate would let us come back and explore sometime."

Kate nodded, bemused. Her house had a secret passage? The old ladies were delighted with their find. The more Kate thought about it the less she liked it. The linen closet sat right outside her bedroom. She had a sudden image of someone or something—like a rat—creeping up the stairs in the middle of the night. And then creeping into her room.

"Come on, Mil." Enid turned to the door. "We can't keep Ms. Keane waiting."

Muriel rose reluctantly, throwing one last glance into the cupboard. Kate nudged a path through the scattered cleaning supplies with her foot.

"I'm so sorry, dear." Enid looked stricken as she surveyed the mess. She plucked a dish towel off the floor and folded it into a precise rectangle that Kate knew she would never be able to replicate even with twice the time.

"I'll clean it up when I get home," Kate said, taking the towel and placing it on the table. She gave Enid a reassuring smile. "Don't worry about it." She was glad, in a way, that Muriel had found the secret passageway. Now she knew it was there. Once Muriel and Enid explored it, she would nail it closed. Properly this time.

The traffic wasn't so bad going into the downtown area—everyone was leaving it—and they arrived at Keane's Funeral Home around 5:40 p.m. Kate held the car door open while Enid and Muriel climbed out of the backseat. Grabbing her purse, she followed the sisters up the walkway to the ornately columned building. Enid charged ahead, her back already stiffening with indignation. Kate forced herself to keep up. She'd thought she'd excised her old fears with her last visit, but they surged again, tangling her feet.

Anna Keane met them at the door. She was wearing a pale pink skirt, crumpled from the heat of the day, and a light silk blouse. Kate bet the funeral director had been waiting for them, waiting to finish with this one last client before going home to enjoy the gorgeous May evening. She hoped that Enid would give Anna Keane a chance to explain her actions.

"Miss Richardson," Anna Keane said warmly, but her gaze slid past Enid to Kate. Surprise and something else flashed through her eyes before she shook Enid's hand and ushered them all in. "You said on the phone that you had a change of mind?" she asked, leading them to her office.

"Yes, we need to discuss some things," Enid said briskly. "I brought my lawyer with me."

Anna Keane threw a startled glance at Kate. "Ms. Lange is your lawyer?"

"You know her?" Enid asked.

"I've met Ms. Keane on a different business matter," Kate said. She kept her tone casual, warm. She didn't want the meeting to get off on the wrong foot.

They filed into Anna Keane's office. This time the flower arrangement on the conference table was a grouping of pale yellow daffodils. Their petals wilted in the warm, airless room.

"Please, have a seat," Anna Keane said. "May I offer you some tea or coffee?" Kate watched Anna Keane go smoothly through the motions of making her "guests" comfortable.

"No, thank you," Enid said. She pulled out a set of

papers from her purse. "Ms. Keane, I would like to cancel my contract with you and get a full refund."

Kate watched Anna Keane's face closely. She gave nothing away. She was probably used to having irate customers. Death was a touchy subject for some people.

"I'm sorry you have changed your mind, Miss Richardson." Her eyes searched Enid's face. "May I inquire why?"

Kate held her breath. Enid was working herself into a snit. Bright spots of color burned under her carefully applied face powder. "Because you tried to trick me into signing over my sister's body!"

Muriel blinked. "My body? You are taking my body?" She wrapped her arms around herself. "No, no. You can't do that!"

Enid placed a hand on her arm. "No, Mil, it's okay. That's not what I meant." She turned her gaze to Anna Keane. "A poor choice of words on my part. But according to my lawyer—" she threw a quick glance at Kate, her eyes seeking reassurance "— I cannot sign a consent form to donate my sister's—" she jerked her head in Muriel's direction "— you know."

Kate nodded. "That's correct—"

"I never suggested you could," Anna Keane shot back.

"Pardon me?" Enid recoiled. "You most certainly did. You said that since I had power of attorney for my sister I could sign the consent form."

"I am afraid you misunderstood me, Miss Richardson," Anna Keane said. Her tone was gentle, patient. She threw Kate a concerned look. "I said that Miss Richardson could sign a form for herself. I never suggested she sign one for her sister."

"That's not true!" Enid glared at her, then turned to Kate. "I told you she was trying to deceive me!"

Anna Keane threw Kate another concerned look. Her brows rose meaningfully. Neither Kate nor Enid could miss the implication that Anna Keane thought Enid was suffering from the same disease as her sister.

Surprise shot through Kate. She thought the funeral director had more empathy than that. She returned Anna Keane's look with a cool frown. But the funeral director's implication wormed its way into her mind. Was Enid showing the first signs of dementia? Alzheimer's ran in families, didn't it?

Kate glanced sideways at Enid. Her cheeks were pink, her mouth a tight line. She didn't look as if she was suffering from dementia…but didn't these things creep up slowly?

She gave herself a mental shake. Enid was as sharp as she was. Probably sharper.

"I can assure you that I acted in good faith, Miss Richardson," Anna Keane said. "I apologize if you misunderstood me. But I never, ever counsel family members to donate their relatives' bodies to science. That would be unethical." She folded her hands in front of her. "If you would like me to refund your deposit, I would be happy to do so." Her tone suggested that not only would she be happy to refund the money, she would be relieved to get rid of them.

Enid stood. "I did not misunderstand you, Ms. Keane," she said stiffly. "I can see you are unwilling to admit to your deceit." Kate flinched inwardly at Enid's choice of words. The funeral director continued to give Enid the same concerned, patient look.

Enid scowled. "You can send the check in the mail." She picked up her bag. "Come on, Muriel, we need to go."

"Yes, Enie." Muriel rose and held out her hand to Kate. "It was a pleasure." Kate took her hand and led her gently to the door.

Kate glanced back at the table. "Did you want to keep the book, Ms. Keane?" It was lying off to the side.

"No. Thank you. I don't require it." Anna Keane smiled again at Kate. The message was clear: it wasn't Anna who had gotten things wrong.

Enid's shoulders stiffened. She hooked her arm through Muriel's and the two women headed toward the main entrance.

Kate strode back to the table and picked up the book, aware of Anna Keane's eyes on her. The funeral director had let her down today with her blatant condescension toward the elderly ladies.

As if she sensed Kate's irritation, Anna Keane stepped around the table and laid a hand on her arm. "I am sorry for the misunderstanding. I think Miss Richardson may have some problems herself."

Kate studied Anna Keane's face. Her expression was bland, but her eyes looked tired. A sheen of sweat gleamed on her forehead. The air was stifling. Today's heat had been unexpected. The air conditioners hadn't caught up to it.

"These things happen," Kate said. It was entirely feasible that Enid had misunderstood Anna Keane. But she didn't think so. Enid was a pretty sharp bird. Anna Keane hadn't said anything to convince Kate that Enid was wrong.

She gently removed her arm from Anna Keane's grasp and walked to the door. "Goodbye, Ms. Keane. I hope you get to enjoy the sun while it lasts."

Anna Keane glanced through her window. The sun had performed its final magic trick for the day, transforming into a fiery orange ball, its rays gilding the roofs of the cars driving by. "By the time I get out of here, the sun will be gone."

Her words echoed in Kate's ears as she hurried to the entrance. The walls of the foyer pressed in on her. She needed to feel the sun one final time today. She flung open the main door, forcing herself not to run down the stairs. Sunshine warmed her hair as she strode to her car. Enid and Muriel were already there, waiting for her.

"That woman!" Enid said as soon as Kate was close enough to hear. "She's a liar!" She gripped her purse with white fingers.

"I know." Kate opened the door for her. "I think she made a mistake and she can't own up to it."

Enid guided Muriel into the backseat and slid in next to her. "Oh, no, it wasn't just a mistake." She looked up at Kate. "She tried to trick me."

Kate studied her face. "Are you sure?"

Enid pulled a folded paper out of her purse. "I picked this up on my way out." She waved it in front of Kate's nose. Kate unfolded the document—making sure she stood behind the open door of the car so Anna Keane couldn't see her from her window.

She scanned the text. Enid had taken a consent form for donating bodies. Kate silently admired the elderly lady's gumption. When she reached the final words at the bottom, she had to reread them to make sure she had understood them correctly: *You can make your loved one's final act benefit the good of mankind. Donate his or her body to the Neuromuscular Motor Study, headed by renowned Hollis University researcher Dr. Ronald Gill, and help change people's lives.*

"What did I tell you?" Enid said. "She's a liar."

"Where did you get this?" Kate asked. She hadn't seen this in the funeral literature displayed in the foyer.

"There's a drawer in the table that holds the usual brochures. I saw Anna Keane get the form out of there the first time so I knew where to look. She thinks I'm losing my marbles, but there's still juice left in this old noggin." She tapped her head.

"May I keep this?" Kate asked. "I'd like to pay a visit to Dr. Gill."

Enid's eyes gleamed. "You do that. See what he has to say for himself." She glanced at her sister, who gave her a tremulous smile. "And make it clear that no matter what greatness he thinks he's doing for mankind, he is doing it at the expense of vulnerable people like us." Enid took Muriel's hand in hers.

Kate closed the back door of the car and slid into the driver's seat. It was stuffy in the car. She rolled down the window, then, remembering the ladies in her backseat, rolled it up halfway. She eased out into traffic, her mind on their meeting with Anna Keane.

The funeral director must have been lying. Man, she was good. Kate had completely fallen for her compassionate funeral director shtick. And yet, was it all an act? She really thought she had glimpsed some empathy warming Anna Keane's eyes.

But empathy only went so far. She had tried to trick Enid into signing over Muriel's body to Dr. Gill's research program. Was it just an overzealous attempt to help medical research? Or was there some other agenda in play?

Kate glanced in her rearview mirror. Enid was brushing some lint off Muriel's old black coat. Muriel must be boiling. She bit back a smile when she saw Enid roll her window down all the way. No frail old ladies in her car, at least not in the typical sense.

Twenty minutes later she pulled her car into the Richardson sisters' driveway.

"Would you like to come in for tea?" Enid held Muriel's door open for her.

"Could we have tea on the weekend?" Kate asked. "I really need to get home right now." She was longing for a shower. She wanted to stand under the stream of warm water and wash off the sweat of the day, the rankness of her meeting with John Lyons, the sourness of her encounter with Anna Keane.

"Of course, dear." Enid touched Kate's arm. "Thank you for coming." She pulled Muriel's hand. "Come on, Mil. It's time for supper."

Kate watched them walk together into their house. The front porch, although sagging in a few spots, was framed by a vibrant show of spring flowers. Muriel's handiwork, Kate guessed.

She drove to her home, a scant three houses away. She was struck by the contrast of her property with the Richardsons'. There were no spring bulbs in front of her home to refresh the drab olive paint. She really needed to get the house painted. Of course, she really needed to have the money for it.

Then she noticed the gleaming black truck of Alaska's dog walker. It was parked by the curb. She sighed and swiped her hair off her forehead. She wasn't in the mood for Finn. What she really wanted was to take that shower, have a glass of wine, relax over a magazine. And figure out how she could have been such a dupe.

Her lips twisted as she put the key into her lock. She was angry with herself. Angry that she had let herself be swayed by John Lyons' big promises—didn't she know better? Angry that she'd been fooled by Anna Keane's brown eyes.

35

Kate unlocked the door. Alaska came bounding through the kitchen doorway, his tongue lolling. He stuck his damp nose in her hand. She patted him, staring through the empty doorway. Everything was silent.

She walked into the kitchen. "Finn, are you in here?"

An off-key whistle made her jump. *Geez.* Any and every little thing was spooking her. She needed to relax. Finn still hadn't seen her. He was leaning into the closet. He was wearing a pair of faded jeans and a T-shirt. The T-shirt had hiked up around a strong, muscular waist. The whistle changed into a cheerful version of "California Dreamin'."

"Hi, Finn," she said loudly.

"Oh, hi." He turned, swinging a paint can in each large hand. Kate noted he still wore the leather thong around his wrist. It emphasized the corded muscles and tendons in his forearm.

She glanced at the pantry. Her mop and broom leaned obediently against the wall. The bucket and dustpan were pushed to the side. "You've been busy."

She knew she should feel grateful that Finn was helping clean up Muriel's mess. But instead, her stomach was a tight ball. It hadn't occurred to her when she gave Finn her house key a week ago that he would go inside her home. But of course he would. He had to get Alaska, find his leash, make sure he was okay. But still…did he just go into the kitchen when he picked up Alaska?

Or did he stroll through the upstairs, checking out her medicine cabinet, her filing cabinet, her underwear?

Stop it. This was Finn, not some psychopath.

And yet her unease remained. She eyed him. He looked his usual laid-back self. How could a guy like Finn be a creep? Then again, how could her mentor screw her like that? How could Anna Keane deceive vulnerable elderly ladies?

Had Finn deceived her, too, when he denied seeing her at Lisa's funeral? But if so, why?

"I brought Alaska back. He was really thirsty since it was so hot out. I went to fill up his water bowl and then I saw all this stuff—" He jerked his head in the direction of the mess. "I couldn't leave him alone." Finn kept his tone light but there was reproof in his gaze.

"I was in a rush." She felt as if she'd just been caught for being a delinquent mother. *Was that how Judge Carson felt?* The thought flashed like quicksilver through her mind, startling her. She banished it. She wouldn't think about Lisa MacAdam or her mother anymore. Case closed, at least for her.

She picked up a can from the floor and smiled sheepishly. "You're right. I should've thought of that. I'm still new at this."

He glanced around, his gaze falling on the collapsed bookcase. "So were you practicing your karate moves?"

A laugh escaped her. It had the unmistakable note of unease in it. "No, my neighbors did this."

"Fierce neighbors."

The thought of Enid and Muriel karate chopping the

bookcase made Kate smile. "They used to play in this house when they were little. They're elderly now. Anyway, they wanted to show me—" She stopped. She hadn't meant to tell anyone about the secret passage. Certainly not Finn.

"This?" he asked. He stepped into the closet.

"Yeah." She nodded. The door was pretty obvious now that it wasn't hidden behind paint cans.

Finn tugged at it. It swung completely open.

"Cool." He stuck his head in the opening. "Holy crow, there's a set of stairs!"

He pulled back and faced Kate. Boyish excitement shone from his eyes. "Have you gone up there yet?"

"No." She peered through the opening. Stale, musty air tinged with a rotting smell—she bet there was at least one dead mouse in there—met her nostrils. It was dark. Gloomy. In the dimness she could make out the first three steps. "I'm not sure I want to go up. It just leads to the linen closet."

"Oh, come on, Kate."

She did not have the energy for this today. She was still in major piss-off mode. "No." She added for good measure, "In fact, I'm going to nail it shut."

He eyed the doorway with a final, longing glance. "You sure I can't convince you?"

She could tell by the look in his eyes that he was caving in. The tension eased out of her neck. She nodded. "Yes."

"Then I'll help you board it up."

"Finn, you don't need to do this. I can handle this." She wanted to be alone. "Besides, I don't have any nails."

He gave her a little smile. "Hang on a sec. I've got some supplies in my truck."

He came back a minute later with a box of nails, a hammer and a handsaw. The hammer was paint splattered and obviously an old favorite. The saw, however, gleamed with the pristine shininess of new ownership.

He put them down carefully and retrieved a long plank from the broken bookcase.

"You're going to use that?" Kate eyed the busted board.

"Once I clean up the edges it'll be perfectly fine," he said. He braced the plank on the edge of the counter and picked up the saw. "Isn't it a beauty?" he asked her. "I just got it."

"Very nice," Kate murmured. She wasn't going to deflate his obvious enjoyment of his new tool. *Men and their tools.* She thought longingly of her glass of wine. Her magazine. A hot shower.

He carefully sliced off the ragged edges of the plank, humming "California Dreamin'" under his breath. "There," he said, carrying it to the closet. "I need your help," he added pointedly.

"All right," she groaned. She followed him reluctantly into the cramped cupboard.

Finn handed her the plank. It was heavy. "Now, if you just hold this up against the door, I can nail it shut."

She bent over and held the plank against the door with one hand.

He stood behind her. "No, I need you to brace it, like this." He knelt down in front of the door and held the plank against it, his arms spread-eagled.

He got up. "Got it?"

"Yes." *Sir,* she almost murmured. It was easier for him—he wasn't in a skirt. She got down on her knees, and held the plank the way he demonstrated. *I better start doing weights again. This is harder than it looks.* Her cheek was pressed against the plank, her arms spread-eagled against each edge.

He backed away. She heard him breathe deeply.

From the very corner of her eye, she saw him pick up the saw.

He fingered the blade. The humming stopped.

He turned. And, in the silence, Kate suddenly thought of Lisa MacAdam. Her limbs had been cut off.

As had the killer's other victims.

There was a blond guy, Shonda had said. *With dogs. Asking about Lisa.*

And the funeral… *Hadn't Ethan said the killer was there?*

He stepped toward her.

There was something in the air between them, something that sucked the oxygen out.

It was fear.

She dropped the plank, scrambling to her feet as the board crashed to the ground.

He jumped. The saw jerked in his hand. "What the hell?" He looked at Kate in alarm. "Are you okay? Did you hurt yourself?"

She backed out of the closet and rubbed her hand. Blood welled in a scratch on her palm. "I snagged it on a nail, I think."

"Here, let me see." He put the saw on the counter and took her hand. "You need some antibiotic cream on this. Let me wash it for you."

He seemed for all the world like a concerned father. And yet, for a moment in the closet, Kate felt something else. Something that had terrified her.

It was his saw. Why had he picked up the saw and not the hammer? "I thought you were going to nail the board," she said, trying to keep her voice casual.

"I was." He stared at her in surprise. "But when you held up the board I noticed I'd missed an edge. I was just going to touch it up first."

Had she overreacted?

She studied his face. There were no signs of deadly intent in his eyes, no sign of murderous rage, no sign of malice. Just his usual warm, friendly gaze.

How could she have thought all those things about him? She couldn't believe what stress and exhaustion could do to an otherwise rational mind. She hoped he hadn't seen the fear in her eyes.

She gently tugged her hand free. "It's okay. I was going to get a shower this evening, anyway."

"Me, too."

He threw that tidbit toward her. She knew she could rise to the bait and they'd be naked in the shower before she could say "pretty please." And it was a ludicrous thought after the paralyzing terror she had felt being alone in the closet with him. But because of its ludicrousness, it was reassuring. It showed her, more than anything else, how extreme her reaction had been. She felt the tension ease out of her. "Thanks for all your help today."

He gave a rueful grin. "Sorry about trying to use the old plank. I'll get some two-by-fours next week."

"Thank you."

Alaska padded toward him. He stroked the dog's head. "See you tomorrow, buddy." He picked up his toolbox and pushed open the kitchen door. "Bye, Kate. Have a good evening."

"You, too." She watched him cross the deck. The evening carried a light breeze with a hint of damp in it. Fog was moving in.

She closed the door. Then locked it. She tottered over to a kitchen chair and sank into it. She felt chilled despite the lingering heat of the day. She doubted a hot shower would be the ticket. The chill went deeper, beyond the skin and into the bone. And every time she walked into this house, it burrowed even deeper.

36

Tuesday, May 15, 8:00 p.m.

Ethan walked casually down Agricola Street, his eyes skimming the doorways and alleys. The old north end street was lined with buildings that had gone from being elegant and proud a century ago to derelict and forgotten. But the street was on an upswing. In the past five years, interior design and antique furniture businesses had "rediscovered" Agricola. New paint in updated historic colors picked out the beautiful Victorian trim on the houses. During the day, the street didn't look half-bad.

At night, it was a different story. The trendy businesses hadn't been successful in doing away with the some of the more established enterprises. When dusk fell, crack whores and pimps crawled out of the woodwork.

He strode toward a pair of women, one black, one white, both stoned. They were leaning against a wrought-iron railing in front of a weed-filled yard. A derelict rooming house loomed above them.

"Want somethin', hon?" one of the women called out.

He stopped in front of them. "'Evenin', ladies," he said.

The black woman shimmied forward. She seemed less

stoned than the white girl, who looked barely sixteen and was so out of it that Ethan wondered how she remained standing.

He fished around in his pocket. The black woman smiled encouragingly. "Fifty for a blow, a hunred for anythin' else."

There was an edge of desperation in her gaze that made Ethan want to take her away someplace safe. God only knew what she was willing to do for a hundred bucks. "Not tonight, hon." He smiled to take the sting away.

She stepped back, tottering in her latex stiletto boots. Her gaze flickered over him. "You're a cop."

"Yeah." He pulled out a photo. "You seen him 'round?" It was a mug shot of Mark "the Shark" Arnold.

The prostitute barely glanced at the picture. "Nah." She stepped back against the railing and began scanning the street for possibilities. Ethan pocketed the photo. "Do you know where Shonda is?" he asked.

She jerked her chin toward the corner.

"Thanks." He slid his hands into his jacket pockets and headed down the street. The day had been clear, but fog was moving in. He wanted to find Shonda before it became hard to see.

A girl stood with her back to him, talking to a prostitute. The woman glanced over the girl's shoulder, said something hurriedly under her breath and left.

The girl stuffed a bag in her pocket and began to walk down the street. Ethan hurried after her.

"Shonda," he called her name softly. He didn't want to scare her away.

She quickened her pace. He broke into a light jog. "Shonda! I just want to talk. That's all."

She glanced over her shoulder. Her gaze was cool, direct. Ethan was relieved. She wasn't high. He might get some information from her.

He fell into step next to her. "You're Shonda, right?"

She nodded.

He smiled. "I'm Ethan." They walked past a little hole-in-the-wall coffee shop. "Can I buy you a coffee?"

She stopped in front of him. "I already spoke to the cops."

"I know. We just have a few more questions."

She crossed her arms. "What about?"

"About the guy who killed your friend Lisa."

"Yeah?"

He'd got her attention. Hopefully, he'd get the truth with it.

"You were the last person to see Lisa alive. Did you see anyone pick her up that night?"

She shook her head. "I already told the cops I didn't."

"What about Krissie Burns?"

She chewed her lower lip. Ethan noticed that her teeth were large and very white. "I didn't see her at all last weekend."

"And Karen?"

She shrugged. "She disappeared. We thought she was out west."

"So you never saw anyone pick up these girls?" Ethan tried to contain his frustration. How could the killer pick off his victims and no one notice him?

"The only time I ever saw anyone pick up someone was with Vangie."

Vangie? The name was familiar. "What was her last name?"

Shonda pulled at her lip. "White. I mean, Wright."

Vangie Wright.

Suddenly he heard Kate's voice: *There was another girl. Her name was Vangie Wright. She's still missing. But*

*the police told Shonda that she took so long to file the
report she'd be hard to track down."*

He remembered passing this information on to
Ferguson. Had she given it to Vicky?

Could Vangie Wright be their still-unidentified victim
number three?

Vangie Wright went missing a year and a half ago, if he
remembered Kate's information correctly. But victim number
three's body wasn't decomposed. She'd been killed recently.

The killer could have held her captive for months and
then butchered her.

He breathed out slowly. "Tell me what she looked like."

"Real tiny, like a bird."

This did not sound like their latest girl. "How old was
she?"

Shonda shrugged. "'Bout thirty. But she looked like
an old bag."

This definitely wasn't the newest victim. "Tell me about
Vangie. What happened to her?"

"She went off in a car with some guy and disappeared."

Ethan searched her eyes. They were bloodshot but clear.
She was telling the truth.

"When was this?"

She frowned. "A coupla years ago?"

He pulled out the photo of Mark Arnold, although he
hadn't been released from prison when Vangie Wright went
missing. "Did the guy who picked up Vangie look like this?"

She shook her head. "Nah." She chewed her lip. Finally
she said, "I dunno. I never saw the guy. He just pulled over
and Vangie got in the car with him. They drove off."

"What did the car look like?"

"I dunno." She squinted off beyond Ethan's shoulder for
a minute. "It was just a car, ya know?"

"Big, small, hatchback, sedan?"

"Medium. I guess a sedan?"

"Do you remember the color?"

She gazed past him for another second. "It was a dark night, kinda drizzly. All I remember is that the car was shiny."

"Metallic shiny?"

"Yeah."

"Gold, silver?"

"Dunno." She pulled at her lip. "Silver, I think."

Ethan put the photo of Arnold back in his jacket and gave Shonda his card. "If you see your friend Vangie again, or if you remember anything else, call me."

She nodded. Ethan was reassured to see her slip his card into her back pocket. "Ya think Vangie got knocked off by this guy?"

"Hard to say." His gaze sought Shonda's. She looked so young and yet so old. "If you see the car again, call the cops right away, you hear me?"

"Yeah." She studied Ethan. "Besides that lawyer, you're the only one who seems to give a shit 'bout Vange."

"What lawyer?"

"Kate somebody." She stuffed her hands into her pockets. "I thought she was gonna figure out what happened to Vange." She shrugged. "But she passed it on to the cops."

He smothered his surprise. So Kate had listened to his concerns. "I'm gonna look into it." As an afterthought, he added, "Has anyone else approached you about Lisa?"

She shrugged. "Just a friend of hers."

Jesus. "A friend?"

"Yeah. A blond guy. He had a couple of dogs with him. I think he walks them or somethin'." She shrugged. "I don't remember his name. But I saw him at Lisa's funeral."

His mind raced. A blond guy at Lisa's funeral? He remembered a fair-haired man, edging his way toward Kate when she was fainting. "If you remember his name or if he comes around again, call me." He felt a stirring of alarm for this too-old kid. "Don't talk to him, okay? And in the meantime, keep an eye out for yourself."

She hunched her shoulders. "Yeah, like you care."

He watched her go up the street and disappear into a house. Time for another hit.

He walked back to his car. His gut was churning big-time. It was either a sign he'd had too much pizza or he was on to something.

His cell rang.

"Drake here."

"Ethan? It's Deb. We ID'd our girl." Ferguson's voice sounded perturbed.

"Yeah?" He switched on the ignition. The car rumbled to life.

"You better come down."

37

Tuesday, May 15, 9:00 p.m.

Kate put the vacuum back into the closet and leaned against the door. She was so tired she could barely move.

But the house was clean.

Boy, was it clean.

Once Finn left, she had wolfed down her dinner. The terror she'd felt in the closet had given her a new appreciation for life. It filled her with restless energy.

She washed the dishes, tidied up the rest of the mess in the kitchen, scrubbed the floors and vacuumed round one of Alaska's shedding.

While her body worked, her mind sifted through the layers of intrigue that had suddenly been revealed. John Lyons had blown all of her previous assumptions about her position in LMB out of the water. She'd been stunned initially, as if she had bitten into a cake she'd been craving and discovered it was full of pepper.

But then it became abundantly clear that John Lyons knew something about TransTissue that he didn't want her to find. It was the only explanation she could come up with. Why else would he settle a case that could clear his client's reputation? Why else had he been deliberately obtuse about her efforts to trace the supply chain of tissue?

She had the sinking feeling he hadn't expected her to do that. That her initiative, her smarts, had surprised him.

Was that why he'd given her the case? Because he thought she wouldn't dig deep enough?

Was that why he hired her?

She straightened.

She needed to find out what was going on. If Brad Gallivant and Denise Rogers had in fact been infected by contaminated tissue from TransTissue, there could be any number of people also infected by tissue products that TransTissue hadn't screened properly.

The implications of this were far-reaching. Alarming. Much bigger than a lone bad batch of product. Under normal circumstances the first person she should call would be the firm's managing partner.

But Randall Barrett had shown he was capable of deception.

Who knew, he could be in on whatever this was.

And there wasn't anyone else at LMB she could trust. She was the outsider. Everything would get back to the senior partners.

If she was going to get to the bottom of this, she needed to do it on her own. Pretend that she bought John's story lock, stock and barrel, while gathering enough information to notify the authorities.

At this point, all she knew—rather, all she *suspected*— was that John was covering up something. She didn't know what, if anything, TransTissue was covering up. It would be a breach of her fiduciary duty to her client to jump the gun until she had more proof than five identical viral-screening reports.

What kind of proof she was looking for, she didn't know. But she had a feeling that TransTissue's tissue supplier might have that answer.

"Who is she?" Ethan asked. He strode toward the group of detectives clustered around the boardroom table.

Ferguson turned. The strain of the investigation was showing. Her freckles stretched across her cheekbones. "Her name was Sara Harper." She stepped around the group and waved him over to the other end of the table. "I've just finished briefing the team. I'll give you an update."

He leaned a hip against the table. "Who ID'd her?"

"Her parents." Ferguson's gaze flickered to Lamond. The constable was sitting at the other end of the table, by himself. Telling the parents that their daughter had fallen prey to a sick and savage killer—one that they had failed to catch after two victims—would be something that would probably stay with him for the rest of his life.

"So what's the story on her?" Ethan pulled out his notepad.

Ferguson flipped open a file on the table. "She's from Montana. She was doing summer courses at Hollis U."

Ethan's brows rose. Not the killer's usual victim. No wonder Ferguson looked stressed. A different victim typology was like a mutating virus. They wouldn't know where the killer would strike next.

"So how'd he get to her?"

"She went downtown with her girlfriend. The girlfriend hooked up with some guy, and she was left to go home on her own. She didn't have much money so she walked."

"Shit." He could picture this all too easily. A struggling student spends her cash on a few drinks, then discovers her friend has made other plans. "Why wasn't she reported missing earlier?"

"The parents were away in Europe, and the victim had planned to go to Toronto the next day—hence the reason she was saving her money—so her friends assumed she'd gone." Ferguson shrugged. "She lived alone. A perfect storm."

"Tell me about it. Where'd she get picked up?"

"She was caught on video surveillance walking down Barrington. She lived on Fenwick. We think she was picked up on the south end of Morris."

Close to the granary. And the cemetery. Ethan drained his coffee. "How'd he kill her?"

"Same way. He drugged her, then strangled her."

"Any signs of sexual assault?"

"No."

"So his M.O. is the same except for the victim?"

"Yeah. He seems to be getting a little sloppier. The victim wasn't laid out as straight as the last time. Looked like he was in a hurry."

A tingle of excitement ran through him. This was good news. He peered over Ferguson's shoulder at the M.E. report she had in her hand.

"Any trace on the body?"

"A fiber in her hair."

"That's it?"

"Yeah." Ferguson put down the report. "The lab says it matches the one found on Lisa MacAdam. Probably car seat fiber."

"So he killed them in the car, and then took them somewhere else to cut them up."

"Just like the others." She pushed her hair back. It was lank. Like everyone on the team, no one was getting home. "What's your status?"

"I finished tracking down Arnold. I spoke with Judge Carson—she just got appointed to the Supreme Court—"

Ferguson gave a low whistle.

"She says Arnold threatened her fifteen years ago. She hasn't heard anything from him since."

"So is he the type to stalk quietly or does he need the attention?" Ferguson's gray-green eyes probed Ethan's.

"He killed his girlfriend in a fit of passion. He's not the type to plan this all out."

"Have you located him?"

That's where things didn't look too good for Arnold. "He's disappeared."

Ferguson raised a brow. "We need to track him down."

"I've alerted the other jurisdictions. There's a warrant out for him already." He leaned forward. "Listen, did Vicky get back to you about that missing prostitute? Name's Vangie Wright."

"Not much to it," Ferguson said briskly. "Her friend filed a missing persons report months after she went missing. Her trail was cold. Vicky did a cross-jurisdictional check for the past five years and no one's seen her. She checked the prisons. No sign of her in the past two years. She's got a request in with Cold Case. As well, she called Vangie Wright's sister, who told her she was really heavy into crack before she disappeared. And that she'd been diagnosed with some kind of illness that affects the brain." She shrugged. "She was a sick, heavily addicted crack whore from the sounds of it. She probably OD'd somewhere. But just in case, Vicky's put a call into the rehab centers and the loony wards."

"I don't know." Ethan rocked back on his heels. "I don't think Vangie Wright's in some ward."

Ferguson's gaze sharpened. "Why do you say that?"

"I took Arnold's mug shot to that drug dealing buddy

of Lisa MacAdam's—" He could see the girl's face per-
fectly in his head but her name just wouldn't come to him.
That's what a week of no sleep did to you. He flipped
open his notepad and searched for the name. "Shonda
Bryant. That's her street name. Found her on Agricola
Street selling dope. She hadn't seen Arnold around." His
eyes met Ferguson's. "Confirms our suspicions about him.
She said she saw Vangie Wright being picked up by a john
in a silver sedan—but that was before Arnold was released.
It was the last time Vangie Wright was seen."

"She never put that in the missing persons report."

"She's an addict, too, Deb. She probably didn't remember."

"So she's not a reliable witness."

"No…but I think she's telling the truth."

"Why?"

Ethan shrugged. "She has no reason not to."

Ferguson pressed her lips together. Finally, she said,
"Fine. We've got so little to go with right now, we can't
ignore this." She straightened and stepped back from the
table. Looking around the room, she announced: "All right,
everyone, we've got a new lead."

Lamond and Walker came over. "Is it Arnold?"

Ferguson shook her head. "No, Arnold isn't a contender.
He's gone AWOL so we've got a warrant out for him, but
that's not the lead." She shot a look at Ethan. "Tell them."

"We think that Krissie Burns wasn't the killer's first
victim."

Walker exchanged glances with Lamond. Ethan read the
look. More bad news.

"There was another prostitute who went missing two
years ago. She was picked up by a guy in a silver sedan
and never seen again." The detectives began making notes.

"She could be the first victim—or there could have been more before her." Ethan shrugged. "But she fits the typology: prostitute, same geographic area, same network of friends. We need to find her body."

Ferguson picked up her clipboard. "Lamond, get the lab on the phone and see if we can match the fiber to a silver sedan model, at least two years old. Walker, liaise with Vicky and get all her reports on this woman. Redding, I want you to go over the surveillance footage from the funeral and see if we can get a match on the car."

The detectives began writing down their tasks. "Ethan." Ferguson tapped the M.E.'s report with her fingernail. "We need to find the kill site. That's the key to this."

Adrenaline surged through him. This was the action he'd been craving. "The M.E. thinks that the killer has some specialized skill with dismemberment." He glanced around, a smile tugging his lips. "Anyone got plans to go under the knife?"

"Walker needs a boob job." Lamond smirked, reaching over and squeezing Walker's pec. Ethan bit back a snort. Walker was a body builder and he was always bragging that his pecs looked like the Rock's.

"Hey, don't knock 'em. The ladies love the look." Walker flexed his chest and threw Lamond a dirty look. "At least I don't need brain surgery."

"You'll both be getting lobotomies if you don't stop," Ferguson said briskly. They were feeble jokes, but everyone smiled. It helped ease the strain of the past few weeks. "Ethan, you're on the right track. I want you to go to the hospitals and check out the surgeons. See if there's been anything going on. Lamond, when you finish talking to the lab, you go with him to assist."

Ethan slipped his notebook back in his pocket. He tried to keep the elation from his face. He was back in action.

He couldn't wait to find out what those surgeons were up to. Scrub gowns could hide a multitude of sins.

38

Strangely, she had a great morning run.

After spending most of the night awake, Kate thought she'd lose steam halfway through the park, but her body hummed with energy. Next time she saw Finn, she'd have to thank him for scaring her out of her mind. It'd given her a real adrenaline rush. When she got home, Alaska flopped on his bed and refused to move until she poured his food.

She knew she'd pay the price later but right now she was filled with a sense of purpose. She put on her favorite suit. The new cream-colored one. She remembered she had it on the day Randall had assigned her the MacAdam case. She remembered the way he'd looked at her, the speculative gleam in his eyes. How the next time she met with him the speculative gleam had changed to a look that both terrified and excited her. And then John Lyons had assigned her the TransTissue file. She'd been so eager to show him what she could do.

But John Lyons had tried to use her. He had thought that if he put her on the TransTissue file—a newly admitted lawyer, an associate on probation with a lot to prove *and* a lot to lose—she'd be more concerned about pleasing him than digging too deeply in her client's ambiguous dealings.

It wasn't TransTissue that concerned her right now. It was John Lyons. He was hiding something.

She was going to find it, if it was the last thing she did. And she knew it would probably be the last thing she did at LMB.

Alaska lay on his bed, already dozing after his vigorous run and filling breakfast. She patted him goodbye. He thumped his tail softly.

She locked the door carefully and drove to her office. It was foggy, but there was a brightness behind the gray. The sun would break through later.

She pulled into the parkade and walked briskly to the elevator. A thought suddenly hit her. Maybe Bob Duggan hadn't asked her to be taken off the file. Maybe John Lyons had lied. Maybe he was trying to undermine her confidence so she wouldn't ask any more questions.

Jesus. Maybe, maybe, maybe. She glanced at her reflection in the mirrored wall of the elevator. No more maybes. Whatever John was up to, she wouldn't let him get away with it.

She'd spent the past fifteen years trying to regain her life. No one was going to screw with it.

It was time to hit the computer and see what kind of slimy trail her mentor had left behind.

Dr. Marilla Olsen shook Ethan's hand with a grip that was warm yet unrelenting. "Detective Drake, Detective Lamond," she said. "Please have a seat." She led them through her office door, which looked the same as all the other doors dotting the southwest corridor of the GH2.

Ethan and Lamond sat on the green office chairs facing

her desk. Ethan glanced around. Numerous framed diplomas and awards hung on the pale green wall behind her chair. A large photo was placed on one end of the credenza. It showed two smiling little girls, one with glasses and the other whose puff of black hair was pulled to the top of her head with a red elastic. The older girl had her mother's eyes, round and wide set.

Wouldn't he love to have two little girls to tickle. He'd thought he'd be a father in the next couple of years, sharing the joys and sleepless nights of a little Drake with Kate.

He tore his gaze away from the photo. Dr. Olsen moved behind her desk, folding her hands in front of her. She wore no wedding band. No jewelry at all, which he supposed was due to the nature of her work. She'd need her hands free and clear to handle the drills and saws required for orthopedic surgery.

"What can I do for you, detectives?" Dr. Olsen asked. Her voice was cool, as were her eyes. The police were never welcomed with open arms at the GH2. Dr. Olsen, Division Head of Surgery, had agreed very reluctantly to meet with them. He was sure she'd been thoroughly debriefed by the hospital administration's risk management team about what not to say. She now surveyed them with an expression that Ethan knew did not bode well for their investigation.

"Thank you for meeting with us on such short notice, Dr. Olsen," Ethan began. It was crucial to set the right tone with her. Intimidation or demands would just get her back up. Today would be about finesse; about two professions overlapping due to circumstances beyond their control; about each professional trying to do their job as best they could. "We are here regarding an investigation into the recent murders of several young girls."

Her eyebrows rose slightly. "Do you mean the judge's daughter?"

"Yes."

She processed that silently. She was not a woman who was easily discomfited, he could tell.

"Why does your investigation involve the hospital?" she asked finally.

"Based on certain findings that all the victims share, we have reason to believe the killer has a surgical background."

"I see."

He wasn't going to wait and see if she would add anything to that noncommittal response. He knew she wouldn't. He got straight to the point. "We would like to know if any of the surgeons operating out of the GH2 have been recently disciplined or have been behaving in a concerning manner."

There was a slight tightening of her hands.

Bingo.

"As you know, Detective Drake, disciplinary matters are held in strictest confidence. I am not at liberty to answer your question."

Lamond shifted in his seat. They'd expected this response, but Ethan had hoped that the brutality of the cases might loosen Dr. Olsen up a bit.

"Dr. Olsen, we have three dead girls. All of them were dismembered." She held his gaze but he thought he saw a flicker of uncertainty in her eyes. He leaned forward. "We need to catch this guy before he kills another girl."

"I understand." Her fingers tensed. "But you need to understand that I cannot disclose confidential information." She stood and walked around her desk. "I'm sorry."

"You must understand the gravity of the situation. This guy is on the prowl. And he knows what he is doing."

Her expression remained stony. "I am sorry, Detective." She walked to the door. "I wish I could be of help."

He made one last-ditch attempt. "You are in the business of saving lives, Dr. Olsen. That's what I try to do, too. We're on the same team."

She shook her head. "No, Detective, we are not. I have a duty to protect my staff." She held open the door. "Good day."

He glanced back at the photo of Dr. Olsen's daughters. He waited until her gaze followed his. "And I have a duty to protect the public." She couldn't miss his meaning. He turned toward the door. "If you decide you can help us, here's my card."

She nodded brusquely. "Good luck, Detective." She took his card and closed the door on their heels.

"Damn," he muttered. He'd hoped he could crack her.

Lamond said softly, "She knows something."

"Yeah. But how are we going to find out?"

They walked in silence down the long corridors, stopping to grab a coffee at the ubiquitous Tim Hortons counter in the lobby. His double-double didn't inspire any great ideas. They rode down the elevator.

Ethan drained his cup and tossed it in the garbage. "I think we'll have to start from the ground up and hope we hit on something."

"I thought this was the ground up." Lamond glanced around the underground parking.

Ethan rewarded his joke with a brief smile. He appreciated his partner's efforts to not let their latest disappointment defeat them. "A surgeon couldn't do a dismemberment in an O.R. suite, could he? Too many people around."

Lamond stared at him. "Yeah. You're right. So where do you think he'd do it? In his garage?"

"Maybe…" He waited until they were in his car. "Or

maybe he'd just go down to where the bodies were waiting for him." He threw Lamond a sideways glance.

When Lamond gave a rueful moan, he slapped Lamond on the back. "This time, though, don't throw up."

Dead ends. One after another.

She had a knack for finding them.

This time, John Lyons had led her on a merry chase. And so far, he was way ahead of her.

She stared at the Registry of Joint Stock Companies Web page and jabbed the Enter key on her computer dispiritedly. She had hoped that John Lyons might have inadvertently left a paper trail that would show his business interests. And possibly illuminate his connection to TransTissue. If ever a case reeked of conflict of interest, it was this one.

But as soon as the site loaded, she saw the first wrong assumption she'd made. She couldn't search by individual name. It had to be by business name. And she doubted that John Lyons would be listed in any official capacity with TransTissue.

The results scrolled on to her computer screen. She was right. TransTissue's registration was free and clear. No mention of John Lyons.

So TransTissue was a dead end. And since she couldn't search by an individual's name, John Lyons was a dead end. She nibbled on her lower lip. The U.S. cases had found the tissue suppliers—not the processors—guilty of negligence.

She straightened. She was starting at the wrong end. She needed to track down BioMediSol, see if she could get her hands on the original reports BioMediSol sent with the tissue used to make the product in Brad Gallivant's knee.

She typed *BioMediSol* in the Registry of Joint Stock Companies search engine. The results loaded on to the screen. She stared at them, puzzled. She'd expected BioMediSol to have an industrial address, a large corporate structure and company headquarters based in Toronto or the U.S.

Instead, BioMediSol was owned and operated by a man named Craig Peters. His civic address was an apartment on Church Street, Halifax. The business mailing address was a P.O. box.

She printed out the record. Church Street was in a densely populated south end neighborhood filled with old Victorian homes like hers. In fact, it wasn't too far away from where she lived.

Was this Craig Peters actually harvesting body parts in his apartment? She pictured blood dripping through the ceiling of the tenant beneath him.

Don't be ghoulish. It could all be perfectly legit.

There was only one way to find out.

She grabbed her purse.

39

"Detective Drake?"

The smooth tones of Dr. Olsen's voice filled Ethan's ear. His heart skipped, then resumed in double time. "Yes."

"I only have a minute. Don't ask me to repeat this."

Fortunately, she'd gotten him at his desk. Ethan flipped open his notepad.

"I'm not supposed to say anything, but I can't stop thinking about those girls…"

He waited.

She said softly, "We have one surgeon out on medical leave."

"Who?"

"Dr. Mike Mazerski. M-a-z-e-r-s-k-i. He's a neurosurgeon."

Ethan paused. The way the limbs had been removed from the victims, he'd been expecting an orthopedic surgeon. "Why is he on medical leave?"

"He'd been behaving erratically in the O.R. We put him on leave for psychiatric assessment on Friday."

Ethan's pulse accelerated. "We need to interview him and the O.R. team."

"I've done more than I should. I can't do any more than that, Detective."

The phone clicked in his ear.

The apartment buildings on Church Street were vintage south end Victorian. Sprawling and wood shingled, with attractive trims and balconies, some were nicely kept townhomes. Others were well past middle age and leaned wearily against one another.

Kate paused on the sidewalk and studied Craig Peters' building. It was smaller, more like a large house divided into flats. Run-down. In fact, typical student digs. She double-checked the number. She had the right place. But it seemed bizarre that this was the official domicile of the CEO of a tissue brokering company. Something was not adding up.

She walked up the stairs to the front door. Several apartment numbers were nailed to the wall. But not number four, Craig Peters' listed address.

She backed down the stairs. She double-checked the registry record she'd printed out. It clearly said apartment four.

She scanned the house again. On the far corner of the building by the driveway was a small four nailed to the wall. An arrow under it pointed to the back.

She stuffed the record in her purse and hurried down the driveway. It was narrow, probably an old carriage lane, but wide enough to squeeze a car through. When she reached the back, she saw there was a small paved parking lot. It was empty.

Three second-story balconies hung over the parking lot, jammed with the usual student accessories: empty beer cartons, barbecues and cheap plastic lawn furniture. A tattered Nova Scotia flag hung forlornly over the railing of one.

At the far end of the house she spotted a nondescript door. It sat in the shadow of the flag-draped balcony. She walked toward it. A small number four marked it as the final apartment of the building.

Taking a deep breath, she mentally ran through her story one more time. Posing as a features reporter was flimsy and completely unoriginal, but it was the best she could come up with on the seven-minute drive between Lower Water Street and Church. Her stomach churned. If the bar society found out what she was doing, she'd be screwed.

Remember why you are doing this, she told herself. If TransTissue or its supplier is using tainted tissue, more people's lives could be ruined.

She raised her fist and knocked on the door.

There was silence.

She knocked again, louder.

No reply.

Curtains were drawn across the small window by the door. It was impossible to tell if anyone was home.

She stepped back and gazed up at the other apartments. They, too, seemed empty. Unnaturally quiet for a building housing students.

It was as if everyone had fled.

A chill raised the flesh on her arms. She turned and walked quickly through the parking lot.

You are being ridiculous. You've come in the middle of the morning. Everyone's at work, or in classes. That's why there are no cars here. Or people.

She slowed down when she reached the street. A car drove past her, the driver mouthing the words to a song on his stereo. A cat ran lightly across the front porch of the house and disappeared into the loamy darkness under the stairs.

She climbed into her car and started the engine. With

the wheel under her hands, she relaxed. She drove down South Street toward the old train station and pulled over.

Chasing after BioMediSol wasn't the right way to get to them.

She'd have to get them to chase *her*.

She sat for ten minutes, thinking. Then she pulled out her cell phone and called directory assistance. Within minutes, she had reserved two meeting rooms at the Marley Hotel for the next evening. She'd stumbled a bit when they asked for the contact name, coming up with the orthopedic surgeon who was being sued by Brad Gallivant in the TransTissue file. *The bar society will really love this one—using the name of a co-defendant to cover up fraud.*

She knew she was taking a risk holding the rooms on her credit card, but all she could hope for was that no one at BioMediSol would think to ask.

Then she dialed the business number listed on Bio-MediSol's joint stock companies record.

She cursed herself for being a chicken and fleeing Craig Peters' front doorstep. If she'd stayed here, she might have heard the phone ring.

The line was picked up. She tensed.

"Good morning, BioMediSol, Inc.," a woman's voice said.

Kate cleared her throat. "Hello. I am calling from the Surgical Teaching Institute."

"Yes?" There was a polite hesitation. "I'm afraid I'm not familiar with that organization."

So BioMediSol had a keeper at the gate.

"We operate a mobile teaching unit under the auspices of the College of Physicians and Surgeons," Kate said coolly, grateful for the research she'd done on tissue products to prepare the TransTissue defense. Hopefully it was enough to let her bluff her way through this. "We rotate between all the major teaching hospitals in North America."

"We've never had the College of Physicians and Surgeons request tissue from us before." The woman sounded both suspicious and yet pleased at the same time.

"We usually get our supply from the medical school inventories. However, in this instance, we had a problem with the refrigeration…" She cleared her throat delicately. "And now we have a session scheduled for the day after tomorrow and we don't have any—" She was just about to say *props*. *Jesus*. That one deserved a smack in the forehead. *Think*. What did a doctor call them? Arms? Legs? Body parts? "—limbs. Your company was recommended to us by the orthopedic division of the GH2."

"I see." The woman's voice was definitely warmer. "And how can we help you, Dr….?"

"Dr. Tupper." Kate paused. Sir Charles Tupper was a great man in Nova Scotia's history. She prayed he wouldn't mind her invocation of his name. "I require eight pairs of arms by tomorrow evening so we can set them up for the following day."

"Tomorrow night?" The woman sounded dismayed. "I'm sorry, Dr. Tupper, but that would be very difficult."

"Don't you have any inventory you can draw on? I assure you that you will be well reimbursed for responding on such short notice."

The woman hesitated. "I'll do what I can. I think I have seven pairs I can send for sure. I'll see what I can do about the final pair."

Kate stared at her hand resting on the steering wheel. How exactly was BioMediSol planning to acquire the final pair?

"Where shall we have these delivered?" the woman asked briskly.

"We have a conference room booked at the Marley."

"Right. The delivery should arrive by 8:00 p.m. tomorrow evening. You will need to pay in full by certified check at that time."

"And what is your rate?"

"Fifteen hundred per pair."

"Fine. Who will be delivering it?" She held her breath.

"Our usual courier. InstantExpress."

She breathed out slowly. "Thank you. I'll keep a look out for him."

"It is a pleasure doing business with you, Dr. Tupper."

Ethan slowed his car down. Lamond let out a low whistle. "Nice digs."

"What did you expect? He's a neurosurgeon." Ethan climbed out of the unmarked car and studied the house. Dr. Mazerski lived on a beautiful street. One of his favorite streets in the city.

The long avenue followed the curve of the Northwest Arm. Deep blue water danced behind the large, gracious homes. But what really got his attention was the fact that there was a boat ramp just around the corner. The boat ramp that Krissie Burns's body had been left on.

Built in a nouveau Cape Cod style with pale blue shingles and cream trim, Dr. Mazerski's house was both elegant and homey. They strode up the long walkway, bordered on each side by masses of yellow and orange tulips. The exuberant display unsettled Ethan. Tulips were Kate's favorite flowers. She had told him she loved them because every time they bloomed it gave her hope. He'd never really understood what she meant by that.

Lamond pushed the doorbell. A deep chime reverberated through the house. After a moment, the door opened. A woman gazed at them expressionlessly, a young baby sleeping on her shoulder. The baby was so new it was still curled up like a flower bud. The woman's eyes were deep blue, her skin clear. Clad as she was in lululemon, she would ordinarily fall into the yummy-mummy category. Not today. Her blond hair was lank and carelessly pulled into a ponytail, her eyes puffy and red. A bit of spit-up trailed down her sleeve.

"Mrs. Mazerski?" Ethan asked.

"Dr. Clare. His wife." She spoke softly but directly. "Who are you?"

"I am Detective Drake from the Halifax Police Department. This is Detective Lamond."

The sound of running feet caught his ear. He tensed, his eyes searching past her shoulder into the depths of the hall. A little boy darted toward his mother, toy train firmly in hand. He stood next to her. Her sentinel. His brown eyes fixed on Ethan's.

"We would like to speak to Dr. Mike Mazerski, please."

She stiffened and put a hand on her son's tousled head. "He's not here."

"Could you tell us where we can find him?" Ethan's gaze was drawn like a magnet to the little boy. The train had found its way to the child's mouth. He sucked it softly as he returned Ethan's look.

"Is my husband in trouble?" Dr. Clare's gaze swung from his face to Lamond's. "What happened in the O.R. wasn't his fault."

"We have some questions for him," Ethan said.

"You're too late, Detective." The muscles in her face tightened until her lips quivered. "He was admitted to hospital this morning." The little boy threw his mother an alarmed look. He leaned against her leg.

Pain. Grief. Despair. They were written plainly all over Dr. Clare's face. She wiped her eyes with her sleeve and straightened. "I'm sorry, I'm not usually like this." She nodded toward the baby. "It's the hormones…"

The baby shifted slightly, as if it had a bit of gas, burrowing its downy head into her shoulder.

"Why is your husband in the hospital?"

Her hand gently cupped the translucent skin of the baby's neck. Anguish roughened her voice. "He's losing his mind."

The baby let out a sudden high-pitched wail.

40

"InstantExpress Courier, please hold."

She waited, her fingers tapping the steering wheel.

"How can I help you?" a man finally asked, his voice harried.

"This is Becky from BioMediSol calling. I want to confirm a pickup for 2:00 p.m. Friday afternoon."

"Let me see…"

Kate heard pages flipping. The man came on the phone again. "The pickup is listed for after 5:00 p.m. Thursday night."

She let out a small sigh of frustration. "I don't know who arranged this, but it should be for Friday."

"All right, ma'am, I'll change it for you."

"Can you please double-check you've got the right address?"

"Twelve sixty-six Spicer Drive?"

A little shiver ran up Kate's back. "That's the one. See you then."

She hung up.

Twelve sixty-six Spicer Drive. She'd been there just this week.

BioMediSol was located in Keane's Funeral Home.

And suddenly it all clicked into place.

She understood why Anna Keane had tried to solicit Muriel's body, why John Lyons recommended TransTissue settle with the plaintiffs.

She stared out the window, her mind turning over the scheme, examining its myriad facets. She could find no flaw.

The brilliance of it took her breath away. Anna Keane could ask clients if they were willing to donate their bodies "to science" or, if they were deceased, ask their family. Then she could provide the body to BioMediSol. In turn, BioMediSol would harvest the tissue and supply it to hospitals, researchers, tissue product manufacturers and pharmaceutical companies. Under Canadian law, tissue could not be sold, but the company harvesting it could charge a "fee" for its expenses. And the law of supply and demand ensured that a large fee would not be questioned when the supply was at a premium.

Kate dug around in her purse and found the consent form Enid had snatched from the funeral home. It stated the bodies would be used for a neuromuscular study conducted by researcher Dr. Ronald Gill. There was no mention of BioMediSol.

Could BioMediSol be benefiting from Dr. Gill's research by using his study's remains?

Or, even more diabolically, could the study be a ruse, Dr. Gill a straw man for the purposes of soliciting bodies?

Kate started the car engine.

She owed Dr. Gill a long overdue visit.

The nurses' station was muted. Obviously Dr. Mazerski was well respected to have put such a damper on the staff's spirits.

Ethan and Lamond flashed their IDs to the ward clerk. "We need to speak with Dr. Mazerski."

Alarm flashed over the ward clerk's face. "You will have to speak to the head of neurology before you can see him."

The last thing Ethan wanted was to get mired in the bureaucratic bullshit the GH2 was famous for. He was too close to homing in on the killer. No one was going to get in the way now. "We need to interview Dr. Mazerski in private. What room is he in, please?"

The ward clerk looked around her for support. A nurse flipped a chart closed, his biceps bulging under his greens, and moved behind the clerk. He was a bulky guy with a shaved head. "He's not able to answer questions. Why do you need to see him?"

Ethan gave him a level look. "It's regarding a criminal investigation."

The nurse picked up the phone. "We need to get Dr. Roberts down here. He's Head of Neurology."

"Fine," Ethan said. Lamond threw him a surprised glance. They both knew their chances of actually seeing Dr. Mazerski were slim to none if the administration got involved. Ethan glanced at the clock over the ward clerk's head. "It's visitors' hours. We'll be in Dr. Mazerski's room." He pocketed his ID. "Come on, Lamond."

He turned down the hall, Lamond jogging to catch up to him, ignoring the fluster of activity at the nurses' station he left in his wake. He bet they were calling all the senior staff. And after that, they'd be calling the staff sergeant to complain. He wasn't worried. Staff Sergeant Robbins had been around a long time. He'd smooth it over.

Ethan stopped by an unmarked door. It was slightly ajar. If he guessed right, Dr. Mazerski would be in a room right by the nurses' station where they could keep an eye on him.

He knocked softly. There was no answer. He pushed the door open. His first glance revealed a typical hospital room with a bed, nightstand and chair. The drapes were drawn against the noonday light. It cast the bedridden patient in gloom.

"Dr. Mazerski?" he said softly.

There was no answer.

His eyes adjusted to the dimness. He approached the bed. A man lay under the sheets. He was perfectly still. Rigid.

And staring.

Ethan tried again. "Dr. Mazerski?"

The man did not turn his head.

His stillness was eerie. As if his muscles were poised for flight.

Ethan edged closer.

The man did not move. Did not blink.

Did this disease his wife said he had—CJD, Dr. Clare had said over the wails of her hungry baby—make him so crazy that they had sedated him?

The man's arm lay on top of the sheet. Around his wrist was a hospital ID bracelet. It occurred to Ethan that he'd better double-check that this was, in fact, the man they were looking for. He could just imagine the staff sergeant's reaction if he found out Ethan had bulldozed his way into a suspect's hospital room and then interrogated the wrong guy.

Ethan leaned over the man to read his bracelet.

The man's body spasmed. His arm jumped off the sheet.

Ethan jerked back.

Lamond snickered softly.

"Shut up," Ethan said.

He forced his heart to slow back down and read the name printed on the man's bracelet: Mazerski, Michael Bogdan.

He studied the man's hand. Long fingers, the nails slightly longer than he would've expected. Was this the hand of a killer or a giver of a new chance at life? Or both?

What would drive a man to give with one hand and take away with the other?

He moved his gaze to Dr. Mazerski's face. He looked to be in his late forties. His wavy hair was graying around a receding hairline. His most striking feature was his eyes, deep set and brown under dark eyebrows. His skin was stretched taut over his facial muscles. Ethan suppressed a shiver. The neurosurgeon's face looked like a death's-head. He thought of the round, soft cheeks of Dr. Mazerski's little children. His heart squeezed unexpectedly.

He squashed his pity. If this man had committed the crimes he thought he did, he deserved none.

Dr. Mazerski had not moved under Ethan's scrutiny. His gaze had remained fixed to a spot on the wall several inches to the right of the clock. Ethan moved his hand slowly in front of the neurosurgeon's eyes. He blinked.

Ethan tried again. Same response. He swore softly under his breath. They weren't going to get any answers from the doc in this state. The frustration that had been his constant companion for the past two weeks surged in him.

"We've got a visitor," Lamond said in a muted voice. The room had that kind of effect on a person. It was as if they had entered a twilight zone.

"Detectives." A woman dressed in surgical scrubs stood in the doorway, her broad shoulders and solid frame tense. Her sharp glance took in Lamond stationed by the door, Ethan hovering over Dr. Mazerski. She strode past Lamond to plant herself by the bed.

Ethan glanced at her hospital ID. "Dr. Lachlan. I'm Detective Ethan Drake, Criminal Investigations Unit."

She darted a quick look at Dr. Mazerski's catatonic face, then met Ethan's gaze. "Why are you here?"

"We have some questions for Dr. Mazerski."

"Why?" Her gaze challenged him. She looked like a real fighter, someone who was used to being first in everything and would steamroll her way to the finish line if need be. Looking at her size and speed, he also bet she'd played sports as a kid, probably basketball. Her steely gaze was on level with his eyes. Pale brown hair was pulled back into a ponytail, a few wisps falling around her smooth, strong-jawed face. Her hair was the only soft touch about her, although when she glanced at the patient lying next to them, empathy flowed like heat through the iron of a radiator.

"Dr. Lachlan, we believe Dr. Mazerski may have been involved in a crime we are investigating."

"What?" She snorted. "You're on the wrong track, Detective."

"I don't think so." He jerked his head toward the inert man. "What drugs is he on? You need to take him off them so we can question him."

She cocked her head, a small smile twisting her lips. "Remember doctor-patient confidentiality, Detective," she chided. "I can't tell you anything without the permission of his wife." She glanced at her watch. "She'll probably be back tonight."

Ethan crossed his arms. Dr. Clare hadn't wanted them to come, especially when she realized they were investigating a murder. It had been a surreal conversation, brief and stark over the frantic hunger cries of her baby. Ethan had discreetly turned his gaze away when her breasts began to leak. It was the realization she was at the mercy of her body that made her relent. Her gaze was direct and hopeless. "You won't get any answers from him. He's got advanced CJD."

He couldn't wait until she could disengage herself from the demands of her children to come down to the hospital. "Look, Dr. Lachlan, the case I'm investigating is urgent."

She studied him for a moment. Perhaps she read the determination in his gaze, because she finally said, "I'll call his wife. See if she agrees to me talking to you. After that, I'm leaving. I was just dropping in between procedures to check on Mike." She strode quickly out of the room.

Lamond resumed his post against the door and watched the hallway.

There was a loud grunt from the neurosurgeon. He folded at the waist and sat upright in bed.

Ethan tensed. "Lamond," he said quietly.

Lamond turned and started at the sight of Dr. Mazerski. The neurosurgeon's eyes stared straight ahead. He gripped the sheets in his hands, his mouth working.

His body spasmed.

Ethan caught him before he fell onto the floor. He gently pushed Dr. Mazerski back onto the pillows. The neurosurgeon kept jerking under his hands.

"Shit," Ethan said. "Lamond, get a doctor!"

"Get your hands off him!" Dr. Lachlan cried, barreling into the room toward the bed.

Ethan let go of Dr. Mazerski, panting as if he'd run a marathon.

"He'll keep spasming if he's touched," Dr. Lachlan added in a calmer voice.

Ethan took a deep breath. "Did you talk to Dr. Clare?"

"Yes. She gave me permission to speak to you."

Ethan sized up Dr. Lachlan. Her desire to protect her colleague was written all over her. "I'd rather get my answers from him. We want him taken off whatever drugs are doing this to him. Just for a few hours."

"He isn't on anything." Her voice was flat. "That's what the disease is doing to him."

Ethan threw a disbelieving glance at the catatonic neurosurgeon. "You're kidding. What is CJD, anyway?"

"Its full name is Creutzfeldt-Jakob disease. It's a degenerative brain disease. Incurable. Caused by a prion—"

"A what?" He cast his mind back to his high school biology class. He'd been more interested in how girls worked than frogs. His brain came up empty.

"A protein that the brain cell generates. In CJD patients, it somehow mutates. No one knows how."

Lamond gave a low whistle. "So how'd he get it?"

Dr. Lachlan crossed her arms. "CJD can occur spontaneously in some people or it can be inherited. It can also, in rare occasions, be transmitted from someone or something."

"You mean, like HIV?"

Dr. Lachlan shook her head. "No. CJD is not sexually transmissible, and in cases of classic CJD, there are no reported cases of it being transmissible in blood." She added, "But we really don't know how it is transmitted. However, there is a new form of CJD, called variant CJD, which is believed to be caused by mad cow disease and that may be transmissible in blood."

"So what form does Dr. Mazerski have?" Ethan asked.

"Hard to say. It could have happened spontaneously. Or he may have contracted it while operating on a patient."

"Which means it's classic CJD?" Lamond asked.

"Possibly."

"But he got it from the patient, right?" Ethan asked, staring at Dr. Mazerski's rigid body.

"I don't think he got it from the patient. My own theory

is that it was from the dura mater—the transplant material we used to patch the tissue around the brain." She shook her head. "Most neurosurgeons don't use cadaveric dura mater anymore. But Mike always felt it gave a better patch. So he kept a little supply on hand."

"That had CJD?"

"That's what I think. It most likely was infected with classic CJD, but until we trace the donor, the dura mater could have come from someone who ate infected beef."

Ethan stared at Dr. Lachlan's set features. His mind darted around the facts, looking for the holes. "Isn't that stuff screened?"

Dr. Lachlan's jaw tightened. "It's supposed to be. Those bloody tissue suppliers claim they use the highest screening standards, but I think they're full of it."

"So you can get CJD just by handling the infected tissue?" he asked.

Dr. Lachlan shook her head. "No. I'm pretty sure I know how Mike could have gotten it. About eighteen months ago he was doing a craniotomy. His scalpel slipped as he was trimming the patch. He nicked himself. And if the dura mater had CJD, the scalpel blade would have been loaded with CJD prions." Her gaze swung over to him. "And now here he is."

"What about the patient who received the dura mater? Did he get CJD?"

"We don't know yet," Dr. Lachlan said. "We're tracking her down. And the tissue supplier."

He stared at Dr. Mazerski's masklike features. What a mess. But he couldn't forget one important fact: eighteen months was a big gap between getting infected and showing symptoms. Dr. Mazerski could have killed a lot of girls before he was put on leave on Friday. "Does Dr. Mazerski have periods of lucidity?"

Dr. Lachlan shook her head. "No. His symptoms are progressing very rapidly. That can happen in his kind of transmission, but even so, he seems to be an extreme case." She paused for a moment, then cleared her throat. "I doubt he'll ever speak cogently again. He's also losing his vision."

He glanced at Dr. Mazerski, despair warring with frustration. They'd been so close. So close. But a week too late. They'd never get any answers from him. They'd need to get their information from colleagues, family, hospital records.

Ethan turned to Dr. Lachlan. "How often have you seen Dr. Mazerski in the past two weeks?"

She held his gaze. "We were on six shifts together. A week ago Saturday, Monday, Wednesday, Friday, Sunday, Tuesday and then the past Friday, when he totally lost it in the O.R."

"A week ago Monday—was it a day or night shift?"

"Night."

Lamond rolled back on his heels. That Monday night was when Lisa MacAdam was killed.

"Were you with him all the time?"

"I'd have to check our O.R. records, but if I recall correctly, we operated at 9:45 p.m. We closed the patient around 2:50 a.m., and then we had another patient waiting right after that. So, yes, I believe I was."

Her pager beeped. She glanced down at the number and swore. "Just when I thought I was done for the night." She gave a grim smile. Ethan realized she was making a joke— the clock bolted to the wall showed it was already past noon. She threw one final glance at Dr. Mazerski. "I've gotta run," she said, striding across the room. "We're short staffed." She sprinted out the door, her pager urging her on.

"I'll get the records," Lamond said, "but if she's right—"

Ethan walked toward the door. "If she's right, Dr. Mazerski is not our man. He's just one unlucky bastard." Leaving behind a grief-ravaged wife and two young children. At least the risk of his family contracting it from him was remote. But what a tragic waste of talent, opportunity, life.

How must Dr. Clare feel to see the brilliant mind of her spouse being ravaged so ruthlessly? To see the promise of their lives cruelly dismantled? And yet, she had had a desperate determination in her gaze. The stunned look of a survivor. He realized—with a shock of recognition—he'd seen that same look before. In Kate's eyes.

They left the hospital floor. The watchful gaze of the nursing staff remained on their backs until they got in the elevator. Dr. Roberts must have been held up. Ethan thanked the powers that be for small mercies.

They walked in silence back to the parkade. As soon as they slid into the front seats, Lamond said, "Man, I thought we were on to something." Frustration flashed in his eyes. "If that doc was right, then we've just lost a prime suspect."

Ethan sipped his cold coffee. "Tell me about it." Disappointment added to the burning feeling in his gut. He put the coffee cup back in the holder. The killer was still out there. What were they missing? How could this guy not leave a trace?

He rubbed his jaw. Stubble rasped against his skin. He needed a shave. He needed sleep. Both those things would have to wait. "I still think we're on the right track. Just the wrong guy."

41

Thursday, May 17, 1:00 p.m.

Dr. Gill was no straw man. In fact, he was a big coup for Hollis University. Kate skimmed his bio again. The university Web site listed the numerous research grants he'd been awarded, and noted he was short-listed for the newly endowed one-million-dollar chair in neuromuscular research. A separate press attachment mentioned the possibility of a Nobel Prize.

This guy was a highly respected medical researcher. What was his involvement with BioMediSol—if any? Was he being used?

In a few hours she would find out. Right now, she needed to work on her files and keep a low profile. She'd shown up to work this morning, trying to maintain the appearance of normality and lull John Lyons into thinking that she was as clueless as he thought she was.

She tucked Dr. Gill's address under the case reports on her desk.

Randall Barrett strode past the associates' offices, heading for one office in particular.

He hadn't seen Kate for days. Not since he'd shared an elevator with her. The memory of her eyes raking his face still made his chest tighten. She'd known about the notes. She'd realized he'd taken them. She just didn't know why.

That had eaten away at him ever since.

He stopped in her doorway. She had her back to him and was bent over. He couldn't help himself: his eyes drank in the heart-shaped curve of her bottom.

He forced his gaze away. It looked as if she was packing her briefcase. He glanced at his watch: 3:05 p.m. A little early for her to be leaving. But her caseload had lightened since the MacAdam and TransTissue cases were over.

"Are you busy?"

She tensed at the sound of his voice, then straightened and turned. "No, I'm not busy." She didn't bother to hide the fact she'd been intending to leave. She placed her car keys on her desk. Her gaze was challenging. "Come in."

He surprised himself by closing the door and lowering himself into a chair. She reluctantly sank into hers. "I heard about the TransTissue file, Kate."

She stiffened, a slight flush warming her translucent skin. Then she shrugged. "John advised them to settle."

Randall studied her. She was watching him as closely as he watched her. "He said you did a good job on it."

That didn't have the response he expected. Her lips twisted. "Glad to hear it." Her eyes probed his face. There was something there, under the surface. A totally different dialogue. It was as if he could see the lips moving but couldn't hear what was being said.

He was sure she must be frustrated to lose the chance to work on a case like TransTissue. He leaned forward. "You know, there will be other cases, Kate. Ones that will go through to the trial phase."

"Yes. I know." She seemed to be waiting for something.

"I'll make sure you get assigned to one in the next few weeks."

Her lips twisted again. "Thanks."

Her desire for him to leave was palpable. Her disdain for him was just as thick.

He couldn't leave things the way they were. She needed to understand that she could trust him, despite everything. That he'd tried to protect her. He leaned back in his chair. "You are correct in your assumption."

He'd expected to see anger, disgust even, at his revelation. But not shock. Her gaze flickered over a scrap of paper peeking out from under her case reports, then snapped back to him. There was no mistaking that there was something on her desk she did not want him to see. *What was it?*

"Which assumption are you talking about?" she shot back. He suppressed both a wince at her implication that she harbored many assumptions—which, from her tone of voice, were unflattering—and a surge of admiration at her riposte. Especially given that she was so tense her cheek-bones jutted from her face.

He had to fight the impulse to smooth the curve of her cheek with his fingers. He cleared his throat. "I took your notes."

She drew back. "I know." Those two words repeated what her eyes had flashed at him. Contempt, anger. Underneath it vibrated hurt.

He leaned forward. "I'm sorry, Kate." Her carefully masked surprise at his apology stabbed him. "It was something I was loath to do."

She crossed her arms. "Did Judge Carson put you up to it?"

"I'm sorry. I can't answer that." He wouldn't blame Hope.

Her gaze challenged him. "Will you return them?"

"No," he said softly. "I destroyed them."

"Of course."

He knew what she was thinking. He'd left her dangling in the wind. "The contents were never revealed to anyone. Solicitor-client privilege was not violated. You don't need to worry."

"I see." She glanced down for a moment. His tension ebbed. She understood.

Then she looked up and his pulse staggered. Fury radiated from her eyes. "So you think that makes it all right? You steal my notes, won't tell me why, and then assure me that no one's seen them?" She stood and planted her palms on her desk. Her breasts heaved under her silk blouse. "Why should I believe you?"

He tore his gaze from her chest.

She saw where his eyes had been fixed. Her lips curled in contempt.

His neck burned. Jesus, he was like a teenager in her presence. This associate who was at least a decade his junior. He rose to his feet and crossed his arms. "Why shouldn't you?"

"Because you stole from me, Randall! You came into my office and went through my files and took my notes and left me holding the bag—" She stopped abruptly.

The whole picture suddenly shifted into focus. *She'd wanted those notes for something.* That's why she was so upset.

"True." He let his eyes probe hers. "But it's not like you needed those notes for anything, right, Kate? They were protected by solicitor-client privilege."

A slash of color burned on each elegant cheekbone. She stared at him, mute with fury. And guilt.

Bingo.

"That's right," she managed. "And you took them."

"But I destroyed them. I wasn't planning on giving them to anyone else…" There was only one person in her acquaintance who'd be able to persuade her to give up those notes. Only one person with a connection to both the MacAdam case *and* to Kate. Only one person who would be willing to resort to unethical investigative means in order to further his own assumptions.

Ethan Drake.

A vein throbbed in his temple. "Did your former fiancé ask to have a peek?"

She crossed her arms and tightened her jaw. But the fiery pink of her cheeks spoke volumes.

"How disappointed you must have been when you discovered I'd beat you to it." He was taking a perverse pleasure in angering her now. She'd planned to breach her fiduciary duty to help Ethan Drake. A man who was willing to sacrifice a person's future in order to serve his twisted ideal of justice. "I saved your ass, Ms. Lange," he said, his tone clipped. "Do you think your ex would have protected you if he'd had to make the provenance of his information known?"

Her face tightened.

"I saved your ass, Kate," he repeated. He wanted her to recognize it for what it was. "And I saved it with Child Protection, too."

"So what do you want me to do?" She was so angry she was trembling. "Kiss yours?"

An image of her on her knees in front of him, her hair tumbling over her naked shoulders, slammed through him. Anger and desire were igniting on the same narrow fuse. *Dangerous*. Way too dangerous. "No." He shook his head to clear his mind of that image. That delicious, tantalizing image. It almost toppled him with need. He wanted to grab her by the shoulders. He wanted to attack her mouth with his and plunge its depths. He wanted to lower her onto her desk and cup that heart-shaped bottom in his hands…

He clenched his hands to his sides. He had not felt desire assault him like this in a long, long time. If ever. That sudden realization fueled his resolve. "I'm not saving you anymore."

He yanked open the door. "You are hereby on notice. You cannot afford any more screwups, Kate. This is it. No more chances."

He closed the door behind him.

She grabbed her briefcase and fumbled with the doorknob to her office. Her fingers shook. She flung open the door and stormed down the corridor.

That bastard.

That bloody, bloody bastard.

She punched the button to the elevator. When the door opened, she held her breath. She half-hoped and half-dreaded seeing Randall Barrett in there. If he was…

She wanted to launch herself against him, pound his chest and make him suffer for those words. All those hurtful words.

The bastard.

How did he know how to hurt her so precisely? To twist the knife like that?

The elevator was empty. She stabbed the button to the parkade, leaned her head back against the mirrored wall and closed her eyes.

She'd been stunned when he appeared in her office doorway—just as she was about to visit Dr. Gill. Had he somehow found out what she was up to?

Had he been on a scouting mission to see what she knew about TransTissue?

She couldn't believe his ballsiness. He'd ostensibly apologized for stealing her notes, and then accused her of wrongdoing.

The worst thing was that he'd been right.

She'd walked right into Ethan's trap, had agreed to give him the notes, but had never thought about what would happen if he was forced to reveal the source of his information. Would he deliberately ignore the evidence trail of the Body Butcher in order to protect her?

Of course not.

Randall Barrett had saved her.

And that rankled more than anything else.

She didn't want to be saved. Correction, she didn't want to make mistakes that required someone—and in particular, Randall Barrett—to save her.

She did not want to be in his debt.

She could not afford it. The price was too high. Not just the cost to her career. There was a more personal price. There had been a moment—*another blasted moment*—when his eyes had demanded that she acknowledge his desire. And not only acknowledge it, but meet it. And her body had complied. With a longing so heated she knew it would burn her up. No one, not even Ethan, had ever done that to her.

She hated the fact that Randall Barrett could. To have him be able to immolate her good judgment with a glance and ignite her nerves scared the life out of her.

It was humiliating.

She climbed into her car and sped out of the parkade. She needed to get away from the firm, from Randall Barrett.

The worst thing was, he understood her better than anyone she knew.

That was a fucking scary thought.

He was her boss. He was also one of the best lawyers in the city. That was an even scarier thought. If he was involved in the deceptions of the TransTissue file—after all, hadn't he persuaded John Lyons to put her on it?—would he guess that she was tracking down its suppliers? Would he be waiting for her to come back and reveal her findings?

She couldn't let him know what she was doing.

"Craig." His employer stood in front of him, blocking his path from the fridge to the workstation.

Craig looked up from the tray he was carrying.

Dr. Gill held his gaze. "This has got to stop. Now."

"It's t-t-too late." Craig gave him a little smile.

"It's never too late, Craig." Dr. Gill softened his voice. "You could just stop. Right now. The police have no evidence. No one would ever know."

"Y-You can't tell me wh-wh-what to do," Craig said, pushing around him. "Dr. K," he added for good measure. *Dr. K.* His employer hated that nickname. Every time he used it, Dr. Gill turned ashen. It was amazing what guilt and shame could do to a man.

This time, his employer stiffened, his head jerking back in that irritating birdlike movement. Just as Craig knew it would. He could predict everything.

Every. Fucking. Thing.

"No." The Esteemed Doctor turned and faced him. His hands were actually trembling. *Trembling.* "Please." Dr. Gill's voice was hoarse. "I'm begging you. Don't do it anymore."

Power surged through him, breaking in a frenzied wave through his body. The Esteemed Doctor was actually shaking in his fucking sandals.

He smiled. "You n-n-never complained before." He

leaned against the counter. "You l-l-liked it when I killed them quietly and you got the limbs on the s-s-side."

"No," Dr. Gill whispered. "No, that's not true."

"You just didn't like it when I st-st-started leaving the bodies out. R-Right, Dr. Kill?" The flash of guilt in Dr. Gill's eyes confirmed it.

At first, dissecting Anna Keane's dead bodies had filled the emptiness inside him. But then the emptiness got bigger. He needed the bodies to be alive first.

Then it hadn't been enough to dispose of their remains in the crematorium. He wanted people to know.

Craig Peters was having the last laugh.

"Why did you?" Dr. Gill looked almost afraid to know the answer.

"I f-f-felt like it." Craig would never justify his actions to this man. This puny man. He had no idea of the power Craig had over his victims. The begging. The pleading. The absolute fucking terror.

White spots appeared around the edges of his left eye. Flecks of spume. Jumping randomly back and forth.

He shook his head. They careered wildly. It was happening almost all the time now. Keeping pace with the steady pulse of the urge.

"You've got to stop." Dr. Gill's voice was low, pleading. "They are just young girls."

Craig's body tensed. He was a rubber band. Tight, tight, stretching to burst. He couldn't breathe. His eyes rolled wildly upward.

The elastic snapped.

His limbs jerked.

He swallowed. "It's t-t-too late."

He dumped the tray on the counter and pushed by Dr. Gill. He'd go home, get his briefcase and wait until darkness fell. That's when the whores sold their bodies. They just didn't realize it was a final sale.

Kate parked her car on a side street by Hollis U. Slightly calmer, she forced herself to walk slowly into the 1960s brick science building which housed Dr. Gill's lab. It reminded Kate of her old high school, down to the musty smell that the forty-year-old linoleum expunged whenever she stepped on it. Funny how a certain smell could resuscitate memories she had long thought buried. The familiar feeling of isolation rushed through her. Of trying to pretend the awkward silences and covert glances of her classmates didn't bother her. She almost expected to see clusters of kids hanging around battered metal lockers.

She walked down the hall, straightening her body out of the hunched posture she had somehow fallen into, and scanned the small plastic plaques. A blond man brushed by her. His face was pale, shiny with sweat.

She'd seen that guy before.

Lisa MacAdam's funeral.

The man in the gray suit.

"Oh, excuse me," she said, although he'd been the one to bump her.

He looked at her. He didn't appear to recognize her.

He walked by her without a word. Then stopped. Turned slowly toward her. She felt his eyes on her back.

Kate's stomach tightened. She hurried down the hall. A door opened. An older man dressed in a lab coat carrying a tray of beakers headed down the hall.

The blond man from the funeral began walking again, toward the elevator. She heard it open for him. And let out a deep breath.

He'd had a weird vibe.

She began reading the plaques again. At the end of the corridor she found a sign announcing Dr. Gill's lab. She peered through the oblong window in the door and knocked. A very tall man in the back of the room jerked at the sound. He whirled around, his expression panicked. He collected himself and walked toward her. He opened the door. But blocked the entry.

Kate tilted her head back to meet his eyes, pale blue behind rimless glasses.

"Dr. Gill?"

"Yes." His gaze darted over her face.

She held out her hand. "My name is Kate Lange."

"How can I help you?" His cheeks were flushed. A fine sheen of sweat gleamed on his high forehead.

"I'm here on behalf of my aunt. She is interested in donating her body to your research. But she's too sick to come herself."

"Oh?" He looked down his beaky nose at her. He reminded her of a heron.

"She's really interested in your research. She would like to know more about it." She was hoping he'd relax at her flattering tone and invite her in.

She seemed to have lost her touch. He remained fixed in the doorway. "In a nutshell, Ms. Lange, I am trying to regenerate nerves and their nerve paths," he said, his voice clipped.

"So if you damaged a nerve, it would grow again?" She furrowed her brow, hoping he would respond to her interest.

"Yes. Say, for instance, a nerve in your arm was crushed from a car accident. It would grow back, but at a rate of one millimeter per month, and most likely not following the same nerve path." He recited this quickly, obviously unable to resist speaking about his research, but his hand remained ready to close the door on her. "By regenerating that nerve quickly, and in the same old nerve path, you would regain the function of your hand within weeks."

From the intensity and passion in his voice, Kate had the sudden conviction he would be successful in his research.

But at what cost? She remembered Enid tucking Muriel's coat around her. *Tell Dr. Gill that he cannot save mankind at the expense of people like us.*

"So you use cadavers to conduct your research?" She almost said *experiments*, but she stopped herself just in time. It sounded a bit too Dr. Jekyll-ish.

"Yes."

"But you wouldn't need to use the whole body, would you?"

"Why do you need to know this?" Suspicion narrowed his eyes.

"My aunt would like to know what exactly her body would be used for."

"We use limbs," he said curtly.

"What happens to the rest of the body?"

He straightened his glasses. "It is cremated."

"By whom?"

His eyes searched hers. His struggle was plain on his face; he wanted to share the glory of his research, wanted to recruit more donations to his cause, but didn't like the direction the questions were heading.

Kate gave a little smile and shrugged. "My aunt has certain...foibles. A lot of her friends have died recently and she is picky about which funeral home she'd like to handle her remains."

He paused. "We use Keane's."

She smiled. "Perfect. They are exactly who she hoped for."

Dr. Gill put his hand on the doorknob. "If you'll excuse me, Ms. Lange, I need to return to my work…"

"Of course." She tried to see past the researcher, to get one final look at the lab, but Dr. Gill wasn't budging.

"Goodbye." His eyes revealed what he really meant: *go away.*

"Goodbye." She darted one final peek past Dr. Gill's shoulder. She thought the blond guy had come from his lab. But she could see nothing.

Once she was outside, she took deep breaths of the cool, damp air. Clouds had filled the sky until it was gray and thick.

Dr. Gill's nervousness had infected her. Her own nerves were churning her stomach into a pit of apprehension.

The pit sank deeper when she thought about the implications of what he had told her. She believed him when he said that he sent donor bodies to Keane's Funeral Home for cremation. What she didn't know was whether Anna Keane was cremating them right away.

Was Anna Keane merely an astute businesswoman who was leveraging her funeral home to solicit bodies for medical research and for much-needed tissue transplants?

Or was she a body snatcher?

Her gut was screaming body snatcher. The sum of the whole was not greater than the parts in the body brokering business.

How much did Dr. Gill know of this?

Her legal mind stacked the evidence. So far, it was nonexistent. She had no evidence of Anna stealing the parts from any bodies; she had no evidence of Anna stealing bodies period. She didn't even have any evidence of Anna illegally soliciting bodies. The donor form Enid took was blank.

She needed cold, hard evidence.

A shiver crept up her back. There was only one form cold, hard evidence could take in a funeral home.

She steered her car into the traffic.

42

Thursday, May 17, 2:55 p.m.

It was a long shot, but it was worth a try. After Shonda had told him about the blond dog-walking man, Ethan remembered running regularly past a guy and his pack of dogs in Point Pleasant Park.

At 2:55 p.m. he pulled into the parking lot. The water was calm today. A hulking container ship inched its way toward the outer harbor. He bought a Fudgsicle from the ice cream shack and leaned against the wall. It gave him a good vantage point of the path.

Fifty minutes later, his patience paid off. A large black truck slid into a parking spot. On the doors were the words *Doggie Do,* with paw prints in the *O*s. A blond man got out and opened the trunk. Ethan eyed the closed bed on the back of the truck. There was a tinted window that had been opened to give the dogs some air. It would hide a victim's remains perfectly.

Ethan headed down the path to intercept the man. The dogs whined in excitement as the man attached their leads. They waited until the dog walker gave the word, then they lunged as one toward the path.

Ethan stared in shock. There were five dogs, mostly large, all different colors. But one stood out. The white husky. Was that Kate's dog?

He fell into step beside the man. "Nice dogs."

The man glanced at him. He had a friendly, confident air. "Yeah, they're a good bunch."

"Are they all yours?"

The man shook his head. He was young, in his twenties, obviously in good shape. So far, he fit nicely into Brown's profile. "No. I run a dog-walking service."

Ethan pulled out his badge. "My name is Detective Ethan Drake. I have some questions regarding a homicide investigation. I'd like to talk to you."

The man stared at him. "Are you kidding me?"

"No. I need to see some identification."

The man fumbled in his back pocket while holding the leads in one hand. The white husky tried to take advantage and started pulling. "Alaska. Sit!" the man said hoarsely.

Ethan stared at the dog. It *was* Kate's dog. Kate knew this man. Jesus. Did he have a key to her house?

The dog walker flipped open his wallet and gave Ethan his driver's license. "Is this about Lisa MacAdam?"

"Yes." Ethan read the license. Finn Scott. With an address in the south end of Halifax. He returned the license. Here was the tricky part. He couldn't arrest the guy without a warrant. Instead, he needed to convince Finn Scott that he'd be helping the police if he came for an "interview."

Finn Scott began walking. Three dogs pulled ahead—Alaska, a Great Dane and a rottweiler—while a beagle mix and a Westie with a baby blue satin bow in its bangs straggled behind, sniffing the bushes.

Ethan fell into step next to the dog walker. He didn't

want him to go too far. "Look, Mr. Scott, we think you could help us in our investigation."

Finn Scott shrugged. "I don't know much, but if you think it would help you guys…" He stopped. The little beagle mix had gotten its leash tangled with the Westie and a large prickly bush. "Whoa, there, Mr. Big," Finn said.

Ethan threw him a sharp look. Then realized Finn Scott had been speaking to the beagle. The dog walker turned to Ethan with the leash for the bigger dogs in his hand. "Could you hold this for a sec?"

"Sure." Ethan took the leash. The three dogs at the end of it ignored him. He stared at the white head of the husky. *Now who's in charge?* It was a childish thought, but he didn't care. The dog had seriously pissed him off.

Finn bent down to untangle the beagle and the Westie from the bush. His wrist grazed the bush. "Damn," he muttered. Blood droplets pricked through a scratch on his forearm. Ethan eyed the wound.

"Here." He offered Finn a tissue, holding on to the leash tightly with his other hand. The dogs were getting restless, tugging at their restraints.

Finn threw him a surprised look. "Nah, it's just a scratch."

Ethan stuffed the tissue back in his pocket. He'd hoped Finn would dab the wound, then dispose of the tissue. Once the dog walker threw it away, he could've dug the tissue out of the garbage and run the blood sample through their DNA bank.

Suddenly, his arm was almost yanked from the socket. Alaska had lunged forward as if he was channeling his relatives and pulling a sled in the Arctic. The other two dogs joined him.

He pitched forward. "Jesus Christ!" It was either run

with the dogs or have his arms dislocated. He pulled back on the leash, "Heel…! Sit…! Stay!"

The dogs ignored him. They were on the hunt. A squirrel ran furiously across the grass toward the safety of a tall pine tree.

"Stop!" Ethan called again. Under his breath, he added, "You goddamned dogs!"

Finn came sprinting up behind him, the beagle and Westie running as fast as their stubby legs allowed. "Alaska. Brutus. Marvin," he called calmly, grabbing the leash from Ethan. "Come."

It was like bloody magic. At the sound of Finn Scott's voice, Alaska slowed down and turned. Brutus and Marvin followed suit. They all looked enormously pleased with themselves, tongues lolling, tails wagging. Alaska and his pair of followers trotted back to Finn and sat by his legs. Brutus, the Great Dane, tried nosing Ethan's leg but he stepped away, throwing the dogs a disgusted look. The husky, as was his habit, ignored him. But Ethan was sure he saw a glint of satisfaction in his ice blue eyes.

When the Westie shuffled over and leaned against the husky, Ethan knew he'd been had. The little white dog cocked her head at Ethan. He was glad to see its bow was muddy. He looked into its beady brown eyes. There was no doubt in his mind what the dog was thinking: *For a detective you're not too bright. You fell for it big time, buddy.*

He turned to Finn. "I'd like you to come down to the station now." His voice was curter than he intended.

"Now?" Finn Scott flashed him a look of surprise. "What am I supposed to do with the dogs?" They gave Ethan an indignant look.

Throw them in the harbor was what he wanted to say. He pasted a smile on his face. "Bring them with you. We'll drop them off on our way." He had a vision of the back door of the car falling open as he turned a corner, his cargo slipping off the seat…

Finn shrugged. "All right, then. They've had a bit of a walk. Come on, boys." He turned with the dogs. Ethan led them to his car and opened the back door.

Alaska stared into the car interior. Then he lay down on the asphalt. The other dogs did the same.

"Go in," Ethan said. His impatience was rising by the minute. He wanted Finn Scott, down in the station, *now*. This guy was their best bet and he wasn't going to let a pack of mangy mutts stand in his way.

"It'd be easier if we went in my truck," Finn said, gazing at the pristine backseat of Ethan's sedan.

"I'll bring you back after our interview." He needed Finn out of his comfort zone. That meant taking him to the station in his car, not Finn's truck. Especially if he found, during his "interview," that there were reasonable and probable grounds to search the dog walker's truck. He didn't want to give him a chance to mess around with evidence.

"Okay, boys, up you go," Finn said.

Four of the dogs stood reluctantly, circling one another. Alaska stretched his front legs out and began licking his paw.

"Alaska," Finn said firmly. "In."

Alaska turned his attention to his other paw and delicately nibbled around his toenail.

Jesus Christ. He'd had enough. The dog needed to learn who was in charge.

He reached forward.

Alaska let out a low growl.

Without a backward glance, the husky stood and jumped gracefully into the car, his tail swatting Ethan on the cheek. Ethan drew back. He swallowed his frustration.

He'd relished the thought of getting his hands around that dog's neck.

"In, Marvin," Finn said, picking up the beagle. The rottweiler leaped obediently into the car. Finn placed Mr. Big on the seat next to it.

"Okay, Brutus, you next," Finn said. The Great Dane looked doubtfully at the backseat. Alaska had claimed one side already, and the rottweiler had forced the beagle into the middle.

Finn took the Great Dane by the collar and urged him forward, while saying cheerfully, "Push over, boys." Somehow the massive dog managed to get its long legs into the backseat. Finn closed the door carefully. Ethan noted that he locked it and stifled his disappointment.

"I'll have to bring Twinkles in the front with me," Finn said apologetically.

"Fine," Ethan managed. He climbed into the driver's seat. Doggy breath surrounded him. He opened his window while Finn and Twinkles settled into the passenger seat.

Without another word, he jammed the car into reverse and spun around, gunning it out of the parking lot.

One of the dogs farted. A smell that rivaled the city dump filled the air.

"Jesus," he muttered. He glanced over at Finn.

Finn gave an apologetic smile. "It's Brutus. He doesn't travel well. He's got a delicate stomach." He glanced pointedly at the speedometer. "Maybe you could go a little slower? Or else…" He reached behind his head and patted Brutus on the nose. "He sometimes pukes."

The Westie placed her paws on the dash and gazed out the windscreen. Ethan could just imagine the reaction if his team saw him with little Twinkles, bow askew, perkily surveying the street from his car.

Despite the fact Brutus was not the closest on the route, he was the first Ethan dropped off. He wasn't taking any chances.

Not with the dogs, not with the dog walker. He accompanied Finn Scott each time into his client's house. He didn't want him making any phone calls without his knowledge. When they got to Kate's house, he was relieved to see that she wasn't home. But it was strange, walking in there, seeing her jacket slung over the staircase, a basket of laundry on the stairs. He couldn't help but notice the lace underwear peeking out under a blouse. He stood in front of it so Finn Scott wouldn't see it. He didn't want his suspect ogling her lingerie. Why had she given this guy a key?

He knew why, but it still rankled.

The dog walker strode into the kitchen, not even glancing at Ethan, checking Alaska's water bowl. The dog nosed Finn Scott's hand. The man seemed very comfortable in Kate's house. Too comfortable. Did he do more than walk her dog?

Ethan eyed Finn Scott as he walked out from the kitchen. He was an attractive guy. Was he soothing Kate's broken heart? Ethan grimaced. That was assuming he'd broken her heart.

He forced his mind from the thought of Kate's lips seeking this young blond stud's and focused on the implications of the dog walker's involvement in the case. Were any of the victims connected to the dog owners? They'd need to get the names of his clients and interview them.

Finn locked up Kate's house, and they got into the car. Brutus's fart had not dissipated. Ethan rolled down his window, shooting a glance at Finn Scott. The dog walker had a perturbed look on his face. He was staring over his shoulder at the backseat.

Ethan threw a look over his shoulder. From the corner of his eye, he could see something dark glistening on the seat directly behind him. He sniffed the air in disbelief.

"Jesus Christ!" He flung himself out of the front seat and yanked open the back door.

A tidy pile of fresh dog shit sat on a bed of white dog hair.

Finn climbed in the backseat from the other side, his hand encased in a doggy bag. "Yikes! Sorry about that, Detective," he said. He wasn't completely successful in hiding his smile. He scooped up the poop and tied a knot in the bag. "Alaska didn't get to do his business in the park."

The car stank all the way back to the station.

After washing their hands and disposing of Alaska's disdain, Ethan took the dog walker to a hard interview room for questioning. He fought to control his temper. He needed to be friendly and laid-back, cajole Finn Scott into trusting him. He forced a smile. "That dog is a real troublemaker, huh?"

The dog walker hesitated. "Uh, yeah, he is. He's a real handful, that's for sure."

If it was one consolation, he now knew the dog walker couldn't lie if his life depended on it.

Unfortunately, he realized after questioning him for ten minutes that Finn Scott's transparent honesty was not going to result in a confession.

The guy had a watertight alibi for the nights of Lisa's and Sarah Harper's deaths. Both times he was working his second job as a bartender downtown. His shifts ran from 9:00 p.m. until 3:00 a.m.

"Why were you asking Shonda Bryant about Lisa MacAdam?" Ethan asked, disappointment weighing his chest. The only turd he'd turned up so far in this investigation was Alaska's. And that had been deliberately planted.

"I knew Lisa MacAdam. She was a nice kid. She didn't deserve to die that way."

"That didn't answer my question. Why were you on Agricola Street, asking Shonda Bryant about her?"

Frustration flashed in Finn Scott's eyes. "Because it's obvious you guys are missing something."

Ethan pressed his lips together. Another cocky guy who thought they could do better than the police. "Do you realize you could jeopardize our investigation?"

Finn shrugged. "Shonda knew I was a friend of Lisa's. I thought maybe if she knew something, she'd be more likely to tell me." He met Ethan's gaze. "I was planning to report anything I learned. But as it turns out, it was nothing. She told me she'd told the police everything she knew." He looked slightly sheepish.

Ethan sighed. "You are just lucky you haven't fucked things up, Mr. Scott."

"Any more than they are now?" He crossed his arms. "I want justice for Lisa, Detective. I want that bastard to pay for what he did to her."

Ethan studied him. In a perverse way, Finn Scott's actions made him feel better. Someone, after all, had cared about Lisa MacAdam while she was alive. "It may surprise you, Mr. Scott. But so do I."

43

Thursday, May 17, 4:00 p.m.

"A woman named Kate Lange just came to my lab. Asking about what happens to the donor bodies. Do you know her?"

Anna closed her eyes. Kate Lange. Why was she digging around in this? "Yes. What did you tell her?"

"That the bodies were cremated."

She tensed. "You didn't tell her that we handled them, did you?"

"I had to, Anna. She asked me point-blank." Ron Gill's voice was tight with defensiveness.

"Damn." She rubbed her temple. Everything was crashing in. First Craig, now Kate Lange. Like dominoes. She wouldn't let it fall on her; she wouldn't be trapped. She'd worked too hard to build O'Brien's dusty funeral home business into something modern and compassionate.

Soliciting body parts for medical research seemed like an obvious offshoot of her core services. Not only that, there was a poetic beauty to harvesting tissue for the living from the dead. Then the act of dying would not be a waste. The dead could rest in peace, having completed the eternal circle of life.

But it had all gone horribly wrong. She'd never guessed that Dr. Ronald Gill, wunderkind of biomedical science, could give the promise of miracles with one hand—and unleash a killer with the other. He'd sent over Craig Peters, his assistant, to handle the disarticulations. Craig did a masterful job. And he turned a blind eye when the rest of the body was sold off to tissue processors and distributors. John Lyons decided to make Craig president of their newly formed company, thinking that it would ensure his silence about BioMediSol's illegal tissue brokering.

Then Craig started showing up after-hours. Anna would discover signs that the upstairs embalming room had been used at night. She'd find extra body parts in the freezer. But not all the time. What was going on up there?

She'd wanted to end it, right then. But John Lyons had warned her not to. They'd all be exposed, he said. She and John would end up bankrupt and in prison for their illegal selling of body parts. And Ron didn't want to go to the authorities. The university ethics committee would stop his research on the grounds that not all his limbs had been legally procured; his scientific career would be over.

Anna had been stupid, naive.

She'd listened to them.

"We've got to do something," Ron said, his voice urgent. "Kate Lange is onto us." His voice lowered. "And Craig is having more of these ataxic episodes."

Despite herself, goose bumps crept along her arms. Dr. Gill scared her. But Craig Peters terrified her. She couldn't let either of them do that to her. She needed to stay in control to get them out of this mess. "What do you think is causing it?"

"I don't know. At first, I thought it was a neurological disorder…but now I'm wondering if it's a disease."

She straightened. "Disease? What kind of disease?"

He spoke so softly she barely heard the next words. "CJD. Creutzfeldt-Jakob disease. He has these spells where he goes rigid, becomes clumsy, can't speak. CJD has those symptomatic behaviors."

"Is it fatal?" She held her breath. Could the solution be as simple as that?

"Yes."

A smile broke out on her face.

There was a pause. A pause so fraught with anxiety that it wiped the smile away.

"We could all have it, Anna." The words came out in a choked whisper.

Her hand tightened on the phone. "What? How could that be?"

"I was trying to figure out how Craig got it. I think he became infected while disarticulating an infected body." He paused. "If I'm not mistaken, we've all handled the bodies."

Her mind raced. The phone became slippery in her fingers and she had to switch hands.

"Did you cut yourself with anything that had been used on the tissue?"

"No."

"Then you are probably safe." Her body went limp with relief. Ron cleared his throat. "I, on the other hand, may not be."

"Can you do a test or something?"

"No. And the disease can be dormant for years…" His voice trailed off as the implications of his words sank in.

She breathed out slowly. "I'm sorry, Ron." It was a lie. She wanted this nightmare to be over. She'd tried to help medical science—and make a small profit—and instead got seduced by an unscrupulous researcher and terrorized by his psychopathic ex-surgical resident assistant.

She needed to cut her losses.

And somehow get the upper hand of this serial killer they'd unleashed.

"Do you think he's still capable of doing the procedures?"

"Yes. The disease hasn't progressed far enough along. What I'm worried about is that he may become careless and the police will find him."

"Which will lead them to us." Her heart thudded in her ears.

"Exactly."

The business line began to blink. She couldn't afford to ignore it. Not when she needed one more pair of limbs to fill that rush order. "Look, I've got a call coming in. I'll call John and see what can be done about Kate Lange."

She hung up and punched the button for the other line. "Keane's Funeral Home." The morgue attendant who answered was a friend of hers. A new body to pick up. A homeless guy. Whenever it was convenient.

Someone was looking out for her today. Her last pair of limbs had just walked into her arms. Now if she could just figure out how to deal with Ron Gill and Craig Peters.

She glanced at her watch: 4:28 p.m. Just enough time to get the body, put together her shipment and have it delivered. She grabbed her purse and headed out to the loading bay.

The traffic crawled along Brunswick Street. Kate tapped the wheel. Should she?

Yes. She should. If she was correct in her assumptions, Anna Keane was running an under-the-table body brokering business that could infect hundreds, even thousands, of people.

The next question was tougher.

Did she have the guts to do it?

Did she have the guts to walk away from her career? Because that's what she would be doing if she was caught. She'd be kissing goodbye her fast-track to the bench, probably her law license if she was convicted of break and enter, not to mention her steady paycheck. Which meant she'd lose her house. Which meant she wouldn't be able to keep Alaska. Especially if she was sent to jail.

She pictured his bright blue eyes. His nose pressed into her hand first thing in the morning, the gentle lick on her cheek to rouse her. The impossibly soft, thick fur that soothed her as she stroked him.

She gritted her teeth. He was the only thing that she loved. The only thing.

And if she lost her home, if she was sent to jail, what would happen to him? Who would look after him?

Tears stung her eyes. She blinked furiously.

Hundreds of people could have their lives ruined because of Anna Keane. Mothers, fathers, children. Could she live with herself if she ignored her suspicions?

Yet could she hold her head up again if she was sent to jail for breaking into Keane's Funeral Home? Everything she'd done to succeed in life was to prove she wasn't like her father.

And now she was contemplating following in his footsteps...

She gripped the steering wheel.

She'd just have to make sure she didn't get caught.

Easier said than done. She didn't have a clue how to go about breaking in. Hell, she wasn't even sure what she was looking for.

By the time she turned onto the residential street behind

Keane's Funeral Home, she'd come up with a plan: she was going to get the feel of the place and see if there was a way into it. Then, later tonight, she would return and somehow break in. She'd look for records that would show Anna Keane was illegally supplying bodies to BioMediSol. Seemed a little optimistic, but that was the best she could come up with. *That's why you're a lawyer and not a criminal. You lack imagination.* That thought cheered her in a perverse way.

She pulled up beside a curb. A deep parking lot fanned out from the back entrance of the funeral home, but there were no other cars to camouflage her, so she parked under a tree. Dumpsters neatly lined one end of the lot.

The far side of the building had a low addition built onto it, with a tall chimney attached. It was the crematorium from the looks of things. Where, presumably, Dr. Gill's picked-clean bodies were turned to ash. On the other end of the building a hearse sat expectantly in front of a loading bay. The car's black doors spread open like beetle wings.

Anna Keane walked through the loading bay, pushing a gurney. Kate hurriedly slid down in her seat. She peered over the dash. The funeral director collapsed the gurney, expertly loading it into the hearse. She closed the hearse's doors, then locked the back entrance to the funeral home.

Kate's heart pounded. It looked as if Anna Keane was going on a call. The funeral director climbed into the driver's seat of the hearse. The engine roared to life. The hearse slowly rolled forward, then stopped abruptly. Anna Keane cut the engine and jumped out of the car. She had her cell phone pressed to her ear, and was trying to talk into it while unlocking the funeral home's loading-bay doors. She used her shoulder to push the door open and disappeared inside.

Kate stared, her mind whirling.

The door had been opened for her—literally.

She couldn't turn her back to it.

44

She jumped out of her car and ran as fast as her narrow skirt and high heels would allow across the parking lot to the shelter of the Dumpster. She crouched behind it. Water ran over her shoes from a puddle. She didn't want to think about what was in that wastewater.

She scanned the loading bay to the funeral home. It was still empty. Anna Keane had been inside for about two minutes. Keeping close to the brick wall, she crept toward the door. Her ears strained for the tap-tap of Anna Keane's footsteps. All she could hear was her blood pounding.

The loading bay was inches away. She took a deep breath and slid through it.

"I've got it." Anna Keane's voice came from around the corner. "Yes, the invoices were all sent today. Don't worry, I'm on top of it."

Kate glanced frantically around for a place to hide. There was a door off the wide corridor. She darted toward it, her hand fumbling for the knob. *Please God, don't let it be locked.*

It turned soundlessly in her hands. She lunged into the

room and closed the door. Blackness dropped over her. *Like being inside a coffin.* She pushed the thought away and pressed her ear against the door.

"I'll talk to you later." Anna Keane sounded a bit out of breath. Her footsteps increased in tempo as she walked past Kate's door. "I've got a rush order. I've got to go."

Kate heard her go through the loading bay. The door snapped shut. She breathed a sigh of relief. It didn't sound as if Anna Keane had set an alarm, so no motion detectors to contend with.

Her hand fumbled against the wall for a light switch. She turned it on. Cool fluorescent lights flickered overhead. She put a hand to her mouth.

The room was full of coffins. Long, short, black, brown, white, ornate, plain.

She took a deep breath. Well, what did she expect? She'd come snooping around a funeral room. *Just be grateful they weren't occupied.* This was obviously a storage room.

She shut off the light and opened the door. A quick glance down the hallway confirmed that it was empty. She walked to the end of the corridor and paused.

Silence.

At least on this floor. She couldn't tell if there was anyone else in the building. It was after five o'clock. She hadn't seen any other cars in the back parking lot. She guessed that Anna Keane had been the attendant on duty.

But who knew how long it would take for Anna Keane to retrieve her latest corpse and bring it back.

She hurried down the hallway. For the second time that day, a smell triggered a memory. This was worse than the last.

It was the way her sister had smelled after she'd been laid out in her coffin.

Formalin. With a faint after-note of decay.

She stopped, her throat tightening. The odor came from a room with an open door. She walked in slowly. It was dark. No windows.

The dark closed in on her again, crowding her with more memories. Of her shame and despair when she was a teenager. Of her aimlessness until she realized her life would never change unless she got her act together. Of her law school graduation, of her admission to the bar. Of her job offer at LMB. Of Alaska greeting her with his goofy grin when she walked in the door.

The dark pounded on her head.

Get away. Get away.

She shouldn't have come here. She should escape while she could. Before she got caught. Because she knew she would.

She'd worked so hard to get to this point in her life, to leave behind her shame. She couldn't just throw it away. She'd find some other way to nail BioMediSol.

She turned.

Stopped.

Squeezed her eyes tight.

"Fuck it."

She flipped the light switch on. Her gaze fell on the metal gurney in the middle of the room.

She stared at its smooth, silver surface. At the drains running down the side. An embalming tank with a thick pink tube wrapped around it sat nearby. No sign that this was where her sister had been pieced together for her funeral fifteen years ago.

She imagined all the dead people who had been bathed, stitched, embalmed, made up and dressed so that their loved ones would be able to grieve without being reminded again of the pain they had suffered.

Was this the same place that people's loved ones were now being taken apart?

If that had happened to her sister…

Her heart began hammering in her ribs.

She had thought she was trying to protect all the living victims who might get infected from tainted tissue. But now she realized she was here to protect the dead victims, too.

It was one thing to choose to donate your body to be used for the greater good of all; it was another to have it stolen after you could no longer defend yourself. She would protect all the sisters, mothers, fathers and brothers that had been entrusted to Anna Keane and were being taken apart, piece by piece, and sold to the highest bidder.

She circled the room, her heels sounding like hammers on the ceramic floor, walking by—but not touching——the equipment. A shelf of green disinfectant soap and pink and orange bottles lined one wall. But there were no filing cabinets in here. Where would the records be kept? She hadn't noticed any filing cabinets in Anna Keane's office, either.

Then her eye caught something. It was a red button set in a panel on the far wall next to a light switch. She hurried over to it. As she neared it, she saw that an elevator door was recessed into the wall, barely noticeable from across the room. Maybe the elevator led to Anna's—or, better yet, BioMediSol's—offices.

She pressed the button. The elevator door slid open silently and she walked in. She couldn't shake the feeling she was being lured into a trap. She pushed the lone button in the elevator, battling the fear that mushroomed as the elevator climbed upward.

The elevator stopped at the attic. The doors opened. She stepped gingerly out of the lift into darkness. The elevator slid back down to the bottom floor. She stood for a moment in the dark, the odor of decay crawling into her pores.

She patted the wall. Relief cascaded through her as her fingers hit a light switch.

Light flickered over the room. The opaque glass of the attic's lone window reflected her tense face back at her. The light would be visible from outside. She needed to hurry.

Her gaze skimmed the room. It was small, probably a secondary office in another life. Now it had been converted into an embalming room. It had the same setup as the embalming room below, but it didn't have the long counter: just a gurney, a sink mounted over a cupboard, a small filing cabinet and three meat freezers all squeezed together.

She hurried over to the filing cabinet and yanked the top drawer open.

Bingo. These were BioMediSol's records. This room must be where BioMediSol did its tissue harvesting.

She pulled out the first three records. They appeared to be for leg parts.

She would try to match the ID numbers on the records to the body parts in the freezers. The body parts might still have the names of the decedents on them. She could trace them back to Anna Keane's clients. Then she could contact family members and find out if consent was ever given. And if it wasn't, Anna Keane and BioMediSol would be toast.

She eyed the freezers.

Took a deep breath.

Here goes. Goose bumps chased her nerves as she pulled open the door of the first freezer. Long knobby strips of yellow flesh in clear plastic bags lay jumbled carelessly on top of one another. She stared at them, confused. Then she realized what they were: spinal cords.

They were each labeled with a tag, on which was scrawled a name and an identification number.

She closed the lid and pulled open the next freezer. A scream welled in her throat. She bit it back just in time. Eyes glared balefully up at her. Two dozen pairs of frozen eyeballs, at least.

She slammed the door closed. Sweat trickled down her sides. It had a rank smell, one she'd never smelled on herself before, like that of a trapped animal. She prayed that she would find legs under door number three. She could deal with legs.

She flipped open the lid.

A foot stuck up from the pile of legs. It looked as if it had tried to kick the door open.

She jumped back.

She could have sworn it moved. She swiped the sweat from her face. She needed to get out of here.

But first she needed to match the ID numbers she had on the BioMediSol records with those dismembered legs. She checked the kicking foot. It did not match any of the three ID numbers. She reached in and quickly pulled up the bagged limb under it. The ID number didn't match. Nor did the next one.

Damn. Maybe BioMediSol had already sold the batch for these records.

She reached down into the freezer to return the limb. A tattoo on the inside of the ankle caught her eye. It was a small hummingbird fluttering next to a honeysuckle. The colors were dulled, the brown skin no longer providing a rich contrast to the reds and oranges.

She stared at it.

A hummingbird.

"A little bird. With little wings that fly really fast."

That was how Shonda had described Vangie Wright's tattoo.

She checked the name. The leg was identified as belonging to Mary Littler. The foot was so small it looked childlike. But no child would sport a tattoo. She stared at the delicate design. Her breath caught in her throat. The vine trailing away from the honeysuckle was subtly curled to form the initials *V.W.*

She closed the freezer and ran over to the filing cabinet. She needed to find the record for Vangie Wright/Mary Littler.

The deep rumble of the hearse vibrated from outside. The engine died.

A door banged shut downstairs.

45

Her fingers fumbled over the handle of the filing cabinet drawer.

Be calm. You still have time.

She yanked open the drawer. Tabs separated groups of files by the hundreds. She searched frantically for 1429. A glance confirmed the number matched the ID on the leg labeled Mary Littler.

She pulled the forms, stuffing them in her waistband. Running to the elevator, she flipped off the light and jabbed the button.

But what if Anna Keane had seen the light and was waiting for her at the bottom of the elevator?

Fear weakened her legs. Until now, she'd only been afraid of what Anna Keane could do to her career if she caught her. But seeing Mary Littler's/Vangie Wright's dismembered leg had cast a whole new light on the funeral director. She didn't have proof—yet—it was Vangie Wright's leg, but she was damn sure it was. Vangie Wright had gone from being a missing prostitute to a cadaveric product.

Had Anna Keane killed her?

The thought stopped her heart. When it resumed beating, it skittered like a mouse running across a marble floor.

Stop panicking.

She took a deep breath and kicked off her shoes. Snatching them from the ground, she stepped away from the elevator, achingly conscious of the vibration her footsteps would make on the ceiling below.

She slipped through the doorway of the mini embalming room and into a big storage area. It was full of boxes and tools. A narrow wooden staircase ran along a side wall.

She crept down the stairs. They ended in a small kitchenette. It looked like a staff room, with a table and chairs, a microwave and a refrigerator. She hurried into the hallway. The lights were dim but they shone like spotlights after being in the dark.

She hugged the wall and began inching her way along the plush, ornately patterned carpet. To her left was the chapel. A soft light glowed within. On her right was a private reception area. In a few moments, she would pass Anna Keane's office and then she'd be home free.

She crept closer to the funeral director's office. The light was on. Was she inside?

She paused, listening.

She could hear nothing. The funeral home was silent.

She crouched down and crawled past Anna Keane's door.

A door banged loudly.

Her pulse jumped in her veins.

Was it the front door or the back?

She took a deep breath and ran to the main door. No sign of Anna Keane or her staff. The banging must have come from the back. She grabbed the doorknob. The door wouldn't budge.

It's after five o'clock; it's locked.

She scrabbled around the knob and found the dead bolt. It slid back smoothly just as her shoes fell from her arms.

Jesus.

She snatched them from the ground and yanked the door open.

Damp air brushed her face. She darted outside, closing the door behind her. Rain fell on her hair.

She slid on her shoes and walked quickly to the sidewalk. A car drove down the street. Then another. Relief swept through her. Anna Keane couldn't hurt her now. There'd be witnesses.

She veered to the right, crossed over to the shadows of the newly leafing trees and approached her car from the other side of the street. She jumped into it and locked the door.

She was just about to turn on the engine when a silver sedan drove past her. It turned into the funeral home parking lot. She slid down in her seat again.

The sedan parked next to the hearse. A man got out of the car. She peered desperately through her rain-blurred windshield. She couldn't make out more than his tall, dark form. But she bet it was BioMediSol's president, Craig Peters. With a sudden shock she realized he was probably overseeing the order she'd placed with them. He disappeared inside.

She began to shake. That was too close a call. When she'd decided to sneak into the funeral home, she had totally forgotten that the fake order she'd placed with Bio-MediSol would mean that they would be trying to get the order ready—at the funeral home, where BioMediSol's operations were based.

So much for thinking you were so clever. You almost walked into your own trap.

She peeled away down the street, her body working

into one big shiver by the time she reached her house. She could barely get the door open. Alaska bounded toward her. She buried her face in his fur. He let her hold him until her shivering stopped.

She pulled the BioMediSol forms from her waistband. Mary Littler had died in a car accident, the form said.

She sank down on the floor. Should she call the police? She had a form with a fake name on it.

But was that really Vangie Wright's leg? Tattoos were a dime a dozen. And even if it was, had Vangie been murdered? Maybe she really had died in a car accident. Heck, maybe her real name was Mary Littler. Prostitutes used street names all the time.

There was only one person who could tell her the truth.

Vangie's sister.

46

Friday, May 18, 4:00 p.m.

"Randall, it's CreditAngels on line two." His assistant, Virginia, allowed a hint of puzzlement to creep into her usual efficient tone. CreditAngels was a company that gave credit to people the banks turned away—in exchange for usurious interest rates. They didn't want a person's first-born, Randall thought. Too expensive. He pushed away the nagging irritation that rose whenever he thought of the revised order for custody support his ex-wife's lawyer had delivered two days ago.

He punched line two. "Randall Barrett."

"Mr. Barrett, this is Ashley Dickson from CreditAngels." She spoke with practiced staccato.

"Yes, Ms. Dickson, how can I help you?" He used his smoothest tone. Perhaps the tables had been turned on them and they needed some legal assistance.

"You are the managing partner of Lyons McGrath Barrett, correct?"

Randall didn't like her tone of voice—as if she was honing in for the kill. He frowned. "Yes. And may I inquire as to why you are calling me?"

"We are calling in a bad debt. We demand repayment of $182,000, which includes $57,000 interest on a principal amount of $125,000."

He loved how the loan company called in the loan at the very last hour before the weekend started. He pitied the real Barrett they were after. "You must have me mistaken with a different Barrett. I have no loans with your company."

"But your firm does."

"I can assure you that our firm does not. We deal with a different banker." He allowed a hint of condescension to creep into his voice.

"Mr. Barrett." Ashley Dickson's voice was discomfiting in its absolute confidence. "We have your signature as managing partner on the loan document authorizing LMB to be a guarantor for the loan to BioMediSol, Inc."

"I've never heard of that company." But he sure as hell was going to find out what BioMediSol was about. "I most certainly did not sign the loan, Ms. Dickson. I'm afraid you've been a victim of fraud." He could guess what had happened. Not only was CreditAngels not too fussy about to whom they lent money, it appeared they weren't too particular about getting proper ID, either.

"I don't think so, Mr. Barrett," she said. "The co-signee was John Lyons." Randall's gut contracted. And suddenly the picture crystalized. John Lyons. Surely he wouldn't do this just for revenge. He was sinking the whole damn ship. "He's the one who took the loan. And now he's in default. We want our money, Mr. Barrett. There will be interest penalties accruing as of tomorrow."

He had no doubt that a company named CreditAngels would demand its pound of flesh.

"I'll look into it and get back to you. Please fax me a copy of the lending instrument."

"I'll call you first thing Monday morning."

So John Lyons had faked his signature on a loan document. He doubted the document would ever hold up in court, but the very fact John had resorted to fraud and involved LMB was extremely disturbing. John'd been acting strangely recently. Stressed, uncommunicative, not his usual suave self. He'd even seemed to distance himself from his little protégée, Kate. Randall had been secretly pleased by these developments. He had thought it demonstrated John's awareness of the new order in LMB.

He'd been wrong. Not only that, he'd been duped. And by John Lyons, the man who envied him his success.

Had John duped them in more ways than one?

Had John had been hiding a conflict of interest with BioMediSol?

He picked up the phone. "Virginia, I need all of John Lyons' client records for the past two years. ASAP."

"Right."

He thought for a moment. "And did Kate Lange ever return my call?"

"No."

Was she somehow embroiled in this? Was this her way of getting back at him for stealing his notes?

His gut told him she wasn't the type to be petty. Life had dealt her too many hard knocks.

Then a thought stopped him cold. Maybe John cooked this up with Kate before she joined LMB. Kate would be the perfect recruit: toiling away in a dead-end firm, desperate for success. And then, in a masterstroke, John feigned an interest in Kate whenever he was with Randall—knowing that it would needle him, but never knowing how disturbing Randall found the thought of Kate being intimate with John—in order to distract him from their true intention: to defraud LMB and exact John's ultimate revenge.

He had a sudden image of her amber eyes. They dug so sharply into him and didn't reveal a thing. Whenever he looked into them he had the sensation of staring into a pool of water, of seeing himself reflected in all his flawed nakedness. But never being able to see what was underneath.

She hadn't returned his phone call.

There'd be hell to pay when he saw her next.

Friday, May 18, 4:00 p.m.

"Someone's playing games with us." Anna fought to keep the panic from her voice, but John could hear it.

"What do you mean?"

"I mean that a person pretending they were from a phony company called the Surgical Teaching Institute placed an order."

"Damn." John stared at his desk in disbelief. What the hell was going on? "Who was it?"

"She said her name was Dr. Tupper. I believed her until the delivery times were changed around. No one met our delivery company. Then I discovered that there is no such thing as the Surgical Teaching Institute. And—" her voice rose "—it gets worse. I think someone stole some of Bio-MediSol's files last night."

"What?" Shock accelerated his heart.

"Not only that, but Ron said Kate Lange had been at his lab, asking questions."

"You think she did all this?"

"I don't know who else would." Anna paused. "I just don't know why she's doing it."

"I do," John said softly. "I know exactly why. She's figured it out, Anna."

"Are you sure? You told me no one would figure it out if we put Craig as president."

"There was no paper trail between Keane's Funeral Home and BioMediSol. Nor with me. I didn't think anyone would figure it out." Especially Kate. That's why she'd been the perfect associate for the TransTissue file. He thought she'd be more concerned about getting hired on with LMB than snooping around BioMediSol.

He'd been wrong.

"We've got to do something." Anna's voice was definitely panicked. "Craig's been acting bizarrely. Ron thinks he's got some kind of brain disease. I knew we should have stopped him when we had the chance."

John closed his eyes. "Anna," he said heavily, "we never had the chance."

"But when he first started bringing those dead prostitutes in—"

"He was psychopathic even then. He's been a psycho all his life. Look at how he got kicked out of the surgical residency program. The only way to stop him would have been to call the police. You know we couldn't afford to do that."

"You mean you couldn't," she said bitterly. "You'd lost a few too many times at the blackjack table, right, John?"

Her dig hit home. He flushed. "Don't be ridiculous. If we'd involved the police, they would have begun investigating BioMediSol. They would have found out that some of those body parts had not been donated."

She exhaled in frustration. "Then what the hell do we do now?"

"I'll deal with Kate. You handle Craig."

"Jesus, John, he's a friggin' serial killer!"

"Anna, you have to be calm about this."

"How can I be calm? He's out of control. We could be next!"

She was right. He needed to be dealt with. "Look, just get him to the upstairs embalming room and inject him. Then stick him in the crematorium." He leaned back in his chair. "Simple."

She exhaled deeply. "Okay. But you better be there, too. He's a maniac."

"Fine. Tell him to come for 8:00 p.m."

47

Friday, May 18, 4:45 p.m.

The fog flirted with the Narrows. It billowed up from the outer harbor toward the slim band of water, dulling it. Within minutes it would enshroud the bridge that connected Halifax to its twin city, Dartmouth.

Kate turned on her headlights and took the exit to Windmill Road. It was one of Dartmouth's working-class areas, lined with small but neat houses and low-rent apartment buildings clad in brick. The neighborhood was inhabited by blue-collar workers, single mothers and retirees whose final years were not tinged with gold. Windmill Road was modest, not destitute. But despite its ordinariness, violent crime was growing at an alarming rate. If there was a murder or assault, chances were good it took place in the north end of Dartmouth.

Vangie Wright's sister, Claudine, lived in an apartment building perched on a slope that rolled down to the water. The building was called, fittingly enough, Blue Water apartments. What the name lacked in imagination was made up for by the view.

Kate parked her car and headed into the foyer. Checking

the security code she had written down, she punched in the number and waited for Claudine to answer.

It had been a stroke of luck to find Vangie's sister. After her narrow escape from the funeral home last night, she had called Shonda, worried that she'd be so high she wouldn't be of any use. But Shonda hadn't answered.

Kate spent the night in suspense, wondering what the reaction of Craig Peters and Anna Keane had been when they realized someone had placed a fake order with them. The clock had started ticking the minute the delivery man was not met.

She just prayed that Anna Keane would not notice that BioMediSol's files had been breached.

The clock would tick in double time then.

Kate spent the morning in LMB's library, pretending it was business as usual. At lunch, her assistant handed her a pink message slip with Randall's name. He'd called first thing this morning, Liz told her.

Kate sat behind her desk and stared at the phone. Had Randall found out that she'd broken into Keane's Funeral Home? The only way he could possibly know was if Anna Keane had told him—which meant he was in collusion with John Lyons.

Yet, with their rivalry, it seemed improbable. Although, they could have started out as partners…

She shook her head. She'd found zero evidence to connect him to either BioMediSol or TransTissue. But she didn't dare call him back. She still didn't trust him. And he always seemed to figure out what she was hiding.

She called Shonda repeatedly throughout the day, her anxiety growing as Shonda's cell phone replayed the same message: "The customer you are trying to reach is not available."

At 4:39 p.m. Shonda answered the phone. She was wary, tight-lipped. But she did tell her that Vangie had a sister named Claudine. The last she'd heard she was living in Dartmouth.

It seemed ironic that after all the risks she had taken to get her hands on BioMediSol's paper trail, she had found Claudine's phone number with a quick flip of the white pages.

Friday, May 18, 5:10 p.m.

John Lyons sat in his car. He studied Kate's house from across the street. Nice neighborhood, but the house needed a bit of work. Whoever bought it would have to put a chunk of money into it.

Every few minutes he spotted Kate's dog. The white husky would stand against the living room window and stare straight at him. As if he knew John was waiting for his protégée.

Why hadn't she just accepted the settling of TransTissue's case gracefully and moved on? She had potential. He bet that she could have had a good career at LMB.

But not anymore.

He glanced at the clock on his dash. It was 5:10 p.m. What was taking her so long? She'd left the office half an hour ago.

If he sat by the curb much longer, people might get suspicious. For once he regretted his luxury vehicle.

His cell phone rang. He jumped. Jesus. He was tense.

It was probably his wife, Lorraine. Wondering if they were still going to the casino tonight.

He needed to act normally. And give himself an alibi. He flipped open the phone. "Hello."

"Lyons."

His heart jolted. "Barrett."

"We need to meet. Now. How soon can you get back to the office?"

His brow broke out into sweat. Damn. He knew from the tone of Barrett's voice that the game was up. Credit-Angels must have contacted Barrett. They'd been threatening to, but he didn't think they'd do it. He thought the money he'd given them as a good-faith payment would keep them quiet.

He didn't want Barrett to think he could be ordered around so easily. But he needed to put out this fire. Fast.

Before everything came crashing down.

But what if Kate tried to contact Barrett before John had a chance to deal with her?

He thought quickly. He'd wait for Kate a bit longer. She must be on her way home. Then he'd handle Barrett.

"I'll be there as soon as I can."

Friday, May 18, 5:10 p.m.

The security door buzzed and Kate let herself into the hallway of Blue Water apartments. She took the small elevator to the second floor. The smell of bacon frying tantalized her nose. She heard a baby crying.

She knocked on 214 and the door opened immediately. A small woman with skin the color of almond biscotti answered. A TV babbled in the background.

"Ms. Wright?" she asked.

"Yes." Her face had a wary look that Kate was becoming all too familiar with. She reminded Kate of a fawn, her delicate frame poised to flee.

"I'm Kate Lange." She smiled and held out her hand. "Thank you for agreeing to see—"

"Who's that, Mama?" A tiny little girl poked her head

around Claudine's legs. She had rows of little pigtails all over her head. Inquisitive brown eyes stared up at her. Kate wasn't good at guessing kid's ages, but she thought she was about six.

"Hi. I'm Kate," she said to the little girl.

"I'm Tania."

"Tania, you go watch your brother," Claudine said. "I've got to talk to this lady for a few minutes." Kate wondered how such a tiny child could be responsible for watching anything.

"Do I have to?" Tania said. "He's so annoying."

Claudine gave her a warning look. "Do as I say."

Tania turned reluctantly from the door, throwing one last look over her shoulder at Kate. Kate gave her a sympathetic smile. She remembered with a pang what it was like babysitting her younger sister.

Claudine held the door open. "Come in."

She walked into the apartment. It was smallish and cheaply furnished, but clean and bright. Tania scrambled over an old velour couch and whispered something into the ear of a little boy who looked twice her size. A cartoon blared but they both ignored it.

Claudine threw them a stern glance and turned to Kate. "We can talk over here." She pointed to a table and chairs set up by the galley kitchen. "Coffee?"

Kate smiled. "Yes, please."

Claudine poured two mugs and brought them on a tray with a small pitcher of milk, a sugar bowl and a plate of sugar cookies. She had obviously set it up in anticipation of Kate's visit.

"Thank you." Kate added some milk and sugar to her mug and took a sip.

Claudine sat down close to her. She cupped her mug

between her slender hands. "You said you had some questions about Vangie?" Her voice was low.

"Yes. First of all, did she ever use the name Mary Littler?"

Claudine shook her head. "Not that I know about. She always stuck with Vangie."

That did it. Mary Littler was a fake name, Kate was sure of it. But just to make sure, she asked, "Did she have a tattoo of a hummingbird on her ankle?"

"Yeah, she got it when she was seventeen. Why do you want to know? Have you seen her?" Her eyes searched Kate's face anxiously. That question slaughtered any lingering doubts Kate had about Anna Keane's guilt.

She swallowed. She had been practicing what to say during her drive over, but telling Claudine that her sister's body had been sold for parts stuck in her throat. "I believe she is dead."

Claudine looked down into her coffee. "I thought so." She raised her chin and met Kate's eyes. "She was pretty sick by the time I heard about it."

"Sick?" Kate stared at her. "With what?"

Claudine pulled out a letter. "I never heard of it. Kratz-filled Jacob or somethin'. Here, you read it."

Kate unfolded the letter. The logo of the Nova Scotia Department of Health was at the top.

"They sent the letter just after Vangie went missing."

"To you?"

"They tried to reach Vangie but she was on the streets by then. I was her next of kin."

Kate put her coffee down and skimmed the letter:

Dear Ms. Wright:
The Department of Health has received information of grave concern to recipients of the human growth

hormone. Our records indicate you received human growth hormone from a donor who subsequently developed Creutzfeldt-Jakob disease. You may be at risk for developing CJD. Please contact us immediately upon receipt of this letter.

Kate put the letter down slowly. "Did Vangie know she'd been exposed to CJD?"

Claudine shook her head. "No. But I think she had it. I seen her a few weeks before she went missing and she was acting strange. She'd been strung out for months, so I figured it was the crack, and I got real mad at her. I didn't even know she'd gone missing till the police called me. One of her friends had filed a missing persons report." She sipped her coffee. Her eyes were sad. "When I got the letter, I called the health people. They told me some of the symptoms."

"And she got it from human growth hormones?"

"Uh-huh. Vangie was real little. Kind of like—" She jerked her head in Tania's direction. "We're all little in my family, but she was the smallest. The doctors gave her these shots when she was eight. To help her grow."

But the shots had been infected with CJD. Kate's mind whirled. If Mary Littler was really Vangie Wright, her infected body had been cut up and distributed by BioMedi-Sol. Who knew if any of her body parts had been implanted into other people. People who had thought they would be healed, not harmed, by the surgery.

"So she's dead?" Claudine's doelike eyes probed hers.

"I'm afraid so."

"I thought she was. But I hoped—" Claudine looked down into her coffee cup. "I hoped maybe she'd gone into rehab somewhere and kicked the crack. She'd done it before." Tears welled in her eyes. "But somethin' told me she was dead." A tear trailed down her cheek. She didn't wipe it away. "She was my big sister. My half sister. She sent me money, you know, helped me get a job at the drugstore before she got so strung out." She looked helplessly around her apartment. "I wouldn't have any of this if she hadn't helped me. And then when I tried to help her…" She wiped her cheek with the back of her hand. "I really tried to help her. But she wouldn't listen…she just wanted the crack. She kept hangin' up on me…"

"I'm sorry," Kate said softly. "You tried."

"But it didn't make any difference. She's dead, isn't she?" Claudine looked at her, anger in her eyes. Anger not at Kate, but at herself.

Kate understood it only too well. That was how she'd felt. Still felt.

"You did your best."

Claudine looked away, out the window at the fog-brushed water. "Maybe."

"Maybe she didn't want you to save her," Kate said softly. Imogen's angry eyes flashed through her head.

"*I don't want to leave yet. Stop bossing me around, Kate. I can make my own decisions!*"

"*Yeah, right. Like snorting up?*"

She'd looked away in shame. Then her righteous anger returned. "I like it! It's not hurting anybody!"

She'd run back to the porch of that house they'd gone to. The one with the party that all the kids wanted to be invited to. Kate had stared after her, fear battling with anger. Her sister had ignored her, was running off into a den of lions. Her sister didn't want her to protect her anymore.

She'd banged on the door and forced Imogen to come with her, threatening to call the cops if anyone interfered. Knowing that she had sealed her fate socially. She was furious her sister had put her in this position. She'd never get asked to another party again.

Both of them were simmering with rage when she peeled away from the curb.

"I hate you. I hate you! Do you hear me?" Imogen had shouted. Her face twisted with anger.

Kate had flinched. Never in her life had her sister said those words to her. After all they'd been through with their father, it'd been an unspoken pledge between them to never hurt each other. They had protected each other.

Until that night.

Imogen seemed to realize how deeply she'd wounded her. She retreated into sulky silence.

Then she blurted out: "I need it, Katie. It makes me feel good. It makes me forget. Don't tell Mom, please. Please."

Despair had flooded through Kate. She understood now her sister's secretiveness. This wasn't the first time. It wasn't the second time, either. Her sister had been withdrawing for months. "You don't need it, Gennie," she'd said fiercely. "We have each other. You don't need it."

"I do. I want it. Nothing else makes me feel like that."

Fear chased away her caution. "No! It's wrong, Gennie. It'll kill you!"

"No, it won't," she'd said. "I'm going to do it whether you like it or not!"

Then the anger came. How could her sister do this to her? She'd made her the bad guy. She'd made her a social pariah. Why couldn't she see she was playing with fire? "Don't do it again. I'll tell Mom—"

Something warm trickled down her sleeve. She looked down, her heart racing. The trembling of her hand had made the coffee slosh over the rim. Two separate streams of liquid ran down her wrist.

She placed the mug on the table and hurriedly wiped her hand. Claudine had gotten up and returned with the coffeepot.

Kate shook her head. She needed to leave before Vangie's sister asked her for details. Claudine didn't need to know what had happened to Vangie's body. It had already been ravaged by drugs and disease. She didn't need to know it'd been ravaged after her death, too. That the no-man's-land Vangie had existed in for most of her life had swallowed her up after death, leaving only traces of her.

She stood. "Do you think I could borrow this letter and make a copy of it?"

"Okay." Claudine rose, looking doubtfully at the letter.

Kate walked to the door. She had the paper trail she needed. Vangie hadn't died in a car accident. And since Claudine hadn't even known her sister was dead, she obviously hadn't given consent to her body being "donated" to BioMediSol.

But how had Vangie died? Was it the crack? Was it CJD?

She had got in the car with some guy and no one had seen her again, Shonda had told her.

Something bad had happened to Vangie. She needed to find out from Ethan what Vicky had learned about Vangie's disappearance and convince him there was more to this than the police thought.

"The police will probably be in touch with you," she said at the door.

"Yeah. They've spoke to me before. But they did nothin'."

The children turned on the sofa. "You goin' Kate?" Tania asked. Her little brother stared at her, obviously used to letting his older sister do the talking.

"Yes. It was nice meeting you." She looked at Claudine. "You have lovely kids."

Claudine allowed a small smile that couldn't hide her pride. "They're okay."

"Take care."

She left the apartment and returned to her car. She had gotten what she came for. In more ways than one.

She'd seen through Claudine's eyes what the path of addiction led to. She had tried to stop her own sister from being lured down that path. Her sister hadn't wanted to be saved.

Her cell phone rang. She started violently. "Hello?" Her voice was trembling. She swallowed.

"Kate. It's Randall." There had been no mistaking his impatience, but now he paused. "Are you okay?"

Her breath caught. She wanted, more than anything, to tell him no. She wasn't. The pain of her sister's abandonment—for she now realized that was what her sister had done: she had abandoned the silent, struggling partnership they had forged after her father's imprisonment for the oblivion of drugs—was spilling through the cracks of her reserve. Threatening to reveal the depths of her pain at being left alone. The sole survivor of the destruction her father had brought down on their heads.

She forced herself to inhale. She could not, would not, let her boss—this man who had both stolen from her with one hand and offered comfort with the other—know that, at this moment, her heart was riven. Wide open and raw. For all and sundry to see.

She needed to pull it together.

She needed to help Claudine and the families of all the other victims that BioMediSol had stolen from. And that meant keeping her boss at a distance until the job was done.

"I'm fine." She made her voice as cold as possible. It worked this time.

There was silence. "Did you get my message?" he asked warily.

"Yes." Again, cool, distant.

"Why didn't you return my phone call?"

"It seemed pointless." The words came out before she could stop them. But she was glad she said them. She hoped it would eradicate whatever concern Randall might feel about her. They both needed to retreat behind the professional divide of boss and employee, managing partner and first-year associate.

There was a stunned pause. She allowed herself a flash of weary triumph. It wasn't a response a man like Randall got very often. If ever. He inhaled sharply. "What do you mean?"

"Nothing." She could sense his antagonism building. She shouldn't have been so brusque. She didn't need to offend him, just keep him away. She added, "I'm sorry I didn't return your call earlier."

"You can give me a full explanation in my office," he said curtly. "I need you to come in now."

Damn. "I can't come right now, Randall. I've got an urgent matter to attend to."

"I'm not asking, Kate." His voice was steely. "Come now. Or don't bother coming back at all."

The phone went dead in her ear.

She threw it on the seat. "Damn him!" But she was really damning herself.

She headed toward the new bridge, debating her course of action. Police cars flashed up ahead. The traffic had slowed to a crawl at the tollbooths. Cars were veering away, racing to the old bridge. A gap in the traffic showed there had been an accident.

"Damn." She abruptly turned down one of the exits, heading for the old bridge. Her frustration—and her pain—

threatened to boil over. She had wanted to avoid Randall until she'd presented her case to the criminal investigations unit. But Randall's phone call had reminded her of something she'd forgotten.

She drove over the bridge, turning off Hollis Street toward Lower Water Street. The gleaming monolith housing LMB was five minutes away.

Once she presented her case to the police, it would blow the lid off BioMediSol and, in turn, TransTissue. Legal ethics dictated she give her firm warning of what was about to go down with one of their top clients.

And resign before the shit hit the fan.

48

Friday, May 18, 5:50 p.m.

Kate Lange still had not come home. Where the fuck was she? He couldn't wait for her any longer. John Lyons' mind raced as he drove against the tail end of rush hour traffic to his office.

Despite his resolve, cold sweat ran down his back. Had Barrett found out about the withdrawals John made on his clients' trust accounts? John had paid them back with the money he'd borrowed for BioMediSol. BioMediSol had never needed the money—their overhead costs were minimal thanks to Anna Keane's on-site facilities—but he'd convinced Anna that the money was needed for future expansion. Eager to grow her empire, she was all over that suggestion.

But he hadn't been able to pay the loan back. He'd been actively buying properties in the U.S., leveraging them to the hilt to buy more. He'd been like a kid in a candy shop. And then everything crashed. The banks were calling in their loans. One after another. He hadn't been able to recover.

He drove into the parkade and took the elevator to LMB's reception area. He stopped, gazing around. He had helped build this firm. He remembered when they moved into these offices. Right on the water, the top two floors. He loved being on the penthouse level. Stunning views of Georges Island and the mouth of the harbor. They had furnished it as befitting a firm of their reputation: with high quality, tasteful and expensive pieces, thick carpeting, stylish cubicles for the support staff and an extensive legal library staffed with their own librarian.

John had personally chosen every piece of artwork on the walls. It was a collection that had taken ten years to build, but it was worth it. He had enjoyed the thrill of scouting emerging Canadian artists, convinced that the value of their paintings would jump exponentially over time.

Everything he had built, had strived for, was teetering on the brink of disaster. His partnership in the firm was his final reserve. The last bastion that could hold the wolves at bay. And now Randall Barrett had called him.

It rankled. Deeply.

He strode into Barrett's office. He'd always hated the stark modernism Barrett surrounded himself with. Harsh angles, hard materials. Barrett had blatantly ignored the design aesthetic John had chosen for the firm.

Barrett swung his chair around, surprise flashing across his face. "I was beginning to think you'd changed your mind about coming in, Lyons." Barrett kept his gaze cool, but John could feel the anger emanating from him.

John had rarely seen his partner show emotion. He'd have to tread carefully. He lowered himself into a leather-and-metal chair that was so ingeniously constructed he couldn't figure out the seams. He kept his features blank. He wasn't going to give an inch to this upstart bastard.

"You said you had something to discuss." There was only one way to conduct this meeting: on the offensive.

"I had a phone call this afternoon. From a lending agency called CreditAngels."

John tried to lean back in the chair but it was almost impossible. "And?"

"They are calling in a loan. One you signed on behalf of the firm. Fraudulently, I might add." Barrett's tone was casual. He could have been recounting a golf game.

No point in lying about it. Barrett would have seen the loan document by now. "I'll repay it. With interest."

"Of course you will. The question is, are there other loans out there that we don't know about?"

"No." He held Barrett's gaze. "Just that one. I was short on cash. I needed it to invest in a promising new company." He made his voice earnest. "It was such a good opportunity, I couldn't walk away from it. The tissue industry is booming. I'll be able to repay the firm within six months."

"What I want to know is whether you advised Trans-Tissue to settle because it would further your interest in BioMediSol."

John recoiled. His back hit the metal frame of the chair. He cursed it silently. "No! Of course not. I would never do such a thing."

Skepticism radiated from Barrett's face. "Don't bullshit me. I want the TransTissue files on my desk tomorrow morning."

Tomorrow was Saturday. John fought to control his reaction to Barrett's arrogant demand. Ordering him around like a fucking articled clerk. He forced his voice to remain neutral. "Randall, I've been practicing for twenty-three years. I have never in my career given legal advice that was contrary to the best interests of my clients." It pained him to think that all those years of success would be undermined by this son of a bitch. Ever since Barrett had joined the firm, he'd done his best to sabotage his power. To the point that he had been voted managing partner last year. Instead of John. It had wounded him, more than he'd ever let Barrett know.

He felt a perverse pleasure knowing he caused the smooth bastard grief. "I admit I made a mistake regarding the loan. I can pay that back. I'll draw up the terms tonight."

"I'll draw them up," Barrett said sharply. "But I'm more concerned about the TransTissue case, Lyons. If you've exposed the firm to a conflict-of-interest suit it won't matter whether you repay the money. It'll cost us a lot more to defend it. The damage to our reputation will be incalculable."

John forced himself to meet Barrett's gaze. He didn't want Barrett to see that he'd found his weak spot. Because if Barrett knew he'd compromised his legal advice—just this once, to keep BioMediSol's practices away from the magnifying glass of the judicial process—Barrett would start digging around his other clients. And then he'd discover he'd been dipping into their accounts.

If that happened, there was no question that he'd be kicked out of the firm. The bar society would suspend or disbar him. His reputation would be in shreds. He'd lose any chance of earning the kind of income he needed to pay back the debts looming over his head.

Barrett placed his palms on his desk. "I'm calling an emergency meeting with the partners tomorrow afternoon at 2:00 p.m. We expect a full accounting of the situation. Don't try to cover anything up, Lyons. It'll just get worse for you."

Twenty-three years of legal practice had taught him one thing: never show them when they've got you by the balls.

"I've got nothing to hide," he said, rising to his feet. He

turned on his heel and left the bastard's office. Sweat beaded his brow. He wiped his hand impatiently across his forehead.

He walked to the reception area and got into an elevator. But instead of punching the button to take him to the parking garage, he went down one floor to the level occupied by associates and junior partners. Taking the stairs two at a time, he slipped back upstairs and hurried down the hallway, going the long way around to his corner office. Never before had he been so grateful that his office was in the opposite corner to Barrett's.

He grabbed his briefcase, flung open his filing cabinet and began stuffing papers into it. His ears strained for the sound of Barrett's footsteps.

The hallway was quiet.

Sweat drenched his shirt to his back. He snapped his briefcase closed. He had brought a coat with him, and now he draped it over his arm, covering the hand holding the briefcase. He closed his office door, locking it. He knew that Barrett could probably jimmy the lock but it was more of a delaying tactic than anything else. He'd think that there were files worth protecting inside John's office. By then, John would have destroyed them in his shredder at home.

He walked lightly on the balls of his feet to the stairwell, taking the same route as before. The pressure in his chest eased. He had the documents. Kate was next on the list.

A plan formulated in his mind. One that killed two birds with one stone.

She would be the Body Butcher's next victim.

After Craig took care of her, they'd kill Craig and dispose of him in the crematorium. Anna wouldn't be pleased with this change of plans; she wanted to kill Craig right away. But they could wait a few hours until he'd disarticulated Kate's body and inscribed his signature.

Then they'd inject him, and slide him into the crematorium. There'd be one less serial killer to prey on the world.

John would drive Craig's car to a spot in the south end and dump Kate's body.

When Kate's body was found the next day, the firm would be in an uproar and the meeting would be postponed. The wind would be taken out of Barrett's sails. The partners would be reacting to losing one of their own; they'd be in a more charitable mood. He'd been a role model and a mentor to many of them. He'd plead stress and his wife's spending habits. They wouldn't want to believe he'd been living a lie for the past five years. They'd give him a chance.

But only one. There'd be no forgiveness if they knew he'd compromised TransTissue, or that he'd borrowed clients' money.

He took the elevator down to the parkade and hurried to his car. It was parked along a back wall, a lone silver symbol of status and wealth that had never failed to give John satisfaction. It was sleek, fast and played hard. He was always careful to leave his car parked away from the high-density areas where it could get scratched or bumped. He opened the trunk, placing the briefcase inside.

A car rumbled up the ramp.

He froze.

The car slid into a parking space opposite the elevator.

He glanced at it from the corner of his eye.

His heart leaped with adrenaline.

It was Kate.

Why had she suddenly shown up here?

Had Barrett called her in to question her about TransTissue—and sent her straight into his arms instead? What perfect justice.

She got out of her car.

He picked up the tire iron in the trunk and pressed it against his trouser leg.

"Kate!"

49

Friday, May 18, 6:20 p.m.

At the sound of John's voice, Kate started. She couldn't see him at first. It was dim in the parkade. Then she saw his form silhouetted against his car.

"Oh. Hi, John." She gave a nonchalant wave and turned toward the elevator. Her heart pounded furiously. He was the last person, the very last person, she wanted to see right now. She hadn't figured out his connection to Bio-MediSol but she was sure there was one. And if he was connected to them, then he was involved in some very dirty deeds.

"Wait, Kate!" He walked hurriedly toward her.

She stopped and turned. "I have a meeting, John. I have to go." She forced a smile.

"I need to talk to you before you speak to Randall." He stood stiffly, his arms rigid at his sides, next to the trunk of a very nice car. Randall's, in fact.

"I don't think so."

"Kate." Disappointment, pain, concern were all wrapped up in that one syllable. "Don't be like that. I want to help you be successful."

"Help me?" Anger at John's betrayal—of her faith in him, of his callous disregard for people's health, of his criminal use of the dead—flooded through her, capturing in its torrent her grief and pain. "I think you'd better help yourself."

She knew it was the wrong thing to say the minute it came out of her mouth.

He stared at her.

Finally, he said, "What do you mean?" His voice was dangerously soft.

She felt the hair on her arms rise. "Nothing."

"Oh, I think you do know, Kate," he said. His eyes hardened. "If you are as smart as you think you are, you'll keep your mouth shut with Randall."

It was the first time Kate had ever heard him speak without his usual courtliness.

She tensed. She wanted to run. But his next words pinned her to the spot.

"You do have a secret, don't you, Kate? One you wouldn't want him—or the bar society—to know."

She felt her skin go clammy. "I don't know what you are talking about." She wanted him to keep talking, to confirm her darkest doubts about him, but her body wanted to flee. She took a step back. "Look, I've got to go—"

He smiled. "I won't tell anyone that you broke into Keane's Funeral Home and stole confidential records—"

She felt her insides turn icy. She had heard all she needed to hear. He could only know about her theft if he was in collusion with Anna Keane. And if he was in collusion with Anna Keane, it meant he knew she was onto him. It meant he had every reason to keep her quiet.

"John, I don't know what you're talking about—"

He smiled. "Don't bother bluffing, Kate. We know what you did. So here's the deal—you keep our secret safe, and we'll keep yours. Otherwise, you can kiss your legal career goodbye."

What he didn't realize was that she'd already said goodbye to it.

He leaned against Randall's car. He began to tap something against the bumper.

She glanced down. And froze.

It was a tire iron.

Slowly, but very surely, it was hammering a long dent into the gleaming chrome of Randall's Jag.

"I don't mean to rush you, Kate, but I believe Randall is waiting for you."

She swallowed. "No deal."

Then she gathered every ounce of energy she had and spun around. She bolted down the parkade ramp to the stairwell. John lunged after her.

Something clattered out of her pocket. She could hear John's footsteps, surprisingly light and frighteningly fast.

She reached the door to the stairwell. Ragged breathing filled her ears. Was it hers? Or was it John's?

It was John's.

He was closing in on her. She wrenched the door handle, pulling it with all her strength. It opened and she threw herself forward. Her body moved faster than her feet. She pitched headfirst down the damp concrete steps. John grabbed her arm. Righting her.

Relief rushed through her. Followed by sick realization.

He raised his arm.

Out of the corner of her eye, she saw it. The tire iron.

Fear made her legs weak. She yanked herself free of his grip.

She felt the whoosh of air being displaced by motion. A sob broke free of her throat. "No—"

The tire iron cracked down on her head.

The stairwell engulfed her in black.

50

Pain. Throbbing, taunting, exploding in waves. She had never felt pain like that before. It consumed her. Made her long for unconsciousness.

She tried to open her eyes. The lids were weighted with lead. Dizziness overwhelmed her. She let her lids fall. It was easier to succumb than to fight it.

"She's coming to." It was John's voice.

Panic welled in her. Where was she? What was wrong with her?

She tried to open her eyes again. Dizziness slammed into her.

She breathed deeply. A smell taunted her consciousness. Strong, unmistakable. *Imogen.*

It made her nausea worse.

"Quick, is it ready?" That was a woman's voice.

"Here," John said. "You do it. I'm no good with these things."

"I'll bet," the woman replied, disgust in her voice.

The woman's name was right on the tip of her tongue. Which was dry, so dry. She needed a drink of water.

Someone grabbed her arm, pushing her sleeve quickly

up to her bicep. It was the woman. Her fingers were businesslike, practiced.

"Look, while she's out, I've got to check in with my wife. So she doesn't get suspicious."

The woman's fingers tightened. "No. You need to stay, John. I can't face him alone."

"Don't worry. I'll be back in plenty of time."

"John!" The woman's panic was evident in her voice. "Wait. Please, don't go."

There was a pause. Then John said in his most soothing voice, the voice Kate knew even in her groggy state was his most dangerous, "Don't worry, I'll be back."

The door thudded before the woman could respond.

Cool air rushed over Kate's skin. A piece of tubing pinched her above the elbow as it was tightened.

Sweaty fingers tapped the skin over her vein. She wanted to pull her arm away but couldn't. She turned her head. The white spots tilted sickeningly.

Jab. Despite the woman's palpable anxiety, the needle slid into her vein smoothly. Anna was good at this. *Anna.* That's who the voice belonged to.

Nausea surged through her. She moaned. Then came the undertow of sleep. A heavy, rolling sleep.

Don't. Don't.

Fight it.

The heaviness rolled over the pain in her head. It rolled through her muscles, holding down her limbs.

She let it take over.

Blackness floated through her.

Friday, May 18, 7:16 p.m.

He couldn't believe it.

She'd stood him up.

Randall glanced at his watch again: 7:16 p.m. He'd called her more than an hour ago.

Damn it. He needed her to cooperate. He ran a hand over his face. He'd let his anger override his professionalism and now this was the price he was going to pay. He'd thrown her an ultimatum and she'd stamped on it. Out of anger? He wasn't sure. She'd sounded on the verge of tears. Maybe she was taking a few minutes to collect herself. Because he knew she wouldn't appear in his office teary-eyed and vulnerable. No, she would stride in and give him a curt excuse for her tardiness, her gaze defiant in her red-rimmed eyes.

At least he hoped so. Otherwise, there was only one conclusion to draw from her failure to appear.

She was on John's side, after all.

Friday, May 18, 7:20 p.m.

"Ethan. Come to the war room pronto." Ferguson's voice was tight with excitement. "The lab just called."

"I'll be there in five." He threw his cell phone onto Lamond's lap, checked his rearview mirror and did a quick U-turn. "They've got the results from the last victim," he told Lamond.

"Finally," Lamond muttered. They were both frustrated. It'd been a fruitless day. Ethan had been interviewing surgeons, Lamond had been going through morgue records. So far, everyone was above reproach.

They made it to the station in three minutes. Ethan and Lamond jumped out of the car and ran into the building. The war room was buzzing when they arrived. Ethan felt adrenaline surge through him. Something had finally broken on the case.

Ferguson stood at the head of the board table. The other detectives crowded around her. As soon as Ethan and Lamond reached the table, Ferguson cleared her throat.

They fell silent at once. Their usual banter had been worn out from the strain of too many days with too many disappointments.

"Our killer has finally slipped," she said. Her eyes gleamed with anticipation. "The lab found trace evidence on victim number three's body."

"Semen?" Lamond asked.

Ferguson shook her head. "Embalming fluid."

51

Friday, May 18, 7:24 p.m.

He walked into the embalming room. The familiar smell embraced him, tantalizing his senses. It was like coming home. It *was* home.

He strode across the room. The elevator door was sitting open, waiting for him.

This was a good sign. He punched the button and waited, glancing at his watch: 7:24 p.m. He was early.

But he couldn't wait any longer.

Adrenaline pumped through his body.

Anna had called him in tonight for an "extra case."

There had been something in her voice—fear, desperation, anxiety—that he had never heard from her before. But he wanted to hear it again. When he was tightening his grip on her.

He was happy to come in, he said.

The elevator stopped. She would be on the other side of the door. His muscles tightened in anticipation. Spots flecked and foamed around his vision. The door slid open. His legs would not bend. *Jesus.* He didn't know what was happening to him, but it couldn't happen now. Not when the need was so great. Using all his strength, he staggered forward.

Anna turned.

His muscles relaxed in a liquid rush. Urge swamped his brain.

Her eyes met his. Her face changed to a look he craved. Fear.

She backed away. "Craig? You're early."

Friday, May 18, 7:27 p.m.

Randall tapped his desk impatiently, staring out the window. Halifax Harbour at one corner, the Citadel at the other. They were the city's two main strongholds: the navy commanding the water, the army manning the fortress. It was a fitting view.

He thought of John Lyons. He'd held on to his superior harbor view with the tenacity of a two-year-old holding a lollipop. He didn't even realize that Randall had no interest in it.

Was he also blind to the fact that Randall was onto him? Randall hadn't been fooled for a minute by John's declaration that he'd only defrauded LMB with the CreditAngels loan. There were more skeletons in his closet. And they were just waiting to drag all the partners into their danse macabre.

He glanced at his watch again: 7:27 p.m.

His jaw tightened. She wasn't coming.

He certainly wasn't waiting for her. He'd given her the benefit of the doubt. Whatever had upset her was no excuse for failing to appear. She'd have a hell of a lot to answer for come Monday morning.

He strode to the elevator, punching P2 on the panel. The parkade was almost empty. He walked to his low-slung E-type, its gleaming green finish improving his mood. God, he loved driving that car.

Despite his irritation, a small smile curved his mouth.

It quickly faded when he noticed the other car sitting three spots away from his.

It looked like Kate's.

He peered through the driver's window. The car was empty. He scanned the interior. The backseats were covered with white dog hair.

That confirmed it. It was her car.

He pulled out his phone and dialed her cell number.

A phone chimed in response. Somewhere around the corner.

His flesh rose.

He strode down the ramp, his heart slamming into his ribs. Kate must have come to meet him.

Where was she?

The chime was getting closer.

He slowed down, scanning the parking lot.

Silver gleamed against the concrete. He ran toward it, the chiming now sounding eerily foreboding.

He snatched the cell phone from the ground and hurried to the elevator.

Kate had been in the parkade.

What happened to her? Could she be in her office, going through the TransTissue file? Could she have dropped her cell phone and not noticed?

He punched the elevator button, practically diving through the doors when it arrived. The elevator climbed to the associates' floor. His heart rate climbed with it. He ran down the hallway to her office. There was a stillness in the corridor. Where the fuck was everyone? Didn't they have work to do?

He was disgusted with the disappearance of the associates on a Friday night. The smell of burned coffee reached his nose. Someone had left the coffee on in the kitchenette.

His heart rate bumped up a notch. If Kate had been here, surely she would have turned the coffee machine off. The smell was so pervasive, so foul.

He lunged through her office door.

His stomach sank. Her desk looked untouched, the files neatly stacked in preparation for Monday. No sign of her jacket or briefcase.

What the hell had happened to her?

A picture of her lying bleeding, her creamy skin waxy and white, flashed through his mind.

With it came fear. Pain.

And a shocking realization.

It almost killed him to think of her being hurt.

He took a deep breath. He needed to be calm. He needed to figure out what could have happened in that parkade. Something had made her run in panic. He was sure of that now.

The hair on his arms rose.

Had she run into John?

Randall tried to put himself in John's shoes. The man was desperate. Randall could smell it on him. Randall had pushed at that desperation, had fed it, effectively boxing John into a corner. He had wanted John off balance for the partners' meeting.

Had he pushed him too far?

He hadn't thought so. But he hadn't anticipated that John would see Kate in the parkade. He'd called John at 5:15 p.m., expecting him to come right away. When he hadn't shown forty-five minutes later, he was seriously pissed off. He wouldn't wait any longer. He wanted answers. Now. He called Kate. She could fill him in on TransTissue. But her refusal to come in had ignited his fury. And then John showed up. At that point, he was so consumed with anger at the mess his fucking partner had gotten LMB into—and that Randall hadn't spotted—that he hadn't even thought about the fact that he'd ordered Kate to come right away.

What an idiot he was. He'd assumed Kate had given him the finger. He hadn't put two and two together. But he was sure John had. He would know Kate would be his bête noire.

He would have every reason in the world to want little Ms. Lange silenced.

52

The pain was duller when she awoke. But in some ways she felt worse. Her body was sluggish. Her limbs felt as if weights sat on them. She was also freezing. Cold metal ran under the length of her body.

She shivered. Her breasts jiggled.

She was naked.

She forced her eyelids open. A light glared directly into her eyeballs, drilling shards of white-hot pain into her nerves. She squeezed her eyes shut.

An obnoxious smell flooded her nose.

It was a smell of death and decay.

She knew where she was.

She was in Anna Keane's little shop of horrors. She was lying on a gurney. She flexed her hands. Tubing secured her wrists together. She tried to move her legs. They were bound as well. Panic welled in her.

"Craig?" a woman asked. It was Anna Keane.

Kate's pulse began to throb through her veins. *Craig*. It could only be Craig Peters. President of BioMediSol, Inc.

The man who signed the disarticulation record of Vangie Wright/Mary Littler.

There was a mumble. Then Anna Keane said, "Why don't you come back in half an hour."

Silence.

Someone stumbled. A body thudded. There was a muffled grunt. She needed to see what was happening. She turned her head away from the light and forced her eyes open again.

Two blurry figures moved jerkily into her line of vision.

She squinted. A man staggered, pinning Anna Keane against one of the freezers.

"Jesus Christ! Get the hell off me!" Anna Keane pushed the man away from her. He fell backward against the gurney that Kate lay trussed on. She flinched.

It was then that she saw his face.

It was the blond man.

The man from Lisa MacAdam's funeral.

The man from Dr. Gill's lab.

His face contorted.

This was Craig Peters.

"Craig, your girl is right there. Behind you," Anna Keane said. Her voice was low, but fear caused it to tremble. "Look, she's ready for you."

Craig Peters started mumbling again. He still hadn't moved away from the gurney. The weight of his body pressed against Kate's legs. She lay perfectly still. But her flesh rose at his words. "I need you…"

Anna Keane backed away, stumbling into a meat freezer. Craig Peters pitched toward her. There was a loud crash as his arm caught the tray of instruments laid out by the gurney. The instruments that were meant to end her life and plunge her body, piece by piece, into the cold depths of BioMediSol's freezers.

The instruments went flying. She jerked as a hot needle of pain dug deep into her thigh. Something had stabbed her. She peered through slit eyes down her prone body. The handle of a scalpel was visible. The blade had embedded itself in her leg. The other instruments had clattered to the floor around her.

"Craig, you don't need me. You've got her. She's waiting for you," Anna cried. Then she added, "She wants you to!" The fear was unmistakable now. Kate could smell it in the close air of the room.

"Doesn't hurt," Craig Peters panted. "Promise." He sounded like an animal. A robot. His body was stiff, rigid, as if he was doing a grim impersonation of Frankenstein. It would have been laughable except for one thing: the look in his eyes. Anna Keane was dead meat.

The funeral director turned and ran out of the tiny embalming room. Craig Peters catapulted himself after her. Kate looked frantically around.

She was alone…for as long as it took Anna Keane and Craig Peters to have their battle to the death. Whoever survived would make her their next victim.

Boxes crashed to the floor outside the embalming room. She tried to block the sounds of Craig Peters' attack, of Anna Keane's desperate cries. The scalpel blade in her leg burned flame into her muscle.

You must get out of here. Focus.

She bent her knees. Pain shot through her quadriceps. Her hands strained toward the scalpel.

She couldn't reach it.

She pulled her knees toward her stomach. Thank God for all her running. Even though her right quad trembled violently, she was strong enough to hold her legs in position while her hands fumbled along her thigh.

Blood warmed her fingertips. She was getting close.

A muffled scream broke through her concentration. It was a desperate, angry cry. Her fingers began to shake. Anna Keane was losing. Panic clenched Kate's stomach. She desperately needed to pee.

Shit. Shit. Shit.

She repeated it in her head.

Anna Keane began to beg. "No. Please, Craig. No."

Kate squeezed her eyes shut and repeated her mantra, trying to block out Anna's pleas. Her fingers scrabbled for the scalpel's handle. She grabbed it. And pulled hard. It resisted, then slid out with a weird sucking sensation, as if her flesh didn't want to let go of the source of its misery.

Blood gushed over her hand. Warm, spurting. She ignored the weakness seeping into her quadriceps and turned onto her side. Her head buzzed.

Focus. Look at the spot on the floor.

It took her a second to realize it was her blood she was looking at.

She bent her elbows and brought her bound wrists up to eye level. She carefully put the handle of the scalpel into her mouth and clamped her teeth above the blade. Then she aimed the point of the scalpel into the knot of tubing binding her wrists together.

The knot swam in and out of focus. Sweat ran into her eyes.

Fuck it.

She rammed the point of the scalpel into the knot. It nicked the rubber.

Yes.

She moved her head back and forth. Vertigo dogged every move as she sliced through the knot. Sweat slid down her chilled cheeks.

Boxes crashed in the next room. Anna Keane was putting up an almighty fight. But she couldn't last forever.

The tubing snapped. Kate braced her hands on the gurney and pushed herself to an upright position.

Spots filled her vision. She felt herself tipping.

Don't. Don't. Don't.

The spots began to recede. She reached down carefully to her ankles. It took only a few seconds to slice through the tubing. In those few seconds, everything fell silent. No boxes crashed. No bodies thudded.

The silence pounded at her nerves.

What was going on in the other room?

Then she heard it. Breathing, harsh and ragged, on the other side of the wall. The victor.

Craig Peters would be searching for her now.

53

Friday, May 18, 7:38 p.m.

Randall squeezed his eyes shut. Think. Where would she be?

She could be anywhere.

He grabbed the phone on her desk and dialed security. "Put me through to the police station."

As soon as the police switchboard answered, he said, "I need to speak to Detective Drake. It's urgent."

He stood behind her desk, waiting for Ethan Drake to come on the line. He never thought he'd be in this position. That he'd have to ask Ethan Drake for help. The man who'd put his oldest friend behind bars.

He wondered what had driven Kate and this guy apart. Whatever it was, he hoped it wouldn't cloud the detective's judgment.

"Detective Drake."

"It's Randall Barrett." He fought to keep his voice calm.

"Yeah?" The detective's voice was unsurprisingly hostile.

"Kate has disappeared."

His words had the effect he wanted. The hostility was gone, replaced by wariness. "What?"

"I believe she's been kidnapped."

"When?" Drake was now all business, although Randall thought he detected a hint of fear in his voice.

He glanced at Kate's clock. It was small, battered. Looked as if it had a few tales to tell. Right now it was urging him to hurry. "Approximately an hour ago."

"By whom?"

"John Lyons."

"The motherfucker." Drake's voice was hard, angry. "Would he hurt her?"

Randall pictured John's silver hair and suave countenance. The desperation in his eyes he'd tried to hide. "He's got nothing to lose," Randall said softly.

"Why would he kidnap Kate?"

"He's been defrauding our firm to finance a company that supplies body parts to one of our clients." He'd found that out after his phone call from CreditAngels. "Kate had worked with that client. I think he wants to prevent her from revealing what she knows."

"What's the name of the body parts company?"

"BioMediSol."

"Who else is involved?"

"A man named Craig Peters and a woman named Anna Keane." She'd been the co-signee of the loan although her name hadn't appeared in the Registry of Joint Stock Companies search. Impatience pounded through Randall's veins. Drake didn't realize how off balance John had been. They needed to hurry.

"Of Keane's Funeral Home?" Drake asked sharply.

"Yes."

"Holy shit."

From his stunned reaction, Ethan Drake had made a connection that Randall had missed. "Why—"

"The embalming fluid's from Keane's Funeral Home," Drake called hoarsely. "Get the fuck over there!"

The phone went dead.

A cold sweat ran down Randall's back. He bolted out of Kate's office to his car.

54

Friday, May 18, 7:38 p.m.

She bit the scalpel sideways between her teeth, keeping her hands free, and lowered her feet to the floor. It was icy. But where her blood spattered, the tiling was warm and slick. Vertigo tilted the room. She put a hand out, her palm meeting the reassuring solidity of the meat freezer.

Move. Move. You have no fucking time. Get to the elevator. Now!

A low moan broke through the pounding in her ears.

She scrambled toward the elevator. It was six feet away. Her hands pulled her along the sides of the freezer.

You can do it.

That wasn't her voice urging her forward.

It was Imogen's.

A small warmth spread from inside her chest. It flowed down her arms, her legs. She pushed off from the freezer and threw herself against the elevator button. Her legs gave out. She slid down the wall. But her fingers gripped the door frame, ready to propel her inside when the elevator came.

The gears whirred. Slowly. Each second was a year of

her life. She saw it with frightening clarity. The lost years after Imogen's death. The desperate years of trying to regain her early promise. And maybe find joy, or at least peace, once again.

Instead, this.

The gears clanked.

Hurry. Hurry. Please hurry.

Blood dripped down her leg.

Craig Peters staggered into the room.

He lurched toward her.

She gripped the scalpel with one hand and pressed the elevator button frantically with the other.

Where the fuck was the elevator? She didn't want to die waiting for an elevator.

He grabbed her by the throat.

He lifted her off her feet, slamming her back against the wall. The elevator button pressed into her spine. The door slid open.

"It won't hur…" he mumbled. His eyes stared into hers. Kate wasn't sure if he really saw her. His face twisted. Saliva dribbled down the corner of his mouth.

His hand spasmed, tight against her throat. Spots exploded in her vision.

Her spine ground tight against the elevator button, metal on bone. The elevator door buzzed in alarm.

Dark spots spun and cartwheeled, outlined in electric pink and yellow.

He was killing her. She was going to end up just like Vangie Wright.

Craig Peters panted. His whole body was rigid, so tense she thought he might snap against her, smash his body into hers and crush her into the wall.

The spots had exploded into neon. The pressure was

building. Blood and tissue pushed against the wall of her skull.

Stop him. Stop him taking one more victim, Katie.

I can't. He's killing m—

Protect the victims. The voice was urgent. *Like you used to look after me.*

But I didn't!

You did, Katie. You did. The voice became sad. *I just wouldn't let you anymore.*

The voice faded into spinning dots. Black melded with white. The hand around her throat remained rigid. Unbending. Unyielding.

The scalpel. She couldn't feel its cool metal between her fingers anymore. Her arm was numb.

Do it. He's winning!

She lifted her arm. She forced her arm to tense. Then she plunged the scalpel into Craig Peters' chest. He stared at her. He still didn't seem to be seeing her. She pulled her arm back. The scalpel popped out with a sudden, sucking give of his tissue.

The choke hold around her neck remained rigid. Her brain was about to explode her skull. It could not possibly stay in her head with all this pressure.

She plunged the scalpel again, deeper. Harder.

Craig Peters' mouth opened. A gurgling noise came out. She wrapped her fingers around the handle of the scalpel for one final attempt. But she was too weak. She couldn't get it out.

She waited, staring into Craig Peters' unseeing eyes.

She had no breath left. It was gone. Gone.

So was her sister. She tried to hear Imogen's voice one final time. But she was mute.

She had a sudden image of being underwater. In the

pool. She and Imogen were holding their breath. Who could hold it the longest? She'd always been good at that game. One. Two. Three. Four—

Craig Peters' hands spasmed. The fingers loosened around her neck. She jerked free of his grip, ducking under his arm and rolling onto the floor.

Run. Run. Run, goddamn it!

But she couldn't. Her lungs screamed for air. Everything else was numb. She lay on the floor, gasping, sucking in the air.

Waiting for his fingers to finish the job they had started.

But he tilted forward, smacking his head against the wall. The scalpel jammed deeper into his chest.

His eyes were open.

Wide open. Unseeing?

She stared at him, unable to move. Gulping in the air. Fresh. Sweet. It rushed into her lungs. They burned, the oxygen fanning the sputtering flame of her life. As her head stopped buzzing, she realized that the buzzing of the elevator had been silenced without her spine to press the button.

The elevator door slid closed.

No! Push the button...

Craig Peters fell sideways to the floor. Blood ran down his chest, spreading in a slow pool.

She rolled to her hands and knees. Forced her body upright. Slammed her palm against the elevator button.

The door opened. She dove into the elevator and reached upward, through the dark, dizzying pain that crowded her head. Her fingers fumbled for the lone button on the panel. Punched it. Her hand dropped. Her eyes closed.

Stay awake. You can't give up now. John Lyons could be downstairs, waiting for you.

She forced her eyes open.

She had to get out of here.

The elevator landed with a gentle bump on the main floor. The door opened. She peered into the main embalming room. No sign of anyone.

Relief weakened her legs. She stumbled toward the door. A set of shelves built next to the wall caught her eye. Scrub gowns were stacked neatly on one of them. She grabbed one, clumsily thrusting her arms in the sleeves. The back gaped open, threatening to fall off her shoulders. She snatched another gown and put it on back to front. Being clothed gave her strength. Like she was one step closer to the living.

She staggered through the door into the hall. The building was silent. What time was it? She had no idea how long she'd been unconscious. She stumbled down the hallway, her hand holding the wall for support, her right leg becoming heavier as if it was filled with water.

Go faster.

John Lyons was somewhere in here.

She forced her feet to move one after another. The dots had receded to the edge of her vision, leaching color from the walls. Everything had a shadow.

Her heart raced, urging her forward, yet begging for reprieve. She eyed the final corner. Was John waiting around the curve with his tire iron raised?

She inched forward, her leg now dragging.

Get ready to run.

She tried to psych herself. She couldn't run. Her leg could barely move. Fear put her heart into overdrive.

She reached the corner. Pressed her back against the wall. Listened.

Was that John's ragged breathing on the other side?

Or hers?

A minute passed.

Then another.

Her leg was numbing. If she didn't move soon, she wouldn't be able to.

On the count of three.

One.

Two.

Three—

55

Friday, May 18, 7:49 p.m.

She barreled around the corner, head low. She'd take him in the middle, take the tire iron on the back, not the head.

The momentum pitched her forward.

She fell onto her hands and knees.

She scrambled to her feet, staggering against the wall, and looked around frantically.

She scanned the shadows. The dots in her vision converged, then pulled apart. She rubbed her temple.

John was not here.

The hallway was empty.

Where was he?

She didn't know. All she knew was that she needed to get out of here. Now. Before she collapsed in this hellhole.

Her strength was ebbing like sand through fingers.

She would not die in this funeral home. She wouldn't give Anna Keane and John Lyons the satisfaction.

The doors to the loading bay loomed in front of her.

She threw herself against the doors and they swung open. The scrub gowns clung wetly against her legs. She stumbled through the doorway, falling to her knees.

Air. Freedom.

She was alive.

She pushed herself to her feet.

The dots careered wildly. She put a hand against the building.

You cannot stay here. Move. Move. You're almost home free.

She staggered forward. One foot. Lurch. The other foot. Her muscles did not belong to her. They belonged to someone else. Small pebbles of gravel dug into her feet.

Warmth. On her leg.

It was blood. The wound on her thigh was still bleeding. Gushing.

Wait. No.

She froze.

A man's silhouette, black against the trees. Silver hair that gleamed—

The spots spun themselves into a fury.

Not now. Not now.

Not now...

Pavement struck her arms, then her face.

The spots careered into a black hole.

56

Friday, May 18, 7:53 p.m.

Ethan slammed the brakes so hard the car spun around. It narrowly missed crashing into Ferguson's car behind him. His eye had caught something green sprawled on the ground, lit by the streetlight on the edge of the parking lot. He jerked the wheel hard. The car lunged over the curb and into the parking lot.

The green came into focus.

His heart jammed into his throat. It was Kate. She lay in a bloody heap.

He leaped out of his car, running faster than he'd ever run in his life. Sirens blared around him. Tires squealed. The rest of the team careered into the back parking lot of Keane's Funeral Home.

She lay facedown, her arm crumpled under her. Blood seeped through the scrub gown she wore. Her legs and feet were bare. She looked so vulnerable, so exposed, he had to fight hard to keep himself from scooping her into his arms and holding her tight.

Because if he moved her, and if she was—he could

barely imagine the words—if she was dead, then he would disturb evidence that might ultimately convict the killer.

He threw himself to his knees and pressed a hand against her neck. Her skin was still warm.

"Please, Kate," he whispered. "Please."

His fingers probed the delicate lines of her throat. He couldn't find her pulse.

He couldn't find her pulse.

He pressed further, his fingers desperate.

Please God. Please.

No matter how frantic his fingers, he couldn't find her pulse.

Ferguson knelt down on Kate's other side. He felt her gaze on him. He wouldn't look up, couldn't bear to see the compassion in her face.

His eyes stung with tears. Tears of loss. And of regret. He had turned her away. He had failed to forgive her.

This was his punishment. *Nice work, God. You really know how to put it to a homicide cop.*

An ambulance veered next to them. The paramedics ran out, pulling a stretcher. Ferguson moved out of the way. Ethan remained where he was.

The paramedics knelt down. Ethan reluctantly removed his hand from Kate's throat. It still held the warmth of life. Once her skin cooled, she would be another homicide victim. She would be part of a process that would talk about her life in terms of her cause of death, her injuries, her final moments, not dwelling on all the moments leading up to this. That was reserved for the victim impact statements. But those could never do justice to all the little ordinary things that, together, made someone extraordinary.

Ethan rocked back on his heels. He couldn't watch the

paramedics trying to put air into lungs that no longer breathed. It would make him hope. And that was too painful.

He turned, desperately scanning the scene playing out in the parking lot. It had taken on a surreal quality. Cars blocked the entry, officers stormed the funeral home, guns ready. Several patrols had been sent to block the front of the home.

But it was too late. They were too late to save her. He hadn't been able to save her. This woman, who'd been brought down into the darkest trenches of life and had fought her way out of them.

He saw that now. He wished he'd seen it before.

He hadn't understood how that past had made her prove her worthiness, over and over again. She deserved so much more.

Why the hell did he have to figure this all out now, when it was too bloody late?

He turned back to the paramedics and waited for the verdict. The male paramedic checked her blood pressure. Kate's arm hung from his grasp. "She's tachycardic. Heart rate one hundred and twenty per minute. Blood pressure seventy-eight systolic. Respirations present."

Ethan's blood began pounding in his ears. The paramedic looked over at him. "She's still alive."

Tears broke free of Ethan's eyes and trickled down his face. He squeezed his eyes shut. Then opened them and grabbed Kate's hand. "I couldn't find her pulse." Her fingers curved limply in his palm. He never wanted to let go.

"Her blood pressure was too low," the other paramedic said, tying a tourniquet above the wound on Kate's leg. "She's lost a lot of blood," she added. "She's got trauma to her head and a bad break in her arm. She's not out of the woods yet."

Her partner checked Kate's pulse and her airway. "Eye

movement to sound. She's withdrawing to pain. Verbal responses incomprehensible." He began inserting an IV into Kate's arm.

Ethan held her other hand. It was still warm. It would always be warm.

She was alive.

The paramedics lifted her carefully onto the stretcher. Ethan walked with them to the ambulance, his hand gripping Kate's until they lifted her inside. The ambulance drove away, its sirens almost drowning out the sudden ringing of Ethan's cell phone.

He yanked it out of his pocket. He was in no mood to speak to anyone, but the only people who had this number were the C.I. team and Kate.

"Detective Drake?" The voice on the other end of the phone made Ethan's blood pressure rise. "It's Randall Barrett."

"How the hell'd you get this number?" His fear had passed, leaving him with a burning anger at all the people who had put Kate in this situation. Randall Barrett numbered high on his list.

"Is Kate okay?" The urgency in Randall's voice cut through Ethan's anger.

"She's hurt, but she's alive," Ethan said curtly. "She's been taken to the hospital."

"What about Lyons?"

"The team's in the building. We'll soon find out."

"Look, I'm sitting at the intersection. The police won't let me near the place. Can you tell them to let me through?"

"Stay away, Barrett. This is no place for a civilian. If John Lyons isn't in there, I'll let you know. Under no circumstances should you have any contact with him. Call the police instead."

"I'm not a fool." Randall didn't bother to hide his frustration.

A bitter smile curved Ethan's lips. Randall Barrett was used to being in control, taking charge of a situation. When would he learn he had no place in a murder investigation?

"I've got to go," Ethan said. "I'll be in touch."

They both knew what he'd left unsaid: *when hell freezes over.*

57

Saturday, May 19, 8:00 p.m.

It was dark when Ethan got to the hospital. Shadows had deepened to indigo an hour before as the sky darkened. Ethan hoped the gift shop was still open.

It wasn't. Damn. No flowers for her tonight. Tomorrow he'd make sure to send her a hundred tulips, her favorite flower. He thought of Dr. Clare. Of the tulips lining her walkway. An ebullient welcome to spring, to the season of rebirth. But for her, it was a season of grief and loss. Her husband would be dead within weeks. Her children would probably not even remember him.

He hurried to the elevator and pressed the button for the orthopedic ward. His fingers slid into his jacket pocket, hesitating. Screw it. He turned off his cell phone. So what that he was breaking his own cardinal rule.

He was still stunned by the discoveries the team had made about the TransTissue fraud. And shamed that Kate hadn't trusted him enough to share her suspicions. He had failed her as a lover, friend. And as a cop.

He stopped at the nurses' station. Unlike the last time he was visiting the GH2, the ward clerk went out of her way to give him Kate's room number. He strode down the hall, his pulse leaping at the thought of seeing her. Touching her. Hopefully holding her.

Her door was half-open. He couldn't hear any voices in the room. He knocked softly.

"Come in," she said, her voice drowsy.

He walked in, his heart in his throat. She lay in the bed, a stack of newspapers next to her, untouched. A large bouquet of lilies and roses sat on her bedside table.

When she saw him, her eyes widened. Her face was a mess, her cheekbone swollen and bruised, one eye black, a bandage wrapped around her head. A monitor was hooked up to her chest and an oxygen tube ran from her nose to a tank. The arm that had been broken lay by her side, the cast a stark white against her gray skin. Her fingers were swollen.

His throat constricted.

"Kate," he said softly. "Sweetheart." He took her uninjured hand in his own.

Her skin was warm, soft. Alive. He rubbed his thumb gently over the back of her hand.

"How are you feeling?"

"Terrible." She smiled. His heart swelled in gratitude.

"You look beautiful."

The smile grew more lopsided. "Liar."

"You are beautiful." His voice was husky.

The smile left her lips.

"Kate…" There was so much he wanted to say. She had taken the curveballs life had thrown at her with grace. Unlike him.

I don't blame you for not telling me about your sister. You were right. I would have blamed you. I did blame you.

Not anymore. He squeezed her fingers gently. The words that flowed so freely in his head jumbled in his throat. He managed, "I'm sorry."

"Me, too." Her words were thick.

"I miss you."

She looked at him, her eyes dulled with drugs but still searching. Searching. It struck him to the core. She had spent her life searching.

He took a deep breath. "I love you." He cradled her fingers in his.

She stared at him for a moment. Tears welled in her eyes. She turned her face away.

His throat tightened. "Kate, please, look at me."

She slowly turned her face toward him. A tear slid crookedly down her cheek. He wanted to wipe it away. But the look in her eyes froze him. A look of resignation. Sadness.

"I know this isn't the right time—" It sure as hell wasn't with her being on opiates and him having no sleep for days on end, but suddenly he was desperate to let her know how he felt. He had to say it before she had a chance to say something he didn't want to hear. "But we've never been good at timing, have we?" He smiled.

Her eyes searched his. "That's been the whole problem, Ethan. I don't think anything's changed."

But it has, his heart roared. It has. "When I saw you lying on the pavement…"

"Don't," she whispered. "Don't say anything you'll regret." She squeezed his hand, her grip so weak it was almost nonexistent, but he felt it, as unflinching as the vise of pain closing around his heart.

Yesterday he had thought she was dead. But she had survived. Like a phoenix rising from the ashes. It was a sign. He couldn't let her get away again. He had learned from his mistakes—

"Ethan," she said haltingly. "I will always love you." Another tear slid down her cheek. He wanted to put a finger on her lips to stop the words he sensed were coming, but he realized he was too late. Too damn late. "But I don't think we were meant to be together."

She closed her eyes, as if the sight of him was too much to bear.

His own tears burned his eyes. He would not make her pay for his mistakes anymore. He bent down and kissed her forehead. "I made a mistake I will always regret, Kate," he said huskily. "I'm sorry."

"Me, too," she whispered.

After he left, she let the tears come. Slowly, trickling a tentative path over the swollen terrain of her face.

What had she done?

She finally had what she had hoped for. She had turned it away.

There had been too many hurts, too many betrayals, on both sides for the careless happiness they had enjoyed to continue. When they did not have that to share, they had little else. They were too different. To become the same, one of them would have to compromise too much of their intrinsic self. It would result in more disaster for both of them.

She knew that. She believed that. And yet she couldn't help but probe her heart one final time.

The pain was there. Deep, silent, waiting for her to approach. But not reproachful. It was the pain of having something that had been lodged deep in her flesh finally removed.

It was a healing pain.

Her tears ran over her lips. She tasted their warmth, their saltiness. They were strangely comforting.

Sleep pulled at her. She let it carry her away.

58

In addition to a body that had been left on display for visitation at the funeral home, two other bodies had been discovered by the C.I. team. The first was Craig Peters' body. The second was Anna Keane's. She'd been strangled to death with an embalming tube. Just like all of Craig Peters' other victims.

But John Lyons wasn't in the building. He was found the previous Saturday morning, floating in the Halifax Harbour. He'd jumped off the bridge.

One of Anna Keane's employees identified Craig Peters as the man who "disarticulated" the bodies. His car, a silver Chrysler, was found and its plate run. The seat fibers matched the ones found on the victims. The Forensic Identification Unit began the laborious process of scouring the funeral home, the car, his apartment and Dr. Gill's lab for evidence.

"So the kill site was the embalming room," Lamond said, a touch of amazement in his voice. "Friggin' genius."

"Craig Peters was a smart man," Ethan said. Very smart. He had been at the funeral, after all. They matched his photo with the coverage they'd shot at the funeral. "The embalming room was a perfect place to dismember the bodies. The room was sterile, so no trace evidence."

"And he even had a nice cold spot to store his trophies."

They hadn't matched all the body parts yet, but Ethan had no doubt some of those bagged legs, eyes and spines belonged to their victims.

No wonder they had came up empty.

"It seems likely that Vangie Wright was ground zero for spreading CJD," Ferguson announced, walking into the room. "Her sister confirmed that the Department of Health suspected she had the illness."

"Jesus," Lamond muttered.

"We are still trying to track down some of her brain tissue to do a biopsy. The GH2 thinks it might be able to find some."

"So she was the starting point of all this." Ethan shook his head. "And the end point. How did she get it?"

Ferguson glanced at the report. "Apparently she got it from human growth hormone when she was a kid."

Lamond gave a low whistle. "You think Dr. Mazerski caught it from her? Did he cruise?"

Ethan slapped him on the shoulder. It felt good to get back to the usual banter. He slapped him again. "Get your mind out of the gutter, Lamond. Remember what Dr. Lachlan told us? It's not sexually transmissible. Dr. Mazerski either got it spontaneously or cut himself with a scalpel while handling the brain tissue. He must have gotten infected through that."

Ferguson flipped the file and scanned another report. "Craig Peters' brain biopsy came back positive, as well."

"I saw his invoice for BioMediSol," Ethan said. "He conducted the dismemberment of Vangie Wright. He must have gotten CJD while handling her tissue."

"How many killers get to invoice a company for a murder?" Lamond shook his head admiringly. Craig Peters had charged his own company for "professional services rendered."

"Yeah. Kind of crazy," Walker said. "Just like him."

"We did a check on him. He'd been a surgical resident, but he'd been kicked out of the program," Brown said.

"No shit." Lamond rolled his eyes. "Guess that explains why he was so good at what he did. Why did he get kicked out?"

"The program will not divulge details, but it was on the grounds of professional misconduct. That was two years ago. Then he came back to Halifax and worked for Dr. Gill. Shortly after that, he killed Vangie Wright. She was his first victim for BioMediSol. That must have been a trigger. The BioMediSol records indicate he'd begun disarticulating bodies a few months before. It might have unleashed his killing urges." She glanced around the table, a flush of excitement on her cheeks. "And five or six years before that, his brother went missing. We've got Cold Case looking into it…"

"Once a psychopath, always a psychopath," Lamond said. "Some of the limbs were found under the bathtub in his apartment."

"Yeah, but throw in the CJD, and we got a psychotic psychopath," Ethan said.

"Do you think Dr. Gill got infected with CJD, too? He used Vangie Wright's arms for his research," Lamond said. He and Ethan had found the records for that, too. BioMediSol kept meticulous paperwork, like the Nazis, detailing their crimes in the name of science.

Ethan and Ferguson exchanged looks. "You get to tell the bastard about Vangie Wright," Ethan said. For a change, it seemed like justice—or at least retribution—had been served in some small way. Dr. Gill would have to live with the fear that he had been infected. It could take decades for the symptoms to manifest themselves, like it did for Vangie Wright. Or like the other victims who caught it from Vangie Wright, he could show symptoms tomorrow. Either way, every time he bumped into something or forgot something, his scientist's mind would no doubt play it over, examining it endlessly to determine if it was the first symptom of CJD.

"Better get the fucker to trial before he's declared mentally unfit," Ethan added.

"How's the neurosurgeon doing?" Ferguson asked, looking at Ethan.

He shook his head. "He's on his deathbed."

"What a waste of talent," Ferguson murmured. "And how about the patient who received the transplant?"

"They can't confirm it without an actual postmortem biopsy, so the patient's scared shitless. Dr. Lachlan thinks there may be more people out there."

All these people killed or infected because of corporate greed. And the government had done little or nothing to control it, putting the onus on tissue processors to report irregularities. He hoped this was the wake-up call. Otherwise the government deserved to have the lawyers going for blood.

59

Ten days later

Liz knocked on the door. "Kate…" She smiled hesitantly.

Kate glanced up from her mail, suppressing a smile. Liz's newly discovered warmth toward her was startling, but to be expected, she supposed. It was one of the benefits of being the country's latest national darling.

"Mr. Barrett wants to see you."

"Oh. Thanks, Liz."

"And welcome back." Her assistant upped the warmth in her smile and shut the door softly behind her. That would take some getting used to. She felt a touch of nostalgia for the old, frosty Liz.

So, Randall wanted to see her. Hardly surprising. It was her first morning back at work. She was glad he'd summoned her. It was a chance to let him see that she was starting over with a clean slate. And that included him. No more disturbing looks. She was going to cement the professional divide between them once and for all.

And remind him of why she'd been hired in the first place. She flipped open her compact. She was going into his office guns blazing. She didn't want him to take pity on her; she wanted what was her due.

She dabbed some powder over her bruises, balancing the compact in the palm of her casted arm—she'd already tried holding the powder puff in that arm and had been rewarded with a knock in the head. It had taken a little practice. Everything took a little practice with a cast. Getting a shower, drying her hair, making a meal, getting her clothes on. She made a face at herself. She looked a sight. She didn't need her mirror to tell her that; her picture was plastered on the front page of every paper in the country.

She knew the press would start leaving her alone when the next big story broke. It'd only been a week since she came out of the hospital. A week of Bruised and Battered: Lawyer Takes Justice Into Her Own Hands, Killer Eludes Law But Can't Escape Lawyer and so on. A week of constant phone calls, interviews and a horde of reporters waiting to speak to her every time there was a "latest development."

And there had been many of those. The whole body-parts-for-sale scheme had fallen apart, bringing down a host of other players. TransTissue had been temporarily shut down while the police combed its facilities to find the stolen body parts of murder victims and clients who never consented to donate their bodies. TransTissue was now on the line for failing to screen its tissue properly. Legitimate tissue banks were frantically scrambling to restore their image, until Kate issued a public statement announcing she had signed a tissue donor card. That had taken a lot of soul searching. But she realized that there was a greater good. She couldn't let BioMediSol get away with perverting it. All the lawyers at LMB had followed suit.

Hollis University lost its endowed one-million-dollar chair for neuromuscular research after sources reported that Dr. Gill had been in breach of ethical standards before, but the university had turned a blind eye to his methods—hoping to share the glory of a Nobel Prize.

Dr. Gill himself was in bad shape. He'd had a nervous breakdown, was on antidepressants and had been released on bail for charges of offering an indignity to human remains. He faced a prison term of five years, but Kate guessed that his own mental hell would last until the end of his life.

She walked slowly out of her office and down the hallway. Voices greeted her on both sides—support staff from the cubicles, lawyers from their offices. There was genuine warmth in the greetings. She was one of them. They were glad she was back. She was cynical about their sudden friendship, but decided she might as well enjoy it. Who knew, maybe she'd grow to like them.

She took the elevator instead of the stairs to Randall's office. She was still a little wobbly in heels. She'd had a concussion from the tire iron. The wound in her thigh throbbed under the stitches. Her body had never been so battered in her life.

But she couldn't lie around at home. Although Alaska was devoted company, there were limits to the amount of conversation you could have with a dog. Enid and Muriel had visited every day, bringing casseroles and cookies, until she was sure she'd be twenty pounds heavier before she could run again. Finn had been gold, taking Alaska for long walks and feeding him, even while she was in hospital. She'd been well taken care of.

It had helped to take her mind off Ethan. Even though she knew she'd done the right thing, telling him they were over had been unplanned and agonizing. She'd been excited when he'd come to her hospital room, not sure of what she felt. But when he told her he loved her she realized that there was no going back. There never was. They had thrown something precious away. She was as much to blame as Ethan. She knew now she couldn't pretend her past hadn't existed. If she ever found another person to love, they'd have to know the truth. And love her, anyway.

She paused in front of Randall's door. Her nerves jangled. She didn't want to talk about John Lyons, about what happened in the parkade. She'd already given her statement to the police—not to Ethan, that would have been too painful—and it'd been hard to relive what had happened. The sudden, bone-chilling knowledge that someone wanted to hurt you.

Kill you.

And you couldn't run fast enough. The knowledge that a steel bar was going to crash down on your head. Exploding pain. Blackness. And that strange vision she'd had before she passed out in the funeral home parking lot. She'd been convinced she'd seen John. Of course, she'd also been convinced her sister had been talking to her while she was fighting for her life. It must have been from the drugs Anna Keane had shot her up with.

Her head throbbed. There was one thing she hadn't spoken about to anyone. Except her doctor. And that was the fact that when she stabbed Craig Peters, she was sure she got his blood on her. And she'd had an open wound on her thigh...

The fear had welled up inside her. What if she'd contracted CJD?

Come on. Remember what the doctor said?

How could she forget. She was lying in her hospital bed. Her surgeon had come to visit.

"I need to discuss something with you," he'd said, his expression grave. "Craig Peters had CJD."

After explaining to Kate what it was—and in her groggy state that took some time—the surgeon said, "I'm telling you this because you need to know there is a possibility you were exposed to Craig Peters' blood."

"Oh, God," Kate said. After fighting for her life, she now had this to deal with? She closed her eyes.

"Kate, it's not as bad as you think. The type of CJD that Craig Peters had has never been transmitted by blood as far as we know. And even if it was, the chances of having actually contracted it are extremely low."

"But his blood was on me. I felt it spatter me." Kate forced the words out. Remembering the violence, the primal urge to survive, the absolute terror, was something she did not want to do.

"Even so. Let me give you an example. HIV is a blood transmissible disease, and yet it's a one in one thousand chance of getting HIV from a needle stick injury. So you don't automatically get the disease if you are exposed to infected blood. And in the case of classic CJD, as far as we know, no one has ever gotten it through blood exposure. So you can see the odds are in your favor." He patted her hand.

"I see," she murmured. But she couldn't erase the memory of what CJD had done to Craig Peters in his final moments.

Just don't think about it. I have a much better chance of being hit by a bus.

With that reassuring thought, she took a deep breath and knocked on Randall's door.

"Come in."

She walked into his office. Its clean lines and sharp angles calmed her mind. She had been a lover of Victorian architecture for years, but this modern aesthetic seemed so confident of its own inherent strength, she felt herself drawn to it.

Randall stood and walked around his desk. "Kate!" He ushered her into his office, solicitously holding her elbow. His grip was sure, strong. She swallowed. Despite the tempering of her resolve, his proximity made her pulse hammer.

She gently pulled her arm away and lowered herself into one of his ingeniously designed chairs.

"How are you feeling?"

She didn't want to get into the details. No more personal stuff. This was her boss. She gave a brisk smile. "Better. Thank you."

He sat behind his desk and studied her. "You took a beating." His gaze was frank, not pitying.

It pierced her reserve. *Damn him.* She looked away. "Yes."

"Kate…" There was something in his voice that made her gaze swing back to him. "I was very concerned about you."

The memory flooded her. So. It hadn't been her imagination.

It had been dim in her hospital room. She'd been dozing, the drugs from the surgery dulling her pain. Then she'd heard footsteps. Quiet. Too quiet. She stiffened. Was it John? A whimper of fear escaped her. Her fingers scrambled for the help button.

"Kate. It's okay," the voice had murmured. It was a familiar voice. It was unexpectedly tender, soft. A hand hesitated over her brow, then lowered. It smoothed the hair off her forehead.

Then he was gone.

She'd thought it had been a dream. Had assumed the arrangement of roses and lilies had been delivered by a florist during her surgery. Not by him. "Thank you for the flowers. They were beautiful."

She had told herself it was an act of compassion. Or an act of repentance.

But when he said, "You are welcome," she knew.

It had been something else.

She looked away, her heart pounding. She forced her voice to sound cool, collected. "I understand you were the one who tipped Ethan off."

He nodded.

She didn't want to imagine *that* phone call. It must have cost Randall a lot to call Ethan for help. "Thank you."

He ran his hands through his hair. "I feel somewhat responsible for putting you in that situation."

She had thought about that in the hospital. Randall hadn't been part of the TransTissue conspiracy. That was a relief. But Randall had wanted to use her against John to build his case. Even though it was his responsibility as managing partner to protect the firm's interests, there had been a personal element to involving her. It had been one final power play, a master stroke to turn John Lyons' protégée against him. And it hurt that he would still try to do that.

"I didn't know you'd run into him in the parking garage, Kate." His eyes sought hers. "I swear it."

"But you insisted I come in and meet with you."

"I had received information that Lyons had a financial interest in BioMediSol. I knew that he had settled TransTissue's claim. I wanted to find out what you knew." He leaned forward. "But when I called you, I thought he'd bailed out on me. I would never have insisted you come in if I'd known he was still in the building."

She studied him. He hadn't meant to put her in danger.

He was asking for forgiveness. And she wanted to tell him she forgave him. But to do so would acknowledge an intimacy that made it all the more imperative to retreat.

Instead, she shrugged. Then smothered a wince when

pain shot down her arm. "I knew more than John wanted me to. I was a threat."

To her relief, he followed her retreat. "How did you find out about the criminal activity at BioMediSol? Didn't John take you off the case before the settlement?"

"Yes." She leaned back in her chair. "But I'd done some research and had heard about U.S. cases where there was fraudulent screening. Then I learned that the funeral home was trying to convince families to donate bodies. I realized something was up." She made no mention of her break-in at the funeral home. When the police came for her statement in the hospital, she told them about the BioMediSol records she stole. She also told them about the Department of Health letter from Claudine Wright. Then she waited for the charges to be laid.

Instead, she received a phone call from Detective Ferguson, informing her that the police had decided they did not have enough evidence to proceed with charges—which she knew was untrue—and with a strict caution to not ever again attempt to investigate potential criminal activities. The message was clear: they were covering her butt this one time. She wondered if it had been Ethan who'd pulled the strings for her.

Randall's gaze had not left her face. She wished she knew what he was thinking. Despite his apology for the danger he'd put her in, he was still her boss. She'd breached a few ethics and broken a few laws to uncover the fraud.

But he'd be a fool to fire her when LMB was desperately spinning its image to mitigate the scandal from John Lyons' criminal activities and suicide.

And he was no fool.

She waited.

He cleared his throat. "Kate, you have integrity, a need

to find the truth that sets an example for our firm." Admiration warmed his eyes. "I know you've been wanting to move to the litigation group."

"That's what I was hired to do." She couldn't resist the arch look she gave him.

"When you are able to take on some files, let's have another chat." He stood. He held her eyes with his own. And despite her resolve, a flush heated her chest.

He said softly, "Welcome back."

She braced herself for what she knew she would see in his gaze. *Be strong.*

But his eyes were questioning. Not demanding. And in those brilliant depths she found something entirely unexpected: tenderness.

What was even more unexpected was her reaction.

She liked it.

She eased herself out of the chair and walked to the door. She turned. "Thank you. It's good to be back."

She felt his eyes on her as she limped into the corridor. *So much for resisting him.*

If she wanted to continue at LMB—and she most certainly did, after Randall's promise to move her into the litigation group—she had to learn to deal with Mr. Barrett. Right now, she had the upper hand. She knew it, he knew it. She'd been through a hell most people did not physically survive. If they did, they emerged with trauma that ruined their lives.

But not her. Hell had tempered her confidence, strengthened her resolve and eradicated her fear. Her wounds— both old and new—were now healing. She was ready to plunder everything that her life promised.

She would no longer hide from things that threatened her. That included Randall Barrett.

She was ready to be all that she'd wanted to be.

She luxuriated in the knowledge that her career was finally going in the direction she wanted it to go. Finally she'd get the files she yearned for. Triumph bubbled inside her. She knew it was short-lived champagne fizz. She'd had time to do some thinking over the past week. Recuperating at home had shown her what she'd been missing: the simple companionship of her dog, the undemanding friendship of Enid and Muriel, the pleasure of sharing a meal with someone. She wanted more challenging work but not at the expense of the rest of her life. Hopefully, Randall would respect that.

If not, her options were looking good. She'd generated a lot of litigation business for firms across Canada. Class-action suits against TransTissue were springing up all over the place. TransTissue was screwed; law firm profits were on the rise. The law of supply and demand was alive and well.

She returned home at 5:30 p.m. Alaska greeted her with his usual delight. "Come on, boy." She grabbed an apple and they sat together on the steps of her back porch. The sun was warm on her neck. Alaska lifted his nose to the breeze. The earth was pungent, full of promise. Tiny buds in vibrant green poked through the soil.

The little buds were brave and bold, sure of their place in the dark depths of her garden. She would get some fertilizer. She would weed the garden. She would invite Enid and Muriel to tea and let Muriel crumble the earth between her fingers.

Spring always came late in Halifax. Now that it was here, she would soak up the sun.

* * * * *

AUTHOR'S NOTE

DAMAGED was inspired by an actual tissue brokering case that originated in the U.S. but had ramifications in Canada. Despite the sensational facts of this case, and my fictionalization of it, tissue and organ donations help many people. My husband and I have signed our tissue and organ donor cards, and have encouraged our children to do the same.

ACKNOWLEDGMENTS

I wholeheartedly thank those who took time from their busy schedules to share their expertise with me:

Constable Jeff Carr, Media Relations, Detective Curtis Pyke, Forensic Identification Technician, and Sergeant Jeff Clarke, Major Crime Unit, all of the Halifax Regional Police Department, who patiently took me through police procedures;

Dr. Martin Bullock, M.D., FRCP, who helped me understand the forensic pathology process;

Ms. Cindy Burchell, who broke down the blood testing process for me; and

Ms. Judith Ferguson, LL.B., who graciously gave me an impromptu briefing on child protection while we waited for our kids' soccer practice to end.

Any mistakes in this book are mine alone and I apologize in advance to those who generously shared their expertise.

I want to thank everyone at MIRA Books for their hard work to make *Damaged* the best it can be, with especial thanks to my editor, the fabulous Valerie Gray. I am so fortunate to be guided through the publishing process by such a fine editor. Her enthusiasm and gentle coaching have made this a truly wonderful experience.

I also want to thank my fantastic, hard-working agent, Emily Sylvan Kim of Prospect Agency, whose encouragement and advice have been invaluable.

Writing is an act of faith. I am blessed to have had so many friends support me:

My talented critique partner, Kelly Boyce, who shares the same passion as I;

Authors Julianne MacLean, Cathryn Fox and Stella

MacLean, who I'm lucky enough to have as mentors *and* friends;

My RWAC chapter: the road would have been longer—and lonelier—without them;

My father and my sister, who have always been there for me;

My brother (and best friend) who always makes me laugh; and

My fellow traveler, best friend and creative sounding board, Linda Brooks.

Last, but foremost in my heart, I want to thank Dan, Julia, Katrina and Peaches. They are the ones that live with me every day, yet love me, anyway.

J.T. ELLISON

Homicide detective Taylor Jackson thinks she's seen it all in Nashville—but she's never seen anything as perverse as The Conductor. He captures and contains his victim in a glass coffin, slowly starving her to death. Only then does he give in to his attraction.

Once finished, he creatively disposes of the body by reenacting scenes from famous paintings. And similar macabre works are being displayed in Europe. Taylor teams up with her fiancé, FBI profiler Dr. John Baldwin, and New Scotland Yard detective James "Memphis" Highsmythe, a haunted man who only has eyes for Taylor, to put an end to The Conductor's art collection.

the cold room

Available wherever books are sold.

INTERNATIONAL THRILLER WRITERS INC.

When some of the top thriller writers in the world came together in *THRILLER: STORIES TO KEEP YOU UP ALL NIGHT*, they became a part of one of the most successful short-story anthologies ever published. The highly anticipated *THRILLER 2: STORIES YOU JUST CAN'T PUT DOWN* is even bigger. From Jeffery Deaver's tale of international terrorism to Lisa Jackson's dysfunctional family in the California wine country to Ridley Pearson's horrifying serial killer, this collection has something for everyone. Twenty-three bestselling and hot new authors in the genre have submitted original stories to make up this unforgettable blockbuster.

THRILLER

MIRA®

STORIES YOU JUST CAN'T PUT DOWN

REQUEST YOUR FREE BOOKS!

2 FREE NOVELS
FROM THE SUSPENSE COLLECTION
PLUS 2 FREE GIFTS!

YES! Please send me 2 FREE novels from the Suspense Collection and my 2 FREE gifts (gifts are worth about $10). After receiving them, if I don't wish to receive any more books, I can return the shipping statement marked "cancel." If I don't cancel, I will receive 3 brand-new novels every month and be billed just $5.74 per book in the U.S. or $6.24 per book in Canada. That's a saving of at least 28% off the cover price. It's quite a bargain! Shipping and handling is just 50¢ per book.* I understand that accepting the 2 free books and gifts places me under no obligation to buy anything. I can always return a shipment and cancel at any time. Even if I never buy another book, the two free books and gifts are mine to keep forever.

192/392 MDN E7PD

Name _____ (PLEASE PRINT)

Address _____ Apt. #

City _____ State/Prov. _____ Zip/Postal Code

Signature (if under 18, a parent or guardian must sign)

Mail to **The Reader Service:**
IN U.S.A.: P.O. Box 1867, Buffalo, NY 14240-1867
IN CANADA: P.O. Box 609, Fort Erie, Ontario L2A 5X3

Not valid for current subscribers to the Suspense Collection
or the Romance/Suspense Collection.

Want to try two free books from another line?
Call 1-800-873-8635 or visit www.morefreebooks.com.

* Terms and prices subject to change without notice. Prices do not include applicable taxes. N.Y. residents add applicable sales tax. Canadian residents will be charged applicable provincial taxes and GST. Offer not valid in Quebec. This offer is limited to one order per household. All orders subject to approval. Credit or debit balances in a customer's account(s) may be offset by any other outstanding balance owed by or to the customer. Please allow 4 to 6 weeks for delivery. Offer available while quantities last.

Your Privacy: Harlequin Books is committed to protecting your privacy. Our Privacy Policy is available online at www.eHarlequin.com or upon request from the Reader Service. From time to time we make our lists of customers available to reputable third parties who may have a product or service of interest to you. If you would prefer we not share your name and address, please check here. ☐

Help us get it right—We strive for accurate, respectful and relevant communications. To clarify or modify your communication preferences, visit us at www.ReaderService.com/consumerschoice.